MURDER
IN TEXAS

MURDER IN TEXAS

Ada E. Lingo

COACHWHIP PUBLICATIONS

Greenville, Ohio

Murder in Texas, by Ada E. Lingo
© 2016 Coachwhip Publications
Introduction © 2016 Curtis Evans
No claims made on public domain material.
First published 1935.

Front cover: Taft oil well blow-out, 1920s (L. M. Clendenen;
    USC Libraries)

ISBN 1-61646-397-X
ISBN-13 978-1-61646-397-7

CoachwhipBooks.com

FOR
CLARA R. POOL

SOCIETY
EDITOR

MURDER
IN TEXAS

·

ADA E. LINGO

A *Black Band* MYSTERY

TEXAS TWISTER
Ada E. Lingo (1908-1988) and *Murder in Texas* (1935)

Curtis Evans

Ada Emma Lingo's only known detective novel, *Murder in Texas* (1935), is an engrossing tale of criminal mayhem in a Great Plains oil town and a prime example of the between-the-wars American regional mystery. The novel was praised by noted critic Robert Van Gelder as a "good story with a lot of atmosphere" and by *New York Times* mystery reviewer Kay Irvin for the authenticity of its setting. "There is the smell of oil and the breathlessness of Southern Summer throughout this Texas tale," observed Irvin. "There is, also, the atmosphere of a singularly unpleasant small town, and, particularly, of the small town's newspaper office, whose society editor is the novel's heroine." Admiration for the realistic and evocative milieu in *Murder in Texas* was frequently expressed in contemporary reviews. In William C. Weber's notice in the *Saturday Review*, to cite another example, the mystery critic, who went by the name "Judge Lynch," rendered this pithy verdict on the novel: "malodorous mazes of small-town scandal form the pungent background for a quick-moving, plausible yarn."

Like the great hard-boiled crime writer Dashiell Hammett, who before he commenced writing in the 1920s his tales of tough crooks and even tougher 'tecs had served as an operative with the Pinkerton National Detective Agency, Ada Lingo—a Texas native who graduated from Big Spring High School, the College of Industrial Arts (where she learned how to operate a linotype machine), and the University of Missouri—knew of what she wrote in *Murder in Texas*, having worked at the local newspaper in Big Spring,

7

the *Daily Herald*, the *Fort Worth Star-Telegram* and the *New York World*, Joseph Pulitzer's legendary "sensational" newspaper. In 1931 Pulitzer's heirs sold the *World* to Roy W. Howard, of the Scripps-Howard chain, who promptly shut down the paper's operations, administering a swift coup de grace in which he laid off a staff of over 3000 individuals. That same year in Manhattan, however, Ada wed Charles Trabue Hatcher, a University of Virginia graduate and electrical engineer eleven years her senior. The next year she gave birth to the couple's daughter, Jean, but the marriage ended in divorce later in the decade, after what appears to have been an early separation, and Ada soon forged an entirely new path in life for herself.[1]

At some point during her short-lived marriage Ada's thoughts turned, like those of so many other possessors of fertile brains in the 1920s and 1930s, to the idea of writing detective fiction. While working at the *Big Spring Daily Herald* in 1934, she produced the manuscript of *Murder in Texas*, and in the spring of 1935 it was accepted, as part of a two-book deal, by Houghton, Mifflin, who slated it for publication in the fall as part of its newly launched "Black Band" mystery series. (Aside from *Murder in Texas* and several novels by the popular veteran British thriller writer Valentine Williams, the series, which apparently lasted merely two years, included Katherine Woods' *Murder in a Walled Town* and Faraday Keene's *Pattern in Black and Red*, both reprinted by Coachwhip.) On the novel, which Ada dedicated to Clara R. Pool, her high school English teacher and the "first person . . . to encourage her in writing," the neophyte author was given an advance royalty of $250 (about $4300 today), with five percent profits on movie rights. Upon its publication in October, *Murder in Texas* received praise not only nationally (as indicated above), but locally as well—though admittedly the interest of the *Big Spring Daily Herald* seemed mostly to lie with the matter of to what extent the book was based on Big Spring. "As a thriller it keeps one guessing until the very last," the *Herald* reviewer pronounced. "But it is not as a thriller that 'Murder in Texas' will be perused by most of The Herald readers. . . . the story is laid in a West Texas town strongly

DOROTHY HOMAN	ADA LINGO	AGNES CURRIE
"Dolly"	"Rusty"	"Ag"
Pep Club; Girls Reserve.	Pep Club; Tennis '24 and '25	Pep Club; Girls Reserve
"Possessor of friends and pals galore, Ever gaining more and more."	"Clever indeed, yet sometimes queer, One couldn't emagine her shedding a tear."	"Agnes is a friend indeed, Ready to help when one's in need

ADA'S HIGH SCHOOL ANNUAL

ANTONIO IRISARRI   Colombia, S. A.
A. B., University of Missouri;
Delta Sigma Phi; Sigma Gamma
Epsilon; Alpha Zeta Pi.

ELIZABETH JANES   Columbia
A. B., University of Missouri;
Delta Delta Delta; Delta Phi
Delta; Delta Tau Kappa; Sketch
Club; Secretary-Treasurer Fine
Arts School '26; Y. W. C. A.;
W. A. A. '26; Cwens.

ADA E. LINGO   Dallas, Tex.
B. S., College of Industrial Arts,
Denton, Tex.; Southern Methodist
University; Chi Omega; Theta
Sigma Phi; Delta Phi Delta; Texas
Club; President Graduate Women.

H. H. LONDON   Denton, Tex.
B. S., Teachers College, Denton,
Tex.; University of Texas; University of Colorado; Southern
Methodist University.

ADA'S COLLEGE ANNUAL

HANSEN   O'LEARY   BEERY   BENNETT   SWARTZ   PARSONS
JANES   DRUMM   SONNTAG   WEBER   LASHLEY   LINGO
ANKENEY   MARTIN   OLMSTED   SCHWABE   ALMSTEDT   COTTINGHAM

ADA IN DELTA PHI DELTA, AN ART STUDENTS FRATERNITY

TRIMBLE   SHAPIRO   SAVILLE   AHRENS   HOFFMAN
RAMSEY   LINGO   READ   McDANIEL   SHEARER
PRICE   NIEHUSS   HUBBARD   PRATT   CROPPER   BIDWELL

ADA IN THE WOMEN'S SELF-GOVERNMENT ASSOCIATION

resembling Big Spring. . . . Fitting the characters to people in town will be great indoor sport for those who read the book, for many months to come. . . . 'Murder in Texas' will make the swellest Christmas present that one Big Spring person could give to another—in or out of town."[2]

Ada was not content to rest on her newly-won detective fiction laurels, however; she had already enrolled in the fall of 1934 in the pre-med program at Baylor University in Waco. After completing her coursework at Baylor in the spring of 1935, Ada spent her summer partially in visiting at Big Spring with her grandmother Ada Evans and her uncle Reuben Louis Price, president of the town's First National Bank, and partially in vacationing with her young daughter and a friend, Ethelwyn "Ditty" Gilluly, at the mountain resort of Ruidoso, New Mexico, where she planned to complete her second novel before enrolling in the fall at Texas University Medical School at Galveston. With her second projected detective novel, which had the working title of *Murder by Minims* and was set at Ruidoso, Ada obviously intended to take advantage of her burgeoning medical knowledge, but the book, though it seems to have been eventually completed, apparently was never actually published.[3] After obtaining her medical degree in Galveston, Ada, presumably with her young daughter Jean, moved to Los Angeles. There she interned at a hospital, becoming a member of the Los Angeles branch of the California Medical Association in 1942. Presently she established her own highly successful family practice in the city, winning a prominent reputation as an LA cancer specialist. Later in life she settled at Olympia, Washington, where she passed away in 1988, at the age of 79.

Ada's granddaughter Elaine Waller recalled her grandmother in 2007, twenty years after her death, as "a family doctor, writer, environmentalist, animal lover, techno geek, and photographer" who "was also a lesbian." In her later years Ada was keenly interested in computers, an interest that proved handsomely remunerative:

> I remember plunking away at the keyboard of her
> brand new Apple IIe in the early 80's. She was in

her 60's [actually 70's] at the time and knew more about computers and the impending PC boom than many young Americans. She had a knack for spotting trends on the horizon and investing accordingly. She invested in Apple computers when the company was in its infancy, and you can guess how she made out on that venture. Unfortunately, she never got to experience the internet. She also never got to use a digital camera. I imagine how impressed she would be by both innovations and how she might choose to employ them in her daily life—following her beloved [Seattle] Seahawks' [football] season online, day trading, blogging about environmental issues, color correcting her photos in Photoshop. But mostly I imagine her loving lolcats.[4]

To all appearances red-haired Ada Lingo was an outgoing, ambitious and active woman who throughout her life made a strong impression on those around her. Jim Lockart, Ada's first cousin once removed, has characterized her as a "brilliant" Renaissance woman with a personality as outsized as her native state, who entered the medical profession because she deemed it a "challenge." At Big Spring High School, where she was nicknamed "Rusty," Ada was an outstanding student scholastically who belonged to the pep club and the women's tennis team, though she appears to have bemused some of her fellow students. During her freshman year, when she was a new arrival in Big Spring, her classmates voted her runner-up as the school's "Biggest 'Hot Air' Artist," while during her senior year she was summarized in the school annual, in a poetic couplet befitting a future crime fiction writer, as "Clever indeed, yet sometimes queer/One couldn't imagine her shedding a tear." In graduate school at the University of Missouri, where she studied journalism, Ada was a member of the student government association and several athletic groups, including the "Missouri Mermaids," a team of women who were devoted to furthering and promoting "interest and excellence in water sports."

It is easy to see the dynamic Ada as her own model for Joan Shields, the energetic and no-nonsense "girl reporter" in *Murder in Texas*, who "takes time off from writing up local bridge parties to investigate the sensational murder of John Fordman, the first citizen of the town."

Ada Lingo's own family background was as varied and colorful as one might expect to find even in the heart-palpitating pages of crime fiction, including not only pacific Pennsylvania Quakers on her father's side of the family, but well-born frontier killers on her mother's. Ada's parents were David Clayton and May Evans Lingo, who wed in 1907 in Fort Worth, Texas, where Ada was born the next year. The son of David Allen Lingo and Emma Holton Yarnall,

MEMBERS

DOROTHY ALLEY	ELIZABETH McREYNOLDS
ISABELLE COEN	ELAINE SCHENK
LELIA FIELDS	ALICE TODD
BENESPRINGS HANGER	DOROTHY WAGNER
HELEN HESSLER	MARGARET WELDON
ADA LINGO	ESTHER WITT

THE Missouri Mermaids, founded in February, 1926, to further and promote interest and excellence in water sports among the women students of the University, is an organization of girls especially proficient in swimming. They work for the betterment of speed swimming, form swimming, and diving; and they are co-operating with the Red Cross Life-Saving Corps in the encouragement of life-saving work. One of their requirements for membership is that the prospective member must have either passed or be ready to pass her Senior Life-Saving Test. Each year they sponsor a novice swimming meet in the fall, an interclass meet and a Mermaid Revue in the spring. They are working with other schools in their efforts to form a national swimming organization for women.

WITT   TODD   SCHENK   McREYNOLDS   WAGNER   LINGO   ALLEY   FIELDS

ADA AND THE MISSOURI MERMAIDS

David Clayton Lingo was born in Peoria, Illinois, in 1876 and grew up in Keokuk, Iowa, the southernmost city in the state, where his father was an engineer on the Keokuk and Western Railroad. Emma Holton Yarnall was a daughter of Holton Clayton Yarnall, an Ottuma, Iowa, merchant and devout Quaker, whose creed was, according to his 1892 obituary, "malice toward none and charity toward all." At the time of the Lingo-Yarnall marriage, the Yarnalls were a family of hoary lineage, by American standards, extending back nearly 200 years to the founding of Pennsylvania. (Indeed, through a common ancestor, Richard Buffington, who settled in Chester County, Pennsylvania, in 1681, May Lingo and my maternal grandfather, Daniel Milton Knohr, were, no doubt unknown to both of them, seventh cousins.)

For a brief space of time during the Spanish-American War, young David Clayton Lingo, descendant of Quakers, served as a musician in Company A of the 50th Regiment of Iowa Volunteer Infantry. The 50th Iowa Regiment spent six miserable months in the disease-ridden "Cuba Libre" camp in Jacksonville, Florida, 32 of its number dying of disease, before being sent back to Iowa and disbanded. A few years after leaving the army in 1898, David went to work as a salesman for the Monarch Telephone Manufacturing Company, incorporated in Chicago in 1901. Transferred by Monarch to its branch house in Dallas, Texas, the salesman there met and in 1907 married young May Evans, born in 1887, one of the twin daughters of the thrice-wed and soon again to be widowed Ada Manning Price Desel Evans, who resided in nearby Fort Worth. David and May Lingo later moved with their only child, Ada Emma, who was named after both of her grandmothers, to Oakdale, Louisiana, where David was employed by the Oakdale Ice and Light Company, founded in 1913. Tragically, May Evans Lingo died in Oakdale at the age of 31 in 1919 (possibly a victim of the flu pandemic), leaving ten-year-old Ada motherless.

Evidently it was decided that a widowed salesman was not the person to raise a ten-year-old daughter, so Ada went to live with her mother's Texas relations while David Lingo relocated to Houston, where he later married a second time, this time to a widow

with an adolescent son. In the 1920 census, taken a year after May's
death, Ada is listed as residing in affluent Highland Park, near
Dallas, in the household of May's twin sister, Daisy, and Daisy's
husband, James E. Lockart, then the head of the Dallas branch of
Dun & Bradstreet's credit rating agency. The couple's son, James
E. "Jimmy" Lockart II, born in 1915, served as Ada's model in
Murder in Texas for heroine Joan Shields' younger brother
"Jimmie," who plays a key role at the novel's climax.[5] By 1922,
however, Ada was living out west on the barren Texas plains with
her maternal grandmother and one of May's half-brothers, Reuben
Louis Price, an officer in the First National Bank of Big Spring.
Due to the discovery of oil in the region, the decade of the 1920s
was one of robust growth for Big Spring: between 1920 and 1930
its population increased by over 200%, from 4273 to 13, 735.

Symbolizing the growth of Big Spring was the grand opening
in 1930 of the fifteen-story Hotel Settles, then the tallest building
between Forth Worth and El Paso. The $700,000, 170-room grand
hotel, with "running iced water" and bathrooms decorated in
"Egyptian color schemes of black and white," was financed by a
pair of individuals—William Rowan Settles and his wife, Lillian
Greer Settles—whom Ada Lingo in *Murder in Texas* briefly fiction-
alized as a married couple named the Hathaways. Oil had been
discovered on the Settles cattle ranch in 1928, bringing the owners a fortune that others cajoled them into lavishly disbursing on
economic development projects over the next few years. Unfortunately for the Settles and their business ventures, the Depression
diminished their once ample oil revenues, resulting in the sale of
the hotel in 1932. The Hotel Settles survived under new ownership, however, emerging as a local bright spot during the drab
Thirties. Lawrence Welk and his orchestra performed at the hotel
in its early years and, according to a 2013 article in *Texas Monthly*,
people in Big Spring "still talk about the day" in 1935 (the year
Murder in Texas was published) when "former president Herbert
Hoover and his son Allan stopped in [at the Settles] for a lunch of
fried eggs and hash, interrupting the luncheon club's weekly bridge
game." In *Murder in Texas*, Dick Fields, the private detective

pal whom Joan Shields brings to the fictional town of Fordman to help solve the murder of its leading citizen (the local sheriff being an idiot), upon his arrival stays at a suite "at the town's newest hotel," presumably a stand-in for the Hotel Settles, just as Fordman is a stand-in for Big Spring. At the hotel he and Joan thirstily drink a libation of White Rock and ice supplemented by gin from Dick's pocket bottle, prompting Joan to declare: "It's swell to drink something besides corn [whisky] for a change."[6]

By 1935 Ada Lingo's uncle and her grandmother were the acme of respectability in Big Spring society, yet hidden in the family past was a dark scandal concerning the old woman's late elder brothers and the vicious killing in El Paso over a half-century earlier of Federal Marshal Dallas Stoudenmire (1845-1882). Adelaide "Ada" Manning was born in the Tennessee Valley town of Huntsville, Alabama, in 1844 (though her death certificate, in addition to giving the wrong names for her parents, listed the year of her birth as 1846), one of two daughters of Peyton Manning—oddly no relation to the great modern football quarterback with the same name—and his wife Sarah Weeden. Ada's family background placed her in the elite of Huntsville society. On her father's side of the family, her grandfather, James Manning, was "the largest slaveholder in the county" and resided in Huntsville at Oak Grove, a great columned brick mansion, while her uncle Bartley Lowe was a cotton broker and president of the Huntsville Planters' and Merchants' Bank. On her mother's side of the family, her grandfather, William Weeden, also was a wealthy planter and her youngest maternal aunt, Maria Howard Weeden (1846-1905), was a noted watercolorist and poet.[7] However, Peyton Manning's economic position deteriorated before his death in 1853. Manning had owned 93 slaves in Madison County in 1840, but by 1860, after his widow Sarah had removed to a plantation in Montgomery County with the seven children from the marriage (Julia Henrietta, 1835-1911, George Felix, 1837-1925, James, 1840-1915, Francis, 1842-1925, Ada, 1844-1936, John, 1846-?, and William, 1851-1875?), the family slaveholdings had diminished substantially, to 42.

In 1870 Ada Manning was married for the first time, to Benjamin M. Price, son of Caleb Price, a prominent merchant and Republican mayor of Mobile, Alabama. After Benjamin's death around 1875, Ada moved with Reuben and Edmunds, her two young sons from her marriage, to the town of Belton, Texas (about seventy miles northeast of the state capital, Austin), where her sister Julia had already settled with her own family. There in 1877 Ada wed Bachman Desel, a bookkeeper descended from a prominent South Carolina family, and with him had one son, Charles Manning Desel. Bachman Desel's paternal grandfather, Charles Desel, was a noted Charleston cabinetmaker of German origin, while his father, Charles Lewis Desel, was a wealthy lowcountry planter and friend of John Bachman, a Lutheran minister and naturalist who collaborated with John James Audubon. (Bachman Desel was named in the minister's honor.)

Like Benjamin Price, Bachman Desel died just a few years after his marriage; and in 1883 Ada entered the state of matrimony for a third and final occasion, this time with 33-year-old Morgan Evans, a Welsh immigrant and highly regarded Abilene, Texas, building contractor six years younger than Ada, who may have begun to misrepresent her true age at this time. The couple moved to Fort Worth, then undergoing an economic boom as a railroad hub and a center of the cattle trade, and there they had their twin daughters. Ada would survive her final husband by nearly three decades, Evans passing away in 1907 at a Texas spa town, Mineral Springs, where he had gone to recover after "an acute attack of dropsy of the heart and diabetes."[8]

As Ada Manning Evans established for herself and her children lives of everyday respectability in Fort Worth, her five brothers took a markedly different path in life, one of vivid color and calamity that has long found its place in sagas of the frontier American West. In his biography of Dallas Stoudenmire, the Texas gunslinger and lawman who in El Paso became locked in a dance of death with the Manning boys, Leon C. Metz declares that "[t]here is little in the Manning background to indicate a bent toward violence."[9] One might beg to differ somewhat with this assessment.

From Col. James Edmonds Saunders' *Early Settlers of Alabama* (1899), we learn, for example, that one of Ada's uncles, Robert J. Manning, was a "dissipated husband" who gave his wife "many trials" before his death at the age of 42. Additionally, Lowe Davis, Ada's first cousin (once removed) through the Manning line, was an opium addict and compulsive gambler who in 1882 was shot and killed at the age of 21 by his estranged wife, in a case that made regional newspaper headlines, the *Chattanooga Daily Times*, for example, calling the tragedy the "Most Remarkable Killing of the Age." Davis' wife was Lucy Virginia Meriwether, a daughter of Lide Meriwether, a trailblazing southern feminist, and her husband Niles Meriwether, Chief Engineer, before the Civil War, of the Mississippi and Tennessee Railroad and, after the Civil War, of the Memphis and Charleston Railroad. Lucy Meriwether had eloped with Lowe Davis after graduating from seminary at the age of twenty, but she left him when she discerned the true nature of his disturbed character. Upon his trailing Lucy from their home in Memphis to the village of Rhea Springs, a popular health resort in eastern Tennessee where she had gone under the care of her mother, and threatening her, outside the hotel at which she was staying, with death if she did not return to him, Lucy, according to the *Chattanooga Daily Times*, "quietly slipped [a pistol] from her pocket, placed it against [her husband's body], and fired" a shot into his bowels, mortally wounding him.

Although Lucy—"a mere girl, of very handsome appearance"—in shooting her husband was determined to have acted in self-defense (on his deathbed Davis placed the blame for the tragedy entirely on himself), her behavior after the shooting was deemed to have been queerly cool for a fair flower of southern gentility:

> "She then walked deliberately to the hotel, informed the proprietor of what she had done as coolly as if she were relating some trivial incident, and left for her room. She exhibited not the least excitement [that] night, although many ladies [at the hotel] were

in hysterics. . . . She related the circumstances as calmly as if she were telling an anecdote, and at midnight inquired after [her husband], and slept soundly until morning." One is reminded of the declaration about Ada Lingo in her high school annual, "Clever indeed, yet sometimes queer/One couldn't imagine her shedding a tear."

Four years after killing her husband, Lucy—who, like her in-law Ada Lingo five decades later, had decided to pursue a career in medicine—graduated from the Women's Medical College of the New York Infirmary for Women and Children and became one of New York's first female physicians. She later married influential modern American artist Arthur Bowen Davies. In an unusual gender twist, Lucy's wealthy family, who kept the Lowe Davis scandal a secret from Bowen, required the then impecunious artist to sign a prenuptial agreement renouncing any claim on Lucy's money in the event of a divorce.

The taint of wildness and violent impulse that was discerned in Robert J. Manning and Lowe Davis also can be detected in Ada Manning Evans' male siblings: Felix, Jim, Frank, John, and William. All but William, the youngest of the brothers, served in the Civil War, in which, according to family accounts, they were zealously committed to the southern cause. With both their parents dead after the war, the hardened veterans, so family legend runs, collected young William and traveled to Mexico, where they fought as mercenaries on behalf of Emperor Maximillian. After the defeat of the Imperial forces and the deposed emperor's execution by firing squad in 1867, the Manning brothers hightailed it to Texas. Felix, who before the war had been educated in medicine at the University of Alabama and in Paris, completed his training at the Medical College of Alabama in Mobile and started a practice in Belton, while Jim, Frank, John, and William led cattle drives between East Texas and Kansas. After William purportedly was bushwhacked and murdered in 1875, Jim, Frank, and John, it is said, implacably pursued the villain who killed their young brother, vengefully slaying him in return.

By 1880, this tough trio had settled in the booming southwest Texas town of El Paso (then known as the "Six Shooter Capital" on account of its lawlessness and general mayhem), where they were joined the next year by Felix, who already had a dangerous reputation of his own on account of a bloody knife fight in which he and a rival doctor had engaged in the 1870s. In spite of his quick temper ("as sharp as a scalpel," as Leon Metz puts it) and propensity for violence, however, an admiring contemporary speculated that the well-educated, violin-playing "Doc," as he was known, was "probably the most accomplished gentlemen in early El Paso." Doc established a new medical practice in the troubled town, and according to city council minutes "he was one of the few doctors ministering to the impoverished sick," including sufferers from smallpox, a disease, notes Leon Metz, which laid waste to more people in El Paso "than Indians or outlaws ever did."[10]

For their part the other Manning boys, Frank, Jim, and John, became important players in El Paso, opening saloons, buying real estate, rustling castle on the sly (it was said) and dabbling in politics. (Jim ran for mayor, finishing fourth in a field of four.) Soon the Manning boys and their supporters clashed with El Paso's new town marshal, the fearsome, six-foot-four gunslinger Dallas Stoudenmire, who also came originally from Alabama. Machinations by the Mannings and others in the town spurred several shooting melees between the town marshal and Manning allies, including the infamous "Four Dead in Five Seconds Gunfight" (April 14, 1881), which left casualties on both sides and resentment between Stoudenmire and the Mannings constantly simmering, threatening to boil over at any time. Town fathers pressed the two warring factions to sign a peace pledge, by which they agreed to let bygones be bygones and "meet and pass each other on peaceable terms," but unsurprisingly this agreement did not hold for long.

Although Stoudenmire was forced out of the office of town marshal, he remained in El Paso as a deputy US Marshal. The long-feared Stoudenmire–Manning death match took place on September 18, 1882 (less than a year after the more famous Gunfight at the O. K. Corral), when Doc and Dallas, after exchanging hot words in the Manning Saloon, both went for their guns and fired, gravely wounding each other in an exchange of bullets. The combatants closed and grappled with each other in mortal combat, until Jim Manning appeared and managed to shoot Stoudenmire in the head (after first hitting a barber's pole), killing him instantly. Both Doc and Jim Manning were acquitted of murder at separate trials, and not long afterward the two men, along with Frank, left El Paso for Flagstaff, Arizona. (Whatever happened to John Manning—seemingly the silent partner in the Manning clan—currently seems unclear.) Doc and Frank died in Arizona in 1925, while Jim, who later resided in Washington and Glendale, California, passed away from cancer a decade earlier, in 1915. A Manning descendant has asserted that the famed silent film western actor William S. Hart once asked Jim Manning for permission to portray his life story, but that Jim turned him down because he "didn't want his past to follow him or his children into California." (Hart, who starred in his first hit western in 1914, a year before Jim Manning's death, later struck up a correspondence with Wyatt Earp of O. K. Corral fame, hoping to make a film about the legendary lawman. His 1923 film *Wild Bill Hickock* featured Earp as an important character and was the first film to portray Earp's ally Doc Holiday.)[11]

Did the enduring Ada Manning Evans, who survived all her siblings by a decade or more, impart any of this lively and lurid family lore to her granddaughter Ada Lingo, thereby helping to stimulate on the part of an inquisitive and ingenious young woman disenchanted with her small-town surroundings an interest in literature of crime and mystery (or, for that matter, in medicine, both Lucy Virginia Meriwether and George Felix Manning having not only become involved in murders but also pursued careers as doctors—killing *and* curing, as it were)? Certainly Ada Lingo's *Murder in Texas* offers an illustration of how a slaying in a small town enlivened life for one young woman residing there. The novel opens

in the office of the Fordman *Daily News*, where society page editor
Joan Shields is going about her generally tedious job, which mostly
consists of detailing the activities of Fordman's seemingly innumer-
able women's social organizations, like Mrs. W. H. Shaw's Laff-a-Lot
Bridge Club. An exasperated Joan finds that even when John Fordman—multimillionaire oil man, rancher and newspaper owner—is
found shot dead in his luxury Isotta–Fraschini limousine, in which
he had been viewing the shooting of his latest oil well, Mrs. Shaw
believes that her club activities are more "fit to print":

> . . . [Joan] winced at the thought of having to ex-
> plain the omission of Mrs. Shaw's party from last
> night's edition. She rescued the story from a pile of
> dusty copy paper on the desk and rushed back into
> the shop with it. Leaving it impaled with its heading
> on one of the linotype operator's "hurry" hooks, she
> dashed back and called the irate Mrs. Shaw. That
> began a long session of calls. The garnering of news
> relating to the crop of parties, sewing-bees, and
> church-circle meetings which made up the life of the
> women of Fordman. Joan copied down lists of
> names, took details of scores of parties large and
> small, sorted out her notes, and typed rapidly dur-
> ing the rest of the morning. The party lists were long
> and the entertainments were many, for the July
> Fourth holidays despite the heat bred as many
> bridges and brides' showers as did Christmas. More
> than one hundred women had entertained as many
> as one thousand of their sisters—had worked franti-
> cally through the day before and the morning of the
> party, cleaning their little box-like houses, counting
> decks of cards, moulding Jello salads, numbering
> tallies, cutting bread into hearts and spades and dia-
> mond shapes, tying prizes into tissue-paper bundles
> with pink, green and lavender ribbons. More than
> one hundred husbands ate suppers of leftover Jello

salads and the slightly curled-up fancy sandwiches,
amid a littler of dirty dishes and crumpled Madeira
napkins stained with lipstick. Mrs. Johnson won a
wall vase. Mrs. Sanders won a boudoir pillow. Mrs.
Evans won a nest of brass ashtrays, made in Japan.
And so it would go on, forevermore, thought Joan.

In this striking passage concerning what might be termed the
evil of banality, which wryly includes a "Mrs. Evans" among the
prizewinning clubwomen of Fordman, Ada Lingo's own frustration
with the limitations imposed on her as a "girl reporter" in Big
Spring is palpable. Like Ada, Joan Shields previously worked on a
New York newspaper before returning to her Texas plains home
town; and she longs to return to the more open outside world. To
Dick Fields, Joan's private detective chum from her days in New
York, Joan complains about the dullness of her life in Fordman
(indicating in passing that she shares Ada's interests in reading,
swimming, and tennis):

"Drink and play bridge—isn't there anything else to
do in this burg?"
"Not much. We have no library. I read about
twenty magazines a month and import as many
books as I can afford. We play golf, the swimming's
lousy, and the tennis courts are monopolized by the
high school children. Some Sundays we spend the
entire day just riding up and down the Main Drag,
out East Highway and back by Lover's Lane. It gets
rather boring!"

A perplexed Dick asks Joan, "Why do you stay, kid?" To which Joan
shrugs and explains, "Mom wants me here for a while, anyway, and
she hasn't been well, you know. Besides, it's a good job and jobs
are scarce as the dickens now, in the newspaper business."
Once again, it is easy to imagine parallels to Ada's own life in
the early 1930s, when Ada, who had lost both a job with the *New*

York World and a life with her husband, returned to Big Spring,
where her elderly grandmother was ailing. Like a contemporary
Oklahoma mystery writer, Todd Downing (1902-1974), a presumably gay author who had a very close relationship with his maternal grandmother in the small town of Atoka, Ada Lingo appears to
have harbored some decidedly ambivalent, if not downright negative, feelings about her native ground. Unlike Downing, however,
Lingo permanently cut the provincial cord, when she moved out to
the more cosmopolitan Pacific Coast.[12]

In *Murder in Texas* Joan Shields is attracted to men, though
the love element remains fairly muted throughout the novel. Dick
Shields is clearly interested in Joan, but Joan does not reciprocate
his interest. The two former denizens of the Big Apple are, however, great comrades in crime investigation, sharing common taste
not only in booze but in books. After "two colored boys" bring in
their dinner at the hotel, she and Dick eat and talk "of New York
and the people they had known there and of the better movies and
the few better books that Joan had been able to procure in the little
town. Joan discovered that Dick had never read Olive Schreiner's
"The Story of an African Farm" and he in turn moaned over the
fact that she had not seen "Maedchen in Uniform." It is telling, as
it relates to the author's own personal interests, that this related
discussion between Joan and Dick revolves around a book recognized as one of the first feminist novels and a pioneering and then
controversial German film concerning intimate relationships
among women.[13]

After the novel's second murder, Joan and Dick again find time
during their investigations to discuss books, when Joan espies a
library of most intriguing tomes at the dead man's house:

> [Joan] . . . squatted to peer at the titles of the books
> under the bay window. She gasped when she saw
> "The Antichrist' by Nietzsche, several volumes of
> Schopenhauer, a small leather-bound edition of
> "Alice in Wonderland," Mrs. Buck's classic "The
> Good Earth," both volumes of Emma Goldman's

autobiography, Joel Sayres's "Rackety Rax," and a
complete set of Romain Rolland. She smiled to see
Marie D. Scopes's "Married Love" standing on the
bottom shelf between Havelock Ellis's "Little Essays"
and Dr. Logan Clendening's "The Human Body."

She revised her secret estimate of the [second
murder victim] and regretted that she hadn't known
him better. . . . she showed [Dick] the books and he
laughed.

"You'd judge the Lord himself by his taste in literature. When you get to heaven you'll go around
squatting in front of all the archangels' bookcases."

"I'll bet the most interesting literature will be
found in hell, darling. All of the 'antis' will be in
heaven and they'll censor the books that are imported from this earth. Can you imagine an archangel from Boston allowing me to enter with
Faulkner's 'Sanctuary' under my arm?"

Hardly," he laughed. "But how about the Songs
of Solomon? Wouldn't it be funny if a Boston archangel banned the Bible?"

This passage, which wryly alludes to the once-common phrase
"Banned in Boston" (a reference to the zealous efforts of Boston's
Watch and Ward Society to censor books and the performing arts),
is of interest not only for its mentions of people who were in the
revolutionary vanguard of radical culture, like sexual theorist
Havelock Ellis and political anarchist Emma Goldman, but for its
inclusion of Joel Sayre, whose *Rackety Rax* (1932), a satirical novel
of corruption in college football, was made into a popular pre-Code
film. Sayre had worked as a crime reporter at the *New York World*
and the *New York Herald Tribune* (during which time he wrote
numerous articles about notorious New York bootlegger Jack "Legs"
Diamond, who was murdered in 1931) and he likely had known Ada
Lingo when she was employed at the *World*. Sayre later wrote screen-
plays in Hollywood and short stories for the *New Yorker*, including

"The Man on the Ledge," which was adapted into a critically acclaimed suspense film under the title *Fourteen Hours* (1951).

The omnivorous Joan hankers after mystery fiction as well, as we learn when she enviously surveys a work colleague's collection: "Joan fingered Kay Cleaver Strahan's latest thriller, noted Mignon Eberhart's 'White Cockatoo,' Francis Iles's 'Before the Fact,' and Leslie Ford's delightful 'Murder in Maryland.' She felt cheated that she could not take away with her Mrs. Rinehart's 'The Album' which she'd been unable to keep up with in the *Saturday Evening Post*." (Mary Roberts Rinehart's *The Album* was serialized in April-May 1933 and published in June of that year, while the other novels were all published in 1932 and 1933, giving an idea, incidentally, of just when the events in *Murder in Texas* take place.)[14]

While Joan, a true bibliophile, may go positively wobbly over books, she is a jaded and fairly hard-boiled character in other instances—as when she is judging other women, for example. "Funerals embarrassed her, ministers annoyed her, and umbrageous females made her slightly ill," we are tartly informed concerning Joan at one point in the novel. One Fordman woman she dismisses as "a neuro if I ever saw one, to say nothing of being the worst hypochondriac in Texas," while of a couple of others she pronounces: "Both she and Mildred are cases for a good psychiatrist. Not mental cases—I don't mean that. Nymphomania, I believe it's called, isn't it? They can't behave normally where men are concerned."

Of the hypocrisies of Fordman society Joan is unfailingly caustic in conversation with Dick:

> Joan . . . walked to a window [at the hotel where she
> is having dinner with Dick].
> "The orchestra's tuning up," she said.
> "What orchestra?" asked Dick, joining her.
> "Roy's Rascals from El Paso, to be specific. Don't
> you know what day this is? It's the Fourth of July
> and the local roisterers always dance on Independence Day. It's another excuse for drinking."

"Drinking seems to be the main occupation of the majority of your citizens."

"Yes, isn't it amazing? Senator Morris Sheppard's state, stronghold of the W.C.T.U., and I've grappled personally with more drunks here than I *saw* during two whole years in New York. Though repeal is nation-wide, I'll bet dollars to a drink of corn that we'll have local enforcement here. It's as paradoxical as Kansas with her Jake-leg cases."[15]

Joan does have her "soft" moments, however. Clearly she is fond of the members of her family, particularly her irrepressible younger brother, Jimmie, an "avid reader of mystery stories" who seems intent on following his journalist sister into the newspaper trade. The relationship between the two siblings—based, as mentioned above, on Ada Lingo's own real-life relationship with her younger cousin Jimmy Lockart (who as a child, Ada humorously told his son, "used to follow her around like a puppy dog")—is portrayed with gruff charm in several vignettes, including one involving a scrumptious plate of strawberry shortcake:

"I'll get your strawberry shortcake, Sis," said the boy.

"Thanks."

He returned from the kitchen a few minutes later with the dessert, its crisp short biscuit covered with crushed berries and topped by a mound of cream.

"It's kind of rich, Sis," he said. "Sure you want it?"

She said "yes" and ate half of it while he watched her sadly. "Here, bum," she said, and pushed the rest to him.

Joan admires the "Nordic handsomeness" of her recently "finished" friend Marion Fordman, the privileged daughter of the murdered millionaire oil man, though the naïve Marion is sometimes perplexed by what she deems oddness in Joan:

"What can we do, Joan? *I* don't know any detective, I'm sure."

"Ah," replied Joan, "but *I* do."

"You always did know such queer people. I remember that party you had for me in New York. Why, there was even a gangster there."

"Not a gangster. Mike was just a nice college lad paying his way through Columbia by selling very poor Golden Wedding rye."[16]

On the whole Joan gets along better with the male population of Fordman, including, besides her brother Jimmie and her buddy Dick, her editor at the *Daily News*, Edward Frank, to whom she is romantically attracted. After Frank looks down at her at the office and puts "a slim hand over hers as they rested on the typewriter," telling her "You're a sweet kid, Joan," before walking quickly away, Joan stares after him, "excited and pleased." What follows is an impressive passage evoking the intensity of hidden passion: "An inner voice keened out, 'He touched you, not casually, but deliberately. He wants you, he's yours now.' Her fingers were cold and trembled against the hard, positive keys of the machine. She jerked them up and lighted a cigarette. When she smoked it through her heart was still pounding but her head was clear. She worked again."

Today's readers likely will find patronizing the attitude which Joan exhibits toward Fordman's black and Jewish inhabitants. Potentially implicated, variously as culprit or witness as the case may be, in the murder of John Fordman are the three members of a prominent local Jewish family, the Levys, comprised of Joseph "Joey" Levy, "the town's leading merchant"; his wife, Etta; and their eight-year-old daughter, Rea. Joan offhandedly dismisses Joey Levy as a plausible suspect in Fordman's murder, as she deems him "a pretty harmless fat Rotarian. The only thing I have against him is that he pats me on the back and shakes my hand every time he sees me. And often he sees me two or three times a day!" Certainly the initial description in the novel of Levy is indicative of Joan's distaste, for stoutness at least: "He was perspiring heavily—

large, plump man that he was—and his bald dome glistened with tiny beads of sweat. Dark crescents of perspiration showed under his arms, on his pale blue shirt. . . . His shirt billowed limply over the top of his trousers and his fat stomach bulged forward, straining the tight linen." Levy's wife, Etta, is described in decidedly mixed terms, as "large and darkly Jewish. . . . Her lovely face, with its clear-white skin and its contrast of smooth black hair, rose incongruously from her squat, uncouth body." Daughter Rea gets off lightly, relatively speaking, with Joan summing her up as "quite intelligent, if a pest." Still, Joan is much more disdainful of the "tall, militant English wife" of the Christian minister Reverend Brush, whom she bluntly describes to her mother in one word: "awful." One suspects that with Joan disdain is ecumenical.

The two most notable black characters in the novel are Fordman's chauffeur, Texas Wills, described as "a small mulatto, very dapper, always courteous, and quite well-educated according to the standards of the Southern negro." Joan addresses him familiarly by his first name, as she does all the black people of the town. (Some locals do not even bother to refer to "Texas" by his given name, instead simply calling him "the nigger man.") At a later point in the story, Joan in pursuing a clue tries to wheedle information out of a black washerwoman named Belinda. She promises the enterprising Belinda to write a news story about her laundry business for the newspaper and later thinks to herself ruefully that she will actually have to follow through with her pledge, her mother having always lectured her, "Never promise a child or a negro anything unless you intend to do it. They are too easily disappointed." Some modern readers may cringe at the paternalistic attitude that this moral injunction signifies, but there is, on the other hand, a certain poignancy present as well, when one reflects on the position of genuine dependence so many black Americans were pressed into at this time in American history, and not solely in the South. Intriguingly, Jim Lockart recalls that later in life, when Ada lived in a fine home in Los Angeles, complete with a swimming pool and tennis court (reflecting her lifelong athletic passions), she one day announced to her cousin Jimmy that a "nice negro gentleman" had

moved in next door. The "nice negro gentleman" turned out to be
Harry Belafonte.[17]

Aside from providing fascinating portrayals in *Murder in Texas*
of both a rather hard-boiled heroine and of social relations in a
Texas oil town in the 1930s, Ada Lingo, an ardent environmentalist, effectively evokes the southwestern landscape of her novel's
setting: the "Mexican choppers" in "variegated clothes" showing
"brightly in the young green" of the cotton fields; the "fat, red cattle
with white faces," stretching their "short necks upward" to reach
the beans in the red seed pods hanging from "ragged mesquite
trees"; the jackrabbits leaping "like giant grasshoppers under the
barbed-wire fences and into the mesquite clumps." At the dramatic
climax of the novel, when a desperate and dangerous murderer
stands perilously close to exposure, a sandstorm bears down re-
lentlessly on Fordman, a natural menace memorably portrayed by
the author:

> ". . . the air was heavy and dead. Small funnel-shaped
> whorls of dust twisted crazily about the streets, and
> these miniature cyclones, swirling papers, weeds,
> and dead leaves, dipped from lawn to roadway,
> caught at flowers, and twisted the tops of trees. Joan
> looked across the north at the reddish wall of ap-
> proaching dust. It had grown in height and would
> probably envelop Fordman within an hour or two.
> She looked at the clock on the dashboard. It was
> four-forty-five."

As for the mystery itself, you will find that you have a real Texas
twister on your hands when you open the pages of *Murder in Texas*.
In the perplexing affair of John Fordman's murder, there is no
shortage of potential suspects in the broiling Texas oil town, what
with journalists, town fathers and even a mistress or two in the
offing as people who had ample reason to want the town's not
altogether admirable kingpin put six feet underground. With
Murder in Texas, the enterprising and acerbic Ada Lingo evidently

intended to blow the lid off small-town hypocrisy with an enter-
taining and clever detective story, and in this effort she admirably
succeeded.

FOOTNOTES

[1] The name of the College of Industrial Arts was changed in 1934
to the Texas State College for Women (now known as Texas
Women's University). Ada Lingo's ex-husband Charles Hatcher
married again in 1940. Ada continued to use the surname
"Hatcher" in her professional capacity as a doctor, though she
published her detective novel under the name "Ada E. Lingo." Jim
Lockart, Ada's first cousin, once removed, humorously recalled
to me one day when Ada, having gone out with his mother and
returned home with her to find a great mess that had been left
there by his father, remarked humorously, "Well, honey, I guess
that's why I'm still unmarried."

[2] *Big Spring Daily Herald*, 13 October 1935, 5 (Review of *Murder
in Texas*). The *Herald* reviewer noted several telltale similarities
between Big Spring locales and places in the novel: "The newspaper office is the former cubby hole occupied by The Herald. The
road to the oil field where the murder occurred in chapter one, is
the road to Forsan. The court house, a red sandstone atrocity . . .
etc." Forsan is a small community located a dozen miles southwest of Big Spring. Oil drillers struck four "pay sands" on a local
ranch in 1926, leading to the coining of the village's name ("four
sands"). The red sandstone courthouse at Big Spring, dubbed an
"atrocity" by Ada Lingo in *Murder in Texas*, was built in 1908
and demolished 45 years later, in 1953. Doyle Phillips of
TexasEscapes differs from Ada in her estimation of the 1908 courthouse, calling it, rather, "beautiful and architecturally tasteful"
and its "Soviet-style" Fifties replacement a concrete monstros-
ity. See "Howard County Courthouse," TexasEscapes.com,

athttp://www.texasescapes.com/TOWNS/BigSpring Texas/
HowardCountyCourthouse.htm. In an author's note at the beginning of *Murder in Texas*, Ada declared that all of the characters
"have been drawn *entirely* from my imagination," but the *Herald*
reviewer was not buying that declaration: "They say that all writers have to do this."

[3] Jim Lockart's father told him that Ada wrote two detective novels, both of which he read. Ethelwyn "Ditty" Gilluly also traveled
with Ada and Jean to Los Angeles in 1939. Twelve years older
than Ada, Ethelwyn grew up in Big Spring and graduated from
the School of Nursing at Texas University Medical School in the
1920s, after which she moved for a time to San Diego, California,
where she worked as a private nurse. After her widowed mother's
death in 1935, she moved back to Big Spring, where she died unmarried at the age of 89 in 1986. Her parents, James and Mary
McMahon Gilluly, moved to Big Spring from Michigan with their
three children in 1899. James Gilluly, who worked as brakeman
with the Texas & Pacific Railroad, died in a train crash in 1908,
after which her mother supplemented the family income by taking in boarders. Ethelwyn's photo in her college annual reveals
an attractive woman with an apparent soulful bent, judging from
the adjacent poetic caption: "With this poor life, with this mean
world/I fain complete what in me lies/I strive to perfect mine own
self/My soul's ambition to be wise." Possibly Ethelwyn's mother
was an admirer of the once-popular Canadian poet Ethelwyn
Wetherald (1857-1940).

[4] Elaine Waller, blog entry, 4 July 2007, *Know the Lingo*, at
http://knowthelingo.blogspot.com/2007/07/i-am-easily-
amused.html.

[5] Jim Lockart to Curtis Evans (email), 25 October 2016. Before
the Second World War Ada's cousin Jimmy also worked at a Texas
newspaper, the *Dallas Morning News*. During the war he "served

in the Army Air Corps, spending most of his military service in the Pentagon," according to his 2003 obituary in the *Austin American-Statesman*, for which he was awarded the Legion of Merit. After the war he went to work for Southwest Airmotive in Dallas, becoming Chief Operating Officer of the company. Jimmy's son recalls that his father and Ada remained close late in their lives, conversing monthly on the telephone. Throughout his life David Lingo maintained a relationship with Ada, even though this ultimately plunged him into family litigation in the 1950s. On October 4, 1951, David and his ailing second wife, Rose Darnell Lingo, made wills naming each other as principal beneficiaries and Rose's three daughters from her first marriage as contingent beneficiaries. Ada Lingo and Rose's son from her prior marriage, Curtis Darnell, were omitted as beneficiaries from both wills. After Rose's death on February 18, 1952, David destroyed his will and made another, in which he named as beneficiaries not only his three stepdaughters but Ada as well. Rose's daughters sued David, alleging that he had broken his pledge to his wife to exclude Ada from the will. In *Richardson v. Lingo* (1955), the Court of Civil Appeals of Texas, Galveston decided in David's favor. David Lingo died three years later in Los Angeles, at the age of 82. After his death Ada ordered from the US army a bronze marker, based on his brief military service sixty years previously in the Spanish-American War, for his grave in Houston, which lay beside Rose Lingo's. May Evans Lingo is buried in Fort Worth, in the same cemetery with her parents and twin sister.

[6] Bryan Mealer, "Up with the Old Hotel: How a Fabulously Wealthy Native Son of Big Spring Came Home to Save the Settles," *Texas Monthly* (March 2013), at http://www.texasmonthly.com/the-culture/up-with-the-old-hotel/. Closed in 1980, the Hotel Settles, once seemingly doomed to oblivion, since has been gloriously restored. At one point in *Murder in Texas*, Joan Shields discourses about the Hathaways, who seem clearly drawn from the Settles:

"That's the Hathaway place," explained Joan. "They made their fortune in oil leases and spent it in two years. Never thought that the money would quit coming in. They had a little ranch out southeast of town and the discovery well of the Hathaway pool was sunk in the chicken-yard, much to old Mrs. Hathaway's sorrow. She loved her chicken-yard. She raised grand fryers too. We used to buy 'em from her. . . . When the slump came . . . they found themselves destitute. They'd built and donated the new Episcopal Church, put up an eighteen-story office building that has four offices rented, and a slick grafter who handled their affairs got out of town overnight with around five hundred thousand dollars. That's the local gossip, any-way."

[7] Daniel S. Dupre, *Transforming the Cotton Frontier: Madison County, Alabama, 1800-1840* (Baton Rouge and London: Louisiana State University Press, 1997), 37. The Weeden's Federal-style Huntsville townhouse, which was built in 1819 and purchased by William Weeden shortly before his death in 1846, is preserved today as a house museum. Maria Howard Weeden, who in her work drew inspiration from Huntsville's community of freed slaves, published four books of poetry, illustrated with her watercolors: *Shadows on the Wall* (1898), *Bandanna Ballads* (1899, with a foreword from Joel Chandler Harris), *Songs of the Old South* (1901) and *Old Voices* (1904). In *Black Like You: Blackface, Whiteface, Insult and Imitation in American Popular Culture* (2006), John Strausbaugh deems Weeden "a self-taught artist of considerable skill" whose "portraits of Negroes . . . are extraordinarily realistic, sympathetic and sometimes even insight-ful," even as he dismisses Weeden's poetry as "some of the sweet-est, most genteel, and weepily nostalgic of all Negro-dialect verse. . . ." (p. 174).

[8] *Abilene Daily Reporter*, 31 August 1907, 5.

[9] Leon C. Metz, *Dallas Stoudenmire: El Paso Marshall* (1969; Norman, OK: University of Oklahoma Press, 1993), 93.

[10] Leon C. Metz, Metz, "Stoudenmire: El Paso Marshal," in *The Shooters* (1976; New York: Berkeley, 1996), 96; Metz, *Dallas Stoudenmire*, 96.

[11] Barbara Astorga, 1 July 2008 comment to "Back to El Paso," 15 October 2007, *The Life, Times and Adventures of Rambling Bob*, at https://ramblingbob.wordpress.com/2007/10/15/back-to-el-paso/; Paul Andrew Hutton, "Wyatt Earp's First Film: William S. Hart's *Wild Bill Hickok*," 7 May 2012, *True West: History of the American Frontier*, at http://www.truewestmagazine.com/wyatt-earps-first-film/. For the best accounts of the Stoudenmire–Manning machinations in El Paso see Metz, *Dallas Stoudenmire*, Metz, "Stoudenmire: El Paso Marshal," and Eugene Cunningham, "Two-Gun Marshal: Dallas Stoudenmire," in his classic *Trigger-nometry: A Gallery of Gunfighters* (1934; Norman, OK: University of Oklahoma Press, 1996). For a succinct internet account see "Dallas Stoudenmire," 10 October 2014, *Jeff Arnold's West: The Blog of a Western Fan for Other Western Fans*, at http://jeffarnoldblog. blogspot.com/2014/10/dallas-stoudenmire.html. In *Murder in Texas*, Lingo on the first page of the novel passingly mentions Flagstaff, Arizona, the city where Felix Manning prominently established himself and his family after leaving El Paso in 1887. Coincidence?

[12] "Cosmopolitan" was the word Ada herself used to describe Los Angles, according to Jim Lockart. Todd Downing's nine detective novels, originally published between 1933 and 1941, have been reprinted by Coachwhip Publications. For more on Downing see my book *Clues and Corpses: The Detective Fiction and Mystery Criticism of Todd Downing* (2013).

[13] In one of his works of mystery fiction Todd Downing, who spent time in early 1930s New York visiting his sister, a student at

Columbia University, similarly makes reference to *Maedchen in Uniform*.

[14] Presumably the Kay Cleaver Strahan novel referenced is *October House* (1932). On Leslie Ford's *Murder in Maryland*, see my review of the novel at my *The Passing Tramp* blog, at http:// thepassingtramp.blogspot.com/2013/06/mind-your-murders-leslie-fords-murder.html. In my review I praised the novel's "nicely-attuned social observation about life and manners in a small southern town" and its woman doctor protagonist, elements which I suspect greatly contributed to Ada Lingo's pronouncing it "delightful" in her own *Murder in Texas*, the very title of which Ford's book probably inspired.

[15] As the author of the Eighteenth Amendment, Senator Morris Sheppard of Texas was known as the "father of national Prohibition." The W.C.T.U. (Women's Christian Temperance Union) was a leading force in the temperance movement. Local enforcement, or local option, allows local political jurisdictions, typically counties or municipalities, the authority to decide whether or how alcohol will be sold within their jurisdictions. "Jake-leg" was a phenomenon mentioned in Kirke Mechem's detective novel *The Strawstack Murder Case* (original title *A Frame for Murder*), which was set in Wichita, Kansas and published a year after *Murder in Texas*. In my introduction to Coachwhip's 2013 reissue of the novel I discussed "Jake-leg" in a footnote, which I quote below:

The novel's references to Jamaica Ginger may not be familiar today, but certainly would have been so in the United States in 1936, particularly to Kansans. Jamaica Ginger, or "Jake" as it was popularly known, was a highly intoxicating preparation (160 proof) of the fluid extract of ginger. It had long been marketed to Americans as a patent medicine said to relieve headaches, chronic coughing, flatulence and other maladies (and not incidentally making quite a potent tipple). As Cecil Munsey has noted, Jake "was readily available in local drugstores, groceries, and even dime stores; and anyone, including preachers and schoolmarms, could slip the little flat aqua or clear glass bottle into a pocket for a discreet nip at home or away." As a putative "medicine," Jake initially was exempted from the 1919 National Prohibition Act (popularly known as the Volstead Act). However, in 1925 the Treasury Department ruled that Jamaica Ginger could be sold over the counter only if the level of ginger root extractives in it was doubled, making the concoction extremely unpalatable. Not surprisingly, enterprising bootleggers immediately began selling illicitly adulterated Jake. Unfortunately, two Boston brothers-in-law chose to adulterate their Jamaica Ginger with a neurotoxic substance, tri-ortho-cresyl phosphate. TOCP was "a plasticizer used to keep synthetic materials from becoming brittle." Imbibers of Jake adulterated with TOCP became afflicted with paralysis of the hands and feet. This condition was dubbed Jake Paralysis or Jake Leg/Jake Walk, for the lurching gait of victims. In 1930, the year the events in *The Strawstack Murder Case* likely take place, Wichita recorded some of the earliest instances of Jake Leg sufferers, including "nine women, members of a bridge club in the fashionable College Hill district," who drank punch their hostess had spiked with Jamaica Ginger. By March, five hundred cases (about one percent of the adult population) had been reported in the city. Wichita's poorhouse was soon overrun with indigent victims of Jake Leg. In Memphis on May 5, 1930, the Allen Brothers recorded *The Jake Walk Blues* ("I can't eat, I can't talk/Been drinkin' mean Jake, Lord, now I can't walk"); the song sold over 20,000 copies. John Kobler, *Arden Spirits: The Rise and Fall of Prohibition* (1973; rpnt, New York: Da Capo, 1993), 301-302; Cecil Munsey, "Paralysis in a Bottle: the 'Jake Walk' Story," in *Bottles and Extras* 17 (Winter 2006): 7-12; "'Jake' Paralysis New Dry Era Malady," *The Delmarva Star*, 11 May 1930, 10; "Jake Paralysis Hits One in 100 in Wichita, Kan.," *Berkeley Daily Gazette*, 18 July 1930, 20.

[16] Schenley's Golden Wedding rye whiskey was an extremely popular brand of liquor before Prohibition and during the putatively dry years of the Twenties "American bootleggers sold an inferior whiskey that they called Golden Wedding." See http://www.prohibitionrepeal.com/history/bb_america.asp.

[17] The most regrettable passage in the novel in this regard takes place when Joan—caught in the act of snooping for clues in another person's home—attempts to imitate the voice of a black maid on the telephone.

MURDER IN TEXAS

If any character or name used in this book resembles that of any living person it is merely a coincidence, for all have been drawn *entirely* from my imagination.

The Author

CHARACTERS

John Fordman: *Victim Number 1—For him they changed the front page.*

Samuel Ross: *A banker—"Alice in Wonderland" sat beside "Married Love."*

Clarence Jones: *Grocer—They called him "Chick."*

Agnes Jones: *His wife—Cherchez la femme?*

Mildred Jones: *Their daughter—Men were her forte.*

Mitchell White: *Reporter—Whiskey saved him.*

Edward Frank: *His boss—Nothing meant much to him!*

Joan Shields: *Gal reporter—The cynic or the "dick"?*

Marion Fordman: *Heiress—No local belle, she!*

Gerard Drexell: *Fordman's assistant—No local Don Juan.*

Mrs. Glieth Lawrence: *Fordman's fiancée—Her happiness was brief.*

Joseph Levy: *Merchant—Do fat men ever kill?*

Texas Wills: *Chauffeur—He cursed and cried.*

Jimmie Shields: *Joan's kid brother—In at the kill!*

Val Day: *Driller—His truck backfired.*

Richard Fields: *Private detective.*

Jim Read: *Sheriff.*

Tom Harte: *Deputy.*

Judge William Connor Millbank: *County Attorney.*

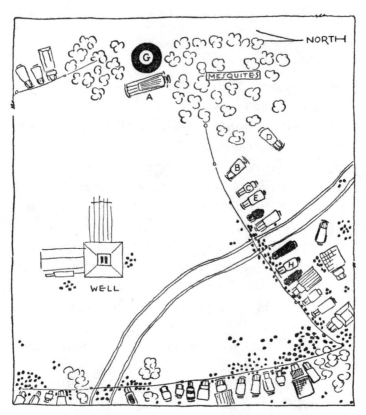

A. Fordman's Fraschini   E. Levy's Buick
B. Jones's LaSalle   G. Storage Tank
C. White's Ford   H. Trotter's Car
D. Ross's Cadillac

I: MONDAY, JULY 3: 2.15 P.M.

"Yes, Mrs. Shaw. I got that. And who'd you say won high-score prize? Mrs. Hall for members and Miss Vanna Belle Smith for guests? Yessum. I'll remember to put in about Janice giving tallies. Thank you so much, Mrs. Shaw. Good-bye."

And Joan Shields, society editor of the Fordman *Daily News*, dropped the receiver of her telephone back onto its hook and leaned back in her hard desk chair with a sigh of relief. Damn Mrs. Shaw and her Laff-a-Lot Bridge Club, anyway.

It was hot, hot as hell, she thought, as she lighted a cigarette and then wiped her damp face with her handkerchief. The brassy afternoon sun seemed hung forever motionless just above the parched locust tree across the street in front of the little building. It concentrated intense heat fiercely on the plate-glass front windows of the office, and the little room, with its crowded desks and filthy paper-littered floor, was like an oven. The acrid odor of hot lead and scorched shavings stung Joan's nostrils and left a flat metallic taste in her mouth. The incessant clatter of the linotypes and the shouts of the back-shop men came distractingly loud over the top of the wall-board partition that divided the office from the newspaper plant.

Joan rose and went to look at the A.P. printers in the front of the room. Lord, but the news was dead. Dallas was typing through:

Flagstaff, Ariz., July 3 (A.P.). Fifteen persons were injured seriously, two perhaps fatally, and 26 others

43

received minor hurts in a miscalculated explosion
of black powder and dynamite . . .

Flagstaff was too far away, thought Joan. No one in this hot,
dusty, depressed little Texas town really cared how many people
were injured in an explosion a thousand miles away. They were
more interested in the daily business of their neighbors—in the
fact that Mrs. Harris was pregnant again; that Doc Ross had taken
the new manicure girl at the Frederick Hotel to the movies last
night; that John Fordman was bringing in a new gusher right on
his Paw's old farm and out of soil that even the hens had refused
to scratch.

She turned to the clock, 'Correct Time By Western Union,' and
noticed that it was already two-thirty. Mitchell should be back with
the story on the well soon. The paper was being held up until three,
waiting for confirmation on the story of the new strike. The story
itself, written several days before, had been in type for hours.
Fordman had known that there was oil in his well, but he preferred
to tell the world about it dramatically on the front page of this
paper he owned—immediately after the public strike had been
made.

Joan decided to type the story of Mrs. Shaw's party now, while
it was still fresh in her mind, so she returned to her desk, turned
the little cushion in her chair, sat down and pulled her machine
toward her on its rolling stand.

"Soc. #1," she pecked in the upper left-hand corner of the yellow sheet, and under that, "Mrs. W. H. 18 pt." She threw the carriage back into position with a bang, spaced five times mechanically, and began rapidly:

Mrs. W. H. Shaw, 305 West Eighth Street, was hostess to the members of the Laff-a-Lot Bridge Club at its last meeting of the season
Saturday afternoon. She used a tasteful color scheme of red, white,
and blue in her decorations and refreshments.

Flowers of patriotic colors carried out the July 4th motif. The
hostess served white mountain cake squares and red, white, and

blue brick cream. Small American flags were used as plate favors. Mrs. Shaw's little daughter, Janice, dressed as Martha Washington, stood at the door and presented the guests with hand-painted tallies.

Joan groaned aloud, seeing Janice, her straight, straw-colored hair powdered white, presenting hand-painted tallies to perspiring women who had gathered to partake of Mrs. Shaw's red, white, and blue ice cream and her bridge prizes.

The screen door slammed at her back.

She turned to see Mitchell White, general news reporter, walk unsteadily toward his desk behind her.

She glanced at the clock. 'Correct Time By Western Union' proclaimed it to be two-forty-five.

White dropped into his chair and pulled his typewriter to him.

"Hi, snooty," said Joan. He had not glanced toward her.

The reporter pushed his dusty brown felt hat back from his wet white forehead and passed a dirty hand across his mouth. The hat had a dark crescent of greasy dampness where the sweat had soaked through from his forehead. Joan could smell the mingled odors of creosote, perspiration, dust, and gin that clung to his rather untidy clothes.

"Well, hi, snooty," she said again, more slowly. She decided that he was pretty stewed.

"God, it's hot, honey," he replied, clearly enough.

"Did Johnny's gusher gush?" she asked.

He stared at her for a moment, then beyond her. "Did it gush!" he replied. "It's raining the damned stuff out there yet."

"Well, that's his fifth producer and his second gusher. He's never even drilled a dry hole, has he?"

"No, and he won't," Mitchell said flatly. "He's dead."

"Dead?"

"Yeah, dead. Shot. Dead."

"Aw, pooh, Mitch, I don't believe you. You shouldn't drink that lousy gin out in the hot sun, anyway. You'll be sick. You look sick now."

She leaned toward him over her chair-back and looked at his white face closely. He was good-looking, she decided, with his large, deep-set brown eyes and his thin, oval, sad face. Dissipation had left small dark pouches under his eyes, and exhaustion from being on the job constantly, day or night, had drawn his features until they were rigid and set. By contrast, his full rather sensual mouth was hanging slackly with a cigarette in its corner, his left eye squinted against the smoke. He grinned wanly at her, and said, "Oh, I'm O.K., baby."

"What'd you mean, Mitch, about John Fordman?" Joan asked, curious now.

"What I said," he replied. "He's dead. Somebody shot 'im when the well came in. I sent A.P. a flash as I came by Western Union."

"Who? Was he murdered, you mean? It was an accident."

"No, it wasn't an accident. The sheriff says he was murdered."

"Murdered! Great day, Mitch, what a story!" Joan's voice rose with excitement. She bounced quickly from her chair and ran to the door into the back shop. "Mac!" she cried, "hold the front page! Mitch has the biggest story we ever cracked. Somebody shot the Old Man."

Mac, short and stocky, dressed only in trousers and an under-shirt, appeared at the door. He shifted his quid of tobacco and said laconically, "Bad hurt?"

"Dead," said Joan.

"My God!" he murmured; then turned and shouted into the shop, "Boys, hold PI, somebody just shot the Old Man!"

Mitchell had pulled his machine closer to him and inserted a sheet of yellow telegraph paper. Joan and Mac crossed over and stood behind him to watch him type rapidly:

Special to the Associated Press by Mitchell White
add—Fordman Murder
Fordman, Tex., July 3. (A.P.) An explosion of nitro-glycerine 1300 feet under the ground was the clever and effectual shield used by the murderer here today

to mask the noise of the pistol shot which took the life of John Fordman, multimillionaire oil-man, rancher, and newspaper owner.

The three hundred odd spectators who had gathered to watch the one o'clock shooting of Fordman's newest oil well were unaware of the tragedy until Fordman's daughter, Marion, who discovered the body slumped into a corner of the family's Isotta-Fraschini limousine, screamed and fainted. No one heard the shot. In fact, it is impossible that anyone could have done so, for it was obvious that it had been timed to coincide with the explosion of the nitroglycerine which sent oil and mud high into the air, deluging everyone within a radius of several hundred feet with its spray. The attention of almost everyone was riveted to this monster fountain of liquid gold.

Here White reached the end of his sheet and stopped typing. He took a cigarette from the pack which Joan held out to him, lighted it, and then said, "Twist that Western Union call buzzer, honey. I want a boy here by the time I finish this."

All sounds of work in the back shop had ceased and the linotype operators and pressmen were crowded together in the small doorway, looking curiously at the group in the outer office.

Mac, who had been as engrossed in the story as Joan, remembered his own obligations and swore quickly. "Hell," he said, "I've got to rip up that front page and get this damn paper made over and to bed. When can you give us our copy on this, Mitch?"

"I'll copy Mitch's first page, Mac," said Joan, "and he can give you carbons on the rest. Then we'll have something to work on and the telegraph office can get the story off, too."

"Lock that front door, Mac," said the reporter. "There'll be a mob around here when this gets out in town. We can't afford any interruptions. I beat everybody else back, but they'll be in before long. I wish Ed would come. We could use his help."

"Oh, well, he's just the editor," said Joan, pulling Mitchell's completed first page from his machine. "We've put the sheet out without his aid before."

Mac closed the front doors and pulled down the large green shades in the face of the smouldering sun. The office was dim in the greenish light. Joan lighted the desk lamps under their green and white cones. They swung slowly back and forth on their long cords from the high ceiling.

"We'll have to have the fan, even if it does blow things," she said as she lifted it off the counter, put it on the floor and flicked its base switch to 'on full.' It swung slowly in a broad semi-circle, gaining power. The balls of crumpled yellow paper on the floor rolled quickly out of its path and the loose sheets of a discarded newspaper caught under Mitchell's feet, fluttered in the strong, hot, artificial breeze.

Mac went back to prepare for this unexpected change in page one's sensation from the shooting of an oil well to the shooting of its owner, and Joan began to copy White's first sheet.

The lock on the front door clicked and the door was flung violently open. Ed Frank, the editor, looked in and then vanished. In his place appeared a stout, weather-beaten country woman. She peered into the dim office and then came slowly in, followed by a younger woman in a limp calico dress, and a farmer in new blue overalls. Frank came in after them and urged them around the counter to his desk.

He glanced at Joan and Mitch, the latter lost in rapid composition on his machine. To Joan's inquiring look he said, "I suppose you know what's happened? Is Mitch doing the outside stuff?" Joan said "yes," and he replied, "Then here's something for you. This is Mrs. Millie Trotter, who saw Marion discover the body. She seems to be the only one who was looking at her. She'll tell you about it in her own words and you can use it for a local story. I'll do the lead, while you take what she has."

Joan smiled at the flustered woman and her frightened family and led them to the chairs in the advertising department's corner.

MURDER IN TEXAS

"Now," she said to the woman, "take your hat off and be comfortable and tell me what happened. I'm dying to hear about it, you know."

Mrs. Trotter wiped her red face on her sleeve and sat down, but refused to remove the rusty black straw hat which perched at a surprised and raffish angle on the side of her head.

"No'm," she said, "I'll jest set down, though. Crystal, you an' Paw set down, too," she directed the man and the girl. They looked embarrassed, but they sat down and the man took off his large felt sombrero.

"He said," began Mrs. Trotter, jerking a large red thumb at Frank, who was on his way into the back shop to talk to Mac—"he said as how I'd git five dollars if I'd tell all about what I seen. Will I?"

"I'm sure you will," said Joan, "if he said so. He's the boss. Now you tell me just what happened. Begin at the very beginning." She looked at her pad of copy paper and her pencil on the desk, but did not make any motion toward them, as she was afraid of checking the spontaneity of Mrs. Trotter's story which was obviously about to burst forth. "Just begin at the beginning," she said again, encouragingly.

"Well," said Mrs. Trotter, hitching forward in her chair, "it was thisaway. We-all come in town from the ranch early this mornin'. We done our shoppin'. Me 'n' Crystal boughten some piece goods an' Jason, he's my husband, boughten a sack o' oats an' a block o' salt down to Miller's Feed Store. We-all started home about twelve. The road to the ranch runs through the oil field an' we got into the crowd of cars that was goin' out to see the well shot off. We reckined we'd stop an' see it too, so we pulled up at the rope to the left of the road."

"What time was that?" asked Joan.

"About twelve-thirty, I reckin, don't you, Jason?" said Mrs. Trotter to her husband. Jason mumbled that it was nearer twelve-thirty-five, but Mrs. Trotter had swept on, growing more and more confident of her ability to tell her story.

"About twelve-thirty," she said, "an' we-all got outen the car an' stood by the rope. I seen Mr. Fordman up to the well with a lot

of other men an' pointed him out to Crystal. Crystal hadn't never
seen him before, but I had. I seen him in his bank onct. An' a fine-
lookin' man he was too, so big an' handsome.

"But anyways, there he was. They was a-lookin' at the well an'
pretty soon they started off toward their cars which was parked
across the road from us. They hadn't got but a little piece away,
when a man at the well shouted real loud an' they all begun to run.
They run every which away.

"I kep' a-watchin' Mr. Fordman an' he run too. He had on a
white suit an' a white hat an' I reckin he didn't want to git any oil
on 'em. He run toward his own car. He opened the back door an'
got in an' set down. Then I looked back at the well. They was all
millin' around an' yellin'. In a few minutes I looked back at that
there big car of Mr. Fordman's. I heerd tell it cost over twenty-five
thousand dollars, but it didn't look so different from any other;
jest lower an' longer. I noticed that he had pulled down the window curtains in the back."

Here Mrs. Trotter stopped short and wiped her face off with
her sleeve again. "Kin I have a drink o' water?" she said. Joan went
to the cooler and brought her water in a Lily cup. She drank a swallow and set the cup down.

Crystal said, "Kin I hev one too?" Joan nodded to her and said
to Mrs. Trotter, "Yes, yes, go on."

"Well, as I said, he had pulled down the curtains. I thought,
that's funny, don't he want to see his own well shot off? An' then
there was a big hullabaloo at the well an' the explosion went off. It
like to of scared me to death. Everybody was a-shoutin' and a-
blowin' their car horns. Jason was a-blowin' ours.

"Then after a little while I looked back at Mr. Fordman's car,
a-wonderin' what he thought with all this new oil an' the money
an' ever'thing an' I seen Miss Fordman, all in white, walk over from
another car near-by and start to git in hers. I poked Crystal an'
said, 'That there's Miss Fordman,' an' right then she must of found
her father dead because she sort o' crumpled up on the runnin'-
board, an' half into the car, an' then slid out onto the ground. She

must of screamed because people begun runnin' toward her an' they all crowded up so I couldn't see nothin'.

"But in a minute I could see that Miss Fordman's faintin' wasn't all the excitement, because somebody busted outen the crowd around their car an' come runnin' over our way an' he was a-yellin' for th' sheriff.

"Then the sheriff pushed up past me an' he run over to the Fordman car. He stayed there a while an' then he come back. Everybody got kind of quiet an' he said, real loud, 'Is there a doctor here?'

"Doctor Phillips got outen his car next to us an' said, 'Yes, I'm a doctor. What's the matter?'

"The sheriff said, 'Come on,' an' then he turned 'round to us an' says, 'Did anybody here see anybody gettin' into or out o' th' Fordman's car?'

"An' I spoke up an' said, 'No, but I seen Miss Fordman gettin' in. Did she faint? What made her faint?' An' the sheriff jus' said, 'Never mind,' an' he an' Doc Phillips started away. But I was real interested, so I said to Paw an' Crystal, 'Come on,' an' we ducked under the ropes an' follered 'em.

"There was some more cars parked by th' Fordman's, but not so close, an' I seen Mrs. Levy an' Mr. Levy an' lots of other people all crowded around. I crowded up close, too, an' there stretched out on a coat was Miss Fordman. She had come to an' was lookin' white an' faint-like an' starin' up at the car. Then I looked up, an' through the open door I could see the sheriff an' the doctor bendin' over somebody on the seat.

"Pretty soon they got out, an' by that time Miss Fordman was standin' up. The doctor said, 'Yes, he's dead,' an' at that she jest nodded an' burst out cryin'. The doctor tried to hush her up, but she couldn't stop, so he an' she got in the car with Mr. Fordman's mortal remains an' the sheriff got in front with the nigger man, who was a-cussin' under his breath an' a-cryin' at th' same time, an' they drove off towards town.

"We was jest standin' there when Mr. Frank come up. He knowed my husband, Jason, you see, an' he says, 'Didn't I hear you say you saw what happened?' An' I says, 'Well, I seen part of it.' So he ast us to all come in here, an' here we are," she concluded rapidly, and looked at Joan expectantly.

"But," objected Joan, "who shot Mr. Fordman? Didn't anyone know?"

"Well, now, I'm sure I don't," said Mrs. Trotter, as if the idea was new to her. She looked crestfallen that Joan should have picked on the one weak spot in her story. "But," she said triumphantly, "the sheriff don't know neither, 'cause he said to th' doctor, after they got outen th' car, 'Now who in hell could have done this?' an' th' doctor said, 'Lord knows, but I'm surprised somebody ain't done it sooner.'"

II: MONDAY, JULY 3

Mrs. Trotter beamed expectantly at Joan again, and Joan said, "Well." She rose and went over to Frank, who was now seated at his desk up front. He looked at her. "Get it?" he inquired shortly.

She nodded and said, "Mrs. Trotter expects five dollars."

He handed her a bill and she went back to the Trotters. She gave it to Mrs. Trotter and watched the excited woman herd the limp Crystal and the lackadaisical Jason out of the front door into the late afternoon heat.

Feeling Frank's eyes upon her she turned and smiled down at him.

"Her stuff any good?" he asked.

"Make a feature," said the girl. "She didn't actually know anything, but what she saw was interesting."

"Yeah. I thought so, too. She gave me an outline coming in. I had to ride in with them. White went off and left me." He glanced at the reporter with amusement in his eyes and then looked seriously up at the girl. "Drunk?" he questioned.

"Not very," said Joan. "I think he's sort of sick, don't you?"

"Whatsa matter with him lately?"

"He's in love, Ed."

"Marion Fordman?"

"Yes."

"No go?"

"No go."

"He isn't bearing up so well. No guts."

53

"What would you do under the circumstances?" asked the girl hotly.

Frank smiled and said: "Well, I wouldn't make myself a laughing stock, anyway. I'd say, 'Well, what th' hell!'" He snapped his long fingers.

Joan smiled too and regarded him more favorably. "But you're older, Ed, and things don't mean much to you, anyway, do they?"

"Not much," he agreed.

"Not anything?" inquired the girl curiously.

"Well, maybe one or two things." His voice dropped, but he held her blue eyes steadily with his intense brown ones.

Joan's composure was a little shaken, so she said, "Well, I've got to get that story out. It's late." She looked up at the clock.

'Correct Time' said four o'clock. The paper would be hours late tonight, thought Joan. Then she became aware that the telephones were clamoring for attention. "Daily News," she said into the first one she reached. An excited voice inquired, "Can you please tell me who won the baseball game between Dallas and Fort Worth?"

"No, I cannot," said Joan, and hung up. The telephone promptly jangled again, but she unhooked the receivers of all three instruments and sat down to her machine to write her story.

Mitchell was still typing rapidly, a wide-eyed Western Union boy beside him. Joan reached over and took the completed yellow sheets that lay on his desk. His story continued from the first page that she had seen:

People were slow in reaching Miss Fordman and she had slipped to the ground before the first arrived. Only after she had been revived was the lifeless figure of the multimillionaire discovered on the back seat. He was sitting back in the rear, or left-hand, corner of the seat, his head sunk on his chest and his white Panama hat pulled low over his forehead. His left arm lay along the arm-rest and his right arm was in his lap.

He had been shot through the heart. The shades at the two door windows, as well as at the seat windows, had been lowered completely. The interior of the car was dark and cool and the small electric fan mounted against the back of the chauffeur's partition was whirring softly.

The chauffeur, Joe (Texas) Wills, had left the car sometime before the explosion was scheduled to occur, with a note from Mr. Fordman to his chief driller, Val Day. When he returned and was told of the tragedy, the colored boy almost collapsed. He had been in Fordman's employ for over ten years.

Sheriff Jim Read, of the local force, who also holds the office of local coroner, has the case under his supervision. No definite statement could be gotten from the sheriff at this late hour.

Fordman's body was brought back to a funeral home in the city, where it will rest pending funeral arrangements.

The deceased, who was forty-two years old, left only one close relative, his daughter Marion. She is said to be his sole heir.

Widely known throughout the Southwest, Fordman has been one of the most prominent figures in this section of the state for several years. He has been mentioned as a likely candidate for governor following Governor Allred's present term.

Mr. Fordman's wealth has been estimated at approximately ten million dollars. Twenty years ago he was a reporter on this sheet at twenty-five dollars a week. He had just graduated from the University of Texas. Within a year he had been made editor of the paper and during the next year he married Miss Lillian Schumaker, only daughter of John L. Schumaker, owner of the *Daily News* and its companion paper in Franklin, the *Daily Record*.

When Mr. Schumaker died, two years later, he left his papers to his daughter. Mrs. Fordman died a month later in childbirth. Fordman inherited the papers in trust for his daughter Marion.

Good fortune followed close on Fordman's heels after this tragic beginning of his life. A wildcat oil company struck the discovery well of the Fordman field on the old Fordman Ranch which had been owned by his father, Thomas. Thomas, who died when John Fordman was eighteen, had left the miserable barren farm to his son. Within a few years, Fordman made his first million. With it he bought controlling interest in six other newspapers in this section of Texas.

According to close friends, Mr. Fordman was not known to have any avowed enemies. Thus the reason for his sudden death has proved a puzzle to the local authorities, who admit that they do not know just where to begin the search for his assailant. The theory that Mr. Fordman was hit by a stray bullet and killed by accident was scouted immediately by the sheriff.

Mr. Fordman, as has been stated in earlier dispatches, was attending the 'shooting' of the newest of the Fordman Company's wells, number five B. He was accompanied by his daughter and a party of business men and their wives.

As the time of the event was widely known in the district, quite a large crowd had gathered. Some three hundred spectators stood behind a rope strung across the field at a distance of several hundred yards from the well, and watched the proceedings.

At the exact moment of the shooting of Mr. Fordman, the noise was at its height . . .

Here Joan put the paper down, as she knew the rest of the story. She thought for a moment and then went over to Frank. "Who made up the Fordman party?" she said. "Are you using their names in the local story?"

Frank said, "Yes," and handed her a list scribbled almost illegibly in pencil on the back of an old envelope. Joan saw that it was quite long, and then she noticed the names of Clarence Jones and his wife Agnes.

It was funny, she thought, that they should go with the party as Fordman's guests. Everybody in town knew that Agnes Jones had been Fordman's mistress for the past three years—that is, everyone except Jones.

She wondered if Jones knew it, too. Then she wondered if Agnes Jones knew that Fordman was in love with a young Houston widow and that they had expected to be married within the month. This she knew from Marion, who had told her the story in strictest confidence.

She went to work on her local angle description of the scene of the crime and finished just as Mitchell White looked up from his machine. He gathered the telegraph blanks together and thrust them at the Western Union boy. "Hop to it, son," he said. The boy left on a dead run.

Frank called them both over to his desk.

"White," he said, "you'd better get up to the courthouse. And you, Joan, look things over there, if you like, then go on over to Fordman's. We'll want an inside interview with Marion for the early morning edition. She'll talk to you. Pick up anything you can on that rumor about Fordman's engagement to some dame in Houston. Know anything about it, yet?" he inquired suspiciously.

"Yes," she said, "but it's supposed to be a secret."

"Well, it's no secret now. Everybody's talking and nobody is sayin' the same thing twice in succession. It's up to us to give 'em the first clear story. Get me? Tell the sheriff I'll be up there in a little while."

"O.K.," said Joan as she turned away.

Mitchell grabbed a new pencil, ground half of it away in the sharpener, put it in his pocket with several sheets of paper, and started out. Joan took up her white Panama hat and followed him. In their separate cars they drove to the courthouse, a red sandstone atrocity in the center of the town square.

Pushing their way through a mob of curious onlookers, they entered the building. The traffic cop on guard at the door recognized them and let them by. The office of the sheriff was halfway down the long hall. As Joan and Mitch arrived the sheriff began his investigation, and in response to his genial invitation the men in the room seated themselves about the walls in yellow folding chairs with 'From Scott & Scott, Undertakers' stenciled across the back rest. They stopped talking among themselves and looked toward the officer. There were only four, and Joan knew them all. Samuel Ross, the banker, sat near the sheriff's desk. Chick Jones sat next to him and stared sideways out of the window. Then there was Gere Drexell, Fordman's assistant, and next to him, Joey Levy, the town's leading merchant.

Joan sat down beside Levy, who promptly leaned toward her and whispered:

"Miss Joan, have you seen her yet? How's she taking it? My wife stayed there."

"I haven't had a chance to get out to Marion's yet, Mr. Levy," answered the girl.

He was perspiring heavily—large, plump man that he was—and his bald dome glistened with tiny beads of sweat. Dark crescents of perspiration showed under his arms, on his blue shirt. Like the majority of the other men in the room, he wore neither coat nor vest. His shirt billowed limply over the top of his trousers and his fat stomach bulged forward, straining the tight linen.

He started to speak again, but the voice of the sheriff interrupted him. "I won't keep you-all long," it boomed, and Joan turned from Levy to watch Sheriff Read lower himself into his worn leather desk chair which immediately tilted backward so that he could rest his feet comfortably on a pulled-out drawer of the scarred oak roll-top desk.

The officer was a large man of the type called 'typical Westerner.' He filled the chair completely, and for further comfort hitched his heavy pearl-handled six-shooter in its leather holster around into his lap. He rested a huge hand on it affectionately, but unconsciously. His other hand he brushed softly across the nap of his stiffly roached gray hair. He looked disturbed and uncertain, but began bravely.

"As you-all know, our admired and respected fellow citizen, Mr. John Fordman, was murdered this afternoon." He looked about him gravely, aware of his own rhetoric. "I have asked you gentlemen to come here so that we can get at this thing right away. You was all members of Mr. Fordman's party at the time of the shootin' and somebody must of seen somethin' that might have some bearin' on the matter. Hit don't stand to reason that a man can be shot in a crowd of three-four hundred people without nobody seein' nothin'." Here the sheriff paused and took a long breath. He stared around the circle of faces in a puzzled fashion.

"Now, folks," he resumed, "let's get some facts together." Pulling a scratch-pad and pencil toward him he said:

"First I wanta know who made up Mr. Fordman's private party an' how you-all rode." He indicated Mitchell White and suggested, "You, White, you're a reporter. You tell us how things was."

Mitch scratched his chin and thought for a moment. Then he began:

"Well, Ed Frank and I went out together in my car. Mr. Fordman and Miss Fordman and Mr. Drexell here all rode in the Fordman car with th' chauffeur driving. Mr. and Mrs. Levy were in their car and their little girl was there too; and Mr. and Mrs. Jones and their daughter were in their car."

"You left out Mr. Ross," remarked the sheriff. He turned to the banker and said, "Where'd you ride?"

"My own car," answered Ross shortly.

The officer jotted down his information and, glancing around the room, stated:

"Well, that's that. Now I wanta know if any of you know anything or saw anything that might help us out? Did you, Mr. Ross?"

Samuel Ross, president of the First National Bank of Ford man, was one of the two men in the room wearing a coat. It was gray seersucker, carefully buttoned. Although it and his trousers had been liberally spotted with oil, they did not look untidy, only spotted. He wore nose-glasses which he took off and balanced on his right forefinger whenever he spoke. Their absence gave his thin white face a rather naked look, emphasized the twin furrows between his pale blue eyes.

He took his glasses off now and looked calmly at the sheriff. "Why, no," he said quietly. "Although I have been associated with Mr. Fordman in business, I am not familiar with his private affairs. You know that he did not talk particularly freely with anyone. He was a very wealthy man and must have antagonized any number of people as he rose in power. He was undoubtedly ruthless. But as to knowing who could have shot him, I am afraid that I cannot even essay any conjecture." He replaced his glasses and unbuttoned the top button of his coat. In this sweltering little room, he must have been just as hot as anyone, but he looked exceedingly cool.

He was discreet, thought Joan, and so damned correct. He could cover his feelings, if he had any. She wondered how much truth there was in the gossip about the quarrel that he had had with Fordman in his office last week. The paying teller, Gerald Stokes, had spoken of it to his wife, Juanita, and Juanita, always anxious to make some sort of stir, had promptly spread it over town via the afternoon bridge tables.

The sheriff rubbed his gray fuzz again and then looked at Clarence Jones, seated next to Ross. "Well, Chick," he said, "can you offer anything?"

Jones, never prepossessing, looked his worst. The heat, excitement, and momentary position in the limelight all conspired to bring about his demoralization, and as the sheriff's attention singled him out he crouched lower in his chair and stammered a few words in a low voice. Joan could not hear him at all. What an unfit mate for the lush Agnes, she thought. The thin, unhappy little man with his drawn, white face and his stringy, straw-colored hair looked like an undernourished boy rather than a man nearing fifty years.

Joan could see the perspiration on his upper lip, the great drops rolling down his high, bulging forehead.

The sheriff, leaning forward, repeated kindly for the second time:

"Whaja say, Chick? You ain't sick, are you?"

The little man sat up suddenly and found his voice.

"No, I ain't sick, Jim. This business has kinda upset me, though." He wiped his face on his sleeve and continued, "I ain't one to slander a man that's dead, but you know as well as I do that there's many a one as would have been purty glad to see Fordman put away. But as to who would come right out and shoot him in cold blood—well, I dunno."

He looked about defensively, as if afraid of condemnation, but the group was silent. Everybody liked the grocer and sympathized. To Joan he was the worm that never turned. His wife ran his business successfully. She despised him and mocked him publicly. He was a Caspar Milquetoast to the life.

Joan's reflections were interrupted by Gerard Drexell's voice. It was a smooth, cultivated voice, but strong and authoritative as well. This man, John Fordman's chief engineer and assistant in the oil business, was everything that poor Chick Jones was not. Handsome, well-educated, he commanded the attention of the little group.

"I've worked for John Fordman, as you all know, for about five years now," he was saying. "And though I've often found him high-handed and ruthless, I've never known him to be dishonest or mean. Many of you may not have liked him, but if only for the sake of upholding the law you must forget personal feelings and give the sheriff here a little co-operation."

This rather smug speech fell a little flat and Chick Jones muttered something too low for Joan to hear.

The girl whispered to Mitch, "Nobody wants to know who killed him, do they?"

The reporter shook his head. "As an investigation it's a flop," he agreed, smiling slightly.

Drexell spoke again. "But surely, sheriff, you've done something about this murder. Did you search the field? Have you found anything?"

The officer's face turned red and he looked angrily at Drexell. "Of course," he said, "we've searched the field. We've done everything possible, but that stampedin' mob ruined any chances we might have had at findin' any clues."

"He wouldn't know a clue if he saw one," Joan whispered to Mitch. The corner of his mouth pulled downward in response.

"Now let's get this thing straight," continued the sheriff. "First, I wanta know just where everybody was when Fordman was killed."

He drew the pad toward him and put the tip of his pencil in his mouth. Joan opened her folded scratch-paper and copied the answers in shorthand.

"Well, Mr. Ross, where was you?"

Ross shifted in his chair and frowned. "Why," he answered slowly, "I ran with the rest of the group. I think that I ran toward my car. I know that I came around the edge of the derrick and started that way. I stopped on the fringe of the crowd and turned to watch the well. After the explosion occurred, I started toward my own machine and had almost reached it when I heard Miss Fordman scream. I ran, with others, toward her—and it was several minutes after that before the body of Mr. Fordman was discovered."

The sheriff took his feet from the drawer and shifted his weight forward. The chair tilted to even keel reluctantly.

"Where'd you go to, Mr. Drexell?" he asked.

"I don't know just where I was when the shot was fired, of course. I left the well before the actual setting of the nitro, and went around south to speak to a farmer whom I knew. I was just returning when I noticed the commotion and walked across to learn its cause."

"Who was you talkin' to, Mr. Drexell?" inquired the sheriff.

Drexell's rakish black eyebrows rose, but he answered evenly enough, "Lonnie Stephens." Leaning against the back of his chair, he put his hands in his trousers pockets. He wore a white linen suit, excellently tailored, and like Ross, had not removed his coat. His silk tie was surprisingly blue, but not more blue than his clear, large eyes. His very short curly black hair was sprinkled with gray.

The sheriff noted Drexell's statement down and then turned to Levy. Before he spoke, Levy burst out excitedly.

"I was right behind Mr. Ross," he declared. "I went on over to my own car. My wife was there and she can bear me out!" He looked around the room as if expecting contradiction.

"O.K.," said the sheriff shortly. "An' you, Chick?"

"Me?" The grocer spoke suddenly and turned from the window in confusion. Evidently he had not been listening to the testimony.

"Yeah. Where was you when Mr. Fordman was shot?" repeated Read.

Jones stared at the sheriff, his eyes blank. Rubbing his hand across his face he finally said, "I dunno, Jim. I can't seem to recollect."

"Didn't you hear the explosion when the well was shot?" questioned the officer.

"Oh, yes," answered the little man. "I know now. I was sitting in the car with my wife. I believe that Mildred and Ed Frank were there, too. Yeah, they were there, too." He sighed and arose, saying, "I gotta go, Jim. I don't feel good. I'm goin' home."

There was a general silence as he walked across the room and out of the door without looking at anyone.

The sheriff rumbled in his throat and said loudly: "You, young fella. Where was you?" He pointed a long brown finger at Mitch White, and Joan felt the boy jerk upright in surprise.

"Why, I was everywhere. I couldn't say exactly," answered Mitch, with a short laugh. "A reporter's got to get around, y'know."

"You can't remember where you was when th' explosion happened?" prompted Read.

"No," answered the reporter, shaking his head.

The sheriff shrugged his shoulders and wrote the information down carefully. While he was thus occupied, Ed Frank came into the room and sat down beside White.

Read looked up and grinned at him, saying, "I already know where you was when Mr. Fordman was shot, Ed, but for th' record . . ." he paused, pencil uplifted.

Frank looked about him and said cheerfully, "Well, I don't know what these fellows been saying about me, but if I remember rightly, I believe I was with Miss Jones in their family car when the well was shot, anyhow. She and I had been walking around before that."

"O.K.," declared the officer, writing. He scowled upward through his shaggy gray eyebrows at Joan, and to her surprise said, "Young lady, I hear you're mighty smart—college education an' such—whadda ya' think about this here business? Know who done it, huh?"

"Goodness, no, Mr. Sheriff!" declared the girl hastily, and Ed Frank laughed softly.

Read looked at him and chuckled. "She ain't so smart as she's cracked up to be, is she, Ed?"

"She shines in other ways," answered Frank, glancing at Joan. "A good many other ways," he added thoughtfully.

The girl smiled her thanks at him and looked at her watch. It was five-thirty. She rose to leave, when three men pushed past her and entered the room. They were Tom Harte, deputy sheriff, Doctor C. T. Ross, official county doctor, and Val Day, Fordman's chief driller.

"Well, Doc, whadda ya' say?" queried the sheriff.

"To put it plainly, Jim, Fordman was shot with a gun of surprisingly small caliber, either a .22 or a .25. The bullet entered his heart and is still lodged in his body. Death was probably instantaneous. I haven't had time to go after the bullet yet, but I'll get right at it. Those little guns"—the doctor spoke scornfully—"toys—it's amazing how seldom they kill. It was held smack against his breast and fired only once, as far as I can tell. The cloth around the bullet hole is burned and black with powder discharge. I suppose there'll be a formal inquest tomorrow? I'll do the autopsy right away. He's up at Scott's and I reckon the family'll want immediate interment. This weather, you know—and Scott's ain't equipped to keep 'em long."

"Yeah," agreed the sheriff, and to Harte, "Well, Tom, find anything?"

"Not a thing, Chief," replied the tall officer. "We're pullin' in all of the questionable characters we kin find. That mob out there sure did tromp down everything. It was easy done. The murderer lost himself in the crowd and was safer'n if he'd hopped a plane to Mexico."

"My God," whispered Joan to Mitch, "lemme out of here. The air is foul. Why don't they go into a bigger room!" She climbed over his knees, patted his shoulder, and escaped into the dirty but less congested hall. The drinking-fountain was out of order as usual and an old-fashioned water-cooler, with an inverted tin cup hung over the spigot, stood in the corner of the hallway. Joan went into the county clerk's office to borrow a glass from the girl at the desk.

"Isn't it excitin'?" gurgled the girl, chewing her gum vigorously. Joan said, "Yeah," and went into the hall for her water. It was too cold and she had to hold each sip in her mouth before swallowing. It cooled her tongue and she could feel the first swallows as they slid downward to her stomach. She drank three tumblerfuls and returned the glass to the chewing girl. "Thanks, Mabel," she said.

"You're sure welcome, Miss Shields."

Joan went out and sat in her roadster for a few minutes before starting for the Fordmans'. It was nearly six o'clock and the sun was behind the courthouse. She had parked under one of the locust trees which bordered the sidewalk in front of the building. The leather cushions were hot and the metal of the door burned her bare arm. She looked over her notes and made a careful list of the people, who, to her mind, might conceivably be suspected by the sheriff. Naturally it included the members of Mr. Fordman's party and ran as follows:

Mr. Ross, who said that he was at the cars.

Chick Jones, who was with his family and Ed Frank.

Ed Frank, who was with Jones and his family.

Gere Drexell, who didn't know exactly where he was, but thought he was talking with a farmer south of the well.

Agnes Jones, who was with her husband, daughter, and Frank.

Joey Levy, who was "right behind Ross."

Mitch White, who didn't know.

Marion Fordman.

Etta Levy.

Texas Wills.

Val Day.

Mildred Jones, who was with her family and Ed Frank.

Of course she knew that the murderer might be an entirely different person, one unknown to her or to the police, but it hardly stood to reason that John Fordman would have allowed a stranger or a casual acquaintance to sit beside him in the car. Then, too, if a stranger had been in town recently the fact would have been known, for Fordman was too small to harbor an unknown.

Joan didn't feel at all horrified at Fordman's death. She hadn't liked him. In fact, she had scarcely known him, even though he did own the paper on which she worked. For the past ten years, since her graduation from high school, she had not lived in the village. First college had kept her away, then several years working on newspapers in New York. Until the past year she had only visited her family every year or so, seeing little of the natives on her flying trips. But the opening of a good job on the local paper, which had recently been only a weekly sheet, plus her mother's illness had brought Joan back to her home for an indefinite stay. It had been a boring stay so far, unpleasantly crammed with bridge club items and other unimportant routine events. This, then, the death of John Fordman, was an event.

Joan was starting the roadster when she saw two men come out of the courthouse and recognized them as Gere Drexell and Levy. She waited until they neared the car and then called to Drexell. The men had been in earnest conversation and Drexell looked up, startled. Seeing Joan he waved, and nodding to his companion, stepped down from the curb and came to the car, saying, "Hello, there, Joan. Saw you inside, but couldn't get over to speak to you. Going out to see Marion?"

"Yes, can I give you a lift out?" offered the girl.

The man ran a brown hand through his hair, glanced at his watch and shook his head. "No, thanks," he said. "I'll go out later when all those women leave. I've got a lot to do now, anyway."

"It's sad for Marion, isn't it?" ventured Joan.

"Yes," he agreed, looking beyond her. She could see the small play of muscle at his jaw as he shut his mouth tightly and firmed his lips. Joan could see why he fascinated Marion; why Mitch failed to hold her interest. The reporter was a child in comparison, gauche, unsophisticated, soft. Drexell carried himself with the air of a man who accomplished things. He was well educated, cosmopolitan, and extraordinarily self-assured, an unusual man to find in a small West Texas town.

He did not seem in a great hurry to leave Joan. There was an air of something still to be said between them. He placed a foot on the running-board of the Packard and leaned against the door. The girl waited. But Drexell only asked a question.

"Who is this Mrs. Lawrence?"

Joan was surprised and must have shown it, for he qualified his question with, "I mean, you know, I haven't met her. What's she like? I've wired her to come up as Marion seems to want her. I know that John was going to marry her and I just wondered."

"Well," began Joan, "I haven't met her either, but to take Marion's word for it she must be a pretty swell person."

"Yes?" Drexell asked this politely and left the silence there between them.

The girl broke it. "Why?" she countered.

"Knew her husband during the war," explained Drexell.

"I feel sorry for her," said Joan.

The man's expression did not change. He nodded and said: "Well, I must be going. Tell Marion I'll be there later."

Joan watched his white-clad shoulders as he walked away from her and thought to herself: "Well, I certainly didn't get much out of him. He's a poker-face." A small spasm of excitement unknotted itself under the region of her breast-bone and spread quivering tentacles of delightful shivers down her shoulders and arms. She started the car and shot backward out of the parking place with a roar of exhaust through the forbidden cut-out. The Fordman house was five miles out of town and she wanted to see Marion and get home in time for dinner at seven-thirty.

III: MONDAY, JULY 3

Joan skidded dangerously into the drive leading up to the Fordman home. She shifted into second for the long, winding road up the hill, but soon had to shift into first as the road grew steeper. It was cut diagonally across the east side of the hill.

The mountain, which was in reality only a large finger of rock mesa-land jutting out sharply from the higher ground to the north, overlooked the low rolling prairie land to the south, east, and west. Fordman had built his home near the edge of the serried red sandstone cliffs which marked an abrupt end of the jutting finger.

The house was always amusing to Joan. Formally colonial in architecture, it gleamed white and barren on the red hilltop. Its six slender porch pillars supported a roof of vivid green.

This country, which called for architecture as simple and as solid as the rocks themselves, was insulted by the intrusion of this slender, delicate building. Loud and blatant with its vivid cobalt sky, its red earth and its lush green cedars, it shouted insults at the slim white house perched on its beloved hilltop. The strong prairie winds pushed at it and rattled its green shutters, and the frequent sand-storms enveloped it grimly, but John Fordman's house was truly builded firm upon the rock! It held itself aristocratically aloof, returned no bawdy word.

The car reached the level top of the hill panting, and with relief it turned into the road winding through the young new trees that had just been planted during the past year. They were Chinese elms, very slender and erect. Each had been set out in a pit

68

blasted in the rock and refilled with rich prairie loam. Joan remembered the day that the holes had been blasted out and the small geysers of dirt that had risen incongruously into the sky above the red hilltop. She had been amused by the fact that the geysers had risen and fallen again before the sound of the blast had reached her ears.

The house did not look so odd from the drive, which curved smoothly around the edge of the hill and swept up to the front veranda edged with flower-beds filled with varicolored zinnias. The lawns had been well rolled and trimmed and were as vivid as the roof. An underground sprinkler system was on, and the wind swept the cool geysers of spray over the walks and into the graveled driveway. As the day drew to a close and the sun dropped lower and lower, the air gained in freshness and vitality.

Joan stepped out of her car and cut through the spray, feeling it soak coolly through her stockings and linen dress. She mounted to the veranda on which stood green-and-white striped canvas chairs on tubular frames grouped about a low glass-topped table. A bowl of crimson zinnias stood on the table and a brown-and-white leather bag of golf clubs leaned against a chair.

The girl reached for a cigarette from a red bowl and was clicking the silver golf-ball lighter when the screen door clapped shut behind her. She turned and saw Texas Wills, the Fordman chauffeur. He was a small mulatto, very dapper, always courteous, and quite well-educated according to the standards of the Southern negro. He smiled at her, showing even white teeth between thin, well-moulded lips.

"Good evening, Miss Joan."

"Hello, Texas," the girl replied. "How's Miss Marion?"

"She's takin' it real fine," answered the man. "Now who could have done such a thing, Miss Joan?"

"I don't know, Texas. Where were you?"

"Why, I was looking for Mr. Day with a note from the boss," he replied.

"Looking for him? Wasn't he at the derrick?"

"No'm, he wasn't at the derrick and I never did find him," declared the negro.

Joan looked at him over her cigarette. She thought rapidly, and then changed the subject. "You knew him real well, Texas. Who'd want to shoot him? Who were his enemies?"

"Lawd, Miss Joan, I don' know. Not many people liked him, you know. People was always sayin' that I was his bodyguard, but I wasn't. I never toted no gun. He wasn't scared o' no one as I knew of."

"Who'd you know of particularly that didn't like him?" asked Joan, and added, "Anyone who threatened him, for instance."

"Well, there was a driller back in Ranger that shot at him once over a card game, and a feller in Borger that had sold out a lease to Mr. Fordman an' thought he got cheated, threatened to kill him, but nothin' ever come of it. He was plumb easy to annoy, come to think of it, an' mighty free with his fists. I remember he beat up Mr. Day somethin' awful once, too. You see Mr. Day was drunk. He said he'd kill Mr. Fordman, but when he sobered up they laughed about it an' I saw 'em shakin' hands."

"I mean townspeople, Texas. Did you ever hear anyone in Fordman threaten him?"

"Well, yessum. That reporter man that you go aroun' with—he was here just the other night and they argued something fierce. He didn't even give me a tip when I brought his car around, and I wiped it all off an' washed th' wind-shield. It sure was dirty, too. I brushed out th' inside, an' back of th' seat was two strings of beads and three lady's vanity cases."

Joan laughed. "I guess that's where mine vanish, Texas. Thanks for the tip. Where is Miss Marion?"

"She's up in her room, miss. There's a bunch of ladies in th' parlor, Mis' Levy, Mis' Jones, Mis' Brush, 'n' th' minister."

"Thanks. I'll go up the back way, Texas. I want to see Miss Marion first. By the way, did you ever deliver that note to Mr. Day?"

"Lawd, Miss Joan, I plum' forgot that note! No'm, I never did."

"Why not?"

"Well, miss, you see, I couldn't find him when I went to look for him, and since then—" he stopped sadly.

"Of course. Do you still have it, Texas?"

"Yes, ma'am," replied the man, fumbling in the pocket of his uniform coat. He brought forth a folded slip of blue paper and looked at it. Joan reached out a naturally commanding hand.

He gave her the note without hesitation and she read it without a qualm. Written in a bold hand were the words, "I want to see you before I leave. J. F."

Joan refolded the paper and returned it to Wills. "Better give it to him, Texas," she advised; "and about our little talk—don't say anything to anyone." Then she walked around the house and reached the second story by the servants' stairway.

She found Marion Fordman lying on the quaint four-poster bed in her lovely room, but she was not alone. As Joan entered, she was surprised to see Mildred Jones rise from a wing-chair by the window. She waved at Mildred and went over to Marion.

"Hello, darling," she said. "I came as soon as I could get away."

Marion sat up, glad to see her. She and Joan had known each other since childhood, renewed their acquaintance in the East where Marion was attending a fashionable school, continued it warmly during the past few months that the younger girl had spent in Fordman. Joan admired her Nordic handsomeness, her excellent sense of humor, her intelligence. She was a tall, strong girl, with large hands and feet that were remarkably slender and well-formed. Her uncropped hair was ash blonde, with glinting highlights of silver. The undiscerning called it 'platinum,' but it did not have that metallic vulgarity of tone. And her eyes, unlike those of most blondes, were a deep sea blue.

Joan took off her Panama, ran her fingers through her own curly black mop. The coolness of the prairie evening was sifting through the open windows. It carried the smell of the spray, the new-cut grass, and the odor of the thousands of tiny prairie wildflowers.

Mildred Jones wanted to talk. "Have you heard anything, Joan?"

"No, nothing new. You-all know as much as I do, I guess."

Marion dropped back on the pillows and sighed. "It's a dam' shame, Joan. He was so alive. I wish I'd known him better. This is the first summer I've been home in four years. And there's Glieth. She'll be coming soon, I hope. I had Gere wire her."

"Listen, Marion. What'll they do at the paper? I mean, who'll be in charge?" Joan had just thought of this.

"Why, Ed Frank, I guess," replied the girl, puzzled. "I don't know anything about it. Mr. Drennan, Dad's lawyer, rang up a few minutes ago. He's coming out right away. There's a will, you know. I'd just say, go on with them like always. He'd want that."

"I'll tell Ed, then," said Joan. "And don't you want to make a statement of some sort?"

"Statement?" she repeated. "Why, no, I guess not. Should I?"

"Not unless you want to, honey. We'll just carry the fact that you had no statement to make and that you've left everything in the hands of the sheriff. Is that all right?"

"Yes. When Mr. Drennan comes, we'll see. There must be trustees. Oh, Joan, who did it, do you suppose? I want it found out. I don't believe that the officers are capable of tracking down a murderer. They might do all right with rustlers or with Mexicans selling liquor—but this is real and clever and deliberate. I'll never forget getting into the car and finding him. It was so dark and cool-looking. I opened the door and stepped onto the running-board and said, 'Well, hail to the oil magnate,' or something silly like that, and when he didn't answer, I looked at him and saw that blood on his shirt. It was so dark red against the white. I never thought I'd faint. It was so silly of me."

"Where had you been?" asked Joan.

"Well, when all of the men left, I went over and sat in the car with that fat Mrs. Levy. Our car was somewhat away from the group and the top is so low that I couldn't see very well. I wanted to see the well shot. I'd never seen one."

Mildred Jones moved out of the wing-chair, to sit on the foot of the bed. She was a large, plump, capable girl. Joan thought her fat, but men liked her roundness. They described her with two out-waving downward sweeps of their hands. She was like that. Full and round. Soft. She liked men. They liked her and called her 'red' or 'rusty' because of her dark-red hair. She had just finished her four years at State University and was home having a good time. She made all of the dances in town and in the neighboring towns, and went often to El Paso or Dallas or San Antonio for parties. She sat on the bed and scowled slightly at Joan, for she disliked her.

"Why don't you offer a reward, kid?" she asked Marion.

"I don't know what to do. I want to see Gere Drexell first. Do you know where he is, Joan?"

"I saw him in town," answered the girl. "He said he'd be out later."

"Well, he ought to call me. Maybe he will soon." Marion got up and went toward the bathroom door. "I'm going to take a shower. I feel so dirty and hot. You will wait, won't you?"

Mildred said "yes," but Joan got up and started out. "I've got to get some supper," she said, "and go back to the office." She went over and kissed Marion and said, "I'm sorry."

At the door she turned. "I'll come up early tomorrow."

She went out and down the long hall to the stairs. It was a double stairway, curving smoothly upward from each side of the large entrance foyer. Joan walked slowly and silently down the right flight and paused at the door of the living-room. Here the voices of the women inside sounded intermittently. She breathed deeply and went in.

Across the room, seated on the deep-red divan, was Etta Levy, large and darkly Jewish. Agnes Jones faced her from an armchair. The Reverend Mr. Brush and his tall, militant, English wife were seated on the chesterfield near the door.

The minister rose at the sight of her and came forward. "Ah, Miss Shields," he said, "and how is Miss Fordman? You've seen her?" His accent was very broad and Bostonian. He was an addition worthy of the new Episcopal Church with its leaning toward ceremony. As tall as his wife, but very thin, he swayed forward and bowed his narrow dark head. "It is hard, very hard, to bear a thing like this," he said.

Etta Levy called to her and Joan went across the room to sit beside the woman. Her lovely face, with its clear-white skin and its contrast of smooth black hair, rose incongruously from her squat, uncouth body.

"There is nothing that we can do, I know, but I do hate to leave Marion, Joan. She is alone." Etta was kind, but so deeply interested in the fortunes or misfortunes of her friends and neighbors that she caused acute discomfort among those whom she desired to aid.

"No," replied Joan, "there is nothing that anyone can do."

Agnes Jones rose from her chair. She was a larger, older edition of her daughter. Her dark, burnt-umber hair was badly mussed and her eyes were swollen and bloodshot from crying. Joan was sorry for her. She had loved John Fordman for years, in the face of public opinion which had branded her with side glances and wise, knowing looks as That Woman! Her position had been made easier since her husband's stores had succeeded so well and the all-powerful money had come to aid her.

She wandered vaguely toward the hall door, caught the eye of the minister's wife, and stiffened immediately. "Joan," she said too loudly, "is Mildred upstairs?"

"Yes, ma'am," Joan replied.

"I will go up and get her. We must go home." She stared steadily at Mrs. Brush, who looked viciously back at her. The minister had risen and stood uncertainly beside his wife.

Agnes Jones turned her back and left the room. It was silent as her footsteps were heard on the stairway.

Etta Levy looked at Joan, and said, "How on earth could she come here?"

The minister's wife snorted violently.

The minister was silent.

Joan said "Good-bye" and went out.

It was almost dark now. The afterglow had vanished and the clouds on the eastern horizon were high-piled purple masses, tipped with silver. Joan shivered, for the prairie wind was cold.

IV: MONDAY, JULY 3

Joan drove slowly down the mountain and into the lighted town. Her own home was on the main street, and, as she drew her roadster to the curb, she noticed that the chairs on the lawn under the large chinaberry tree were empty. The family was at dinner.

She went in quietly, took a shower, and put on another fresh linen dress.

Her father and her mother and her young brother Jimmie were still at the table. They were eating strawberry shortcake for dessert, but even Jimmie looked up eagerly when she entered.

"I don't like you to be involved in this, Joan," said her mother.

"Say, Sis, can I go back to the office with you? I'll run errands an' answer the 'phone if you'll let me," said Jimmie.

Her mother rose and went into the kitchen. "I've kept some supper hot, dear," she said.

"Say, can I, Sis?" begged the boy.

Joan looked at her father, who smiled at her. "It is going to be a pretty big mess, isn't it, Sister?" stated Joan's father.

She nodded and turned to Jimmie. "Yes, you can come with me."

"Does anyone know anything?" inquired her father. "The town is humming."

"Not that I've heard. What do they say?"

"Well, some say the nigger man; some say an escaped lunatic; some whisper Chick Jones, and I've even heard that there was bad blood between Ross and Fordman."

75

Joan nodded. "But he was reported broken off with Mrs. Jones," she offered.

"Maybe so," said Shields thoughtfully, "But—"

He paused and began eating his strawberries as Mrs. Shields entered with Joan's plate.

"Do you have to go back tonight?" she said as she set it down.

"Yes, Mom. There'll be a lot to do."

"Well, I don't like it. A murder! Have you been to see Marion?"

"Yes, Mom—just before I came home."

"Who was there?"

"The minister—Brush, I mean, his awful wife, Mrs. Levy and Mrs. Jones and Mildred."

Mrs. Shields shook her head sadly and rose. "You'll find your shortcake in the icebox. The whipped cream is in a bowl." She looked at her husband. "Let's go out, John," she said. "It's so awfully hot in here and I feel somewhat upset."

They left Joan and Jimmie together, Mrs. Shields's voice returning faintly from the living-room—"Leave the dishes right where they are. Minnie will clear up when she comes home."

"I'll get your strawberry shortcake, Sis," said the boy.

"Thanks."

He returned from the kitchen a few minutes later with the dessert, its crisp short biscuit covered with crushed berries and topped by a mound of cream.

"It's kind of rich, Sis," he said. "Sure you want it?"

She said "yes" and ate half of it while he watched her sadly. "Here, bum," she said, and pushed the rest to him. He gulped it down and caught her at the front door. They called good-bye to the two in the chairs under the dark china tree and drove back to the newspaper office.

There they found work going in full blast. The regular edition had come off the press some half-hour before their arrival and the newsboys were getting their stacks to hawk on the streets. Joan noticed that each stack was twice as large as usual. Jimmie vanished into the melee of the back shop. The machines drew him like magnets.

Frank, looking worn and haggard under his green eyeshade, was sitting at his desk reading a smudgy first section. Mitch White was nowhere in sight. The advertising men were at their desks also reading first sections. Joan went into the back shop and procured one for herself.

A two-column cut of Fordman was set up in the center of the page. A seventy-two-point banner head proclaimed:

JOHN FORDMAN KILLED

The story, under a four-column, thirty-two point head, was the one that Mitch had written, with a little change in the first paragraph localizing the story. Her own interview with Mrs. Trotter had been dropped under the same heading, but to the left of a 'box' which held a short story to the effect that the paper would continue to function under the direct management of Edward Frank, Editor. The story was authorized by Patrick Drennan, Fordman's lawyer, and had been confirmed by Marion.

Frank looked at Joan over his paper and said, smiling wearily, "See you've been home. 'Ja see Marion?"

"Yes. She wouldn't say anything definite for publication. Wants to wait and see Drennan and Gere Drexell."

Frank raised his eyebrows, moving the eyeshade with them. "Drexell, hmm."

"And likewise 'hmm,'" said Joan. "Where's Mitch?"

"He's gone over to the boarding-house to grab some supper and a shower—and a drink, I guess. Goddamn him. If he don't keep sober while this thing is goin' on, I'll fire him." He slapped his hand on the paper in front of him. "I'm goin' home, too," he said. "You keep an eye on things and I'll be back in a couple of hours. Want to see some of these people. If anything breaks, just sit on it and I'll call in every now and then. You c'n head up some of the A.P. stuff. We're goin' to get a mornin' edition out. Won't change much but the front page. That's all anybody'll want to read."

He took off the eyeshade and picked up his coat and hat. "I got oil on everything I have on," he said.

"Yeah, I smell it," sniffed Joan.

"There'll be a mob of fellows from the other sheets down on us soon. Hall has already called from *The News*, and the Fort Worth man wired he'd be over from Abilene right away. Give 'em as much as you know, without openin' up too wide. So long." He banged the screen door behind him and disappeared into the darkness.

Joan straightened her desk and wiped away the inevitable yellow dust that perpetually powdered everything in the country of daily sand-storms. As she crumpled up and threw away the collected paper, she came across the story of Mrs. Shaw's red, white, and blue bridge party. "Omygod," she thought, it missed the evening edition. Still, it could go in the morning sheet if Mac would recast the Soc. page for her. She started writing fourteen-point heads for it—

MRS. SHAW ENTERTAINS
LAFF–A–LOT BRIDGE CLUB

MESDAMES HALL AND—

No—that wouldn't do—

MISS SMITH AND MRS. HALL
WIN HIGH SCORES

The telephone burred at her elbow. She recognized Marion Fordman's voice.

"Can you talk?" it said.

"Yes," replied Joan; "everybody's gone for the moment."

"Oh, Joan, I'm so worried. I don't know what to do. Gere called up, but he said he couldn't come out until tomorrow. Mr. Drennan has come and gone. He said that the will would be read tomorrow. It's in the vault at the bank."

"Are you there alone?" interrupted Joan.

"Right now, but Mildred is coming back to spend the night, and Mrs. Smith, the housekeeper, is here. Mildred went home to take her mother." Here she faltered.

"Hello," said Joan into the silence. "Well, I'm glad that you aren't alone. Is Glieth coming?"

"Yes, I wired her and she will be here tomorrow afternoon, she said. She wired awhile ago."

"Is she in Houston?"

"Yes. I suppose so. She got my wire and I sent it there."

"Of course."

"Oh, Joan, there's so much I want to ask you—"

"Not over the 'phone, Marion. I'll come up tomorrow, early."

"I guess you're right. I imagine that Central is listening in, don't you? Anyway, I don't care much. It's about the police. They are nice enough, but not very bright. Shouldn't I get someone else? You ought to know. Drennan hemmed and hawed, and Gere said 'no,' but—what do you think?"

"I think so. Most decidedly. And I know someone, too. Go to bed now and try to sleep. Lord knows when I'll get to bed!"

"Well, thanks a lot. Good-bye."

Joan sat back in her chair and smiled. Then she pulled a telegraph blank out of her desk drawer and wrote:

TO RICHARD FIELDS
3001 LINDELL BLVD.
ST. LOUIS, MO.
CON TEXAS PAGE ONE'S ACCOUNT LOCAL MESS
STOP FT. WORTH DALLAS SHEETS SURE TO
CARRY STOP IF I WIRE OKAY CAN YOU HOP
HERE BY PLANE STOP MAY MEAN BIG RETAINER
AND BIGGER BRAIN TEASER STOP AIR MAIL
LETTER FOLLOWS
          JOAN

She called a boy and sent the message as a night wire. She knew that Fields read every important paper within a radius of a thousand

miles and that by morning he would be sure to find the story of
John Fordman's murder staring at him from every front page of
the Texas papers, at least.

Joan had known the big red-headed detective during the two
years that she had functioned as refined sob-sister and feature
writer on the New York *World*. The same depression that spelled
an end for that ancient sheet and thus ousted Joan from her post
had sent Fields west to join an agency in St. Louis.

He had been one of Joan's most ardent admirers in his hard-
boiled way, and under the influence of the girl's sympathy had revealed several interesting facts about his early life. He was the only
son of a wealthy hat manufacturer of Danbury, Connecticut, and
to papa's supreme disgust refused to follow in his footsteps and
help cover the heads of the nation's citizens with derbys, svelt top-
pers, straw sailors, and business-man felts. He made a record at
Brown—on the football field, but was firmly expelled during his
senior year after blacking the eye of an official who aroused his ire.

Hesitating to face papa after this fracas Dick had joined the
New York State Troopers and later resigned to become a junior
member of a newly organized private detective agency. Dick, with
his entrée into several top-notch clubs and his acquaintances in
New York society, had been able to bring his agency much welcome business until the depression curbed the desires of wealthy
New Yorkers to hire operatives at several hundred dollars a day.
The agency went rapidly to the wall and Dick was glad to get a good
opening out in the "sticks."

Joan knew that he had done remarkably well there, for several
of his cases had received wide publicity. He had written recently
to say that business was going slack again, however, and why the
hell didn't she invite him to Texas?

Thrusting aside the papers on her desk, she got out her notes
and began to type the letter to Dick. She clipped the stories in the
News and added them to her own résumé. She listed the people
who had been with Fordman and characterized them fully, so that
Dick would waste no time on his arrival. She outlined the rumors

and told of Fordman and Agnes Jones—of Fordman and his fiancée, Glieth Lawrence.

Joan thought about Glieth Lawrence. Mrs. William Cameron Lawrence she had been. But Mr. William Cameron Lawrence had been shot down over the German lines, two days before the Armistice had been signed. The two had been married a week before he sailed for France. Marion had told Joan this. Marion liked her father's fiancée. She had met her in New York and had introduced her new friend to her father about a year ago. Marion said that she was thirty-eight and beautiful. The news of Fordman's sudden death must have been a severe blow to this woman, twice within sight of possible happiness.

She included these thoughts in her letter and was just finishing the long missive, when a shout from the door interrupted her. She looked up and saw two unmistakable newspaper men, both lighting cigarettes, regarding her over the counter.

"Hi, Sister," said one, "I'm Davis, the *Telegram's* West Texas correspondent. This is Jackie Jackson of the *Dallas News* and *Journal*. That Texas Bible has decided to break down and print a murder story. Can you imagine! We jus' got in. Anythin' new happened?"

"No," admitted Joan, "but you boys come on around and sit down. Here's our evening sheet. It has everything so far."

The boys grabbed the paper and read quickly. "Hell," said Davis, "we've got that much!"

Jackson queried Joan, "Who gets the billion berries? The gal?"

"I suppose," she answered.

"You know her?"

"Yes."

"Good-looker?"

"Very."

"Pitchers?"

Joan laughed. "Yes, I've got pictures. I had Mac run some mats off a plate—two-column. It's a good one, too. Steichen did the photo. In New York, you know?"

"Steichen? Holy Gee!" said Jackson. "Then she's no local belle. She's been around. Finishing school—abroad—all that?"

Joan got her index card devoted to the life of Marion Frances Fordman from her files and held it close to her. The boys held out pleading hands.

"No, sirs,' she declared. "You can both copy this. I'll read it out, but I won't let you carry my files away." She read to them the notes she had collected on the activities of Marion Fordman for her own private morgue of individuals of interest to the readers of her society columns.

Both reporters dashed for telephones and each placed calls for his own paper. The calls came through promptly and they relayed this information to their respective city editors.

Joan finished her letter to Dick and stamped it for airmail and special delivery. She called Jimmie from the back shop and sent him off to the post-office with careful instructions as to posting it in the airmail slot. It would go out on the morning plane, east-bound, to Dallas, and from there would go to St. Louis. Dick would have the letter by the next evening at the latest. She sent Jimmie home.

Jackson came and sat on her desk. He bummed a cigarette and offered her some corn from a Woolworth flask. She refused the drink with a wrinkling of her short nose, and said, "The spirit is willin', but th' stummick is weak."

The reporter laughed and took a long swallow. He chased it with a drag from the cigarette.

"Close that flask," said Joan. "The stink will bring all of the boys up from the back and we'll never get out a paper."

He laughed again and corked the flask. "Well, we're goin' up to th' hotel and clean up," he said, "but we'll return!"

"I'll bet," said the girl flatly. She smiled at them both.

"So long," they chorused, and the door banged in their wake.

Joan headed up A.P. copy until Frank returned. She told him about the reporters. He grunted. He was sore. Mitch, he told her, had passed out at his boarding-house. She would have to stay for a while, anyway, and help with the routine stuff. It was ten o'clock.

She stayed until three and then went home and to bed. She wondered about White. Had he passed out or was he ill? He had looked drunk, but he hadn't talked so badly. His story had been coherent and even a little dramatic. But he had looked sick.

V: TUESDAY, JULY 4

Joan's Baby Ben jangled her into wakefulness at six o'clock on the morning of July 4. She got up and shut it off quickly, but her mother had already heard its clamor and appeared in the doorway. She was in her nightgown and slippers and she looked quite cross.

"Are you getting up now?" she inquired.

"Yes, Ma'am," replied Joan.

"What for?"

"I've got lots to do, Mamma."

"You came home at three-thirty this morning," severely.

"Three."

"I heard the clock strike three-thirty about ten minutes after you tiptoed down the hall."

Joan was dressing. Her mother came in and sat on her bed. "Please, darling, don't work so hard," she said.

"I'm all right, Mamma."

"Where are you going at this hour?"

"We are getting out a morning edition and I have to be there."

She finished dressing, kissed her mother, and went through the back to the garage. Jimmie was sitting in her roadster. He had the garage doors open and the motor running.

"Good Lord! How did you ever wake up?" she said. "It usually takes a cold ducking."

The boy giggled. "I set my alarm for five an' I've been up ever since. Are you goin' out to the field?"

Joan looked at him sharply. "Does Mom know you're with me?" she asked.

"Nope."

"How'd you guess that I was going to the field?"

"I just guessed," was the answer.

They drove rapidly out of the silent town and onto the state highway that led toward the oil fields. The sun had been up only a short time and the air was still cool. The West Texas country, an odd mixture of rolling plains and small lumpy hills, stretched clear and vivid around them.

The ground was clayey red and sandy. On one side lay the cotton fields. The Mexican choppers were out and their varicolored clothes showed brightly in the young green. On the other side of the road lay pasture land, the greenish-gray bunch grass tall and dusty. On the ragged mesquite trees the seed pods were turning red. The dark green cedars looked cool and fresh. Fat, red cattle with white faces, stretched short necks upward for the mesquite beans. Occasional jackrabbits leapt like giant grasshoppers under the barbed-wire fences and into the mesquite clumps. A chaparral ran smoothly across the road into a grain field.

About eight miles out, a dirt road turned into the oil fields. It was deep with dust, finely powdered, which lay a foot deep in the hard ruts. The overpowering rotten-egg odor of crude oil hung heavy over the area.

Joan whistled with disgust and Jimmie said, "I like it." He sniffed appreciatively.

The derricks rose on every side—a forest of barren metal trees. At some, there was drilling with full crews, but most of the wells were silent.

The recent legislation limiting or 'prorating' production had made this once frantically busy place into a veritable graveyard, with the derricks standing as suitable memorial shafts. A field with the potential yield placed at eighty thousand barrels per day, proration had limited the actual amount of oil removed daily to a mere twenty thousand barrels. Hundreds of men had lost their jobs. Whole families had moved to other states. The remainder sat hopelessly, with salaries cut, waiting for the price of crude oil to be forced high enough to make profitable the drilling of new wells. With the slump in price resulting in proration legislation had come a corresponding slump in the business of the town. Incomes of ten and twenty thousand dollars a year had dwindled to a microscopic three and four, with the lapsing of fat leases and the cessation of every phase of oil activity.

Joan stopped the car near a red-and-yellow Shell Company's shack with a smoking chimney. A man came out and, in answer to her question, pointed down the road. She would find the Fordman well roped off, he said. He returned to his coffee and his bacon which they could smell cooking in the shack.

About four miles down the dusty road, they came to a Y and Joan turned to the left. A quarter of a mile farther on, the rope which the man had mentioned appeared. Here they stopped the car. Joan could see the crew busy around the tool shack. The ground looked spongy with oil, even as far away as the rope, but the well had been capped down and the flow of oil stopped.

She turned off the little road and parked near a mesquite clump to its right. The ground was marked with many criss-crossings of tire tracks. She and Jimmie ducked under the rope and walked over the oily ground toward the well, where she could see Val Day and the marshal, Tom Harte, talking together.

Harte greeted her smiling. "Howdy, Miss Shields. You come out to write up the pink tea the oil boys had yest'day?"

"You guessed it, Tom," she replied. "Whew, the smell is pretty strong, isn't it?"

"What smell?" said Day, the driller, winking at Harte.

"Don't kid me, Mr. Day." Joan smiled and looked at Harte. "D'ya mind if I look around? I see that the law is on the job."

Day moved away and entered the engine shed.

"Yes, ma'am, Miss Shields. I got to stay here 'til the county attorney comes. Lord knows why! I've been all over this place and I can't find nothin' that would convict a flea, let alone whoever killed Mr. Fordman!"

He sat on the floor of the working platform built into the derrick and swung his feet. His boots were covered with yellow dust and his tight blue serge trousers were spotted with oil and dirt. He wore a blue shirt open at his leathery throat and his Adam's apple jerked convulsively as he cleared his throat and spat into the yellow weeds. His brown face looked like jerked beef, wrinkled and tough. He looked at Joan with his pale blue eyes and said, "You'll shore git dirty if you mess aroun' here, Miss Shields."

"Where was Mr. Fordman's car parked, Tom?" she asked.

"Hit was right over there by that tank, by them mesquites," said the officer, pointing to the left.

Joan thanked him and walked through the dusty weeds to the mesquite clump. The ground was dry and powdery near the mesquites and gnarled little trees were hoary with the dust. She felt a little foolish, but decided to figure things out to her own satisfaction, anyway.

Harte, curious, had followed her and pointed out the heavy tire tracks made by the Fraschini. Joan took out her pencil and made a rough sketch of the relative positions of the cars.

Harte, who had been on hand the previous day, helped her with her diagram. The Fordman car had been isolated from the others with several mesquite trees between it and the nearest car: a LaSalle belonging to Chick Jones, Mitchell White's Ford roadster had been next in line, and Joey Levy's blue Buick sedan had been the last, facing the road and the well. Mr. Ross had parked his Cadillac sedan behind the other cars, facing it toward the town.

Joan left the parking space and walked around the small storage tank. She noticed that the ground was permanently moist from the oil that had oozed out of several leaks in the galvanized iron. A shallow ditch, about a foot wide and six inches deep, black and soft with oil, had been dug around its base.

Near the ditch, on the side farthest away from the wall, Joan noticed a particularly trampled area. She picked up two cigarette butts, noted that they were Luckies, and threw them down again, wiping her fingers on her handkerchief. A small scrap of paper

caught in a weed drew her attention. She picked it up and found it
to be a newspaper clipping, well worn from folding, of the daily
syndicated bridge problem which ran in the *Daily News* and several of the associate papers.

She glanced at it curiously and put it in her pocket.

Harte and Jimmie came up. "Find anything?" asked the latter.

"Not much," said Joan. "I guess I'm no detective."

They returned to her car and she and Jimmie got in. "Thanks,
Tom," she said, "I'll leave you the smell!"

"I wish you could take it with you, Miss Joan," said the wrinkled
Westerner.

Joan and Jimmie drove back to town in silence. The boy knew
that she was thinking and preferred to be left alone. He was surprised when she swung the roadster into the road leading to the
Fordman home.

"Everybody'll be asleep, Sis," he said.

"Maybe not," she replied.

They drove up the long hill and Joan ran her car around the
house to the garage in the rear. The double doors were open, showing the rears of the Isotta, Marion's Packard coupe, and the Ford
roadster in which Fordman had preferred to drive himself to and
from the oil fields.

Texas Wills, in brown coveralls, came to the door of the garage, sponge in hand. He was cleaning the Ford. Joan sighed in
relief and she said sharply, "Don't wash the Isotta, Texas. Don't
even brush it out. There might be something important in it or on it."

The negro looked at her, big-eyed, and shook his head. "I ain'
teched it, Miss Joan, but it's all bloody inside."

Joan got out, leaving Jimmie, and went in to look at the big
car. It was quite dusty. The Isotta had been one of Fordman's prized
possessions, and although he never drove it and seldom rode in
it—it was Texas's particular pride to keep it clean and shining.

Joan looked carefully at the large silver handles on the tonneau doors—especially at the one on the right. They were plain and
heavy, and to her inexperienced eye hopelessly covered with
smudges and dust.

The car itself was sombre, with its rear shades pulled down and its long black body heavy with dust. Several irregular scratches paralleled each other along the entire right side of the body. Clearly, the car had been carelessly swept through the cat-claw bushes on the way into town.

Wills saw her eyeing the scratches and said: "Them was cat-claws, Miss Joan. I drove too close to the side of the road yest'day comin' in. It'll take a pow'ful lot of work to get them marks out."

Joan walked around and opened the left rear door, snapped on the ceiling light, and looked into the tonneau of the car. The little fan was silent, its four blades were still. The deep pile carpet was dirty and the prints of oily, dusty shoes showed clearly on its gray surface. She could see a small dark stain on the edge of the gray seat and a larger dark stain close to the base of the seat, on the floor. Fordman had bled considerably. Joan shivered slightly as she looked at the dry spots, mute witnesses of the hatred of some-one toward the wealthy oil man. She withdrew her head and mo-tioned to Texas. "Let's lock the car all up," she said, "and I'll take the key in to Miss Fordman."

Texas leaned inside and set the locks, turned the key in the handle of the door at the driver's seat and gave it to Joan. She thanked him and went into the house. The kitchen clock showed eight-ten, and Mrs. Smith, the housekeeper, was rattling pans in the pantry. Joan slipped quickly through and avoided the old woman, who was annoyingly garrulous. She went upstairs and knocked at Marion's door, softly.

Marion called "Come in" and Joan entered, to find the girl in a chair at the window, looking out over the lower plain.

"Hello, dear," she said.

Marion had not realized who had entered until Joan spoke. Then she rose quickly and cried out gladly, "Oh, Joan, you did come early. I'm so glad."

Joan said: "I've only a moment. I must go to the office. Mitch was ill last night and I'm sure there's lots to do. I did want to talk to you, however, about calling in someone to help out with this"— she hesitated and then said, flatly—"unfortunate murder."

Marion sat down at the word and shut her eyes.

There was silence.

The younger girl pulled her frayed nerves together with an effort and faced the issue bravely. "Yes, you are right. It was a murder," she said. "I've tried not to think of it with that word."

"I know," said Joan, "but if you want things cleared up, something must be done at once. The local police will muddle along for a day or so and then the county attorney will step in with much publicity, and in my opinion the trail will grow so cold that even Sherlock himself would be baffled."

"What can we do, Joan? *I* don't know any detective, I'm sure."

"Ah," replied Joan, "but *I* do."

"You always did know such queer people. I remember that party you had for me in New York. Why, there was even a gangster there."

"Not a gangster. Mike was just a nice college lad paying his way through Columbia by selling very poor Golden Wedding rye. But to get back to the detective. He is Dick Fields—you may remember him, a big red-headed fellow. I think that he was chief bottle-opener at that same party. Well, anyway, he is in St. Louis with a detective agency. Now I hear that he's a super-sleuth, and even if it's an exaggeration he is bright. Certainly almost any bright lad would be better than Read and Harte, or even County Attorney Millbank and his investigators. If you want me to do so, I'll wire him to come down and look things over. I'm certain that there should be a serious and thoughtful investigation—and immediately."

"Well—it couldn't hurt anything, Joan; but will the local authorities allow him just to sort of take things over?"

"With your permission, they won't be able to help themselves, no matter what they think. But there is no need for them to know— at least, not at first. There is another thing, though, Marion. I've had Texas lock the Isotta and here is the key." She produced it and held it out. "Can you get along without it until Dick can look it over? So far, I don't suppose that the police have thought of it, have they?"

"No, not that I know of—but why is it so important?"

"I don't know that it is," replied Joan, "but it might be, and at least it's the only tangible thing we have to work with." She hesitated, and then went on. "Then you do want Dick to come down?"

"Heavens, yes. Do you think he'll come?"

"I don't doubt it," answered Joan."

Marion rose and tightened the belt of her silk dressing-gown. "Come down and have breakfast with me," she invited.

Joan looked at her wrist-watch and said: "Well, I'll have a cup of coffee, anyway. It's late, but Frank can't afford to fire me for tardiness with his only reporter out like Lottie's eye. And that reminds me. I must stop by Mitch's boarding-house and look in on him. His old she-devil of a landlady will let him starve to death and never lift a finger."

The two girls ate breakfast under the attentive eye of Mrs. Smith and refrained from further discussion of the murder.

As Joan left, she asked, "Will there be a formal reading of the will today?"

Marion nodded and said: "Pat Drennan is coming out with Gere Drexell this afternoon at one. Glieth should get in at twelve-fifteen on the plane from San Antonio. Shall I telephone you when they finish?"

"Yes. Call right away, will you, dear? The paper goes to bed at three sharp, but Frank will want to hold it until he has something definite."

"Oh, the paper. I forgot about it. Does all of this *have* to go in the paper?"

"Well, of course, you could keep it out of the local paper by just closing down and standing firm, but it will be in all of the state papers, so we might as well carry it, too." Here her professional enthusiasm showed itself in her regretful tone as she visualized their publication of the *Daily News sans* the latest developments. "It won't make any difference, darling," she said. "Everyone will talk about it and they might as well have the facts correct. Have any of the out-of-town men tried to see you yet?"

"Someone telephoned last night, but Mildred found out who it was and told them that I wouldn't see them or talk to them. They will probably come out today."

"You'd better let Drennan talk to them," advised Joan, remembering the brutal insistence of the two who had talked to her on the previous evening.

She looked down at the pale, anxious face of her friend and realized the feeling of futility which possessed the younger girl. Years of correct boarding-schools, extended visits abroad—a nomadic, cosmopolitan, but withal well-chaperoned existence, had done much to blunt her native American aggressiveness. She knew little of the people who made up the great mass of Americans. Their habits and their thoughts were as hidden from her as were those of the prairie dog. She was bewildered; yet she was not soft—not childish. She was a polished, finished, cultured young woman; modern in a very pleasant way. Good taste was her chief ikon. She had known so little of her father, of his life and his interests. He had been merely the source of her life, so familiar as to be but a vague background. His existence she had always taken as a matter of course, and his non-existence was unthinkable. She could not embrace the change that it would impose.

She sat wearily at the table, her cheeks cupped in her hands, and stared at Joan. Waving a vague hand she said: "I really don't know what to do next, Joan. All of this . . . this excitement; this unpleasant turmoil"—she hesitated—"I don't—know what to do!" she finished lamely.

Joan leaned across the table and patted her shoulder. "It isn't surprising," she said. "By the way, you're breaking a good reporter's heart and giving Ed and me twice our usual work to do. What's the matter with Mitch lately? He worships you, you know."

Marion smiled a little, then looked cross. "It's his own fault," she declared. "He's so irresponsible. He's such a good newspaper man, but he drinks and neglects his work. You know that Dad was about to let him go, don't you?"

"No," said Joan, "I didn't know. Maybe you could straighten him out, Marion."

"Not me. I've washed my hands. I really tried, but he gets so upset when I see anyone else, and after all Gere is a lot easier to get on with. We've had a splendid time this summer."

Joan nodded. "He is interesting," she agreed. They talked for a few minutes longer and then Joan went out to her car. She found Jimmie eating a large slice of toast spread with marmalade.

"Say, Sis," he muttered thickly, "say, what'll you gimme for a clue?"

She pushed his feet ungently off the seat and slid under the wheel. He flourished the toast and marmalade under her nose and said derisively, "Yah, you're so smart, but it takes little brother to find things. Lookit," and he produced from his sweater pocket a small dull-black automatic. "Yah," he said again as he flourished this under her nose. "*I* found it!"

"Give that here," she demanded. "Where did you get it?"

"Don't you wish you knew?" was the thick reply, as he crammed the last of the toast into his mouth. Joan was rapidly realizing the significance of the boy's find, and his antics angered her intensely, to his evident satisfaction. He leaned back against the door and grinned.

She controlled herself with difficulty and said calmly, "If that is the gun that Mr. Fordman was shot with, you had better give it to me—you have probably ruined any of the finger-prints on it by now."

Jimmie's face became ludicrously blank and he drew his arm around in front of him and stared at the gun, now held carefully by one finger through the trigger guard.

"Oh, gosh, Sis," he said slowly, allowing her to take it out of his grasp without protest. "Gee," he muttered, "I never thought of that."

"Where did you find it?" asked Joan—"if you did find it," she added skeptically.

"Well, I was talkin' to Texas while you were in the house," he began, still sobered by the enormity of his thoughtlessness—he was an avid reader of mystery stories and knew *all* about finger-prints—"an' when he went in to get his breakfast, I went over to look at the big car. I didn't see anything important, so I sat down on the run-ning-board of the Ford. Just then Texas came out and brought me some toast, so I stayed there to eat it. And I was lookin' at the rear end of the Fraschini, when I noticed those two big spare tires on behind. I was just even with them an' I noticed the leather cover on the outside one bulging a little. Well, I went over and stuck my hand through behind and found that between the cover and the tire. And"—he finished impressively—"it was all wrapped up in this." He produced from the same pocket that had held the gun a man's very oily handkerchief.

Joan took the rag gingerly and smiled at the boy. "Don't worry about the finger-prints, darling. I guess that our murderer reads mystery stories, too. I'll wager that the only prints on this gun will be yours."

The back door of the house slammed and Texas Wills stood on the step. "Any trouble with yo' car, Miss Joan?" he called.

"No, thanks, Texas," she replied, dropping the gun and the handkerchief in her lap. "We were just talking." She started the car and they swung around the drive into the steep hill road before either spoke. Then Joan asked, "Did you show it to Texas?"

The boy rebuked her with a brotherly snort. "Of course not, silly," he said.

She let him out in front of their home, for his breakfast, and went on to the office. It was early, but the entire staff was at work. The linotype clacked rhythmically in the back shop and the printers clicked off the news in the front. On her desk lay a telegram. She tore it open, noticed that it had been sent from St. Louis at six o'clock that morning. It read,

DROPPING EVERYTHING COMING BY PLANE AT ONCE STOP DEPENDING ON YOU TO GET CON-FIRMATION STOP THANKS LOVE D. F.

VI: TUESDAY, JULY 4: 9.30 A.M.

Joan figured that Dick should arrive by the middle of the afternoon at the latest, if he had caught the morning air express from
St. Louis to Dallas. She put the thought aside, however, as she realized how much work must be accomplished that morning. Already there were a dozen or more scrawled slips of paper on her
desk, reading:

> Call 729J Mrs. Scott
> Call 2321 Something on Presbyterian Christian
>   Endeavor
> Call Mrs. W. H. Shaw—Important

The last one was underscored and she winced at the thought of
having to explain the omission of Mrs. Shaw's party from last
night's edition. She rescued the story from a pile of dusty copy
paper on the desk and rushed back into the shop with it. Leaving it
impaled with its heading on one of the linotype operator's 'hurry'
hooks, she dashed back and called the irate Mrs. Shaw. That began a long session of calls. The garnering of news relating to the
crop of parties, sewing-bees, and church-circle meetings which
made up the social life of the women of Fordman. Joan copied down
lists of names, took details of scores of parties large and small,
sorted out her notes, and typed rapidly during the rest of the morning. The party lists were long and the entertainments were many,
for the July Fourth holidays despite the heat, bred as many bridges

and brides' showers as did Christmas. More than one hundred women had entertained as many as one thousand of their sisters— had worked frantically through the day before and the morning of the party, cleaning their little box-like houses, counting decks of cards, moulding Jello salads, numbering tallies, cutting bread into hearts and spades and diamond shapes, tying prizes into tissue-paper bundles with pink, green, and lavender satin ribbons. More than one hundred husbands ate suppers of leftover Jello salads and the slightly curled-up fancy sandwiches, amid a litter of dirty dishes and crumpled madeira napkins stained with lipstick. Mrs. Johnston won a wall vase. Mrs. Sanders won a boudoir pillow. Mrs. Evans won a nest of brass ashtrays, made in Japan. And so it would go on, forevermore, thought Joan.

But she thought about the parties only vaguely, for her mind was on the small black automatic in the pocket of her car outside. She was trying to decide whether or not she should turn it over to the sheriff or wait until Dick arrived. It was a losing fight for her conscience. She knew that the revolver would remain where it was until Dick could see it. There was no way of tracing its ownership by its number, she knew. Pistol permits were unheard of in that part of the country. Not that men habitually carried guns, as their Eastern visitors liked to imagine, but at least they could buy and own them without question.

The morning advanced and the heat settled down again on the office. The assistant pressman went out and came back with his arms full of cold Coca Colas. Joan gave him her nickel and drank the stuff with little enjoyment. It only made one hotter in the long run. She leaned over to put the empty bottle by the side of her desk, and rose again to face Mitch White as he came through the door-way from the back shop.

He looked faintly cheerful but decidedly rocky.

"Hello, honey," he said, sitting down at his desk next to hers.

She smiled at him and did not comment upon his morning's absence.

"Where's Ed?" he asked.

"He went out half hour or more ago, at about eleven. Said for you to get the A.P. stuff back as fast as possible—to cut out your column today—just fill in with wire sports—and then to meet him at one-thirty at the sheriff's office. They will hold the inquest this afternoon at about two-thirty and the paper won't go out until afterwards."

"Honey—can't you do the A.P. stuff? I've got to get a shave and a cup of coffee—and I feel like hell." He sat on the corner of her desk and held a cigarette between his fingers—unlighted. He rolled it back and forth slowly and lightly. The tobacco began to spill from the ends and drop into Joan's lap.

"You're ruining that cig," she said.

"Couldn't stand to smoke the lousy thing, anyway." He jerked himself off the desk and dropped the limp white cylinder on the floor.

"Send the Greek down with a bottle of milk and a sandwich," said Joan, "and I'll get the A.P. job over with while the men are at lunch. They were calling for copy a few minutes ago, but my last batch of society will hold 'em until they leave."

Mitch picked up his dusty hat, and waved a limp good-bye at her and was gone. Joan was alone except for the bookkeeper who stayed from twelve to one to answer the telephone. He sat on his big stool in the corner of the office and scratched his ribs reflectively—thinking of the glass of cold home-brew that he'd have when he got home. The linotypes were silent and the printer clacked only intermittently.

A little boy ran in to leave his mother's recipe for the Friday contest. Joan wrote headlines—about the war in China, about Greta Garbo, about Hitler, about the W.C.T.U., about Jim Ferguson. The telephone startled her out of her sleepy consideration of a four-teen-point head for a Prince of Wales story. It was Dick Fields calling from the local airport.

"Come out and get me, honey," he said plaintively. "The taxis are conspicuous by their absence."

Excited, Joan finished up her work hurriedly and then gathered together the few things that she wanted to take to Dick: the bridge clipping that she had found at the field; the copies of the stories run so far in the *Daily News*; her own notes; the sketches of the field and a carbon copy of the letter she had written to him and which she knew that he could not have received.

Driving rapidly out to the airport through the hot blue midday haze, she reflected that the weather was perfect for flying. Calculating rapidly she decided that Dick must have left St. Louis long before the regular transport ship and hence must have come by private plane.

Parking her roadster, she recognized Marion Fordman's coupe and Drexell's Ford among the cars in front of the airport station. A small group of people stood on the cement apron in front of the hangar. Fields came out of the station and walked across to her car. They shook hands and then he laughed and kissed her, saying, "Still love me? God, it's hot here!" The sun gleamed in his red hair which stood wirily on end. Perspiration covered his white forehead as he dashed it off with his hand.

"You look hot," said Joan sympathetically.

His woolen suit was too heavy for the climate and he carried an overcoat across his arm. He grinned, wrinkling his pleasant freckled nose, which was now pink with wind-burn.

"I wasn't too hot up there. See the crate I came down in?" He pointed a finger at a small crimson plane being pulled into the hangar by two of the station attendants. "Chartered it special, on the strength of the case," he added, beaming.

"Good Lord, Dick, what will you do next?"

"How about taking a bath?"

"That might be a good idea. But wait, Mrs. Lawrence, Mr. Fordman's fiancée, is due in here on the transport from Houston at twelve-fifteen. I think I see Marion Fordman and Gere Drexell over there by the hangar, too." She pointed, but Dick, putting his overcoat in the car, deliberately peeled himself out of his suit coat, ripped off his tie, and opened his shirt collar before he would listen to her explanations.

"I can't think when I'm uncomfortable," he stated, smoothing his shirt and adjusting a pair of bright blue braces. "Now this Fordman girl—she's the daughter?"

"Yes."

"And the man?"

"He was Mr. Fordman's assistant, at present rushing Marion. At least she's rushing him."

"There's a difference."

"Yes."

The man covered his flaming hair with his Panama and sadly shrugged himself into his coat. "Might as well meet 'em now and get it over with."

"Why don't you wait until you can see Marion alone?" suggested the girl. "I'll go over and wait until Mrs. Lawrence comes in. The plane's due now," she added, looking at the clock on the dashboard. Then scanning the horizon to the south, she pointed out the incoming ship, a dot of black in the strong blue haze.

The man agreed that the idea had merit, so she hastily got out of the car and ran across to the hangar.

Marion welcomed her eagerly, saying, "I thought I saw your car. Here comes Glieth's plane."

Drexell was staring reflectively at Dick's red ship, pulled up into one corner of the hangar.

"I'd like one like that," he commented.

"Isn't it cute!" agreed Joan.

"The bird who flew it in says he came from St. Louis this morning."

"Yes, I was just talking to him," said the girl.

Marion cried out excitely, "They're coming in!"

Drexell glanced toward the south, then back at Joan. The girl realized that he was definitely nervous and that he did not want her to stay. Her mind worked quickly and she turned away, saying, "I'll come up later, Marion." She cut through the small crowd and walked toward her car. Once, glancing back, she saw that Drexel still watched her. She walked on to the car which was around the corner of the airport office building and called to Dick.

"Wait for me a few minutes longer," she said. "I'm going to try something." She dodged back behind the building and approached the landing apron from the rear of the big concrete hangar. Entering the hangar by a small door, she skirted several planes and slipped carefully to the big folding doors that spread across the face of the building and gave out upon the apron. Peering through a crack between the hinged doors, she found that she was a bare twenty feet from Drexell and Marion as they stood watching the approaching plane.

The big silver transport had settled lightly to the field and the pilot was gunning her across the dirt with explosive roars of the motor. She kicked up a cloud of dust, made a turn and came to rest at the edge of the apron. An attendant opened the door and several passengers got out. Marion ran toward a woman in gray and they embraced. They returned to where Drexell stood, his white hat in his hand. Joan could hear Marion's full, pleasant voice, saying, ". . . and this is Gere Drexell, Glieth. Mrs. Lawrence, Mr. Drexell."

Joan could see Glieth Lawrence's face, dark, thin, thoroughbred, under her gray hatbrim. She could see a quick smile come—and as quickly—go. The woman held out her hand, saying, "It is pleasant to meet you, Mr. Drexell." But Joan did not believe her. She did not seem pleased now. And that smile had been one of surprised and instant recognition.

Joan ran quickly through the hangar, gained her car before the group on the apron moved. She was sitting at the wheel, talking with Dick, as Drexell came up hurriedly, got into his car and drove swiftly away. Joan told the detective who he was and explained what she had seen. He looked puzzled until she added that Drexell had told her only the day before that he had not met Mrs. Lawrence, though he had known her husband in France.

Fields smiled at her. "It was a smart trick, honey," he complimented. "We'll remember that."

Joan changed the subject. "I didn't know you flew," she said as she started the engine.

"I've learned during the past two years," he answered. "I think I'll buy that ship I came down in. It's a dandy."

"Buy it? Dick, your father hasn't died and left you the hats?"

"He died, poor old codger, but thank God he didn't leave me the hats. He didn't think I'd appreciate them and left the whole outfit to a cousin of mine named Percy. But he did relent and leave me a few thousand ducats."

They drove into town, following the car in which Marion Fordman and Mrs. Lawrence rode. It was twelve-thirty when they finally reached the suite that Dick had secured at the town's newest hotel. He immediately set out a bottle and sent for White Rock and ice. Joan sampled her drink and said, "It's swell to drink something besides corn for a change."

Fields laughed and set up a bridge table that he had ordered. They chatted about the past few years as he laid out paper and a fountain pen, a portable typewriter, and a small leather-covered box which he opened carefully.

Joan watched him unload a small microscope, a kit of the standard necessities for finger-print work, including shakers of black and gray powder, brushes, millimeter rules and compass. She fingered some of the other objects from the box—huge bunches of keys, oddly twisted wires, small and large flashlights, and a can of 'Three-in-One' oil, a small bunsen burner, test-tubes, and a dozen small vials of powders and liquids carefully labeled.

"My traveling lab," Fields explained.

"It looks complete," commented the girl.

"It is, pretty well. I may not need any of those things, you know, but then again I may." He arranged the paraphernalia on a glass-topped table in the bedroom and returned to the living-room. Sitting down at the bridge table, he picked up his pen, mashed out his cigarette.

"When's the inquest?" he asked.

"At about one-thirty," said Joan.

"Well, we'll work for a while. I've ordered some sandwiches sent up here for lunch. Will that do for you?"

"Oh, yes," answered Joan; then, "I've got something to show you." She took the small revolver from her brief case where she had placed it before driving out to the airport and handed it to the detective. His gray eyes hardened as he took it from her carefully— still wrapped in the handkerchief.

"The prints belong to my kid brother, Jimmie, and to me," said the girl. She explained where it had been found and that no one else as yet knew about the discovery.

Fields grinned at her, then examined the blue-black weapon in his hand closely. "These are nice little jiggers. A .25 automatic," he remarked.

"It looks like a woman's gun," Joan said.

"Not necessarily," he stated. "This baby is most effective and carries accurately at quite a distance. It's easily hidden, too." He went into the bedroom, stayed there for a few minutes and then returned.

"I tested it for finger-prints, anyway," he said. "There are a few. I'll take yours and Jimmie's and we can then eliminate. I imagine, however, that it was pretty thoroughly wiped off before you touched it. There were six cartridges in the magazine and the one that was fired makes seven. Undoubtedly one was fired recently and the gun was not cleaned after the firing either."

He made some notes, and then asked:

"Do they know what size the bullet was that killed Fordman? I mean, have you heard the results of the post-mortem yet?"

"Not fully," said the girl. "Doctor Ross mentioned either a .22 or a .25, I believe, yesterday, but he hadn't finished his investigation."

Fields laid the gun aside; then as an afterthought he asked another question, "You didn't," he said, "remove the magazine, did you? Either you or Jimmie?"

"I didn't," answered the girl. "I don't think he did. I'll ask him."

Dick sat down and picked up the handkerchief. It was plain white linen of good quality, with two threads, green, drawn into its border for decoration. There was no monogram. It was dirty and oily.

Joan said, "It looks as if he used it to wipe off his shoes!"

"No laundry marks," commented Dick.

"Ain't that somethin'?" remarked Joan.

"It's not so negative as one might think, darling. The handkerchief's not new. Been laundered. Use your brain."

"Clue number one," said the girl. "The murderer's laundry was did by a fat negress named Belinda."

"Will you stop being facetious? What d'you mean—a fat negress named Belinda?" Fields scowled at her.

"It's not so negative as one might think, darling," Joan quoted. "A fat negress named Belinda does the washing for a large part of our population—either she or one of her seven daughters named, chronologically, and geographically, Austin, Mexia, Navasota, Paris—"

Dick interrupted rudely. "You sound like a train caller in the Union Depot. What the hell *are* you kidding about?"

"I mean that Belinda or one of her seven daughters named— well, let that pass—probably washed the hankie, hence the absence of identifying marks. Simple enough."

Dick scribbled on the pad in front of him. "We'll put it down, anyway," he said; and reading, "Check list of Belinda's customers." He tossed the handkerchief over the revolver and picked up the clipping that Joan had found behind the storage tank at the oil field.

It was two columns wide and about seven inches long and was headed 'Your Contract Problems' by J. Thomas Hall, a syndicated piece by a well-known authority which appeared simultaneously in hundreds of papers throughout the country. Dick turned it over. On the reverse side was the left half of a crossword puzzle which had been partly filled in, obviously before the article had been clipped from the paper: obviously, Dick pointed out to Joan, as several of the letters forming the words had been cut in half and many of the words lacked their inevitably accompanying definitions at the top of the puzzle. Definitions for only twelve words remained and few of those bore numbers that would place their answers in the half which Dick held.

He read the eight-point type that filled the left-hand column and frowned.

Joan took the paper from him and read a few lines. She laughed and said: "It's the continued story—our daily Hairbreadth Harry bilge. I've read proof on that thing too many times not to recognize it in my sleep. This part is just after the heroine, Jacqueline, has soundly slapped the villain, Mr. Carew, and started walking home."

"Is this from your sheet?" inquired Dick.

Joan looked at the clipping closely and said: "It looks like it, but I wouldn't swear to it. The bridge article and the puzzle are both boilerplate, you know. We carry them, but so do some of the other papers in our chain. I can easily find out, however." She pointed to the small date mark under the puzzle, and said: "It ran in the edition of July first, which was Saturday. I can compare it with our own edition of that date and if the placements coincide, we'll know that it ran in the *News*. If they don't, we've four other papers in our chain to check over, to say nothing of the dozens of others using the piece."

Dick made another notation on his pad and slipped the clipping away in an envelope which he labeled and added to the other exhibits on the table.

"Get the paper of that date and bring it up here," he said. Joan nodded and handed him the carbon copy of her letter to him. He flipped through the pages and then read with complete absorption, while Joan got up and made fresh drinks for both of them.

"Well," remarked Dick as he finished the letter, "that's what I call a help. I believe I'd recognize these people on the street. Now it's time to fill out our motive and opportunity chart and then I'll get off to the inquest. It's two o'clock now, but those things always start late."

He took a large sheet of paper and turned it sidewise. Without hesitation, he scribbled six headings across the top, and drew five vertical lines.

"We'll take the people just as you have them in your letter," he said, "and examine them closely. Taking for granted that some one of his acquaintances murdered the unfortunate Mr. Fordman for reasons as yet unknown to us, we can at least tabulate as many of his acquaintances as could conceivably have been on hand at the time of the murder. And a murderer must, in most cases in which firearms are involved, at least be on hand."

He wrote the name of Agnes Jones first in the column labeled 'Suspects.' Under the column labeled 'Relation to the Murdered Man,' he wrote 'Mistress.'

"I suppose," he said to Joan, "there's no doubt about that?"

Joan shook her head firmly.

"All right," he continued, "we can dig up some hypothetical motives then, I guess."

Joan said: "Jealousy. Fordman was to have married Glieth Lawrence soon."

Dick wrote, 'jealousy, because of impending marriage,' and skipped to the column labeled 'Opportunity.'

"D'you know where she was at the time of the shooting?" he asked Joan.

"No. She was at the field. That's all I know. We'll have to find out."

Dick made another notation. "Does she play bridge?" he asked.

"Does she!" exclaimed Joan. "She gives lessons at two dollars an hour."

Dick added the words, 'Bridge expert' under the column 'Supporting evidence.' Then he re-read Joan's note relating to her visit to the oil field that morning. "I see," he said, "that you picked up and tossed aside the butts of several cigarettes and that they were Luckies. We'll have to get them just as a matter of caution. For instance, were they smoked by a woman or by a man?"

Joan looked apologetic and said: "Well, if you mean did they have lipstick on them I'd be tempted to say no. I don't remember any, but then I didn't look very closely. I only looked at the brand. I do remember, however, that they'd been put out, mashed or stepped on, because they were still pretty long and couldn't have been smouldering."

"Does Mrs. Jones smoke Luckies?" asked Dick.

"No," said Joan. "She smokes Chesterfields. Both she and Mildred do. I can't remember seeing any other brand at their house."

Dick left the discussion of Agnes Jones and returned to the left-hand edge of the paper. He wrote in the name of Clarence Jones and looked at Joan.

She said: "Well, let's see. He and Fordman have known each other forever. Went to school together out here in the country. Chick's about two or three years older than Fordman, but they were what you'd call contemporaries. Fordman and he both went through high school, but Chick couldn't quite make the grade for college. He went to work instead—in a grocery store—and has been at it ever since. He's moderately successful—owns the Servy Self chain. They've little competition. I believe that his wife is the reason that they succeeded. She's the one with ambition and horse-sense."

Dick lighted a cigarette and sipped his drink. "They've a daughter," he said.

"Yes, Mildred. You must meet her. Men always like her—and her mother, for that matter. Agnes is only thirty-eight. She's still handsome, if a trifle large. We were all out at the Gun Club last Sunday and you couldn't tell them apart, watching from the car as I was. I went over to get the scores for Mitch, who was supposed to cover the shoot but didn't, and found that I'd mistaken Agnes for Mildred all afternoon."

"Gun Club?"

"Yes—we have a trap out here south of town and the villagers while away their Sundays potting the clay birdies."

"How does Agnes Jones shoot?"

"Oh, she's top-hole. The best of the women and better than most of the men." Joan looked at Dick, and then said, "Shooting clay pigeons with a twelve-gauge isn't like shooting a man with a revolver."

"No," said Dick, as he rubbed his chin with his fingers and thumb. "God, but I do need a shave." He got up from the table and opened a bag, saying, "You write this down and I'll make myself presentable." He went into the bathroom and called to her above the noise of water running, "Does Jones shoot too?"

"Yes," replied Joan.

"Well, enter that under 'Supporting evidence' for the both of them. Where did Jones say he was when Fordman was killed?"

Joan looked at the notes she had taken during the informal inquiry conducted the evening before by the sheriff. "He didn't say," she replied. "I'll put that under 'Opportunity' since we know that he was at the field, anyway. And I'll also put it on our list of things to find out. It will probably come out at the inquest this afternoon."

She wrote rapidly for a moment and then called to Fields: "I say—Chick smokes cigars. I've never seen him with a cigarette. At least that should go under 'Contrary evidence,' shouldn't it?"

"Yes," was the answer, "but cigarettes are often resorted to during periods of emotional stress when time is short. They are a solace because they keep the hands busy. A cigar is smoked in a meditative mood and consoles rather than stimulates."

Joan thought for a moment, privately believing that the exceptions to the rule were numerous. There was no time for an argument based on generalizations, however, so she skipped back across the page and added the name of Samuel Ross to the list. In the second column she wrote, 'Business associate and President of the Fordman National Bank.' She communicated this to Dick, who turned off the water and appeared in the doorway, his face white with lather and a safety razor in his hand.

"Oh," he said, "that's Fordman's bank. Now we leave the motives based on love and hate—or shall we say sex—and come to those based on greed. There haven't been any rumors out about the bank's instability, have there?"

"It's said to be the strongest in this part of the country. It's bound to be, with Fordman as chief depositor."

"Still, there may be something fishy somewhere. Murders have been committed before to cover embezzlement."

Joan was slightly shocked. This didn't sound at all like Mr. Ross. She said as much and Dick laughed at her.

"You think," he said, "that murderers must look like criminals before they can be eligible for suspicion?"

"I do not," replied Joan, "but I know Mr. Ross fairly well and I believe that, though he might be a little unscrupulous as to money matters, a murder would be—well, too messy for him to countenance. He is such a fastidious man, cautious and precise. He'd think of the consequences of murder, which are generally messier than the deed itself. He'd never want his brain cluttered up with the afterthoughts that are bound to arise. He's too intelligent to have murdered John Fordman."

"There may be something in what you say, Joan. Besides, what good would it do to murder Fordman to avoid the discovery of bank irregularities? After his death, things are bound to be checked and discrepancies immediately noticed. There might have been something private between 'em—but then, we can say that about all of our suspects. Carry on. What about his opportunities?"

Joan gave a brief resume of Ross's account of his whereabouts during the critical period. "That places him in the 'possible class,' along with the others," commented Joan. She went on: "And as to supporting evidence in the light of the bridge clipping, I am forced to say that he is one of the most interested readers of the column. Called us up and complimented us when we began the series and raised hell just a few days ago when his paper failed to come and he missed the article. We had to send a boy out special with a copy. He plays duplicate contract, which isn't particularly popular here as yet. Sent to Chicago for duplicate boards."

Joan hesitated, and then said: "I don't know whether he smokes or not; possibly does not, but I do know that he keeps a revolver in his desk drawer at the bank. I've seen it. We'll have to check on that."

Dick reached over and patted her hand. "Sister," he said, "you surely are the detective's best friend. I never saw such a mine of information. You're better than any morgue I ever ran across."

"Well, I should hope so," commented the girl.

"You know what I mean," he said, emphasizing the word 'mean.' Then he became aware of the razor in his hand and the lather drying on his face, and dashed back into the bathroom.

Joan said: "It's nearly two. I'll add a note or two to Ross's credit under 'Contrary evidence' and we can finish this thing tonight. You may get some interesting sidelights at the inquest, anyway. We've still got five or six more suspects."

She gathered up the papers and, when Dick emerged from the bathroom a few minutes later, he slipped them all, including the revolver and the handkerchief, into a bag which he locked and put away in a closet, also locking that and pocketing the keys. He handed the key to the bedroom of the suite to Joan and said:

"I'll meet you here between five and five-thirty. If you get here first, just walk in and make yourself at home."

Joan thought of something and went to the telephone, saying, "Wait a second." She called the Fordman home and got Marion on the wire. After listening for a few minutes, she said: "I'll be darned. Thanks. We'll come out this evening, Dick Fields and I. Call you first, though. . . . Yes. He got here about noon. Good-bye."

She turned to Dick, hanging the receiver absently in space several times before it struck the hook, and said: "Fordman left his estate, divided equally, to his daughter and to his fiancée, Glieth Lawrence. He made a trust fund for Marion's half, but left Mrs. Lawrence's part outright. The will was made on Monday of last week and includes a ten thousand benefit for Gerard Drexell, five thousand for Val Day, Fordman's driller, and a hundred dollars a month income for the chauffeur, Wills, for the rest of his life. The five thousand he willed to Day was apparently an afterthought. It was added in a codicil only last Saturday."

They left the room reluctantly. It was cool and breezy and the sun was blazing outside. Joan was glad that she needn't attend the inquest. The courthouse, filthy and bad-smelling at all times, was particularly obnoxious in the summer. She had sat through several trials in the courtroom where the inquest would be held, and remembered all too vividly the sweating men and the panting, overperfumed women jammed together, suffering silently to satisfy their morbid curiosity.

She dropped Dick in front of the building and watched him push his way through the mob that already surrounded the place. Then she returned to the newspaper office. It was two-forty, and since the edition would be delayed until five or six so that the story of the inquest could be included, there was little activity in the shop.

Joan was surprised to see Ed Frank sitting at his typewriter working rapidly. He stopped when she came in, and beckoned to her. In a lowered voice he said:

"This whole town is going crazy—Sam Ross killed himself in his bathroom at one o'clock this afternoon."

Joan didn't sound particularly surprised when she spoke. Too much had happened in the past twenty-four hours for anything ever again to seem surprising. She merely asked, "Why?"

The editor looked at her curiously and said: "We don't know the reason. He didn't leave a note—at least none has come to light as yet. Probably he killed Fordman. At least that's what the police are inclined to believe."

"Do you?"

"Well," he mused, his thin lips drawn down at the corners and his cold eyes hard and expressionless, "it would clear this business up nicely. It isn't impossible."

"I don't believe it," stated the girl. "Tell me how he killed himself."

"Blew his brains out. He was standing in front of the bathroom mirror, fully dressed according to the sheriff. Used a .45 Colt automatic."

Joan asked, "Was he holding the gun when they found him?"

"No," replied Frank, "it was in the hand basin, covered with water. He had left the hot faucet on and the bowl was entirely filled. If it hadn't had a safety outlet the whole place would have been flooded."

"The gun was *in* the basin?" Joan queried.

"Yes. It does sound funny, doesn't it?"

"Funny is a mild word for it," remarked the girl. "Who found him?"

"Oh, the negro girl Sarah heard the shot and ran upstairs. She took one look and ran down again, screaming. Mrs. Ross was at a bridge party and nobody else was at home. She ran over to the Nelsons' who live next door, and put them in a panic, of course. The Nelson boy, Peter, had sense enough to call the police, but, all in all, it was almost thirty minutes before anyone got there. I was with the sheriff when they notified him, and went out in his car. They've postponed the inquest until tomorrow. We'll probably get this damned paper out by midnight. I hope that the next person who dies will wait until tomorrow so we'll have something for another edition. This one's so full now that we'll have to cut out almost everything not relating to the shooting and Ross's death."

"Everything except the society," said Joan, grinning. "Murder or suicide notwithstanding—the bridge parties go on and on and on and on—Lord, it's hot."

"What d'you expect on the Fourth of July?" remarked the man as he returned to his typing.

Joan dusted her desk and wondered how she would get word of this new affair to Dick. The telephone rang.

Dick's voice was low and he asked: "What in hell has happened? The inquest is called off until tomorrow and rumors are floating around about another murder. Any truth . . ."

Joan said: "I'm glad the party was a success, Mrs. Wimple. Can I come out and get your list? It's so hard to hear the names over the telephone."

"What the hell . . . oh, you've an audience. That right?" inquired Dick.

"Yes."

"Well, meet me out front here in ten minutes. O.K.?"

"I'll be glad to."

Joan hung up and swore effectively at the telephone. Frank said, "What is it now?"

"That fool, Mrs. Wimple, wants me to come out after her list. She hasn't time to dictate it over the telephone. As if I have time to dash out to Park Place and back for every party write-up!"

"Oh, go on. Keep the old sister happy. You've nothing else but time this afternoon."

Joan went, and ten minutes later was driving Dick slowly out Main Street toward the little bumpy hills. She explained and he questioned, but her knowledge was limited.

He remarked, "Finger-prints don't wash off just by immersion."

Joan said, "I wondered."

Dick continued: "But unless the sheriff is smarter than I believe him to be, he'll never look for fingerprints."

"He won't," stated Joan with emphasis.

She speeded the car out the highway, cut in at the Country Club gates and parked near the clubhouse. The parched golf course was deserted. They got out of the open car and fled hastily out of the sun to the shelter of the broad porch. The house was also deserted except for a negro boy who brought them ginger ale which Dick spiked from his flask.

Joan said: "We'll give Marion time to get home and I'll drop you there and get back to the office. She'll send you back to town all right. You can look at the Isotta, anyway."

"If this man Ross was the type you described, I can't see him shooting himself—though I must say that a bathroom is the best place to do such a messy job. Do you think that I'll be able to get into that house? I'd rather see that bathroom than the Isotta, and the quicker the better."

"Well, if Marion makes it known that you are working on the case for her, I expect the sheriff will be decent about it. He's a pretty good fellow." Joan finished her drink and continued, "Maybe it's best, anyway. I mean for you to work openly."

Dick pulled himself erect and said impatiently: "Well, I've wasted enough time getting started. Haven't seen a damn thing yet except that gun. Come on. Let's go."

They drove up the hill to the Fordman house and Joan parked in the rear as she had that morning. There were two cars in the front and the three machines belonging to the house were in the garage.

"They must be back by now," said Joan. "I saw Drexell's car out front."

She led him through the side entrance and halted him in the hallway while she sought Mrs. Smith, the housekeeper. That disturbed woman fell upon her with small cries of mournful delight and at her request set off to deliver to Marion the note which Joan scribbled out at the kitchen table.

Marion appeared immediately and led them upstairs, saying, "Let's get away from that madhouse."

"What do you mean, madhouse?" asked Joan.

"They all talk and talk and talk," replied the girl.

She seated them in the upstairs sunroom which was on the south side of the house. Here it was cool, with the long windows thrown open on the three sides and the glazed chintz curtains drawn back. The wicker chairs were comfortable and the dull-green tile floor gave the illusion of water coolness.

Joan explained that Dick wanted to see the Isotta. He interrupted with: "I'd like to take this case, Miss Fordman, and I believe that I'll lose too much time trying to work alone. If you will give me your authorization and introduce me to your lawyer, I'll see to the police myself."

Marion looked at Joan and said, "I suppose it's legal?"

"You're twenty-one, aren't you?" replied Joan. "Did your father appoint a guardian?"

"No," said the girl quickly, and turned to Dick: "The lawyer is downstairs; also Gere Drexell, my father's friend, and Mrs. Lawrence, my father's fiancée. We can go down and talk with them."

"May I ask you a few questions first, Miss Fordman?" inquired Dick. The girl nodded and he glanced into his notebook. "I have here your statement, taken from the story in the *News*, made immediately after your father's death was discovered by you. Have you thought of anything to add to that statement? Isn't there anything you have thought of that might be important? Even the smallest things can be most important. For instance, who reached you first, after you screamed? Or did you lose consciousness immediately and completely?"

"I really don't remember a thing," she replied, "after I realized that something had happened to Dad. That is, until I came out of

the stupid faint and found myself lying on the ground looking up
at hundreds of faces. I didn't remember immediately about him. I
just felt awfully undignified." She smiled.

Dick sighed slightly, closed his little book and offered the two
girls cigarettes. They looked at the crumpled packet and Marion
said, "Not for me—Picayunes—Gere smokes those awful things."

Joan took her case out of her pocket and they both lighted fags
of milder blend. She said: "We've a chap in the office who smokes
those. I tried 'em once."

"Where is Mr. Drexell from?" asked Dick.

"New Orleans, I believe. He hasn't really a home. He was in the
army for quite a while and then he lived abroad—in Russia, I believe."

They went downstairs. Two men and a woman in gray looked
up as they entered the living-room. The men arose and Marion said:
"Mrs. Lawrence, my friend Joan Shields. This is Mr. Richard
Fields." She waved a hand at the men and said, "Mr. Drexell and
Mr. Drennan." The men shook hands and in the silence Marion's
voice sounded clearly, "Let's sit down. I've something to say."

They all sat down, and she continued: "Mr. Fields is a detective—"

Drexell jumped to his feet. "My God, Marion!" he said; "why
couldn't you wait—"

She looked at him and he sat down, coloring suddenly as he
realized that the others were all staring at him too.

Joan looked at Mrs. Lawrence. She was a calm, lovely woman
with long dark hair and classic regularity of features. Her beauty
was Grecian with the long, straight nose and the high forehead of
those unsmiling ladies of the Golden Age. She wore a gray linen
suit, tailored perfectly, with a soft white blouse and a brown-and-
white tie. Joan approved of her poise and of her unmoved calm.
Her hands were in her lap, quietly holding a brown handkerchief,
and her slender feet in brown-and-white pumps were resting on a
low stool in front of her chair.

Marion was talking. She said: ". . . and I have decided that it is
best for us to have this cleared up quietly and quickly. I don't feel
that Mr. Read has had the experience necessary, and even if

Mr. Fields is unable to find an explanation for my father's murder, I will feel that I have done what should be done in such a case. I hope that he will be able to tell us something, however, as soon as he is in possession of the facts."

She smiled at Dick, who arose and thanked her. Joan thought, "It's ridiculously formal."

Dick said: "Mr. Drennan, I understand that you were Mr. Fordman's attorney. Who administers the estate?"

"Miss Fordman does, with my advice and the assistance of Mr. Samuel Ross in financial matters," replied the lawyer. He was a small, thin man with sandy hair and a red mustache. He was nervous and spoke jerkily. "I don't mind saying," he continued, "that I am glad that Miss Fordman has consulted an expert. Mr. Drexell and I differed on this point, but I believe an outsider will see things more clearly. Where are you from, Mr. Fields?"

"St. Louis," said Dick. "I will be glad to submit my credentials," he suggested.

"Oh, no, oh, no. I didn't mean that," said the lawyer. "I am sure that Miss Fordman knows . . ." His voice trailed off.

Joan thought: "He won't antagonize her. He must make plenty running the Fordman affairs."

"Well," said Fields, "if you will come with me, Mr. Drennan, I'd like to get back to town. Miss Fordman, may I see you for a moment before I go?"

They crossed the room together and Joan saw Marion hand him an envelope. He turned and bowed to Mrs. Lawrence, caught Joan by the arm, and the three of them left. Drexell and Mrs. Lawrence stood together in the center of the room and Joan heard the man call peremptorily to Marion as they went out the front door.

Drennan and Joan waited while Dick went around for the roadster. He said to her, "Hasn't something else happened, Miss Shields? We were not told why the inquest was postponed and, as the sheriff had vanished when the clerk made the announcement, I couldn't find out why—"

"Yes," answered Joan, "you see, Mr. Ross killed himself just before the inquest—"

"Oh, my God!" said the little lawyer, badly shocked. "I wonder how the bank—" He stopped suddenly and looked at Joan. "Did he leave any reason, any note?"

"They haven't found anything yet."

The roadster roared around the house and came toward them, scattering gravel into the flower-beds. The zinnias flamed in the sun, and the silence of that amazingly silent country was broken only by the noise of the car. It skidded to a stop and Drennan and Joan got in, he remarking, "Should have brought my own car."

"Whose Lincoln is that?" inquired Joan, pointing to a gray car parked on the oval.

"I think Miss Fordman borrowed or rented it to use in place of the Fraschini," said the lawyer. "Naturally, she doesn't care much about driving about in it."

"No," said Joan. "That must have come from the Ford agency. I'll bet she bought it."

"I wouldn't be surprised," said Drennan, and sighed deeply, thinking of his own battered Chevrolet.

Joan dropped them at the courthouse and went back to the office.

Frank was still sitting before his machine. He looked at her sourly and said: "Old lady Wimple just called. She said that she was sending the list down by her sister-in-law. I told her that you were on the way out like she asked, and she said that she hadn't—"

"Yeah, I know," interrupted Joan, "but I've got something better than old lady Wimple's party. Marion Fordman's hired a detective from St. Louis to track down the dastardly criminal who perpetrated this dastardly crime."

"Who is he?" asked Frank, reaching for pencil and paper.

"One Richard Fields, private inquiry agent extraordinary. Solved the Brindle case in Kansas City, and that army post poisoning in St. Louis last year. Fearless, incorruptible, and so forth."

"You've met him?"

"Met him! I've known him for years."

"Listen. Are you working for a paper or not? What's the idea in holding out on us? This almost missed the night edition."

"Sorry, old chap. It wasn't ripe for publication before now. You might thank me, anyway. Neither you nor Mitch seem to be so hot on the job."

"Hell, I can't be everywhere at once. Mitch is with the sheriff—I hope. He ought to be back soon."

Joan went to work and an hour passed before White returned. He looked fagged and slumped wearily in his chair as he reached for copy paper. His hat was gone and his shirt collar gaped open, the tie pulled into a hard knot and hanging loosely.

He shifted the cigarette in his mouth and said: "Some bird, name of Fields, detective from St. Louis, took a look at that gun of Ross's and said he didn't kill himself. Said he was murdered. Said being in the hot water wouldn't bother the finger-prints and the only ones on it were the sheriff's, made when he fished it out of the basin."

VIII: TUESDAY, JULY 4: 5.45 P.M.

"Good jolly old Dick. He always knows a murder when he sees one, especially if everybody else calls it suicide. I never did believe that Sam Ross would choose such a way to die. He might have killed himself all right, but he'd have taken poison. He's that kind." Thus spoke Joan.

"Don't be funny, kid," said White. "This thing's getting serious. There's a homicidal maniac loose. He may not stop at two."

"Don't be silly," retorted Joan. "You know that these murders must be related. Mr. Fordman and Mr. Ross were too close for it to have been a coincidence. Homicidal maniac nothing!"

White grinned at her. "Don't get sore, baby," he said. "It's too hot to argue with you. Besides, I haven't time." He snatched a sheet of paper and rolled it into the machine.

Frank said, "Have you flashed the A.P. yet?"

"Yes," replied Mitchell, "this is an add. There's a mob of reporters in town now and when this gets out there'll be plenty more. We'll scoop 'em in this area, of course. What d'you know about this man Fields? He turned up out at the Ross place with Pat Drennan and practically took over the investigation."

"Joan knows him," snorted the editor. "'Known him for years,'" he quoted in a smarty falsetto.

Joan defended herself and offered aid when he should come to that part of the story dealing with Dick Fields.

Mitch pounded out the first sheet of copy and Joan picked it up to read.

Special to the Associated Press
by Mitchell White
      add—Fordman Murder

Fordman, Tex., July 4. (A.P.) At about 1 P.M., exactly twenty-four hours after the murder of John Fordman, multimillionaire oil man, his friend and business associate, Samuel Ross, president of the Fordman National Bank, was shot and killed in the bathroom of his home in fashionable Park Place, south of this city.

In earlier bulletins it was stated that Ross had committed suicide, this being the belief held by the police at that time. But now it is known that the banker was murdered.

A private investigator, Richard Fields of St. Louis, called into the Fordman case by the murdered man's daughter, Marion Fordman, pronounced the second shooting a murder after local authorities had unofficially called it suicide.

Fields, who is a finger-print expert, came to his conclusion after examining the gun with which Ross was shot. It was found in the hand-basin where it had presumably fallen when Ross slumped to the floor. The basin was filled with hot soapy water and the tap was still open and the water running when the police arrived. The sheriff himself removed the gun, a .45 Colt automatic, from the water, carefully touching only the trigger guard and the barrel. Fields tested the surface for fingerprints and found only those of the sheriff.

He states authoritatively that mere immersion could not have completely removed the finger-prints which would have been on the gun had Mr. Ross shot himself. This reporter watched Fields and Sheriff Read carry out a test in the bathroom in which Mr. Ross was killed, to determine the accuracy of the former's statement. A revolver belonging to Mr. Fields was wiped carefully and finger-printed by the detective. It was then placed in the basin and the hot water was turned on. Mr. Fields took a piece of soap and, lathering his hands, clouded the water as it had been before. The gun was allowed to remain in the hot soapy water for more than half an hour and then taken out and put carefully away to dry by evaporation.

When it had dried, Mr. Fields tested it for the fingerprints which he had placed on it and exhibited to the witnesses a perfect set brought out clearly by the white powder which he dusted over the revolver. Immersion had not dimmed them.

The only other statement made by the local authorities was one to the effect that Fields would work with the police and the county attorney, Judge William Connor Millbank, in an effort to reach a speedy solution.

Richard Fields, who arrived here by private plane this morning, has become quite well known in the past year for his part in the solutions of the famous Brindle case in Kansas City and the army post poisonings in St. Louis. He is a graduate of Harvard and has been, in his short but varied career, successively, law student, medical student, rancher, and private detective in New York City. He participated in the solving of many cases with the New York and St. Louis police.

County attorney, Judge William Connor Millbank, who arrived here today from San Antonio where he has been visiting friends, will supervise activities of the police. This evening he stated, "This is a terrible thing. For two of the leading citizens of our fine community to feel the sudden hand of death . . ."

Here Joan gave over reading the peroration of the county attorney which was full of rhetoric but little else. She went into the back shop and began looking through the files of past copies of the *News* until she came to the issue of Saturday, July 1. She detached the paper, folded it inconspicuously into another of later issue and went back to her desk.

Frank had gone, but Mitchell still pounded his machine with rhythmic viciousness. The little shop was filthier than usual, and one could not walk without kicking through piles of crumpled copy paper and long curls of discarded teletype news. The edition was ready to run except for White's story which was being set up by the shop foreman himself as fast as the pages could be carried back. The single Mergenthaler clicked and hummed as the matrices dropped and the hot lead was forced into rigid slugs, a column width in length and only type wide. The matrices were carried back into position and dropped into their respective slots with musical tinkles. Mitchell's typewriter clattered on and the air in the room was heavy with smoke from cigarettes and the acrid scorching odor of hot lead from the shop.

Joan read galley proof on Mitchell's story as it came damp from the type. It had few errors. Mac, the shop foreman, was an excellent linotype operator, and would have preferred the job to the more important and hectic one which he held.

The last length of smudgy proof had been read and impaled upon the O.K. hook when the telephone rang. Joan answered and Dick asked her to meet him at the hotel at six-forty-five.

Fifteen minutes later, the girl was seated on the divan in Fields's room, sipping a pre-dinner highball. Dick, dressed in white flannels, sat across from her in an armchair. They relaxed and enjoyed the coolness of the evening wind sweeping through the open suite. The heat was gone, the air had freshened and held an unmistakable odor of the sea. It was almost damp, and one could smell the salt marshes. Joan explained that this phenomenon always amazed the visitors. The altitude, some five thousand feet, she said accounted for the drop in temperature, but where the ocean-smelling breeze came from was a mystery. The Gulf, more than three hundred miles away, could scarcely be considered, and the only other water stood in the chain of shallow 'gyp' lakes that stretched toward the west.

Dick commented politely upon her little conversational attempt and then said: "I've ordered dinner sent up here. We can eat and then discuss this thing. I want a lot of information from you. Can you stay all right?"

Joan nodded and went into the bedroom to telephone her mother.

When she came back, the dinner had arrived and two colored boys were arranging things on the table. She and Dick ate and talked of New York and the people they had known there and of the better movies and the few better books that Joan had been able to procure in the little town. Joan discovered that Dick had never read Olive Schreiner's 'The Story of an African Farm' and he in turn moaned over the fact that she had not seen 'Maedchen in Uniform.' It was almost with reluctance that they settled down at the bridge table a half-hour later, with the door locked, and began on their problem.

"All right," said Dick, "let's clarify what we know and begin our list of what we must do tomorrow. First, we have the Fordman murder and with it, so far, only two actual clues—the revolver and the handkerchief."

"What about the clipping and the footprints and the cigarette butts?" asked Joan.

"They may have no bearing on the case at all. Anyone could have left them there at any time. Of course, we must by no means overlook them. Did you find the issue of the paper from which this was cut?" He produced the clipping of the bridge hand and Joan got the paper. They turned to the daily article and comparison showed them that it was the same. Dick marked heavily around the article with a pencil and they turned the page and placed the clipping beside the square marked on this sheet. Joan shook her head and Dick nodded. The reverse sheet of the local paper carried a crossword puzzle also, but no part of it was taken in by the heavy outline marking the position of the bridge problem on the preceding page.

"Not our paper," said Joan. "I could have sworn to it, but then these things are all syndicated. There is no telling where it came from. I know that it isn't from a Dallas or a Fort Worth sheet. The quality of the paper they use is much better than this and the whole thing looks better—their presses are newer and—well, anyway, I know." She snatched up two of the papers that she had mentioned and showed Fields what she meant. "Then, too," she continued, "neither of these run a crossword puzzle on the editorial page. It's pretty poor make-up, you know. Violates all the rules and whatnot."

Dick had turned the clipping over and was looking closely at the puzzle. "He didn't get any too much of it finished," he said, referring to the partially filled spaces. "Anyway, he knew that the sound of a mule is called a 'bray' and that 'at home' is 'A.H.' Nothing particularly hard about those. I wonder what definition was given for the word 'ephemeral' which is seventeen across. Most of the definitions are missing. Oh, well, this won't get us anywhere." He slipped the clipping back into the envelope.

Joan said, "Why not test it for finger-prints?"

"Not this; the paper is too rough and the newsprint too spotty as a background." He got up and crossed the room to a coat hanging on the back of a chair. "Talking about finger-prints—here's the gun that killed Ross, *sans* prints."

He returned to the table and put the heavy revolver down in front of Joan. The cartridge clip had been removed and he produced it carefully from a large envelope. Placing it on a sheet of paper he dusted it with the powdered aluminum. A few whiffs from a small rubber bulb with a fine black nozzle and the excess powder had been blown away, the remainder revealing a hodge-podge of superposed finger-prints covering the side of the clip. A similar treatment of the other side gave the same results. Dick said: "Well, this isn't entirely negative, but it looks to me as if it's too good to be true. I can't see our murderer leaving *any* prints, much less dozens of them." He got the little camera out of the traveling lab and took two time exposures of each side of the clip under a strong light.

Joan, an interested spectator, said, "You didn't do that with the little gun, did you?"

"Yes, the results were just the same as this." He produced the little revolver from the kit and showed Joan the prints on the clip. Taking a large magnifying-glass he studied both clips in silence for a while.

"They aren't the same, as well as I can tell," he said. "It will be easier to compare them when the negatives are developed and the enlargements are made."

"Has anyone identified the large gun yet?"

"Yes, it belonged to Ross, they think. He kept one at the bank in his desk drawer, about this size. The sheriff's checking on that. I told him about the little one and promised to take it by for him tomorrow when I return the large one. He'll check on that, too."

"It's all so very confusing," remarked the girl.

"What impressed me about the second murder, as well as the first one," said Fields, "was the narrow margin of time which the murderer had. That girl at the Ross place was in the kitchen. Ross had come home for luncheon and evidently went upstairs first to wash up. He left the bank at twelve-forty-five, as he does every day. I understand that the banking people are regular to the minute about lunch or dinner times. Only two leave at a time and Ross never went out until the assistant cashier, Jennison, returned. He has been going home at that hour for eight years, they tell me. Everybody knew it. He must have been killed as he walked into the bathroom. The bullet went through the right temple arid came out just above the left ear. We found it in the plaster near the window. What kind of a woman is his wife?"

"Poor Mrs. Ross. Where was she? I forgot to ask."

"Oh, she was at some bridge party. Nobody even knew where and consequently she wasn't notified until she came home at about four o'clock."

Joan thought for a moment, then said: "She goes to the Idle Hour Club, on Tuesdays. They met at Mrs. Fiske's for luncheon today. I remember her name on Mrs. Fiske's list because there were only two tables and she won high-score prize for members. Bath salts."

"Yeah—bath salts. She dropped them in that foyer downstairs and they broke and went all over the place. Fainted when she found out what had happened. The sheriff certainly is short on tact."

"And Mrs. Ross is long on nerves. She's a neuro if I ever saw one, to say nothing of being the worst hypochondriac in Texas. She's forever away in hospitals taking the baths and the waters and the diets. Did you talk to her?"

"No, she was pretty well broken up and the doctor had her put to bed. She didn't know anything, anyway."

"How did the sheriff welcome you?"

"He wasn't so bad. Said that these killings were out of his line and he'd be glad to have me help him. Both inquests will be held tomorrow. The Fordman in the morning and the Ross in the afternoon. Can you take me out to the oil field in the morning, early? I want to get that place mapped out, and the inquest isn't until ten o'clock. I've never seen a field in action."

"The action here is quite suspended at present," explained Joan disgustedly. "This is a fairly large field with high test crude, but proration has closed most of it down. You should have seen it in the boom days."

"O.K., then—tomorrow at six-thirty. Now let's finish that chart. Where did we leave off?"

Joan rummaged through the papers and remarked: "We left off with Ross, I believe. Well, he's eliminated."

"Maybe," said Dick succinctly. "Never take anything for granted."

"But surely, Dick, he couldn't have killed Mr. Fordman. He was murdered himself," Joan protested. "It isn't logical!"

Dick smiled at her and said: "Murder seldom is. Suppose he killed Fordman and then shot himself? There was a wash-cloth on the basin into which the gun had dropped."

"You mean—he could have held the gun with the washcloth over his hand and so eliminated fingerprints? Isn't that pretty far-fetched?"

"Yes, it is. I just considered it, that's all. People do a lot of freakish things when they commit suicide, you know."

"Samuel Ross never did a freakish thing in his life," remarked Joan positively.

"He got himself murdered."

"That's so; but I mean if he were going to shoot himself he'd do it without any flourishes or story-book details. And he'd leave a memo to the effect that it was 'in his consideration the wisest course, etc.' He was that kind. That's why I was surprised to hear that he *hadn't* left a farewell note. It was out of character."

"Well, we can safely leave it at murder, I believe. Who else did we discuss yesterday?"

"Agnes Jones and Chick."

"Say, my dear—you'll have to start tomorrow and find out where several of your busy townspeople were at one P.M. today."

"Good Lord—you don't want much, do you?" Joan looked at him dubiously. "I can check on the women, but you'll have to find out about the men."

"All right—let's take a few more suspects. Who can be next?"

"Well," said Joan, "I have Ed Frank, the *Daily News* editor, next on my list. I got this at the meeting yesterday, you know. These are all people who made up the Fordman *entourage*."

"All right; Frank. What kind of a bird is he?"

"He's really rather queer. You know I don't like him and we clash constantly, but I do feel sorry for him. He seems so lonely. Yet it's hard to have anything to do with him; he's so bitter. You see he was a big shot with the A.P. for several years and then something happened. Nobody knows what. I think probably it was nothing more than a quarrel with the man above him. Starr, I think it was. Starr is at the head of the whole service now, but then he was only the assistant—in New York, I mean. The reason I say Starr is because of Frank's attitude whenever Starr's name comes up."

"How long has he been here?"

"Ever since Fordman quit managing the paper himself. Several years. They went to school together. After Frank left the A.P. he worked on a paper in Fort Worth. He resigned by request, after a scandal involving the owner's wife, and yet he isn't a man who'd deliberately mix himself up in anything messy. He just got some bad breaks and his temper probably made them worse. I'm the only person on the paper who isn't afraid of him and that's because Mr.

Fordman hired me himself and Frank can't fire me! Maybe he will now," the girl added as an afterthought.

"How do the people like him here?"

"They don't. He lives by himself at the old Mesa Hotel and never seems to go out. He doesn't drink or smoke and I've never seen him anywhere after office hours except in the Corner Drug Store up on Main and Third. He stands in there and talks to Johnnie Scholtze, the prescription clerk, for hours. Johnnie's just about as queer and bitter as Ed, so they make a good pair. In fact, Johnnie is the town cynic. He debunks everything—out-Mencken's Mencken."

"What were his relations with Fordman? Friendly?"

"Fairly so. They never came to blows so far as I know. You see, Ed is a good newspaper man. He's the best Mr. Fordman could get for fifty dollars a week. He knows news, but he's a poor editor. He never organizes things and he antagonizes his staff. That won't get results, you know. I think that he resented Mr. Fordman's success, really. He called him 'God' most of the time. Mr. Fordman was often patronizing, you see, and Ed is quite brilliant. He reads constantly, and writes well."

"He sounds like a fair candidate to me. The monomaniac often kills."

"How horrible, Dick! I didn't mean to give you that impression. Ed could be quite lovable, if he liked. He's fascinatingly attractive."

"To you?"

"Oh, I don't like him, but speaking generally, he honestly is. He's tall and thin, with shoulders even broader than yours; built like a wedge from his shoulders to his hips. He is the most graceful man I've ever seen. But his eyes are so hard and his mouth is so bitter. When he smiles I have cold chills along my backbone."

"Pleasant bird. Anything else? What sort of interests has he? He must have some if he doesn't run around with women or drink or smoke!"

"His hobby is bridge problems; that's why we run the series. He got Fordman to put it in. It's the best and quite expensive. There was opposition, but he took a census of the readers and they all

clamored for it, so Mr. Fordman laughed and gave in. When the
other papers saw what a good thing it was, he had to buy it for four
of them."

"Would he carry a clipping of it about with him?"

"I don't see why he should. He gets it in advance, you know.
We get the whole series for a month, around the first, and cut it up
into 'takes.' They set it up in the shop several days ahead of time.
He takes all of it home when it comes and studies it until it's
needed."

"Humm. Well, if he doesn't smoke, at least he didn't leave the
much-mooted cigarette butts. I hope those things are still there
tomorrow. It was just this morning that you saw them, wasn't it?"

"Yes. I feel as though I've lived through a month today, however.
And a month without sleep. I went to bed at three and got up at
five-thirty this morning. I've kept going on excitement and
highballs, to say nothing of cigarettes."

"Let's finish quickly, then, and get you home to bed. Who is
next?"

"I have Mitch White, our star reporter. Somebody once said
that his epitaph should be:

> 'He was marked when he was born
> To die from drinking too much corn.'"

Dick laughed, and Joan continued, "He's a good kid, though—
sweet, you know."

"You evidently like him?"

"Everybody does. Even his creditors."

"Who are his creditors?"

"Gosh, I don't know. He's the kind about whom it's said, 'Oh,
he owes everyone in town!'"

"Been here long?"

"Just a year. We celebrated the anniversary last week. Four of
us drank fifty-three bottles of home-brew between three P.M. and
three A.M. Said home-brew was found later to have had a liberal
spicing of embalmed ants."

"Joan!"

"Sure enough. We found it in a cupboard in a house that Mitch and a friend of his had taken for the summer. It was the best beer I've ever tasted, heavy and dark with a rich creamy head."

"But the ants?"

"There were four bottles left and the next evening we started to drink those when Kay—she was the other female of the foursome—wandered over to the kitchen door and looked through her glass in the light of the setting sun. There wasn't anything to do then, and, anyway, only two of those four bottles had ants so we decided that if we were still O.K. we couldn't be killed." She added, "We drank the two bottles without ants."

"That's what Prohibition has done to our young!"

"That's putting it mildly, dear. What tales I could tell you about the carousing in *this* town—but, we were talking about Mitch. He's one of the chief carousers, by the way."

"And you?"

"Oh, I'm only an amateur. He's the professional!"

"And how does he happen to be on your list?"

"Well, he's in love with Marion Fordman, and Texas Wills told me that he and Mr. Fordman had a very violent set-to a few days ago. But I don't believe he'd ever stop to plan a crime. He might pop somebody off on the spur of the moment, but this business—it's rather too deep and heavy for Mitch. His murders would be light affairs."

"We'll put down 'Motive unknown' then. And as to opportunity, where was he when the first shooting was going on?"

"Neither he nor Frank has accounted for himself. They were both at the field and in Mr. Fordman's party."

"Well, then, for 'Supporting evidence' we'll note this quarrel. Find out more about it if you can. Does he play bridge?"

"Oh, yes. He *gambles* at bridge is a better word for it, and he was awfully interested in the problem hands for a while. He hasn't talked about them quite so much lately. In fact, he's been pretty down about something for several weeks. I think it's Marion and Gere Drexell."

"Where is White from?"

"Ranger. He went to the University. Jerked soda and worked on the paper to pay his way through. Pledged Sigma Chi, but never quite got the grades to be initiated. Made the better crowd, the faster dances, and the slicker girls on his good looks, personality, and good family. He was always broke and in debt there. Mildred Jones knew him and she must have had a heavy affair with him for a while. She still watches him pretty closely. Doesn't like me because we go around together—or did until he fell for Marion. He was on the Ranger paper a couple of years before he went to State University and had pretty good sports and oil field experience. He is one of the best young sports writers in Texas and turns out a neat column. Even *I* read it, and I hate all sports stories except the ones on tennis and horse-racing. If he'd lay off the liquor he'd be darned good. He smokes too much, too—thirty or forty cigs a day, but no particular brand. Anything except Menthols!" Joan brought her disjointed characterization to a close and walked to a window.

"The orchestra's tuning up," she said.

"What orchestra?" asked Dick, joining her.

"Roy's Rascals from El Paso, to be specific. Don't you know what day this is? It's the Fourth of July and the local roisterers always dance on Independence Day. It's another excuse for drinking."

"Drinking seems to be the major occupation of the majority of your citizens."

"Yes, isn't it amazing? Senator Morris Sheppard's state, stronghold of the W.C.T.U., and I've grappled personally with more drunks here than I *saw* during two whole years in New York. Though repeal is nation-wide, I'll bet dollars to a drink of corn that we'll have local enforcement here. It's as paradoxical as Kansas with her Jake-leg cases."

Dick grunted disgustedly and returned to the table. "Come on, darling," he said, "let's finish this. Who's next?"

"Joey Levy. He's a pretty harmless fat Rotarian. The only thing that I have against him is that he pats me on the back and shakes my hand every time he sees me. And often he sees me two or three times a day!"

"Was he a friend of Fordman's?"

"I guess. He's a director in the Fordman National Bank and I understand that Mr. Fordman holds his notes for a goodly sum. As to opportunity, he seems to have an alibi for the Fordman affair. He states that he was with his wife, in their car, when the well was shot. He was so emphatic about it that I'm inclined to believe him. People seldom push untruths very hard despite the old saws to the contrary. It's harder to make people believe the truth than it is to put over a lie."

"Joan, the philosopher. Isn't it odd how hard it is to take a fat man seriously? I don't believe that I've ever seen a fat murderer, though, come to think of it." Fields paused and looked thoughtful, shaking his head slowly. "Well," he continued, "Drexell isn't fat. Let's consider him. Trusted employee, ten-thousand-dollar beneficiary, questionable alibi, hocus-pocus concerning the fair Mrs. Lawrence—that's a mere outline! Do you say that Miss Fordman is carrying the torch for the gentleman?"

"So I understand. He's the main reason why she stayed on here this summer. She usually goes abroad."

"And does he care for her?"

"Well, I honestly believe he just humors her. He considers her a kid. Still, he may know a good thing when he sees it. A million goes farther than ten thousand. He's a typical adventurer. Spent four years in the army after running away from home at seventeen and enlisting. When he came back, he went to M.I.T., I think, and then abroad to Australia or South America or somewhere with the Shell Oil Company. He was in Russia for a while, and during the World War served in the British Air Force. He cracked up eight times, Marion tells me. After the war he came back here, and with his technical experience got a good job with Fordman handling his oil operations."

"Well, he has a good motive—as good as any—and little alibi, for the first murder, anyway. My God, we'll have to eliminate some of these people soon. They *all* couldn't have done it. I suppose he plays bridge too?"

"Quite well," Joan admitted.

"Drink and play bridge—isn't there anything else to do in this burg?"

"Not much. We have no library. I read about twenty magazines a month and import as many books as I can afford. We play golf, the swimming's lousy, and the tennis courts are monopolized by the high-school children. Some Sundays we spend the entire day just riding up and down the Main Drag, out East Highway and back by Lover's Lane. It gets rather boring!"

Fields looked at her curiously and asked, "Why do you stay, kid?"

Joan shrugged and said: "Mom wants me here for a while, anyway, and she hasn't been well, you know. Besides, it's a good job and jobs are scarce as the dickens now, in the newspaper business."

"In any business." He nodded grimly. "It's the scarcity of jobs that makes more work for guys like me." He walked behind her and tilted her head back against his hard thigh. She smiled up at him and said, "You look funny."

He pulled her hair gently, then thrust her head forward. "G'wan," he said, "I *feel* funny." There was a moment's silence and he put his hand on her shoulder.

"I'm glad you haven't married some guy out here just for the change," he remarked lightly.

Joan laughed. "A change for the worse, I'd call it," she declared. Feeling his eyes still on her, she added: "Let's get on. The next is V. V. Day, Mr. Fordman's boss driller."

"He benefits, too, doesn't he?" asked Fields.

"Yes. His is the five-thousand-dollar legacy that Mr. Fordman added on Saturday."

"I'll have to ask Drennan more about that will. The man hadn't an alibi, had he?"

"Not that I know of," replied Joan. "Texas was looking for him when they shot the well off." She told Dick about the note the chauffeur had shown her and then told him what the colored boy had related as to the fight Fordman and Day had had.

"It didn't sound very serious," she remarked; "he fought with everyone—had a violent temper and hated to be crossed."

Dick continued: "This lawyer bird, Drennan; you don't have him down, so I presume that he wasn't along on the oil well shooting picnic. Does he have much to do with the administration of the estate? I mean did Fordman put much responsibility on him?"

"I don't believe that he did," answered the girl slowly. "He attended to the financial end of his affairs himself. Of course Drennan ran any legal business, just as Gere ran the actual oil business and Ed Frank ran the paper here. Fordman dictated policies and kept a close hand on the newspapers, much closer than on the oil business because he liked it better, I guess."

"Well, we'll check on Drennan, anyhow. Can't overlook any bets."

"I'll find out from Marion just how much he had to do," promised Joan.

Dick began to gather up his papers, stopped and said: "How about that chauffeur? He was unaccounted for, and he benefits."

"Good Lord, Dick! Texas loved old man Fordman with his life. And why would he kill Mr. Ross? Be yourself. You need sleep."

"Well, check his alibi, anyway. I may not be so smart, honey, but I'm thorough. Have another drink?"

"Hope. I'm going home. It's twelve-forty and I'm dead."

Dick put on his coat and together they got aboard the elevator. The operator grinned at Joan and said, "Evenin', Miss Shields. Ain't you goin' to th' dance?"

"Not tonight, Bill," she replied.

"First one I've ever seen you miss," remarked the boy. A red light glowed on his indicator and the buzzer had been sounding ever since they had left Dick's floor.

"Some o' them drunks," said Bill, and stopped the car at the second floor. He opened the doors and three men and a girl crowded on, the men holding the girl upright. She was Mildred Jones.

Even in her dazed condition she recognized Joan and threw an arm around her shoulder. Joan introduced Dick as the car dropped the one flight, and they halted in the lobby. Mildred made no effort to introduce the men and said loudly, "Where's Mitch?"

"I don't know, Mildred," replied Joan.

The drunken girl fixed her with a glassy eye and said, "Like hell, y'don't."

One of the men tried to draw her away, saying, "Come on, baby, le's dance."

She shook him off and turned back to Joan. "You're a snob, see?" she said thickly. "You an' Marion Fordman, an' now her old man's dead an' she's got a million dollars he'll be after her. He's no good, anyway. I hate him." Her voice rose. "I'll get even. I'll tell where he was yesterday when Mr. Fordman was killed. He was right by that big car of theirs. I saw him hiding in the bushes. I called him and he ran. What'd he wanner run for if he didn't have somethin' to hide?" She caught her breath, soberer now, and looked around at them. Her heavy red hair was loose and the powder was caked on her nose. She put her hand to her mouth and cried out, "What have I said? Omygod. I didn't mean—" She turned, and grasping the elbow of one of the men, pulled him toward the ballroom door.

The music had begun again.

Joan and Dick went out into the cool night and the girl said: "That was Mildred Jones. I'll ask Mitch what she meant, but I know it will make him mad. He can't stand her."

"Blowsy wench," remarked Dick as they drove up the deserted street.

IX: WEDNESDAY, JULY 5: 6.30 A.M.

Joan picked up Dick in front of the hotel. Jimmie was occupying the rumble seat, speechless at being in the presence of a real detective. They drove through the empty streets of the little town and out the highway toward the field.

"It's three miles less by the short cut," the girl said as she swung the car off the macadam, over a cattle-guard, and into an old road that cut through a pasture dotted with dusty mesquite and cedar trees. They jolted down into a deep draw, across its sandy bottom, and up the other side. Reaching the top of one of the little hills, they saw the field in the broad valley below them. The derricks rose thickly as far as they could see and the odor of the crude oil swept over and engulfed them.

At the well they found Day and another man. The well was still capped down, and the two men were looking over the tools that had been used in drilling. The huge steel bits were covered with white clay and mud and lay along the platform which extended west of the well.

Joan introduced Dick to Val Day and moved away while the two talked together. She and Jimmie edged toward the storage tank and the mesquite clump. She looked back at the men, but they were engrossed in their conversation, so she, with Jimmie at her heels, walked around the tank and stopped in surprise. The whole area, including the small ditch, had been freshly spaded up and leveled out. A spade was thrust into a mound of dirt banked against the tank, indicating that the job was as yet incomplete. Joan moved

135

slowly through the weeds near the spaded area and looked for the discarded cigarettes. Jimmie watched her curiously.

"What on earth are you lookin' for, Sis?" he said.

She told him, and he helped with the hunt. They found no cigarette butts, but they did discover that the whole area, weeds and all, had been raked and cleaned. They gave up and went back to the derrick. Day was explaining the business of shooting the well.

"Yeah," he boomed, his red face beaming with pride, "we put seventy-five gallons of nitro in 'er an' she come through like a lady." He saw Joan, and his jollity vanished. He said to her soberly: "Miss Shields, I ain't had time to get up to see Miss Fordman yet. I wonder won't you tell her how sorry I am? Mr. Fields here has been tellin' me that Mr. Fordman left me five thousand dollars in his will. I didn't expect nothin'. It sure was a surprise. Nobody's been out here yet to give me any orders, so I'm goin' this afternoon an' see Drexell." His face clouded and his eyes narrowed. "I'd sure like to keep on workin' for this outfit, but I don't know if I can get along with that man. As long as I took orders from old John himself, everything worked fine, but me an' Drexell—we don't think alike."

"I'll tell her, Mr. Day. Everything is still so confused, you know, I don't suppose that anyone has even thought about this end of the Fordman affairs."

"No'm. I went in yesterday, but I couldn't find Drexell nor Pat Drennan in their offices, so I went to the inquest an' wasted an hour or so of my time before I heard about Mr. Ross committin' suicide. Then I come back here because this plug ain't goin' to hold her long, what with the gas an' everything." He waved a hand at the well. "That there pocket we opened with the nitro yesterday is full of gas an' oil. We'll have to let some of the pressure off soon."

"You didn't see last night's papers, then, did you?" inquired Dick casually.

"Nope. The mail comes out this mornin' about nine. We get last night's papers then. Why?"

"It has been discovered that Mr. Ross did not commit suicide. He was murdered—"

"Holy Mother!" breathed the big man, crossing himself quickly. "Him too!"

Joan thought that if Day knew anything he was certainly a first-class actor. He seemed completely deflated.

"Mr. Day," began Dick, "where were you Monday when the well was—er—'shot'?"

"I was here. Why?"

"You understand, of course, that there's no suspicion directed against you at all. I'm merely checking on every person who was in any way connected with Mr. Fordman."

The man looked surprised, but he said: "Well, I was here with the boys most of the time. Th' truck that brought the nitro backed up at that there platform and then before th' stuff was lowered I got in an' drove th' truck over yonder." He indicated a southerly direction, and continued: "When I was gettin' out, some bird said that John Fordman's colored boy was lookin' for me. Said he was talkin' to a bunch of fellers over by th' old well." He pointed to an abandoned derrick about two hundred yards south of the new producer. "I walked over thataway, but I didn't see anybody but a bunch of birds shootin' craps, an' I decided that he should know where to find me, so I hustled back in time to get caught in th' spray when th' thing went off. You see I didn't have nothin' to do with th' shootin' itself. We hire a professional who does the dangerous part." He paused and looked inquiringly at them.

Dick asked, "Did you know any of the fellows who were shooting craps, Mr. Day?"

"Nope. Leastways, I didn't recognize any of 'em, but I was in a hurry. I didn't go up close. Ya know," he said excitedly, "that man of Fordman's mighta been there with 'em an' that's why he didn't find me. I kinda knew what John Fordman wanted, anyway." He grinned at them rather sadly. "Ya see, him an' me an' a bunch o' th' boys planned to play poker last night an' have a quiet little celebration for th' Fourth an' for th' well. He was goin' to let me know if he could come. We played at my place over on th' old lease ever' now an' then."

"And yesterday—where were you before the inquest was scheduled to start?"

"I come in about ten A.M. an' went up to see Drexell. He wasn't in an' neither was Drennan. Drennan's office is in the same building. I waited around in Drexell's place for about an hour and a half an' then went down to th' Busy Bee to eat. When I finished, I went over to Jack's place for a shave an' a haircut, an' then sat out in my car until it was time for th' inquest to begin. It was three-thirty by th' time I started home."

"What time was it when you were in the barber shop?"

"I dunno. Ask Jack. He shaved me. Mebby he'd remember."

"By the way, at exactly what time did the explosion occur? Do you happen to know?"

"Yep, I do. It was scheduled at one o'clock, but I looked at my watch when it went off and it was exactly one-four." He produced a thin gold timepiece proudly, and said: "This here watch John Fordman give me two years ago, an' it ain't never lost a minute since then. I wind it up ever' night at ten P.M. an' check it by the radio. Me an' th' wife listen to Amos an' Andy regular, you see."

Dick had taken the information down in a notebook, thanked Day, and then, in response to Joan's "I'll show you where the cars were," moved off with her.

He produced the map of the area and, pacing off the distances, established the fact that the Fordman car had been over a hundred feet from its nearest neighbor, the Jones's LaSalle.

"Why," he inquired, "was Fordman so exclusive? He parked inside the roped-off area and his friends outside."

Val Day came toward them from the well. "'Scuse me for botherin' you," he said, "but I just thought of somethin'. Tom Harte, th' deputy, told me yest'day that he arrested two boys for shootin' craps Monday, while he was out here. Mebby they'll know about Wills."

Dick thanked him, and asked, "Why did Mr. Fordman park inside the rope?"

"Why, he come before the rope was put up, I believe. I didn't see him because I was over to my shack eatin' lunch until about twelve-thirty and I only got here about twenty minutes before one, an' Mr. Fordman was talkin' to some men. That's why he sent me th' note, I guess. He never did see me."

Joan spoke. "What are you-all doing with the ground around the storage tank?" she asked.

"Why, Jake—that's the boy up there—he's clearin' th' grass an' dry tumble-weeds away in case of fire. We'll start fillin' that tank up today. Th' pipeline connection ain't been made yet. He hoed an' raked around there all yest'day afternoon. Not much else to do."

This was a logical explanation and Joan nodded in agreement.

"That countrywoman," remarked Dick—"what was her name?"

"Mrs. Trotter?"

"Yes. Where is their farm?"

"Oh, it's out north of here somewhere. Why?"

"I'd like to talk to her. She seems to be a pretty observant sort of person. I wonder just how *noisy* this place was before the well was shot."

X: WEDNESDAY, JULY 5: 8.30 A.M.

They drove up the hill to the Fordman home and Joan ran the road-ster around to the rear. Texas Wills came out of the back door and welcomed them.

"Howdy, Miss Joan," he said. "Hit's shore goin' to be one hot day, ain't it?"

The sun had risen in a cloudless sky and already loomed white-hot against the infinite lacquer-blue dome above them.

"It's going to be worse than yesterday," commented Joan; and then to the colored man: "Texas, will you help Mr. Jimmie put my top up? This driving in an open car isn't so pleasant under such a sun."

"Sure, sure, Miss Joan," replied the man, and he and Jimmie turned their attention to the car while Dick and the girl went into the garage to look at the Fraschini. Dick took an envelope from his pocket, tore it open, and produced the key which Joan had given to Marion. He got into the big car and backed it out into the paved courtyard. Then he examined it minutely, front and back, remov-ing cushions, taking up the carpets, and shaking out the light robe which had been folded over the rod along the back of the front seat.

He slipped his hands into the pockets, brought them out empty, and then unfolded the small seat on the right.

"Here's the shell," he said, bending over and picking up a small brassy cylinder which had been mashed flat between the metal seat support and the floor. He put it in his pocket and continued his search.

140

Joan watched him snap the little button that turned on and off the tiny electric fan. He called her attention to the latter. There was a faint clicking noise audible while the fan was in motion.

"Somebody knocked the guard a little lopsided," he said, "and the blade hits it here." He pointed. The fan was fastened high against the back of the chauffeur's partition.

"It really does a lot of good, doesn't it?" commented the girl, letting the breeze set in motion by the little blades blow in her face.

"It only stirs up the hot air," dissented Dick as he shut it off and examined the bent guard. He then got his finger-print appa-ratus out of the roadster and under the admiring eyes of Jimmie and Texas dusted with the powder the door handles, the polished wood set into the window frames, the fan, the silver fittings inside the tonneau and the glass partition between the back and the front seats. He opened the doors and blew the revealing stuff carefully around the metal frame, even at the floor. Then, inch by inch, he went back over the parts so treated, puffing away the excess pow-der with his little bulb.

Joan checked the parts on paper as he called them out.

No prints on right door frame.
No prints on fan.
No prints on right window frame in door.
No prints on right window or door glasses.
Superposed prints on right door handle.
Same, outside. Vague and blurred.
No prints on right window cranks, front or back.
Superposed and single prints on partition glass and
    frame.
None on partition glass crank.
Single and superposed prints on left window and
    door frames, also cranks and door handles.
    Blurred and indistinct.
Numerous prints, inside and out on left window and
    door glasses.

He had focused his camera and taken dozens of exposures as he talked, carefully numbering and marking the print positions on each plate as he set it aside.

"I won't waste time on the outside of the car," he said. "The whole business is pretty obvious, anyway. We won't find the prints we want out of these. He was cautious and smart." Dick ran the car back into the garage and locked it again.

They were getting into the roadster when Marion called to them from an upstairs window asking them to stay for breakfast.

Joan declined, saying that she was due at the office soon and that Dick had several other investigations to make before the inquest. They promised to come that evening and report whatever progress had been made.

From the Fordman home Joan drove Dick to the addition called Park Place where Ross had lived. At his direction she passed the banker's lovely home slowly, turned left and drove down the side of the block. At the alley entrance Dick had her stop for a moment and they drove on. They turned left again and were in front of a large whitewashed brick house with well-kept grounds. The shutters were fastened and the house had a deserted air.

"That's the Hathaway place," explained Joan. "They made a fortune in oil leases and spent it in two years. Never thought that the money would quit coming in. They had a little ranch out southeast of town and the discovery well of the Hathaway pool was sunk in the chicken-yard, much to old Mrs. Hathaway's sorrow. She loved her chicken-yard. She raised grand fryers, too. We used to buy 'em from her."

Joan had stopped the car in front of the house. A graveled drive curved gracefully around to the hack. The flowers were in full bloom and the grass and hedges neatly trimmed. A small sign was planted in the circle between the two walks leading to the wide porch. It read:

For Sale
See Any Broker

"When the slump came," continued Joan, "they found themselves destitute. They'd built and donated the new Episcopal Church, put up an eighteen-story office building that has four offices rented, and a slick grafter who handled their affairs got out of town overnight with around five hundred thousand dollars. That's the local gossip, anyway."

She started the car and turned left again at the first cross-street. The large corner lot next to the Ross place was vacant, the nearest house being across the side street to the east.

"That's where the J. C. Nelsons live. I guess you know how it's all laid out now, though."

"All right. I've a pretty clear impression of it, but I didn't have much time yesterday to fix the outside landmarks clearly in my mind."

Joan parked in front of the Ross's red-brick home. A tall boy in overalls was cutting the grass on the terrace. The girl called to him, "Hi, Joe," as they walked toward the front door, and explained to Dick: "He's the son of the old man who lives on the Hathaway place and takes care of it. They stay in the servants' quarters over the garage." She looked back and saw Jimmie vault out of the rumble seat and join Joe on the terrace.

As they waited for an answer to their ring, Joan noticed that all of the screens and the door frame had been freshly painted a dull and restful green. The screen door still looked damp and had been propped open with a brick. Joan was touching it with a tentative finger when the negro maid, Sarah, opened the door. She remembered Dick from the afternoon before and recognized Joan.

"Mis' Ross is 'sleep," she whispered, but she stood aside and let them enter.

"Where is she, Sarah?" Joan asked.

"She in de downstairs guest-room, Miss Joan. She won't go upstairs no mo'."

"We won't disturb her then, Sarah," said Dick. "We want to examine the upstairs rooms again. They haven't been touched, have they?"

"No, suh," said the girl positively. "Nobody been up dah, excep' de nurse de doctor lef' here to git Mis' Ross's clo's. She stayed heah all night an' slep' in de room wif Mis' Ross. On de chase divan she slep'." The heavy negro woman walked with them to the stairs and stood at the foot watching them go up.

Dick took a key from his pocket and unlocked the door to what had been the banker's bedroom. It was a lovely east room with a large bay window, recessed and fitted with bookshelves and a large comfortable chair. The bath which connected with Mrs. Ross's room yielded to Dick's key, and Joan said, "My, what a mess!" when she peered past him into its cool blue interior. The tile floor was spattered with blood, as was the hand-basin and the lovely pale blue tub.

Dick quickly set to work with his finger-print paraphernalia, and Joan, less interested now, wandered about in the bedroom.

Dick called to her in warning not to touch anything, so she guiltily dropped a copy of the 'Rubáyiat' of Omar Khayyám and squatted to peer at the titles of the books under the bay window. She gasped when she saw 'The Antichrist' by Nietzsche, several volumes of Schopenhauer, a small leather-bound edition of 'Alice in Wonderland,' Mrs. Buck's classic 'The Good Earth,' both volumes of Emma Goldman's autobiography, Joel Sayres's 'Rackety Rax,' and a complete set of Romain Rolland. She smiled to see Marie D. Scopes's 'Married Love' standing on the bottom shelf between Havelock Ellis's 'Little Essays' and Dr. Logan Clendening's 'The Human Body.'

She revised her secret estimate of the little banker and regretted that she hadn't known him better. When Dick came out of the bathroom, she showed him the books and he laughed.

"You'd judge the Lord himself by his taste in literature. When you get to heaven you'll go around squatting in front of all the archangels' bookcases."

"I'll bet the most interesting literature will be found in hell, darling. All of the antis will be in heaven and they'll censor the books that are imported from this earth. Can you imagine an archangel from Boston allowing me to enter with Faulkner's 'Sanctuary' under my arm?"

"Hardly," he laughed. "But how about the Songs of Solomon? Wouldn't it be funny if a Boston archangel banned the Bible?" He wandered about the room, peering into drawers, glancing quickly over papers taken from a suit of clothes hanging in the closet. It was the gray seersucker that Ross had worn on the day of the Fordman murder. The odor of the oil was heavy in the closet.

"Not much here," he said, as he returned the letters and receipted bills to their respective pockets. The drawers of the secretary yielded even less. Scores of checkbook stubs were packed in one, arranged carefully in order. More receipted bills filled another. There was no personal correspondence. The desk pen held no ink and the white blotter was innocent of stains. Dick took the latter out of its leather-covered holder and turned it over. It was just as unblemished on the under side.

"He evidently did his writing at the office," Dick remarked. "I'll get to that desk this afternoon, I hope. And I still haven't seen Fordman's private papers. His office was at home, wasn't it?"

"Yes, he had a study downstairs and did everything there. His secretary should be back next week."

"Secretary? What the hell? Nobody said anything about a secretary."

"Well, he's a pretty retiring sort of fellow. His last name's Squires, but I haven't seen him often. He's on a month's vacation. I should think he'd be back pronto, if he's seen a newspaper."

"What do you mean, retiring?"

"Oh, well, mousey, you know. I never laid eyes on him but once, but you sort of feel his ever-present absence or his absent ever-presence or—Good Lord, I sound positively bats. The man's probably quite normal, with a wife and six kids somewhere in town. Fordman's personality hardly encouraged others to bloom in its presence. Squires just has no personality, anyway. Did you find anything in the bathroom?"

"Nope. Just a precaution. Th' sheriff left some prints on th' far doorknob, inside, and some on the hot-water tap handle when he turned it off and on, but the rest of the place had been wiped clean.

Come into this other bedroom with me. The door's locked from that side."

They went down the hall and into the room that Mrs. Ross had occupied. Almost every object there was fully and formally dressed in white or pale-blue taffeta. The dressing-table stood against a plate-glass mirror panel set into the wall from the floor to the ceiling. It stood stiffly in a white taffeta skirt back to back with its own reflection. The bed was low and mounted, and it was covered with a white taffeta spread which spilled in stiff ruffles over the side. A mass of pale-blue pillows was banked against the gilt head-board. Occasional chairs were blue and a large chaise longue was upholstered in white. The heavy pale-blue taffeta drapes were drawn back from curtains of sheerest net. There was not one bit of evidence to show that the room had ever been occupied.

"This," said Joan, "is the envy of half the women in town. Looks like a kept woman's boudoir, if you ask me."

"Fie, fie, child! How can you be so crass? This room belongs to a middle-aged wedded spinster. It is the mute revelation of her soul," said the man, opening a closet door gingerly with his hand-kerchief over his hand. "Not in bad taste, you know," he added.

"No," admitted Joan; "she paid a decorator enough for think-ing it up. He submitted seventeen sketches, in color, before she decided on this one."

Dick was groping about in the closet without entering, swear-ing softly to himself. "Hey," he said, "where's the light?"

Joan looked for a switch on the outside, but could find none. Dick emerged and, looking in his kit, found a large flashlight. This he trained on the ceiling of the closet and saw, immediately over-head, a large glass square which he identified as an indirect light-ing fixture. He got a small chair from the bedroom and, standing on it, slid the glass panel back, revealing a cluster of incandescent bulbs. He looked at these for a moment and then, covering his hand with his handkerchief, twisted one of them to the right. It glowed brightly, and he swore again triumphantly. "The beggar has been just too damn smart this time. He should have screwed 'em in again." After screwing several more of the bulbs tightly into their sockets, he got down from the chair, leaving the panel open. The closet was brilliantly lighted.

He removed the blue chair, its silken seat holding the imprint of his oily shoes, and with Joan at his side surveyed the tiny room.

It was a model closet. One end was fitted with drawers from top to bottom, all neatly labeled *Shoes, Hose, Slips, Gowns, Underwear, Hats, Gloves, Handkerchiefs*, and so on. Joan sighed and remarked, "Here's where my envy begins. I have four drawers for everything I possess."

The wall in front of them was in reality four sliding doors. Dick stepped carefully across the carpeted floor and opened them successively, revealing dresses, coats, and negligees. He retreated to the doorway again and looked about the floor. The carpeting was a continuation of the heavy-pile powder-blue chenille of the bedroom. It showed footprints clearly, for the threads were soft and easily crushed. Joan could see numerous impressions, mostly those of a small toe and a sharp heel. Then there were several of a larger, broader shoe with a larger heel, and, as Dick pointed, she could easily discern the unmistakable impression of a man's shod foot, crossed and partially obliterated by this second print.

"I've an idea," said Dick, "that these belong to the nurse who 'slep' on th' chase divan las' night.'" He pointed to the sensible print and then to the smaller one, "and this to 'Mis' Ross' who 'slep' on the guest-room bed.'"

"And that," added Joan in a theatrical voice, "belongs to the man who murdered the man whose wife slep' on th' guest-room bed."

"Commendable, my dear Watson, commendable." Dick rose from his knees and went to his kit again. He returned with some white chalk which he used to trace around six or eight of the prints, especially those which crossed. Then, focusing his little camera, he took several time exposures. When this was finished, he entered the closet and examined the floor carefully.

Joan wandered away and was glancing over a copy of Earnest Dowson's poems which she found on the bed-table. She was thinking that this was pretty strong stuff for Mrs. Ross when she discovered an inscription on the flyleaf reading, 'To Sammy from Nell, in remembrance.' Mrs. Ross's first name was Thalia.

An exclamation from Dick brought her back to the closet. He was sitting on the floor with something in the palm of his hand. He held it out to her and she smiled as she took it in her fingers. It was the seed pod from a weed that grew thickly in that section, its peculiarity being that it was formed of thin flexible spikes, each tipped with a barbed point. It was grassy, pale, and wispy, and Joan blew it lightly from her fingers to the floor.

Dick rescued it and said: "There are three of these here. You know what they are?"

Joan replied: "Do I! I've had enough contact with the little devils. They are all over the golf course—in the rough, I mean—and they stick like the dickens. The dogs pick them up and so do the sheep and cattle."

"Does Mrs. Ross play golf?"

"Good Lord, no. But they're likely to be in other weedy spots than the golf course. Still, I can't see Thalia Ross walking in the weeds."

"Humm," murmured Dick as he deposited the 'little devils' in a pill-box and heaved himself to his feet. He got his finger-print outfit and blew the powder all about the lovely closet, revealing dozens of prints which he examined under his large lens. After a moment or two he muttered disgustedly, "Women."

He again balanced himself upon the blue chair and unscrewed two of the bulbs from the overhead fixture. Taking them to a table he dusted them with a black powder and said, quite loudly, "Well, I'll be goddamned!"

"What's the matter?" inquired Joan.

"There are no prints at all on these things."

He tried the others, getting the same result.

Joan grinned at him and said, "Do you really think that he was in the closet?"

"Of course," was the retort. "He had to hide somewhere while Sarah came upstairs to investigate the sound of the shot. He unscrewed the bulbs so that the automatic switch, controlled by the opening and closing of the door, wouldn't flood the place with light in case she happened to open it and look in. Not that there was much chance of it, of course, but he had this one planned perfectly. When she dashed out and made a bee-line for the Nelsons', he merely followed her and vanished in the shrubbery. It was easy. That is, easy to get out. I wonder how he got in." Dick mused for a moment and then said, "Well, let's go outside."

He repacked his kit, locked the doors leading into the two bedrooms, and they went quietly downstairs.

Joan found Sarah in the kitchen and asked her if she might use the telephone.

"De man ain' come yet, Miss Joan, to fix de telephone."

"Is it out of order?"

"Yessum. It ain' work since yeste'day."

Joan called to Dick, who was investigating the arrangement of the kitchen stairs, and told him about the telephone. He laughed shortly.

"I rather wondered about that," he said. "Let's go out the back way."

They went through Sarah's shining kitchen, the screened back porch, and out into the hot sunshine. A small path led from the steps directly to the garage. To the right was the paved drive. The whole yard was thickly grassed and Joan pointed out the small greenhouse behind a screen of hedges to the left. They walked over and looked into the glass building.

Dick pointed upward and said, "Look, there are four panes broken, curved ones, too." The glass was scattered in the aisles and over the beds of yellow marigolds. The delicate deep-red petals of the azaleas lay on the ground and one had been overturned. Dick found near it several large flinty stones.

"Run back, darling," he said, "and ask the admirable Sarah howcome all this." He waved a descriptive hand.

Joan ran, obediently, and found Sarah ironing on the back porch.

"Ah done git so behind yeste'day, Ah's tryin' to ketch up today," she explained when Joan appeared.

"Sarah," she said, "how'd the greenhouse glass get broken?"

"Dem boys, Miss Joan. Yeste'day a li'l' befo' Mr. Ross come, Ah heard a big crash an' Ah ran out dar an' find what you-all seen. Ah goes quick tru' de hedge an' catch 'em playin' ball on de vacant lot. 'You li'l' hellions!' Ah yells, 'what-for you break our glass?' an' dey yells back, 'We ain' break yo' glass, we jes' playin' ball.' 'You-all thow'd rocks an' broke it,' Ah says, 'an you better not let Mr. Ross ketch you.' So dey run home an' Ah come in. Ah sho' dreaded tellin' Mr. Ross, but Ah nevah have to." Sarah picked up her iron and snuffled. She put it down again and blew her nose violently. "Ah's ironin', honey, to keep mah min' off dese sinful happenin's."

Joan thanked her and left before Sarah's temporarily pent-up emotions could break forth, and, as she went down the steps, the negro woman's mournful contralto was lifted in the old chant, "Nobody knows de trouble Ah sees, Nobody knows but Je—sus."

She found Dick on a ladder behind the garage. He hailed her with "Here's where the son of a so-and-so cut the telephone wires and tied 'em up again." The break was completely invisible from the ground. Dick descended from the ladder and said, "Well?"

"Somebody tossed a bunch of rocks through the greenhouse roof at about twelve-forty-five yesterday. Sarah blames it on some kids playing ball in the vacant lot next door, but I have my doubts."

"Good work, Joan. So have I got my doubts—about the kids, but not about how our fellow got in the house. He cut the wires, smashed the glass, luring Sarah outside, and went in while she argued with the boys. If that hadn't worked, he could have used another ruse, equally clever." He dusted his fingers with his handkerchief and continued, "Let's have a look at the alley."

They went through the gate back of the garage and Dick wandered up and down the dusty weed-grown lane. He came back to Joan saying, "Nothing to be seen out here."

When she pointed silently to his legs, he looked down and cried out, "Well, I'll be—" Dozens of 'little devils' had pierced his white flannel trousers legs and clung tenaciously to the woolen cloth. He pulled several of them off, shook his pants vigorously, and said, "They certainly stick like hell, don't they? And they jab my poor bare shanks, too." He removed the rest of the barbs, and they went back into the yard.

Halfway down the drive, he ejaculated, "Ow!" and sat down on the steps leading up to the side door. Two 'little devils' had located themselves in his right sock and were sticking his ankle with experimental viciousness. He plucked them out and held them in his fingers. "That," he said to Joan, "is how those three got upstairs in Mrs. Ross's swell-elegant closet. They jabbed him in the ankle and he absent-mindedly took 'em out and threw them down to betray him."

Jimmie came panting around the corner, calling to them, "Say, what d'ya think, what d'ya think—"

"Calm down, calm down," advised his sister.

"Calm down, nothin'! I bet you don't calm down when you hear this—"

"What is it now?" asked Joan amusedly.

"Well, if you'll quit interruptin' me—"

"*Interrupting* you!"

"Yeah, I said interruptin'—"

"Go on, son. What is it? Joan, shut up," commanded Fields.

Jimmie cast a grateful glance at Dick, gulped and began. "Well, I was talkin' to Joe out there an' he told me that his father'd gone to town to tell the sheriff about a car he saw parked across from th' Hathaway house yesterday about noon. He didn't know th' guy who came along an' got in it about one o'clock, but he says that he came from this way. So he decided that he ought to tell th' sheriff about it so he walked in this mornin'. They haven't got a car. An' he just come back an' what d'ya think! It was Mitch White's car an' th' sheriff arrested him right then an' there."

"Mitch, good Lord!" said Joan; "they're crazy."

"Well, Joe's old man said that White couldn't prove where he was yesterday between twelve and one, an' that th' sheriff knew that he an' Mr. Fordman had had a fight a few days ago an' that Mitch couldn't prove where he was while Mr. Fordman was murdered an' that he is in love with Marion Fordman an' that he owes Mr. Ross a thousand dollars an' that Mr. Fordman threatened to fire him if he didn't keep away from Marion an' that he said, 'I could kill you for that, sir!'" The excited boy took a long breath.

"Doesn't he deny it, Jimmie?" asked Joan.

"Yeah an' no. Joe's old man says he denied killin' them, but that he didn't deny anything else."

XI: WEDNESDAY, JULY 5: 10.30 A.M.

The three of them hurried back to town and Joan dropped Dick and Jimmie at the courthouse. She went on to the office and found Ed Frank banging away at his machine.

"Thought I'd have to get the paper out single-handed today," he greeted her. "You look perturbed. Heard about Mitchell?"

"Yes, I have, Ed. They are crazy to arrest that boy. What do they have against him? The story I heard sounded awfully wild."

The editor pushed his machine away and leaned back in his chair.

"I believe," he declared, "that you are in love with White."

"I am not," denied Joan, "but I'm fond of him. He's a dear. Tell me what happened, Ed."

"Well, this man from the Hathaway place"—he referred to a piece of paper—"name's Josephus Goetz, came in with the story that he had seen a car parked across from the house at around twelve. He was cooking dinner for himself and his son in their rooms over the garage. They ate their dinner and at about one o'clock, when he sallied forth to hang the dish-towel out to dry, he saw, so he says, a man dash down the sidewalk from the direction of the Ross place, enter the car, and drive rapidly away. The man he saw only at a distance, of course, and through the hedge at that, but the car, he swears, was a Ford roadster, sand-colored, rumble seat open, top up, equipped with chromium disk wheels. They flashed in the sun, he said."

"That must be Mitchell's car," said Joan slowly. "What else have they against him? They couldn't arrest him on that."

"No. They have something else. They went up last night and got that chauffeur of Fordman's. He told them that White had quite a quarrel with John Fordman several days ago. He admitted listening, and states that it was over the attention that White was showing Marion. Evidently Fordman had plans for his little girl that didn't include marriage or anything else with a dirty newspaper man." Here Frank grinned sourly and continued: "He threatened to fire Mitch pronto and keep him from getting a job anywhere else in Texas, unless he agreed to leave Marion alone. Said something about his not being fit to touch his daughter after some of the floosies that he'd been with in the oil towns around here. Mitch resented that, of course, though it's pretty much the truth, and Wills states that he said, 'I could kill you for that, sir.' He's positive White said 'sir'! Mannerly kid, eh?"

"Don't joke, Ed. What does Mitch say?"

"Well, on top of that they've found out that he had borrowed a thousand dollars on a personal note from Mr. Ross against his father's estate. The note was due last week and Ross was pressing him for it."

Joan put in: "And when his father's estate was settled, they found that he'd left three hundred and fifty dollars in assets and five hundred thousand or more in debts. Oil ruined him."

"Yes, Mitch has been hard pressed. Owes me a hundred dollars. I don't expect to see it again. Anyway, they nabbed him. He was still asleep, smelling like a brewery, when they went over after him. And here's the crazy part. I'll read the statement he made. Millbank questioned him personally."

Question: Where were you between twelve-forty-five and one P.M. on Monday, July 3rd?

Answer: You won't believe me if I tell you, but I was over behind those stinking mesquite and cedar bushes losing a pint of gin and a perfectly good ham sandwich. The heat and that sulphur smell made me sick, and to save the good name of my lousy paper

I dashed through the trees and just made cover before the worst happened.

Question: Can you prove this by witnesses?

Answer: God, I hope not.

Question: Did you enter Mr. Fordman's car at any time during the day?

Answer: I did not. I was busy with my own affairs, and, besides, John Fordman didn't like me. I never enter cars when the owners disapprove of me.

* * * *

Question: Where were you between twelve-thirty and one-thirty P.M. on Tuesday, July 4th?

Answer: Well, at twelve—

Question: Twelve-thirty please?

Answer: I have to tell you about twelve, first. I left the office and went by the Greek's—it's a greasy-spoon near the office—ate a fried-egg sandwich, drank a cup of coffee, and started up to the barber shop on Main and Second. When I was opposite the Fredrick Hotel I felt so uneasy in my stomach that I went into the hotel and, shutting myself securely into the employee's lavatory downstairs, I again gave up the ghost, or, more specifically, the fried-egg sandwich, the cup of coffee, and a half-pint of rotten corn liquor. You won't believe it, of course.

Question: Didn't you see anyone in the hotel?

Answer: No. The lavatory is just inside the side entrance. There's a small couch in there and I lay down for fifteen or twenty minutes. I naturally felt lousy. Somebody tried the door once, but I was dozing and I didn't get up and let him in. He went away soon. When I could drag myself out, I went over to Ed Frank's room at the Mesa Hotel, slept for a while, got up and shaved and went to the courthouse.

* * * *

Question: Do you own a sand-colored Ford roadster?

Answer: Yes.

Question: How is the top fixed now?

Answer: It's up. It's too dam' hot to ride around—

Question: Answer the questions. Does it have a rumble seat?

Answer: Yes. And it's open, if you'd like to know. It won't stay shut.

Question: Where do you keep your car?

Answer: Anywhere.

Question: Where was it on the afternoon of July 4th between twelve and one P.M.?

Answer: Good Lord! I don't know. Oh, yes, I left it in front of the courthouse on my way to the office in the morning. I stopped in there first and as it's only half a block I walked on over to the office.

Here Frank stopped reading. "That shows you," he said, "why they don't believe him."

Joan sat down for the first time and took off her hat. She ran her fingers through her black curls and said: "He was drinking gin on Monday, Ed. I remember smelling the stuff and noticing how sick he looked when he came back from the field. And he was in here at twelve yesterday and went by the Greek's to send me in a sandwich. He got the corn there. I knew that that old buzzard sold it. It's full of fusel oil. No wonder it made him sick: and with a fried-egg sandwich! Ugh!"

The telephone jangled. It was Marion calling. "Joan," she said, "Gere's here and he tells me that they've arrested Mitchell. Where is Dick Fields?"

"He's at the courthouse now, Marion. Why?"

"I want to see him. It couldn't have been Mitchell. Pat Drennan's to try and arrange bail. I'm so worried. No one tells me anything and I just sit here waiting for the telephone to ring. What do you think about Mitchell, Joan?"

"I think it's a shame. But don't worry. If he didn't do it, they'll let him go soon. It's just unfortunate. I suppose you know why he's drinking?"

"Why, yes. I know that he was unhappy over what Dad said and I told him that it would be best if we didn't see each other for a while, anyway. I haven't seen him since Monday at the field, and I didn't talk to him then. I thought that he was drunk and I was angry with him for being such a baby. I wouldn't even speak to him. I went over and sat with Mrs. Levy so that he wouldn't come near me. I knew that he'd avoid Mrs. Levy because she's the W.C.T.U., you know, and she'd have lectured him. He called me yesterday around lunch time—"

"He called you?" Joan interrupted. "When?"

"Around lunch time."

"What time was it? Can't you remember?"

"No, it was some time between twelve and one. Is it important?"

"Quite. Try to remember. See if anyone else remembers. Who answered the telephone?"

"Glieth did, but she's outside now. I'll ask her when she comes in and call you if I have time before the inquest. We are leaving as soon as Gere comes."

She rang off and Joan turned excitedly to Frank.

"Yes, I know," he said. "You are about to establish an alibi for him. How'll you know where he called from?"

"Well, if he called from your room in the Mesa, the operator will know about it."

"Not if he used the private wire instead of the house telephone," stated Frank, shaking his head.

"That's so," said Joan, "and I expect that he would use it, because the girl there listens in." She sat for a moment without moving; then she said, "Didn't anyone see him go in at the Mesa?"

"He told Milbank that he didn't think so. Everybody, he said was in at dinner and he went right up the stairs and into my room as quickly as he could go."

"Surely there was someone at the desk. What about the switch-board girl?"

"She's in the alcove back of the cloakroom and only comes out when somebody pounds on that old bell on the counter. The clerk was at dinner. You know they serve at half-past twelve and all of the old-timers who usually inhabit the lobby from dawn until dark make a mighty break for the dining-room as soon as the doors are opened."

Joan nodded in forlorn acquiescence. She could picture the lobby of the Mesa, paneled in golden-oak, with the old men planted about in the black leather rocking-chairs, rocking, spitting, shrilly cackling among themselves, reading papers (often several days old). She could see them looking slyly at their brassy turnips, at the hotel clock over the desk, calculating, wondering what would be for dinner that day. She could see the clock hands stretching vertically, pulling out into one thin black line, and hear the single stroke which signaled the unlatching of the screen doors between the lobby and the old dining-room. With one accord, she knew, the ancients had risen, spitting for the last time into the tall brass cuspidors on rubber mats by the leather chairs, and trooped to the table on which the food had already been placed, boardinghouse style. For at least half an hour the lobby would have been deserted and the boy, ill and disheveled, walking quickly, could have crossed the room and mounted the broad padded stairs, unseen.

"A chambermaid might have seen him, Ed," she remarked hope-fully. "At least I'll ask Dick to inquire. Someone might have seen him on the street, too, though at dinner time it's unlikely."

Ed merely grunted and began to type again. Joan remembered her neglected society column and began her daily telephoning. It took longer than usual today, for the women, curious and sure of her unlimited knowledge, questioned her unmercifully.

Frank left for the inquest, stopping to say that he had hired young Billy Barron to help out 'for the time being.' The editor looked down at her and put a slim hand over hers as they rested on the typewriter. He drew her fingers together for a moment, let them go abruptly, and said, "You're a sweet kid, Joan." Then he turned and went quickly away, through the back shop.

The girl stared after him, excited and pleased. An inner voice keened out, "He touched you, not casually, but deliberately. He wants you, he's yours now." Her fingers were cold and trembled against the hard, positive keys of the machine. She jerked them up and lighted a cigarette. When she had smoked it through, her heart was still pounding but her head was clear. She worked again.

Jimmie called at ten-forty to say that the inquest was just beginning and that Fields wanted her to meet him at the hotel for luncheon at one o'clock. The boy shouted, "I'm stayin' for th' inquest. He's holdin' my seat. G'bye."

Mrs. Fiske, who had entertained the Idle Hour Bridge Club on the preceding day, called at eleven-thirty.

"Oh, Miss Shields, did you get my list?" she inquired.

"Yes, Mrs. Fiske. Your sister brought it in, in advance, on Monday, you know."

"Oh, yes. I'd forgot. But you don't know about the prizes or the refreshments, do you?"

"Why, yes, ma'am. Your sister came by yesterday afternoon and left me a note. She said that you used a red, white, and blue motif carried out in refreshments and decorations—"

"And in the flowers, too," broke in Mrs. Fiske. "We had carnations, red, you know, and white, tied with a blue ribbon, at each plate for favors. The flowers came from Fort Worth, you know, by mail, special."

"Yes, your sister put that in," said Joan, moving her mouth away from the damp, sticky telephone.

"And the prizes," continued Mrs. Fiske, "the first for visitors was a kitchen clock, green. Miss Jacks, the new elocution teacher, you know, won that. And for members I gave bath salts, 'Tre Jour.' Mrs. Ross won that." She rushed on: "Isn't it awful about Mr. Ross, Miss Shields? And Mrs. Ross playing bridge here all afternoon and having such wonderful luck! You know she said once to me, 'This must be my lucky day,' poor thing. Little did she know, or any of us. And when she telephoned home—"

"When did she telephone, Mrs. Fiske?" asked Joan.

"Why, I remember exactly. It was just before we served luncheon. She came into the hallway and telephoned, but nobody would answer. It must have been around a quarter of one. She just couldn't understand why Sarah didn't answer. But she didn't try very long because we were electing officers and she wanted to vote. You see," explained the woman, "she had been renominated for president against Mrs. Clarence Jones—"

"Mrs. Jones's name wasn't on your list."

"No, Agnes couldn't come. She called up just an hour before luncheon and said that she was sick. Well, anyway, Mrs. Ross was elected president, of course. She's been president for three years, you know."

Joan listened with growing impatience and got rid of Mrs. Fiske soon by saying that the other telephone was ringing. She promised to give her a number one head on her story, to use all of the details, and then she hung up.

Finishing the day's society news at twelve-thirty, she decided to run over to the Mesa Hotel and see if someone had not seen Mitch on the day before. It was twelve-thirty-five when she entered the dark, musty old building. After the blinding glare outside, the interior was gratefully cool. There was no one in the lobby. The leather chairs were empty as were the circular leather benches built around the pillars that supported the high ceiling. Discarded newspapers littered the floors around the cuspidors and a bridge table supporting a large checkerboard with the red and black counters still in place stood waiting for the combatants to return to the deserted battlefield.

Joan could see no one, but she could hear them at their food. Down the large hall to the right of the lobby were double screen doors, and the noise of dishes rattling against trays, against one another, and being thumped down upon the table-tops almost completely drowned the low murmur of conversation. The broad desk held the huge register, open with the bell upon it, and behind were the rows of pigeonholes for keys and mail. Joan peered across the desk and looked into the pigeonhole numbered 22. The key lay in its box with its identification board dangling outside. Some letters bridged the box, diagonally, above the key. Frank had not been in.

The girl turned to her left and went slowly up the broad green-carpeted stairs. The long hall was empty and piles of dirty linen stood outside several doors. The chambermaid was evidently at her dinner, also. Joan moved down the hall toward the linen closet, peered inside. The light that had attracted her was burning brightly, but the little cupboard was deserted. Ed Frank's room was just across and she tentatively turned the knob. To her surprise the door opened and she stepped inside. The unmade bed and a large pile of soiled sheets and towels on the floor told the story of the unlocked door; the room was in the process of being tidied.

Joan had been in it only once before, and now in the light of her awakening interest in Frank, she looked about with curious eyes. It was a typical bed-sitting-room of the old period hotel type. A large white iron bedstead denuded of its coverings stood near the window to the right. By it was a glass-topped desk table holding two telephones. The rest of the furnishings included a bureau littered with ties, papers, and magazines, and there were several comfortable chairs and a bookcase. The bookcase, obviously not the hotel's contribution to Frank's comfort, was built against the left wall and extended from the floor to the ceiling.

Joan looked at the books and mentally cursed Ed for not having offered some of them to her. The choice was varied and many were recent. His taste ranged from the better mystery stories to contemporary verse. Joan fingered Kay Cleaver Strahan's latest thriller, noted Mignon Eberhart's 'White Cockatoo,' Francis Isles's 'Before the Fact,' and Leslie Ford's delightful 'Murder in Maryland.' She felt cheated that she could not take away with her Mrs. Rinehart's 'The Album' which she had been unable to keep up with in the *Saturday Evening Post*.

She noticed several volumes on short-story writing and that excellent guide '1001 Markets for the Writer.' Frank must be working after hours, she thought, and wondered if he had already sold anything. He'd never tell anyone. She was looking at a book titled

'Problems in Contract,' when one of the telephones shrilled behind her. It startled her badly and she dropped the book to the
floor. The telephone rang again and she walked over to the glass-
topped table, wondering what she should do.

At the third burr of the bell she reached a decisive hand and
plucked the receiver of the French 'phone from its cradle. The bell
was silenced. This was the outside wire. She glanced at the pile of
dirty linen on the floor and said, pitching her voice into a typical
negro treble, "Hello."

A woman demanded, "Let me speak to Mr. Frank."

"Mr. Frank ain' heah," replied Joan.

"Who is this?" asked the woman.

"Dis yere's de chambahmaid."

There was a silence, and Joan wondered what she would do if
Frank were to come in suddenly.

Then the woman spoke again, "Well, never mind. I'll call— no,
is there a pencil there?"

"A pencil heah?" inquired Joan vaguely.

"Yes, a pencil and some paper. I want you to write down a message for Mr. Frank. Will you?"

"Wellum" began Joan; then, "Yassum, there's a pencil right
heah. Ah'll take you numbah."

"All right. It's seven—two—two. Did you get that? What did I say?"

"Yo' said 'seven—two—two.' Ah'l write it right down an' leave
it heah. He'll git it sho'."

"Don't forget it now," cautioned the woman. "It's quite important. Write 'Important' by the number."

"Wellum,' said Joan vaguely, "iffen you'll spell it."

"Never mind. Just leave the number," came the reply hurriedly,
and the connection was broken with a loud click.

Joan replaced the receiver and stood thinking.

Then she snatched up the small directory and turned the pages
to the name, Clarence Jones. The number was 722. But whether
the caller was Agnes or Mildred, she could not say.

XII: WEDNESDAY, JULY 5: 1 P.M.

A few moments later, Joan was out of the Mesa and, driving quickly around the two blocks intervening, she parked in front of the Fredrick Hotel. Dick was waiting in the lobby and they went into the dining-room. A few people gazed curiously at them as they took a small table in a corner, away from the group. A waitress hurried after them and hastily set the table, saying, "We only set those up closer. You sure this is all right?" They reassured her and sent her away with their orders.

Dick took a notebook from his pocket and said, "These are the most important facts brought out at the inquest this morning which, by the way, returned the verdict of murder by person or persons unknown—the old stand-by."

Joan sighed in relief. "They didn't decide on Mitch, then?"

"No, the sheriff didn't press his case. He needs more evidence, and I persuaded him to wait. The jury was a dumb one, anyway. Here's what came out, besides what we already know: first, the .25 automatic belonged to Marion Fordman. She and Drexell were practicing with it after lunch on Monday. They were back of the house, and when Fordman came out and called them to go to the field with him they got into the car and Marion slipped it into the pocket on the right-hand door. Drexell says that the finger-prints on the clip are most likely his, as he reloaded the gun after they finished shooting."

"What was Marion doing with a gun?" asked Joan.

"Her father gave it to her to carry in her own car, she said. She expected to drive down to Houston after Mrs. Lawrence soon. Incidentally, the large gun belonged to Ross and the finger-prints are his. I checked that last night. Forgot to tell you. Also checked on the bullet extracted from Fordman's body. It came from the small gun, and the one in the plaster in the Ross bathroom came from the larger one."

"When on earth did you do all of this, Dick?"

"Last night after I sent you home. I went over to the undertaker's and saw the good doctor who was performing the autopsy. He gave me the slug out of Fordman's body. I brought it back here and checked them both. I had the one that killed Ross. It's pretty rough checking, of course, with my limited paraphernalia, but I sent 'em off by air today to Dallas for an expert to look at, guns and slugs. You see I've only got a comparison 'scope with me, and in almost every case it suffices, but both of the bullets were somewhat battered, the larger one by smashing into the bathroom wall and the smaller by hitting one of Mr. Fordman's ribs and finally lodging in the backbone. I prefer to have 'em verified by an expert with a universal molecular 'scope. And, too, it was hard for me to get companion bullets to use for comparison without flattening them out considerably. They won't have that trouble in Dallas."

"It's Greek to me, Dick. What else came out at the inquest?"

"Nothing of importance. In a case of obvious murder the inquest just furnishes a sort of screen behind which the officers can work. It doesn't tip off the culprit because they seldom allow any important evidence to be given at that time."

"So they brought in the verdict of 'murder by person or persons unknown,'" mused Joan.

"Yes. The jury seemed bewildered by the evidence, especially that of your brother."

"Jimmie?"

"Yes. He was called to tell of finding the .25 automatic. He was pretty thrilled, too."

"Good Lord! Mom will certainly be mad. She thinks he's still a baby."

"He did very creditably and he left you out entirely, on my advice."

"Thanks for that," said Joan gratefully.

"You see," continued Dick, "they probably had some notion of calling it suicide until then, but even they knew that Fordman couldn't have killed himself and then run around and stuck the gun into the spare-tire cover. The doctor testified as to the wound and the bullet extracted, and they took it for granted, even without my testimony, that the little gun was used. A flock of people testified, including the overripe Agnes Jones. She's an odd one, isn't she?"

"Yes. Both she and Mildred are cases for a good psychiatrist. Not mental cases—I don't mean that. Nymphomania, I believe it's called, isn't it? They can't behave normally where men are concerned. I get so disgusted with Mildred. Whenever we have a party or go to a dance, you can always count on Mildred to drink too much and make a fool of herself over some man. By the way," she added, "one of them seems to be after Ed Frank now." She related the incident in the hotel room. Dick was mildly interested. Then she told him what Marion had said about Mitchell's call on the day before.

"You go," he directed, "to the telephone company and get someone in authority. Get their statement as to when they first knew of the break in service and when they sent someone out to look things over. They always keep a record of such things. That kid," he continued, "may get an alibi out of this. That is, if Mrs. Lawrence can remember exactly when he telephoned Marion. It's obvious that he couldn't have called from the Ross place *after* the wire was cut, and he couldn't have called from there *before* it was cut because he wasn't in the house, if he was the murderer. Hence, if he called the Fordman house after the break was reported and before the murder was committed at one o'clock, he obviously didn't commit the murder."

They finished lunch and Dick went back to the courthouse to see the sheriff before the second inquest could begin. Joan went to the office of the telephone company and asked for Mr. Bell, the appropriately named general manager. He heard her request, hurried away, and returned to tell her that Mrs. Ross herself, speaking from the home of C. C. Fiske, had reported that there was no answer at her home, saying that the operator had believed the wire to be out of order. The time, he said, was twelve-forty-six P.M. They had sent no one out until this morning, as it was the Fourth of July and the force was short-handed. This morning, however, the man had found the wires cut near the garage, had repaired them, and reported that the telephone was again functioning properly.

Joan returned to the office and found a note on her desk with Marion's number scribbled on it. She called and Mrs. Lawrence answered. She said, "I understand that you want to know when Mr. White called Marion yesterday, Miss Shields?"

"Yes, it's quite important," said Joan.

"Well, I remember that it was exactly ten minutes of one. I looked at my watch as I came through the hall. I was wondering whether or not I'd have time to dress before luncheon. You see, I had only arrived a few moments before and everything was so upset that I hadn't changed. Marion told me that we'd lunch at one o'clock and then go to town to the inquest." Here her cool voice broke off, but she resumed almost immediately: "So I hurried indoors, leaving Marion on the porch talking with the chauffeur about a new car. As I walked down the hall, the telephone rang. No one was about, so I answered it. It was Mr. White and he thought I was Marion. I finally convinced him that I was not, and went out to call her, but she refused to answer the telephone, so I returned and told him that she was too busy at the moment to talk. He seemed satisfied and, thanking me, hung up. It was five minutes of one before I reached my room. I looked again and decided to change after luncheon." She waited for Joan to comment.

"I thank you so much, Mrs. Lawrence. You'll be willing to swear to this, won't you? You see, Mr. White has been accused of these murders solely on circumstantial evidence, and this conversation which he had with you practically ruins the whole case against him," Joan told her.

"Why, yes," said the woman, "I would swear to it and so for that matter could Marion and the chauffeur. You see, I went to the door and said, 'Marion, a Mr. White wants to talk with you.'"

"That's so, but you were the only one who noted the exact time and it's that that's so important," Joan said. "Will you tell Marion that Mr. Fields and I will come by sometime this evening? It may be late."

Joan hung up, mentally blessing Glieth Lawrence's orderly mind and her calm, healing personality. She would help Marion immeasurably, Joan knew. Her presence relieved Joan of her obligation and left more time for her to do her bit in the investigation. She felt far more fit for the latter than for the former, shy of conventional sympathetics as she was. Funerals embarrassed her, ministers annoyed her, and umbrageous females made her slightly ill. The Fordman funeral was to be held that evening at six o'clock, and everyone in town would attend. The service would be read in the little chapel at Scott and Scott's Funeral Home, and the millionaire would be buried in the local cemetery north of town, near his father and mother and his wife.

There would be little to hold Marion here now. She would probably sell the home and go abroad. This would at least put an end to Mitchell's troubles, as his infatuation could scarcely survive the distance of six thousand miles. Poor kid, thought Joan.

The large table devoted to exchanges caught her eye and she went over to scrabble among the papers tossed a foot or so high upon it. Some had been opened and thrown down again, sheets scattered; others were still rolled and pasted into their address papers just as they had arrived. She sorted them into piles, throwing all of the old and out-of-state sheets to the floor. The only ones she kept were the four companion papers that carried the bridge article and several state papers that might include it. Then she went rapidly through this pile, keeping only the ones dated Saturday, July 1. She had seven papers when she finished and stood knee-deep in the discarded mass. The first one was the El Paso *Banner*. She opened it to the woman's page where the bridge article was run, and found the one she sought. But the back side of the sheet carried only sports news. The crossword puzzle was tucked away in a corner of the last page, with the comics. She crumpled the *Banner* and threw it to the floor.

The next paper was the San Antonio *Light*, a companion sheet, owned by Fordman. It was the one she sought. Her marking around the bridge article included the crossword puzzle and the continued story; as well as she could tell, this was the exact placement shown by the clipping. She refolded the paper carefully and went through the others just to make certain that there was no duplication. She found that there was none, and tossed the mass of discarded exchanges back to the table, thoroughly mixing the chosen six among them.

It was three-thirty. The office was quiet. The bookkeeper sat on his high stool in a corner and, arching his shoulders back, scratched at an inaccessible spot between them. Billy, a local youngster, journalism student at State University during the winter, was conscientiously reading proof at Mitchell's desk. He had been so quiet that Joan had forgotten him. He smiled at her as she looked around, and said, "Did you find your paper, Miss Shields?" referring to her methodical if messy search among the exchanges.

She laughed and replied: "Yes, I keep tabs on the other society editors. One of them thinks of something new every now and then and if I don't see it before Mr. Frank does, he's apt to call my attention to it. We newspaper people are notorious plagiarists, you know. Sure as the Dallas *News* uses a new boxed feature head over an Amelia Earhart story, we try it out next Sunday over two columns of Eleanor Roosevelt human-interest stuff. I'm in search of new ideas for the Friday Market Page. It's the devil to keep interesting. Joyce Maxwell of the El Paso *Ledger* featured fruit soups this week. A banana consommé won first prize. She was certainly hard up for subjects."

The boy laughed and Joan left. She drove out to the negro district and stopped in front of a low whitewashed cottage, its fenced yard crammed with every type of flower that would bloom under the western sun. A negro woman sat in a rocker on the small porch.

"Hello, Belinda," called Joan as she got out of the car.

"Howdy, Miss Shields," cried the woman, coming down the steps toward her. "Come in, come in," she continued. "Hit's too hot out yere in de sun. Come in an' set on th' po'ch an' Ah'll git yo' some lemonade." She raised her voice suddenly and bellowed, "Austin, git Miss Shields some lemonade."

Belinda's daughter appeared in the doorway, giggled, withdrew. When she returned a few moments later, she bore a tall glass of pale-yellow liquid with a piece of mint tucked in the side.

Joan accepted it, thanked her, and they talked about the heat, the depression, and the terrible happenings in town. The girl finally approached her mission casually, with "By the way, Belinda, you wash for the Fordmans, don't you?"

"Yassum," replied the woman. "Ah does all o' Miss Fordman's dresses, lak yo's." She chuckled.

"Do you work for Mrs. Jones, too?"

"No'm. She has a girl who does dey things on de place."

"Belinda, if you saw a man's handkerchief, would you recognize it? That is, I mean, if it was in your work regularly?"

"Mebby Ah would, Miss Shields," said the negress doubtfully, "but if Ah didn't, Dallas might. She's de younges', you know, an' she does the li'l' flat things." Belinda referred to her seventh daughter, who was in the neighborhood of eight years and whose head was extending over the edge of the porch directly behind her mother.

The negro woman thought awhile and then said: "Ef it was dahned, Miss Shields, or of it had a spot or somethin', it would be easier. Did you-all git an extry hank'chief in yo' wash? Ain' nobody complainin' about losin' one. You-all jes' keep it," she advised.

"I hate to do that, Belinda," replied Joan. "I'll bring it by tomorrow and let Dallas look it over. She may know whose it is. Do you keep any record of your customers?"

"Yassum," said the puzzled woman. "Ah has to, else we'd never know when who was who. Whaffo' yo' ask?"

"We'd like to run a story about you and the girls in the paper, Belinda," said Joan rashly. "With pictures and everything," she added. "I might be able to run a list of your customers along with it. It would do your business a lot of good."

The negress beamed at her, delighted. "Well, well, well," she said, "ef yo' ain' sweet, Miss Shields. Ah's got my customers' list right heah." She produced a ten-cent composition book from her apron pocket and held it out to Joan. As the girl thumbed through it, her spirits fell. There were at least fifty names. She copied out into her own notebook about thirty of these—the ones she thought might help—and returned Belinda's list to her.

Promising to send a photographer out next week, she got away and cursed herself roundly, on the way back to town. She'd have to run the story about Belinda, she knew. Couldn't disappoint her. Belinda would be telling her neighbors now, and begin looking for the photograph in the evening's edition. Joan's mother had a saying, "Never promise a child or a negro anything unless you intend to do it. They are too easily disappointed." Well, she thought, if Belinda can identify the handkerchief that Jimmie had found with the gun, she'd have earned a story. Anyway, a few lines on the girls' names were always amusing.

She stopped by the office and Billie told her that Dick had called and asked her to meet him at five o'clock at the courthouse. Ed was still away and Billie was waiting for someone to tell him what to do. It was four-forty-five and he told her that the inquest had just 'let out.' "They brought in the same verdict, Miss Shields," he said. "I called up Dad an' he told me. He was on the jury an' just got back to th' store. He said that it sure was one big mess. Nobody seemed to know anything except that detective from St. Louis who just called you, and he only answered the questions, didn't volunteer anything extra, Dad said."

Frank came in and threw a sardonic smile at Joan. "Well," he said, "they didn't hang Mitch this afternoon, but he's still in the coop. How are things going here?"

The linotypes were silent in the shop and, after a short search, he and Joan found Mac and the boys rolling dice in the pressroom.

"Hell," said Mac, spitting tobacco juice in the pit under the press, "there ain't no copy left to set up. We been waitin' around here two hours. Everything's ready to go but th' front page and an inside I kep' for run-over. We can get it off in an hour and a half."

Ed returned to his desk and started on the story of the second inquest. Joan, knowing that there was nothing more for her to do, waved good-bye to Ed and went to meet Dick.

He was standing in front of the jail talking to the sheriff. They went in to see Mitchell. He was lying on the cot in his cell, reading, by the light of the one small window above him, a newspaper which he threw to the floor and jumped to his feet when Joan called to him from the corridor.

"Hi, Mitch," she said, "you look soberer than I've seen you in days."

"I am sober, honey, and I can't get the sheriff to let me even send out for corn!" He laughed and seemed glad to see them. There was a few moments' silence. He broke it with: "I've been reading the state papers. They've sure got it covered, haven't they? There was a bunch of fellows up this mornin'. The sheriff let 'em talk to me—through the bars. I knew most of 'em." He stopped and then spoke to Dick. "Say, Fields," he said, "how long'll it be before you get this thing cleared up? I'm going to get tired of reading papers soon. An' that cot"—he gestured—"it's sure hard. I'm not looking forward to my night's rest."

"We'll get you out before long, Mitch," promised Joan. The sheriff chuckled behind her. She turned and spoke to him. "Sheriff, I can give you an alibi for Mr. White right now that will cover yesterday's murder. You want it?"

"I'll listen, Miss Shields," said the big man politely.

Joan turned back to Mitchell, who was regarding her with interest. "Mitch," she said, "what time did you say that you went over to the Mesa?"

"I don't know for sure, Joan, but it must have been after twelve-thirty. Those old fossils were in at dinner. It must have been before one, too, because I met Frank at one-thirty in the sheriff's office and I shaved and bathed during the time I was there. Say twelve-forty or twelve-forty-five, I guess."

"What else did you do while you were in Ed's room, Mitch?"

"What else? Nothing that I know of. Why?"

"Think again, Mitch."

The reporter pressed his head against the barred door and they all stood in silence.

He jerked his head up and said, "I didn't want to say, but I guess you mean did I telephone anyone?"

Joan nodded and looked at the sheriff. He moved closer and rumbled in his throat.

Joan said to Mitch, "Who'd you telephone, idiot?"

"Why, I called Marion, but she wouldn't talk to me," he answered slowly.

"What time did you call Miss Fordman?" put in Dick.

"I don't have the faintest idea," replied White. "You see, I called her five or six times yesterday, every time I got near a 'phone. She hasn't let me see her or talk to her since her father was killed. It was a sort of automatic gesture, you know." He stopped and looked at them; then continued: "I thought I had her yesterday, though, but it was that Mrs. Lawrence." He reddened at the recollection. "She must have thought that I was crazy."

The sheriff rumbled in his throat again and addressed Joan. "I can't see as how this makes much difference, Miss Shields," he said. "He coulda called her up from anywhere."

"But Mr. Read," protested Joan, "if Mitchell murdered Mr. Ross, he must of necessity have been in the Ross house between twelve-fifteen and one o'clock. Mr. Fields told you about the broken greenhouse and the conclusion that must be drawn from it, didn't he?"

"Yes, but—" began the sheriff.

"There are no 'buts,'" stated Joan. "The murderer *must* have entered the Ross home when Sarah left it that once. The house was otherwise tightly locked. And he must have left it when Sarah ran next door to the Nelsons'. Don't you agree?"

"Yes, ma'm, but—"

"Well, then," said Joan, "the murderer cut the telephone wires *before* he entered the Ross house because he didn't want Sarah to telephone from there and thus block his only means of exit. He must go out the back door if possible and slip away through the shrubbery, especially since his car was parked in the rear."

"So," she continued rapidly, "the murderer could *not* have telephoned to anyone between twelve-fifteen and one o'clock, because he was inside the Ross home and the telephone service was disconnected.

"Now, Mrs. Lawrence is ready to swear that Mr. White called and asked for Miss Fordman at ten minutes of one. He talked with her for at least two minutes and waited two more while she went to inform Marion that he was on the wire.

"And, furthermore," she added, "I have proof that the Ross telephone *was* out of order at a quarter of one, because Mrs. Ross herself reported the fact at the telephone office. She had tried to 'phone Sarah from Mrs. Fiske's, and when she couldn't get anyone and Central told her that the wire seemed out of order, she called the business office and reported this fact." Joan stopped and drew a long breath.

Mitchell said, "Thanks, kid, I'll do as much for you some day."

The sheriff rumbled in his throat again, brushed his hand across his gray roach, and thought for a moment. "It'll have to be verified, White," he declared, "and if it's true, I'm sure I'll be glad enough to let you go, providin' Millbank agrees." He turned to Joan and grinned: "Ya see, Miss Shields, ya can't blame us. He never told us nothin' about this-here 'phone call an' them alibis he give us was just about the worst I've ever heard. Sick in th' bushes. Sick at th' Fredrick. It didn't sound possible."

"It was a remarkable coincidence," said Joan.

"Call it what ya like," added the sheriff, "but anyway ya look at it, it sounds fishy. An' with all them people out at the field on Monday, we can't find a one who says they saw White."

The four of them stood in silence, and then the sheriff said, "Well, I'll go see Millbank now, if you-all are through here."

They told Mitch good-bye and he watched them walk away, rather sadly. They had reached the door when he suddenly shouted, "Joan!"

The girl looked at Read, who nodded at her, and she ran back to Mitchell's cell.

He said: "Will you see Marion, Joan? If you do, won't you tell her that I'm sorry? She can't believe that I shot her father—"

"She doesn't, Mitch," put in Joan. "She called me today to say that she was having Drennan try to arrange bail. She didn't believe it at all."

He brightened and said, "Thanks. And say, you know that Levy kid, the one who says pieces?"

"Rea?"

"Yes. Well, you know, I just remembered, she followed me through those mesquite trees on Monday. I dam' near had to play hide-and-seek with her before she'd go away an' leave me to my troubles. She might be able to remember it, anyway, and at least it would bolster up my story." He said this rather helplessly, but Joan snatched at it eagerly.

"She's lots brighter than most of the kids her age, Mitch. She possibly will remember. I'll go around there now and talk to her." She turned away, but remembered the incident in the elevator and asked, "Say, didn't Mildred Jones spot you too?"

"God, yes," was the indignant reply. "She yelled like a guinea hen, 'M-i-itch! Mi-itch!' half a dozen times, but I just ran fast as hell the other way!"

Joan laughed and told him what the girl had said. He wrinkled his nose and said, "Poisonous bitch."

"You used to like her, boy; why the sudden change?"

"Ya can't eat ripe olives every meal," was the succinct rejoinder, and Joan left him mumbling.

She joined the sheriff and Dick who had waited for her at the end of the corridor.

They went into the former's office and talked the situation over for a few minutes, Joan telling them what Mitchell had said about the Levy child.

The sheriff looked skeptical, but said: "You might go talk to her, Miss Shields, in front of her mother, of course, an' see what she says. This whole dam' business has me buffaloed, I don't mind sayin', an' with Millbank yellin' for an arrest Well, that stuff about the telephone calls, it oughta spring 'em. I'll go see Millbank now an' you can see the Levy kid an' meet us here in two hours. How about it?"

Joan assented, and she and Dick left the building. They sat in Joan's car and the girl told him about the San Antonio newspaper, producing it from her brief case. He looked at it and then took her list of Belinda's customers. They went over it together, but it yielded only four names to interest them. These were, Fordman, Drexell, Ross, and Levy. Joan went over the list again carefully, and then added Mrs. Getschalk, saying, "I hate to do this, but I see that Mitchell's landlady is also represented. She sends his things out for him, I know."

"Well," announced Dick, "we seem to be getting somewhere. At least the number of our suspects is dwindling. Say, I wired that bird Hall today, the bridge columnist, you know, and asked him who sent in the problem that's presented in our clipping."

"What good will knowing that do you?" asked Joan curiously.

"What good? Say, didn't you read the article through?"

"Lord, no," was the reply. "One bridge conundrum is like another to me. I read the first two or three paragraphs, but that's all."

"You shock me, Joan. And I thought that you had the makin' of such a good detective." He shook his head sadly and climbed out of the car. "Come up and see me sometime. I'll show it to you. In the meantime, mull over it, darlin'. You had the darn thing almost as long as I have. Well, I must away. You go out and quiz the women and children for your boy friend. I've other work to do. See you here at seven."

He did see her there at seven. She was excited and obviously amused over something. Judge Millbank and Sheriff Read were in the latter's office. Millbank, an officious little fat man dressed in senatorial black, wearing a William Jennings Bryan bow-tie, bowed politely to Joan. Her father was a wealthy man and his opinions were highly respected in matters political.

The four of them went over the case and the conclusion reached regarding Mitchell's part.

Joan said: "And I've another bit of proof that should convince you that he is telling the truth about Monday. I went out today and talked to Mrs. Levy and Rea. The child is eight years old, you know, and quite intelligent, if a pest. I began by asking Mrs. Levy where she herself was when the well was shot off. She said that she had not moved from their car at any time and that Miss Fordman had joined her at twelve-thirty. She knew because she asked Marion the time. They agreed that they still had a half-hour to wait.

"Rea, she stated, had gone with her father to get a closer view. She said that her husband returned, without the child, at the moment the well was shot off. He arrived out of breath because he had run to keep from being in the spray that always follows the shot.

"She asked him where Rea was and he said that she had left him quite some time before, to return to the car. They both grew very agitated as the moments passed and Rea didn't show up. But just as Mr. Levy was going away to look for her, she appeared with some story about a man who had yelled at her.

"They were still talking to her, scolding her, when Marion left them and went to her own car, finding, as you know, her father's body. The ensuing hullabaloo drove the thought of Rea's adventure out of their minds.

"But Rea remembered it!" Here Joan laughed and continued. "I'll tell you what she said that the man yelled at her presently. It's really funny. You should have seen Mrs. Levy's face—but, anyway, her story was that she had come back to the car and, noticing that Miss Fordman and her mother were talking, she slipped around and crept into the mesquite thicket to get some mesquite beans to chew.* Her mother considered this a dirty practice, hence the secrecy of the venture.

"She was in the middle of the thicket gathering, and I presume chewing, the beans, when a man came running through the grove. She knew him because he had 'written up' the story about her prize in elocution only the week before and he had been very jolly and pleasant to her. So she called him and ran after him. She didn't remember his name. He turned and saw her, and dashed farther

---

* When ripe, these long reddish beans are considered quite delectable to Southwestern youngsters, who chew and suck them much as if they were sugar-cane.

into the mesquite. She followed him persistently, wondering what he was doing, and if he was hiding from someone.

"Well, to make a long story short, he got sick of it and stopped. Then he yelled at her, scaring her somewhat, and she retreated. He hid behind the cedars, she said, and then, when she thought he wouldn't see her, she went through the trees and peered at him. By that time he was sitting on the ground, leaning back against a tree, and she said that he looked awfully white.

"She watched him until the explosion came—evidently startling both of them and he got to his feet. She said that he went away around the little storage tank and she sucked a few more mesquite beans and went back to her car."

Here Joan stopped. Then she continued: "Let's go down and see if Mitchell can tell us what he said to the child, trying to get rid of her. If it is what Rea says he said, you really ought to let him go, don't you think, Judge?"

The Judge smiled at her and said: "Why, yes, Miss Shields. I don't believe that we can hold the boy with all of this evidence in his favor. Read, here, has checked on the telephone calls and we'll take your word on this, for tonight, anyway. What *did* White say to the child?"

"I'll write it down," said Joan, "and you can read it after he speaks his piece." She scribbled on a piece of paper and handed it folded to the Judge, who put it in his pocket.

They all arose and went down the corridor to Mitchell's cell. He was standing at the window, looking out at the town square, and turned eagerly to greet them.

Joan explained the situation to him and asked, "What did you say to the kid, Mitch?"

"You mean exactly?" he inquired.

"Yes. You tell us what you said to the child when she found you hiding under the mesquites, and we'll tell you whether or not you've an alibi."

"Good God, Joan. I didn't think when I made that kid scram that it would all be made public. What I said won't bear repeating. Suppose Mrs. Levy hears about it?"

"She's already heard it, darling, and she's gunning for you with blood in her eye—but come on, before these men as witnesses—what was it?"

"Well, I said, 'Get th' hell outa here, you little bastard.' Aw, gee, Joan. You know that under normal conditions I don't swear at women and kids—"

The four in the corridor yelled with laughter, and a bum in a cell farther away called out, "Hey, lemme in on d' joke. It's d' foist time I've hoid anybuddy laughin' in dis yere jernt."

Ten minutes later, Joan, Dick, and the ex-jailbird Mitch hopped jubilantly down the steps of the county jail-house and headed for the local Tony's out on the West Pike.

XIII: WEDNESDAY, JULY 5: 7.45 P.M.

Mitchell and Joan and Dick took a small table in the back room of the roadhouse. Mitch recommended the rye, so they ordered highballs and sandwiches and talked about the case.

"What I can't understand," said Joan, "is how the murderer used your car, Mitch."

"I thought about that in jail," answered the reporter. "It was easy. I left it in front of the courthouse at about eleven-thirty and I didn't use it again until one-thirty, when I drove out to the Ross place with the sheriff's party. I never lock the thing, you know. It's pretty well shot and I've got good insurance. I wish that bird had wrecked it."

"Someone must have used it deliberately," said Joan, "to implicate you."

"What came out at the second inquest?" asked Mitchell of Dick.

"Nothing of importance. They only took the testimony of the maid who found the body, the doctor, the sheriff, and myself. Oh, yes, and that of the paying teller at the bank, who says that Ross left there at around twelve-forty-five. Since it was a holiday no particular attention was paid to the exact luncheon hours. Only three or four of the employees were working, anyway. Ross, however, worked every day—even came down on Sundays."

"Have the police checked on the alibis for the second murder yet?" asked Joan.

Dick snorted. "They are trying to do so 'inconspicuously' according to Millbank. Anybody in this place with a little cash in the bank is sacred."

179

"Well, what *are* they doing?"

"For one thing they're looking up the past histories of Drexell and of Day. Both of them are comparative newcomers here. That is, they aren't 'old-timers.'"

"Is that all?"

"Well, we are going into conference tomorrow morning and interview a bunch of these people. Millbank has decided that we'll have to risk offending them."

They finished their drinks and sandwiches and drove back to town. After dropping Mitch at his boarding-house, Dick said, "How long will it take to get out to the Trotter farm?"

Joan looked at him curiously. "About half an hour."

"We'll go," he announced—and they went.

Out the South Pike, through the oil fields and on into the rolling farm country. It was dark before Joan turned the roadster into a sandy lane that ended in a barnyard. They went through the barbed-wire gate and up to the house. The Trotters were sitting on the front porch and a young fellow in overalls, evidently Crystal's beau, arose from the porch step. Joan was greeted effusively by Mrs. Trotter, and they all gazed at Dick when Joan told them that he was representing the police and wanted to ask some more questions.

"Well," said Mrs. Trotter, rising excitedly to her feet, "let's all go in th' settin' room where we kin see."

They followed her into the musty-smelling parlor and seated themselves about the room. Dick took a chair at the oak center table on which Crystal had placed two oil lamps.

Mrs. Trotter leaned forward in her straight-backed kitchen chair and watched Fields solemnly. The others were intensely interested.

Dick produced the sketch of the field, talking to the woman as he did so. "Mrs. Trotter," he complimented, "your story was a marvel of accuracy, but there are a few things that need elaboration—er—I mean, more explaining. The situation, as you probably know, has become even more serious and we need all the help we can get.

"Now tell me . . . you stated that it was between twelve-thirty and twelve-thirty-five when your husband parked near the rope." He pushed the map toward her and continued, "Just where were you, exactly?"

Mrs. Trotter studied the sketch and said: "This-here's real clear. Our car was th' second one in th' line acrost th' road from Mr. Levy's." She pointed, and Dick marked the place. "You see," continued the country woman, "when we drove up, there was lots of cars already parked, an' we thought we'd have to walk up to see anything, but jest as we was backin' off, a car come out of that space an' we got it."

"I see," said Dick, then, "and how long after that did you notice Mr. Fordman?"

"Well," she considered, "we got outen th' car an' watched by th' rope for a while. I seen Mr. Fordman then, talkin' to some men—"

"Where were they standing?" interrupted Dick.

"Right there at th' corner of th' derrick—th' corner nearest us."

"The northeast corner?"

"Yes, I guess that was it. I never do remember directions well."

"This must have been about twelve-forty-five?"

"I guess. It couldn't have been more'n five minutes, anyway."

"Then?"

"Well, we got too hot out there in th' sun. So I sez to Crystal, 'Let's git back in th' car.' We all did, Jason too, an' it was about then that I seen Mr. Fordman goin' towards his car."

"Did you know any of the men with him?"

"No, I can't say as I did. I didn't notice no one in partic'lar. There was people runnin' all around an' some man was tryin' to get 'em outside th' rope. There was lots of kids too, an' I remember sayin' to Crystal that their folks oughta be ashamed to let 'em run aroun' loose where there might be an explosion any minute."

"Then you watched only Mr. Fordman. What did he do?"

"He walked acrosst towards his car an' when somebody shouted at th' well he began to run. Everybody was a-runnin'. He got to his car, opened th' door

"Wait," said Dick. "When he opened the door did he get in immediately?"

"Well, no, not exactly," answered the woman. "I remember he put his foot on th' runnin'-board an' stood there a moment. Then he looked back at th' well an' got in."

"You said in your story that 'he got in and sat down.' Could you see him after he got in the car?"

"Well, now, I reckin I couldn't. I probably said that he set down because that's what anybody does when they git in a car, but now that you mention it I don't suppose—"

"You stated that you looked away then, at the well. Was this at the moment of the explosion?"

"Oh, no. Th' man that yelled must of made a mistake because it was quite a while before th' thing exploded. We kep' a-waitin' an' a-waitin', ever'body gittin' nervouser an' nervouser all th' time. It was kind of like watchin' a kid blow up a balloon, expectin' it t' bust any minute. Crystal had her fingers in her ears 'til she near deefened herself. Then she took 'em out just when th' thing went off."

Mrs. Trotter allowed herself to chuckle softly at the memory.

Dick said, "But you didn't have your fingers in your ears, did you?"

"No," said the woman, "loud noises don't bother me none. Why, Crystal was a-jumpin' ever' time that-there truck back-fired, thinkin' it was th' well."

"What truck was that?"

"The one at th' well. Th' man who got in it to drive it away couldn't seem to git it started an' it backfired all the time 'til he finally got it over back of th' well. That made ever'body laugh."

Dick glanced at Joan, who nodded approvingly. He smiled at her and then said to Mrs. Trotter, "It was particularly noisy then *before* the explosion?"

"Laws, yes," answered the woman. "Ever'body was a-yellin' an' when that-there truck begun its noise, they all laughed an' shouted an' blew their car horns. You know how people act when somethin' like that happens."

Joan knew. She could easily reconstruct the incident: the crowds around the well, the dust, the holiday excitement, the child-ish humor and delight of the audience, the advice shouted at Day and the raucous applause at this simple diversion. Mrs. Trotter was talking.

". . . you see. An' when th' man shouted, ever'body got real quiet, expectin' th' explosion. But it didn't come for so long that th' truck back-firin' sort of loosed up th' tension, you might say, an' ever'one sort of let themselves go."

Dick nodded in agreement and put several more questions. He took her through the part of her story relating to Fordman's actions at the side of the Fraschini. She could add little except that she wasn't at all sure whether or not the shades on the car were lowered before Fordman stepped in or after he had entered and presumably seated himself where he was later found dead.

They thanked the Trotters and started back to town. Joan swung the car capably over the rocky, winding road, silent until Dick should speak.

"Did Fordman and Agnes Jones carry on their affair openly?" he asked suddenly.

"No. They went to great lengths to hide it, but several people seem to have seen them together in Dallas and Fort Worth. Agnes has a sister who lives in Arlington—very conveniently, and she vis-ited her quite regularly."

"She must have been upset when she heard of Mrs. Lawrence. She doesn't appear to me to be a woman who'd take such a blow quietly."

"How about her alibi?"

"Very few of the alibis hold now, darling, in view of what Mrs. Trotter just told us. We must rearrange our time limit. The mur-derer had from twelve-fifty to about one-ten—twenty minutes—in which to act. He or she could have been out of the car and well away from it by one-four, when the well was shot."

"Then you think that Mr. Fordman could have been murdered during the fourteen minutes before the explosion?"

"Yes. With the noise that Mrs. Trotter described in full blast, the crack of that little revolver would easily have gone unnoticed."

Joan applied her brakes suddenly and they bumped over the last cattle-guard and turned into the highway. "What did you do while I went to see the Levys this afternoon?"

"I went through Ross's things at the bank. The only interesting discovery that I made was in his personal letter-file. The space marked 'Fordman' was empty."

"Empty?"

"Yeah. It had been quite full, too. The gap hadn't been shoved together, if you get what I mean."

"Well, I never heard of a gap being shoved together, but I think I understand," remarked Joan. "That's the first actual link, isn't it?"

"Yes," he admitted. "Shall we go by the Fordmans' now?"

"I told Marion we'd come," said Joan.

They drove along in silence until they neared the entrance gates to the Fordman estate and it was Joan, peering ahead of the area lighted by the car, who discovered the commotion at the turn-off. There were several cars lining both sides of the highway and a small crowd of excited people was milling about the gates.

Dick got out of the roadster hurriedly and ran up through the crowd. He didn't come back for some time, but when he did he had Sheriff Read in tow. They were talking and Dick was protesting angrily at something that the officer had said. Joan could hear his last few words: ". . . oughta kept this crowd out, anyhow."

The sheriff waved his hands and replied, "They got here before I did, I tell yuh!"

Dick put his foot on the running-board of the car and began, "Well, what the devil did they move the car for?"

Joan called loudly, "Dick, what has happened? Stop arguing and tell me."

He leaned down and looked in at her, his eyes vague. He was still thinking of his argument with the sheriff, who had gone back to the gate. Without saying anything, he ran around the front of the car and got in.

"Drive on up the hill," he directed. Then: "It's a hold-up. Read says some hoodlum held up Mrs. Lawrence and slugged her. Robbed her, too."

Joan started the car, but did not drive forward. She caught her breath and cried, "Is she badly hurt?"

"Still out," answered Fields shortly. "Go on. The sheriff has the gate open for you."

Joan drove through the crowd and the gates and stopped on the far side. Fields said, "Wait a minute," and climbed out of the car. He and the sheriff talked for a while longer and when he came back he was muttering angrily to himself.

"What's the matter?" asked the girl.

"Damn dumb cops," he explained, "moved the car, let this mob run all over everything. You see Mrs. Lawrence was coming down the hill here and evidently saw the gates shut. When she got out to open 'em, she was slugged and left in the road. That fellow Drexell found her just inside the gates and had to move her car and open the gates so that he could drive in and take her up the hill."

"But the gates are never closed, Dick," said Joan.

"So the sheriff says. They were closed on purpose to get her to stop the car."

The sheriff came up. "I'll ride on the runnin'-board,' he said. "I wanta see if she's come to yet."

"Having trouble with that crowd out there?" asked Dick.

"Gawd!" exclaimed the big man. "Them newspaper reporters sure have been ridin' on my tail. I bet there's fifty of 'em. They swarmed through the bob-wire an' it took me an' six dep'ties t' run 'em out agin. Got 'em all herded up now. When your boss gets here, Miss Joan, won't you please tell 'im to take 'em in hand? I ain't goin' to issue no statement 'til I'm sure what happened." He clung to the side of the car and Joan drove up the hill. She felt a little sick from the excitement of the long hard day and her mind found it hard to embrace this new story of violence.

"What do you think about it, Dick?" she asked.

"I think that Read is nerts if he thinks this is a plain hold-up," answered the man vehemently, and they climbed the rest of the way without other words.

At the top Joan parked next to the coupé which Mrs. Lawrence had driven, and Fields looked it over carefully with his flashlight. The sheriff talked with Joan.

"Where was Mrs. Lawrence going?" asked the girl.

"Wall, fur's I kin make out she was agoin' t' town," stated the officer. "Nobody knowed much about it, an' when Miss Fordman heard about it she fainted an' I ain't been able to see her yet. The fust thing I knowed somebody 'phoned in an' said to come out here quick, that there'd been a stick-up."

"Who 'phoned?" asked Joan.

"I dunno. One o' th' boys took th' call. We come right out an' found this car down at th' gate. I drove it up here."

Dick came over and asked, "Were the lights on when you found that car down the hill?"

"Naw. They was off," answered the officer.

"Did Drexell find them on?"

"I dunno."

"Did he say whether or not the engine was running when he found Mrs. Lawrence?"

"Wall, now," mused the sheriff, "I don't rightly recall whether he said it was runnin' or not."

Dick grunted slightly, and said, "I'll go and find Drexell if I can." He started for the house and Joan followed. The sheriff spat out a quid of tobacco and came with them.

As they entered the deserted foyer, Drexell appeared at the head of the stairs. He came down rapidly, greeted them without enthusiasm, and was going to pass by and go out the front door when Dick stopped him.

"I'd like to speak with you," he said pleasantly. Drexell stopped and looked at the detective without expression. They eyed each other for a long, silent moment before either spoke. In that moment Joan realized that Drexell was in a bad state of physical and mental discomposure. His eyes were bloodshot and puffy and his hands were shaking as he took them out of his pockets to light a cigarette. A three-cornered tear in the side of his linen trousers revealed a bloody cut on his leg. His hands were scratched and dirty and across the toe of one of his white buckskin shoes was a smear of blood.

He got the cigarette lighted, remembered Joan's presence, and offered the pack to her. She refused and he replaced it and his hands in his pockets.

Dick said, "The sheriff told me that you found Mrs. Lawrence. Won't you tell me the story?"

"God! I've told it six times already," was the man's reply.

"I'm sorry," said Fields, "but I haven't heard it yet, and you can appreciate the necessity of my knowing exactly what happened."

"You people should get some order into your investigation. Of all the slipshod methods I've ever seen, those of the police here are the worst." He stared at the sheriff, who protested unintelligibly. Then he smiled a little and shrugged his shoulders.

"All right, let's go into the living-room here and I'll tell it again. There's not much to tell, anyway."

Read asked, "Is Mrs. Lawrence able to talk yet?"

Drexell shook his head. "No," he said shortly.

"Well, I'll be goin'," remarked the officer and stalked across the hallway and out the door.

Joan, Dick, and Drexell went into the living-room and sat down, Fields asking, "Is the doctor still with her?"

"Yes. She's in a pretty critical state. Likely not to live through the night."

"Do you know where she was going?"

"I do not. I drove out from town and, as I started to turn in at the gates, I was surprised to find them closed. My headlights shone through the bars and I could see another car a little way back from the gates on the inside."

"The headlights were not burning on the other car?" asked the detective as Drexell paused.

"No. I thought maybe somebody had got that far and run out of gas, so I started to shove the gates open. The one on my left swung back all right, but the other one only swung halfway. I stepped inside to see what blocked it and found Mrs. Lawrence lying on the ground. I ran back to my car and got a flashlight out of the pocket, and as soon as I examined her I found that she was still living. She had a nasty scalp wound. It was still bleeding when I picked her up, or else had started again, I don't know which. It bled on my coat, so I left it in the car. I didn't want to scare Marion when I carried her in. I put her in my car and then moved Marion's coupé so that I could drive in. When I got her up to the house and carried her in, Marion was in the hallway there and fainted. She struck her head on a chair and everything was pretty hectic for a while. Finally, however, the doctor came, and with him the sheriff." Drexell paused, threw his cigarette butt away, and lighted another.

Dick said, "And you think the motive was robbery?"

"Looks like it, doesn't it? The sheriff told me that her purse was gone and I know that her engagement ring is missing."

"Engagement ring?"

"Yes. She wore an emerald, and when I got her up here both Mrs. Smith and I noticed that it was gone."

The detective rubbed his chin and stared at Drexell. "Was the engine running when you found the car?" he asked suddenly.

"No," answered the man. "No, the ignition had been cut off."

"And the lights?"

"And the lights."

"About what time did you find her?"

"I don't know exactly. It must have been a little after nine-thirty."

"Where were you prior to that time?"

"Working in my office."

"Alone?"

"No, my secretary was working with me."

"I suppose that there is a lot of work to be done getting the estate in shape and all that?"

"Yes."

"Well, Mr. Drexell, that covers things so far as the accident is concerned, but I wonder—have you been quite frank with me?"

The man stared at Fields. "Frank? What do you mean? I've told everything I know."

"We have information that leads us to believe that you and Mrs. Lawrence have known each other for quite some time," Dick stated quietly.

Drexell laughed shortly, scoffingly. "And if," he said, "we have—what about it?"

"You admit it?"

"I don't admit anything."

"Your attitude isn't a helpful one, Mr. Drexell," remarked Fields, rising. "I'd advise you to think things over. Certainly I don't envy you your position."

The man arose also, but he said nothing else.

Joan asked, "Where do they have Mrs. Lawrence?"

"In the guest-room downstairs," Drexell answered. "Marion is in her own room."

Dick said: "I must telephone. Joan, will you show me where the 'phone is?"

They left the room, leaving Drexell standing beside the arm-chair.

In the hall Joan indicated the telephone closet and Dick drew her inside.

"You must go to Marion," he directed, "and find out exactly what led Mrs. Lawrence to drive down the mountain. I'll wait for you here."

"Why, Dick? Surely you don't want me to question her now! This will be far more of a shock than her father's death was. Glieth Lawrence is her closest—"

"I know," he interrupted, "but you must do it. There's something wrong about the whole business. What was she driving to town for—alone—when there's a chauffeur here for that purpose? Why should she go, anyway? To buy something? To send a telegram? No, the telephone can be used for that. To meet someone?" He glanced at Joan and answered his question with another. "Why not meet whoever it was here? Has she ever been in Fordman before?"

"No," said Joan, fanning herself with her damp handkerchief.

"So," he continued, "she could scarcely have been going out to pay a social call. We must know why! That's the reason you will have to see Marion and find out." He frowned. "I don't like the whole set-up. An ordinary hold-up at a time like this is too coincidental."

They came out of the hot closet and Joan looked at him despairingly. "I hate to do it, Dick," she declared.

He looked at her grimly and then glanced down the empty hall. "Look here," he said softly, "I know how you feel, but remember that there've been two murders already and Mrs. Lawrence is in a critical condition. If she dies, that will make three. Three deliberate, cold-blooded murders." He paused, and then went on; "Remember, the gates were closed to stop the car. The woman was struck down. Her bag and jewelry were snatched to make the job look real. Then, to keep passers-by from finding her too soon, the car lights and the engine were switched off. Does that look like an ordinary hoodlum job? You know darn well it doesn't."

"No," admitted the girl slowly. "It doesn't."

Mrs. Smith, the elderly housekeeper, was sitting beside Marion's bed when Joan entered the room. The girl was conscious, but she looked pale and frightened. Mrs. Smith arose, saying:

"I'm glad you came, Miss Shields. She was bound to get up and I couldn't of kept her down much longer."

Joan looked at the blue lump above Marion's eyebrow. The skin was cut and the place was bleeding. She sent Mrs. Smith away for gauze and tape and sat down in her chair.

Marion asked, "How's Glieth?"

"She's all right," lied the girl. "The doctor is with her."

"Wasn't it a shame?" Marion was near tears. The blood dripped in tiny splashes on the pale-green pillow slip and she raised a handkerchief to her forehead, unconsciously.

Mrs. Smith came with the things that were needed and there was silence as Joan bathed and disinfected the lump above Marion's lovely arched eyebrow. She covered it lightly with a square of gauze and fastened the gauze in place with tape. Then she nodded to Mrs. Smith and the woman went away.

"Marion," she began, "why did Mrs. Lawrence want to go to town?"

The girl on the bed looked at her in surprise and answered: "Why, she went to meet you and Mr. Fields. He called her at eight-thirty and asked her to come to the hotel. She had been looking for him since six-thirty."

"Of course," said Joan. "Why did she want to see Dick, Marion?"

"She didn't tell me," answered the girl, shaking her head. "We had dinner downtown following the inquest—Gere took us. Mrs. Smith is all to pieces and it was more convenient, anyway. When we got home there was a letter for her. She read it and immediately tried to get in touch with Dick. When she couldn't locate him by telephone, she had Texas take her to town, but she didn't find him then. They came back within an hour."

"Don't you know what was in the letter, Marion? It might be important."

"I'm sure that it must be, Joan, but I didn't read it. I know who wrote it, however. It was from my father—"

"Your father!"

"Yes. He'd evidently written it several days ago and it had reached Houston after Glieth left to come here."

"How did it get up here so late?"

"It didn't come late. You see we were at the inquest all afternoon. It came in the afternoon mail that Texas brought out from town. Mrs. Smith put it on the hall table and it stayed there until we got home."

"Who else saw the letter, Marion?"

"Why, let me see—Mrs. Smith, Texas, and myself, of course. And Mr. Drennan was here, and Gere Drexell also. I remember I picked it up from the tray on the hall table and handed it to her. It had been forwarded here."

"So she tried to find Dick," commented Joan. "Do you know where she went when Texas took her to town?"

"No. She didn't say."

"When did the call come?"

"You mean, when did Dick Fields telephone?"

"Yes."

"About eight-thirty. We were sitting on the front porch, with Pat Drennan. Mrs. Smith called Glieth to the telephone and when she came back she asked me for the keys to the coupé, saying that she must meet you and Fields at nine-thirty. I didn't want her to drive in alone, but she just laughed at me. Mr. Drennan left in a few minutes and at about nine-fifteen Glieth said that she must go and that she'd be back in a short time. I watched her start the coupe and then I heard the telephone ring. It was Mildred Jones, and I talked to her for quite a while. I was still in the telephone booth when Gere came in with Glieth, calling for me. I was just trying to get him on the 'phone when I heard him calling. I hung up quickly and opened the door. His voice sounded so hoarse and funny. When I saw Glieth, I ran toward them and tripped on the rug. The next thing I knew, Mrs. Smith was splashing water on me and everything was in an uproar." She closed her eyes and the first tears overflowed.

"They tell me that she's very badly hurt," sobbed the girl. "Do you think she'll die?"

"I haven't talked to the doctor, darling," said Joan. "I don't think that she will. She couldn't have been hit very hard."

"Good God, Joan," she said, "what will happen next?"

Joan held her hand tightly and said nothing. She touched the bell-push on the night-stand and in a few moments Mrs. Smith reappeared. Joan got up, saying, "I'll be back right away, dear."

She went downstairs and found Dick waiting impatiently at the front door. He tossed his cigarette butt out into the darkness and said softly, "Is she all right?"

"Yes. I bathed her head and put a bandage on. The doctor is still with Mrs. Lawrence. She should have a sedative."

"Yes? Did you find out why . . . ?"

"Mrs. Lawrence was on her way to meet you," replied Joan.

"The devil . . ." began Dick, but Joan stopped him and related Marion's story.

Dick was thoughtful and took out his notebook to record the times that Joan had mentioned. He snapped the little book shut and remarked: "It's pretty clear, isn't it? Well, our murderer made a slip this time. You stay here with Marion. I want to see that chauffeur and make a quick trip to town. When the sheriff comes, tell him that I'll be right back."

He pushed the screen open, cleared the steps with one jump, vaulted over the closed door of Joan's roadster, and shot it around the oval with a roar of exhaust and a skidding swish of gravel.

Joan stood in the doorway lighting a cigarette, and her mind dwelt morbidly on the details of the catastrophe. Swearing silently, she shuddered, felt her flesh quiver, and drew her thoughts back to Marion, lying unhappily upstairs.

The telephone shrilled as she passed the tiny closet, and she answered it, to hear Mitchell White's excited voice blurt out:

"What in the name of Heaven has happened out there, Joan? We've a report that Mrs. Lawrence had an automobile accident and was killed. It wasn't suicide, was it?"

"You've got it all wrong, Mitch," said the girl. "Mrs. Lawrence was held up at the gates, knocked down, and robbed. She's badly hurt, they say. If you're going to get out an extra just for this, I'd wait for a full report, anyway."

"Oh, she wasn't killed then. How's Marion?"

"She's rather done up, of course," replied Joan, hesitating to mention Marion's fall.

"Poor kid. Would she see me, d'you think?"

"Not now, Mitch. She'd best be quiet."

"Yeah—say, listen, Joan, call me if you learn anything. Ed's on his way out now and I'm covering the telephone in case anything comes up. We'll get out that extra when we get enough dope."

He clicked off, and Joan, brought back effectively into the world of the living, ran lightly up the stairs and opened the door to Marion's room. The girl was asleep, and Mrs. Smith, sitting beside the bed, raised a finger to her lips. Joan nodded and withdrew. The hall was oppressively quiet and Joan walked to a window at the front of the house. She could hear faintly the shouts of men and the sound of cars. Evidently the sheriff was at the scene of the accident. Joan considered for a few minutes and walked to the door of the blue room that had been given to Mrs. Lawrence. She didn't know what she expected to find when she stepped inside and shut the door silently behind her. A small bed-lamp was burning on the night-table. Joan switched on the ceiling lights and saw on the floor near a small knee-hole-desk an open traveler's writing portfolio, its sheets of paper and its envelopes spilled out onto the carpet.

She knelt over it and saw that several letters had been hastily tucked into the pocket of the back flap. That they had been shoved in quickly she judged by the fact that the edges of the letters were folded over and some of them had been crammed in doubled. The untidiness of the portfolio was at such variance with Joan's estimate of the woman's character that she felt assured that it was indicative of excitement and a hurried search by Mrs. Lawrence, or of a ransacking by other hands than hers. A crumpled wad of characteristic yellow caught her eye. It was a telegram crushed into the flap. Taking a nail file from the dressing-table she poked the paper out of the pocket and opened it carefully. It *was* a telegram, addressed to Mrs. Lawrence, care of El Patio Hotel in San Antonio. It had been sent from Houston on Monday, July 3, at 4.46 P.M. and read:

MESSAGE HERE FROM M. F. TO EFFECT THAT F. HAS HAD FATAL ACCIDENT STOP SHE REQUESTS THAT YOU COME TO HER BY PLANE ARRIVING IN FORDMAN AT TWELVE-FIFTEEN SAME PLANE STOPS IN SAN ANTONIO AT ELEVEN-TWENTY-FIVE STOP HAVE ANSWERED THIS MESSAGE FROM HERE SAYING THAT YOU WILL BE ABOARD THE SHIP.

The telegram was signed "Louis."

Joan re-read its amazing contents as she knelt over the scattered sheets of the portfolio on the floor. Dazed, she leaned back against a chair and painfully considered the possibilities arising from this revelation. So Glieth Lawrence had been in San Antonio on the day her fiancé was killed.

It was a bare two hours' drive from San Antonio to Fordman.

Noises downstairs brought her to her feet. She replaced the telegram and went to the door. Taking the key from the inside, she locked the door securely and went down the hall to Marion's room. The girl had awakened and smiled faintly at Joan. Mrs. Smith was nowhere in sight.

"She went down to see who had come," explained Marion.

There was a tap at the door and Mrs. Smith entered, followed by Doctor Ross. He said, "Well, young lady, I'll patch you up now."

"How is Glieth, Doctor?" asked Marion anxiously.

"She's getting on as well as can be expected. I've got a mighty fine nurse with her now, so don't worry."

"Is she conscious yet?" inquired Joan.

"Not yet," was the doctor's short reply. He sat down beside Marion and said, "Let's see what's under this pretty bandage . . ."

Marion cut in with: "It's perfectly all right, Doctor. I'm really not hurt. Miss Shields fixed me up."

Joan left as the doctor began his examination and met the sheriff mounting the stairs.

"Glad you stayed here, Miss Joan," he greeted her. "Where's Mr. Fields?"

Joan explained his absence and told of the letter and of the 'phone call that had almost sent Mrs. Lawrence to her death.

The big man swore heavily, begged her pardon and swore again. "Miss Joan, there's a lunatic a-loose," he stated. "Fields sure it warn't no ordinary hold-up?"

"Reasonably sure."

"Wall, I gotta talk to th' doc. I wonder how long it'll be before we kin talk to her?"

"I don't know. She's still unconscious."

"Too bad, too bad. An', say, when your boss gits here, don't forgit t' tell 'im what I said about them reporters."

Joan nodded and went downstairs to sit out on the front porch. Ed Frank arrived in Mitchell's car almost before she'd lighted a cigarette, and unfolding his long, lean body, came across the central flower-bed.

"What th' hell's goin' on out here, anyway?" he asked.

Joan told him briefly, and relayed the sheriff's message regarding the reporters.

Frank laughed and replied: "Yeah. They were sure sore when I got through down there. I'll go and have a look around. Where's your friend?"

"Who?"

"The boy detective from St. Louis."

"He went to town," replied Joan, ignoring the dig.

"So he's been out here?"

"Yes, we came out together. We didn't know about Mrs. Lawrence until we got here."

"I don't suppose he's so interested in this, is he?"

"Why not?"

"Ordinary hold-up, the sheriff said." Frank's eyes twinkled.

"Ed, you're just trying to find out if I know anything!" Joan declared, laughing.

"Well," he warned, "if you do, remember you're still working for a newspaper. I'd hate to fire you." He grinned at her faintly and left. She heard the Ford skidding around the first turn.

An hour passed before Dick returned. He hurried into the hallway, his red hair on end, gleaming in the light.

"How's Mrs. Lawrence?" he asked. "Any change?"

"I don't think so," said Joan doubtfully. "The doctor is still with her. Did you find out anything in town?"

"I'll say!" He beckoned the girl into the living-room and they sat down on the red divan, facing the door.

"Our trip to the Trotters' was worth less than it should have been," he began. "If we'd come directly here, we'd have been a darn sight nearer the end, and Mrs. Lawrence wouldn't have been hurt."

"How is that?"

"It's easy to reconstruct what happened. When Mrs. Lawrence returned here following the inquest and dinner in town, she found a letter from Fordman written shortly before he was killed. It contained evidence of sufficient importance to make her—an unusually calm and thoughtful woman—desire to see me at once. The fact that she hesitated to wait until we came, as we had promised, is proof that the letter held direct and damaging information. She telephoned the hotel at six-thirty and learned that I was out. Then she called the newspaper office and asked for you, but you were out.

"Then she called the sheriff's office, but he was at a restaurant eating and no one answered the telephone, although a man in the county clerk's office heard it ring. She waited until seven o'clock and then got Wills to take her to the hotel.

"There she asked for me again, and when she was informed that I hadn't come in, requested an envelope and paper. At a desk in the lobby she wrote a message, placed it in the envelope, returned to the desk. The clerk said that it was marked with my name and 'Urgent.' He took it and promised to give it to me as soon as possible. Mrs. Lawrence left and Wills drove her home."

"How did you find out about the calls?" asked Joan.

"I talked to the switchboard girl who handles the calls from here. Naturally she listened in, especially when Mrs. Lawrence called the sheriff's office. You see, she is not only 'operator' from six to twelve, but 'information' as well. Mrs. Lawrence asked her for the numbers of the hotel, the newspaper office, and the sheriff's office. I expect that she telephoned from her room upstairs and there wasn't a book."

"And the note she left for you?" asked Joan. "What was in it?"

"I don't know," replied the man. "I didn't get it. That's why she was attacked."

"Why—what had that to do with it?"

Fields smiled wearily. "Too much. Somebody called the desk at the hotel and told the clerk to send my mail over to the sheriff's office at the courthouse immediately. He knew that I was a detective by that time, so he gave a bell-hop the note and some other mail that had come and sent him off. The call came in about ten minutes after Mrs. Lawrence had left and whoever impersonated me merely asked if there'd been any calls or letters for Mr. Fields. The man told him about the calls and the note and told him further that the note was marked urgent. So he didn't balk at all at the suggestion to send the stuff over by a boy.

"The kid told me that he walked over and knocked at Read's door. He heard voices inside and in a moment the door was opened a crack, a hand reached out and took the mail, first offering a fifty-cent piece. Then the door was promptly shut and he heard the voices again."

"And he didn't see who it was?"

"No. He said that the hall was dark and this fellow just held out a hand."

"Of all the nerve! And Read was eating supper. Why does he go off and leave his office unlocked?"

"It wasn't his office—it was the anteroom, which he doesn't lock until he's ready to go home."

Joan looked puzzled. "How could anyone have known that Mrs. Lawrence left you a note?"

"Somebody was watching her movements pretty closely," answered the detective wearily. "Of course I inquired about in the lobby, of the clerks and bellhops, but they said that they didn't see anyone suspicious. Of course they didn't—since they weren't looking for anyone. And then, it was dinner time and the lobby was crowded."

"You don't think that she left that important letter from John Fordman at the hotel, do you?" asked the girl.

"No," answered the man slowly. "No, I don't. She had it with her when she left here this evening. It was too important to leave at the hotel. But whoever called her on the 'phone, asking her to meet me, knew that she was carrying it—no doubt asked her to bring it. That's why—"

"That's why she was nearly killed," interrupted Joan. "Because of John Fordman's letter to her!"

"Yes, the murderer was afraid of that letter, and of her, because she had read it."

"Why do you suppose she didn't confide in Marion?" asked Joan.

"Because of what was in the letter," answered the man, drawing from his pocket a large square envelope. He handed it to the girl, smiling.

"Dick! You are a devil, leaving me in this suspense," she said crossly as she unfolded the paper. It read:

Saturday night

My Dearest Glieth,
It's good news at last, my darling. I won't go into detail—enough to say that I bought him off. It cost

me a quarter of a million in cash, but it was worth it. He turned over everything—the papers, photographs, and the affidavits that could have ruined me—ruined our future together.

For a year I have been paying—never sure that even the huge payments I made were protection. God knows I've paid in money and in anguish for my two greatest sins—that woman and the desire to make more and more money. It was so easy to pipe off extra oil—hidden pipe-lines or several dummy derricks could increase my production ten or twenty times— the inspectors were crooked and everybody did it, still do it. But I'll swear I quit, when I met you.

And then—when I could see my way clear to run for governor, to marry you and make up for my weaknesses and my failings, this blow fell. It is incredible how a man could have conceived such a thing.

Oh, well, it's all over now. I'm keeping the whole amazing document, however, for you to see. Gave it to Ross to put in safe-deposit. I never thought that anyone could be as thorough. He has watched my every movement for years. There are snapshots from Juarez, Chicago, New Orleans. There are photostats of hotel registers and so on. All of this, my dear, was many years ago, but people would not stop to think of that.

There were affidavits from two inspectors admitting that they'd accepted bribes. There are a dozen photostats of checks. There is even a map of the oil field showing accurately the whereabouts of secret pipe-lines that carried the hot oil.

It makes me shudder to think what the papers could and would have done with this if they'd gotten it. And what could I say to the fine men who are urging me to run for governor? "Gentlemen, I am afraid to run. I have an enemy who would delight to ruin my reputation. He has proof of my dishonesty and my sinful past." Could I say that? Hardly!

Thank God, I can say it to you—have said it to you. You are so wise and understanding. That's why I want to bring you closer to Marion. She needs you and your love, my dear.

How strong and confident I feel tonight! For the first time I believe that I know who this blackmailer is, and what is more, I shall be sure of his identity soon. The money I gave him is marked, and I shall trap him in a web of his own weaving. I am arranging to prove that it was stolen from my library safe and when I send the officers for him, they will find evidence enough to send him up for many years. But enough of this.

Marion tells me that she is planning to drive down next week to visit the Hendricks and will bring you back to me. I count the days!

Always yours

John

Joan refolded the letter and returned it to Dick.

"It must have been an awful blow to get that after he was dead," she said sadly. Then, "Where did you find it?"

"Under the car seat," he answered. "You see, her bag was gone, and I took it for granted that the letter was in that, but on my way back from town I decided to look again. Evidently her purse was too small to take the envelope—it's an extra big one—so she put it on the seat beside her and it slipped behind. Lucky, huh?" He grinned at her.

"I should say," agreed the girl. "But, Dick, it doesn't say *who!* It isn't much help, really."

"No, it doesn't, but I'm thankful for small favors. It clears up the motive, though, and opens several lines of further investigation." He drew out his notebook and wrote slowly, reading aloud as he wrote:

1. The murderer is a man.
2. He has 'watched' his victim for several years, therefore he must be closely associated with Fordman, as he did not excite his suspicion.
3. He has received for a year 'huge payments' from Fordman. This money was paid over either by cash or by check and Fordman's accounts should be examined.
4. The blackmailer has this money. Is it in a bank— as an ordinary account; in safe-deposit; invested; or has it been hidden intact?
5. Where is the 'quarter of a million' in marked bills and how were they marked? Did anybody know that Fordman was raising this much money in actual cash?
6. Where have the photostatic copies of checks, etc., been made? Locally—near-by—far away?
7. What inspectors in state oil commission took bribes from Fordman and were willing to sell the information to the blackmailer? They must have been discharged or resigned.
8. What private detective agencies in towns mentioned might have assisted in the gathering of the 'evidence'?
9. Who could have known of the positions of the pipelines carrying 'hot oil'?

As Dick finished this list, Joan frowned. "It'll take so long," she objected, "to find out all of those things."

"Yes," admitted the man. "But they'll tell us the story!" He paused, and then continued: "Things have been going too fast, anyhow. This hasn't been an investigation—it's been a footrace."

Joan laughed. "It would help to get some sleep," she said.

"Well," said Fields, with satisfaction, "we've learned that the murderer is a man and that he is most methodical and patient. I believe that we know the actual motive for Fordman's killing—the man learned that his victim had given him hot money and was planning to trap him. Undoubtedly that's it."

"How would he know?" asked Joan.

Fields shrugged his shoulders. "Maybe Fordman told him, thinking that he was telling a friend. Remember, he wasn't *sure* as to the fellow's identity."

Joan remembered what she had found upstairs and they went to Mrs. Lawrence's room together. Fields looked about carefully and, stooping, as Joan had done, studied the portfolio and its contents.

Joan urged, "It's the telegram, there." She pointed and he pulled out the yellow paper.

The man read the message and looked up at Joan. "Who is Louis?" he asked.

Joan shrugged. "Maybe," she offered, "Marion knows."

Dick went through the letters and commented: "Here are two from Marion; one from somebody who signs himself 'Sincerely, H.'; a note from Riese and Riese, stock-brokers, stating that they must have eight thousand dollars additional collateral without delay; a bill for eight hundred and ninety dollars and fifty-nine cents from Saks, Fifth Avenue, in New York; but nowhere do I find any communication from her fiancé, John Fordman."

"She must have been rather hard up," remarked Joan.

"Not necessarily," was the reply. "The Saks bill is dated July 1 and shows no unpaid balance. The broker's letter is dated June 29. She may have raised the eight thousand before she left Houston. But I can't understand why she didn't carry any letters from Fordman!" He glanced about the room and spotted a gray fabric-covered case on a stand. It was not locked and he rummaged slowly through its meager contents, carefully replacing Mrs. Lawrence's fragile under-things as he found them. In a blue silk handkerchief case, folded in a lace handkerchief, he found a snapshot. Joan came over and looked at it.

It was one that had been taken by the smallest of folding cameras, and although it was barely two inches square every detail was perfect. A man wearing the uniform of a commissioned officer, complete with boots, visored cap, and crop, stood with his back against the body of a plane, half hiding the emblem painted on the plane's side. He was leaning against the ship, holding his stick in both hands and smiling a little, as if he were embarrassed.

Joan stared at the little photograph, wondering what was wrong with it. Something didn't fit. She was trying to decide whether it was the ship or the uniform when Dick said, "I thought Mrs. Lawrence's husband was a U.S. flyer."

"He was," answered the girl.

Fields pointed a big finger at the snapshot. "This guy has on a British Royal Air Force uniform," he told her. "And that emblem behind him was never painted on a U.S. ship."

The girl stared at the little picture and saw that he was right, but she saw something else.

"That, that fellow," she declared, "is Gere Drexell, or I am crazy!"

Fields looked more closely at the picture and nodded his head. "You're right, Joan," he agreed. "It's Drexell, without a doubt."

"It doesn't look like an old snapshot," commented the girl. "Do you suppose she's had it ever since the war?"

The man turned it over, but there was no writing on the back. "No," he said, "I believe that this has been printed recently." He took out an envelope and put the little picture safely away, saying: "Well, I'll ask that fellow a few more questions. It's sure funny Mrs. Lawrence being engaged to Fordman and carrying this bird's photograph around in her handkerchief case."

Joan sighed. "I'll go home on that," she said. "I'm too tired to stay up any longer."

They walked down the stairs together and Fields told her that he and the local officers would hold an informal court of inquiry the next morning in his rooms, starting at nine o'clock. On the porch they found Ed Frank talking to the sheriff.

Ed said: "Got your car, Joan? I'll take you home."

"Thanks, Ed, I'll let you. Dick, you keep the roadster. I'll get Dad to drive me down in the morning."

They got into Mitchell's Ford and Ed drove more carefully than usual down the long hill, through the crowd of newspaper men and curious townspeople, who had been checked at the gates, and out onto the macadam.

"Want a drink, Joan, or a sandwich?" inquired the man.

"No, thanks, Ed. Just need sleep."

"Come on an' have a drink with me, anyway," he urged. "You've never so honored me. Tonight's a good one to start with."

Joan realized suddenly that he had had several drinks himself. She'd never known him to drink before.

"What are you doing with liquor on your breath, Ed?" she asked. "I thought that you drove the water wagon."

"Had t' drink with the boys back there," he replied. The liquor betrayed him only by its odor and by a slight softening of his usually clipped and acid speech. He wasn't drunk, but he was very near to being.

"Stop at the hamburger place, Ed," Joan commanded. "I would like some coffee. Don't you want a hamburger?"

"Sure," he replied, "sure."

They drew up near the large hot-pig stand, a proud object made of two huge wooden pig silhouettes outlined with electric lights. A comfortable kitchen and long counter had been built between the foot-thick porkers, and over this counter passed a never-ending stream of hamburger, barbecue sandwiches, soda, home-brew, and, to the initiated, occasional Mason jars filled with amber corn liquor.

Joan and Ed ordered coffee and sandwiches and while they waited he took another drink from his flask.

"You know," he confided, "I feel pretty low."

"Why?" asked Joan. "It looks to me as if you ought to feel pretty high. You've got a great story and I expect that you'll soon be general manager of all the Fordman papers."

"Oh, yeah," he shrugged, "that—I mean inside of me. Those things don't mean much."

Joan nodded understandingly. "They really don't," she agreed. Then, "Do you just have the doldrums generally? I do."

"Yeah—" The drink began to take effect and he muttered to himself. Remembering her he said clearly: "My wife died three years ago tonight. She died an' the baby died."

"Oh, Ed. I'm so sorry. I didn't even know you'd been married." Joan put a comforting hand on his as it hung limply on the steering-wheel. Frank immediately brought it to life and clung tightly to her, even while the boy arranged their window tray and pocketed the coins he placed there with his left hand.

He let her have her hand while they drank their coffee in silence, but he took it again when they were ready to drive into town. Joan reflected sleepily that knowledge breeds sympathy just as surely as ignorance breeds distrust and in about the same ratio. She was surprised that she hadn't heard about Ed's tragedy before. Fordman was a small town and usually missed nothing. Still, Ed didn't talk to people generally and tonight he'd had several drinks.

But he was sober when they reached Joan's house. Sober and doubly sarcastic. Annoyed with himself, he snapped: "I'm an ass. Forget it, Joan, whatever I said about myself. Don't want sympathy"—he caught her eye and added, smiling a little—"but I'd like a kiss."

His mouth was eager and he held her firmly and comfortably. They sat quietly in the car until the porch light went on and Mrs. Shields called softly, "Joan."

Regretfully, sleepily, Joan got out of the roadster and left Ed with a soft "good night."

Her mother held the door open for her, saying: "I didn't mean to hurry you, dear, but you haven't had any sleep in so long and I haven't seen you for days. Where on earth have you been?"

Joan realized that her mother hadn't heard about Mrs. Lawrence's accident and decided not to tell her until morning. She drank a glass of milk and ate several pieces of cold fried chicken and a bowl of baked custard with thick cream, before undressing and dropping wearily into bed.

As sleepy as she had been a half-hour before, she found that her mind was abnormally awake and active now that her body was comfortable. The fantastic and unbelievable happenings of the last three days paraded through her thoughts.

She found that she could evolve no workable, plausible theory to fit all of the cases. It was obvious that Mrs. Lawrence had been attacked because of the letter, but the attacker had certainly bungled by not retrieving that dangerous document.

She thought of the telegram found in Mrs. Lawrence's room, and of the snapshot. Suddenly her mind, groping for some familiar fact, recalled the bridge clipping from the San Antonio paper. With San Antonio only two hours away, why not believe that the paper that had carried the clipping had been brought to Fordman by someone who had spent the week-end there? Fordman residents 'ran over' constantly. Who else could have been there on the week-end? She tried to recall paragraphs from her Sunday 'News of Personal Interest' column: Mr. and Mrs. Joe Shotts, and daughter, Betty Joe, are visiting relatives in San Antonio over the week-end . . . Wilson Phillips and family motored to San Antonio Saturday . . . and so on.

She marked this duty in her mind, to scan carefully the *News* and the papers of the city in question for some clue as to who might have returned to Fordman with the clipping that she had found. Then she slid peacefully into the cool current of sleep.

XV: THURSDAY, JULY 6: 10.00 A.M.

Mrs. Shields saw to it that Joan slept until late on Thursday morning and it was ten o'clock before she had breakfasted. She called Dick Fields at the hotel and learned that the interviewing had already begun. He also told her that Mrs. Lawrence had not regained consciousness.

"Joan," he said, "when you come down, let yourself into the bedroom with that key I gave you. I have Millbank and the sheriff in with me and a court stenographer. You can listen without being seen. If the 'phone rings, answer it and take any message that might come to the door. I'll drop in to see you every now and then." He hesitated, and then continued: "Listen closely, Joan. You know these people pretty well and should be able to catch anything off-color more fully than I could. Oh, yes, bring Jimmie with you. I've some errands for him to run." He hesitated again, and then said: "I've got to break this case today. Millbank's had word that the Governor's sending somebody from Austin tomorrow to investigate the progress he's made."

He hung up, and Joan telephoned a friend who would do her routine work at the office. When the woman had agreed, she found Jimmie, called a taxi, and they drove quickly to the Fredrick Hotel.

Deputy Tom Harte sat in a chair tilted back against the wall near the door to Dick's living-room. Joan waved to him and let herself into the bedroom. A table and a chair had been placed at the slightly open door leading into the living-room. Paper and pencils had been provided and there was a note from Dick with a small package. The note read:

> Have Jimmie take this handkerchief out to Belinda for identification. She'll do more for him than for an officer.

Jimmie left, promising to come back before lunch, and Joan settled down at the table. She could see through the crack at the hinged side of the door, and, though the visible field was limited, she could glimpse Dick's white-clad leg under a table in front of which stood an empty chair.

Judge Millbank's suety voice came to her. "Who's next, my boy?"

Fields answered crisply, "I'd like to see Drexell, if he's here yet."

Sheriff Read walked across Joan's line of vision, saying, "He's acrost th' hall."

Drexell came in with Read, and Joan put her eye close to the crack. She could see him clearly. He was in a better humor than he had been the evening before and saluted his inquisitors briskly.

"Anything I can do to help, gentlemen?" he inquired, and added: "But I'd like to get away quickly. The new well's gone on the rampage and broken through the capping. Day sent for me at six this morning and I've only just run in to see what was wanted here." He was dressed in serviceable brown breeches with laced boots and a khaki shirt open at the throat. His black hair, with the white triangle at the temples, was carefully brushed. He carried a moderately sized Stetson, old and faded, but quite clean.

Fields shuffled some papers on his desk table and suddenly began his questioning.

"When you drove out to the Fordmans' place last night, Mr. Drexell, did you see anyone—pass anyone you knew?"

"No."

"And you saw no one on the Fordman property?"

"Not a soul." The man's voice was positive.

"Have you ever seen this?" questioned the detective.

The man leaned forward and then settled back in his chair, holding a slip of paper in his hands. Joan recognized it as the bridge clipping.

"It's Hall's article," he remarked. "I've not seen this particular one." He was silent for a moment as he scanned the clipping. Then he cried out, "Say, did you notice that the problem was submitted by someone in Fordman?"

"Yes," Fields answered. "Who do you think would have sent it in, Mr. Drexell?"

But Drexell did not answer at once. He was still reading the article, and when he did look up, it was not to reply to Dick's question, but to state: "I know this hand. It was played here two months ago during the Contract Tournament at the Country Club. It just about broke up the party. Mrs. Clarence Jones and her partner got it, unfortunately."

"How was that?" asked the detective.

"Why, Mrs. Jones and her partner, Mitchell White, were playing East and West. Mrs. Jones was East. North and South bid and made six hearts, doubled and redoubled, which netted them twelve hundred and twenty points. Mrs. Jones insisted that White could have bid his hand differently, thus giving them the contract at six clubs or, if their opponents insisted on bidding, at seven spades. As Hall says here, seven spades goes down two tricks or two hundred and fifty points, as against twelve hundred and twenty gained by North and South. If they'd got it at six clubs doubled and redoubled, they'd have made a neat eleven hundred and eighty points.

"They argued about it—or rather Mrs. Jones did—for almost an hour. Then the argument got to be general and we had a hard time getting things going again. Frank, the newspaper fellow, was quite interested in it, and so was I. We couldn't decide on the correct form of bidding to arrive at a decent declaration by East and West, so Mrs. Jones suggested that we send the problem to Hall and let him settle it. I think that she did so." Drexell concluded his long speech and looked at his watch.

Dick said, "But you've never seen this particular clipping?"

"No." Drexell leaned forward and laid the paper on the table.

Joan remembered something. She should have remembered it long ago. It was a small item that Mitch had written and tossed onto her desk for the society columns early last Monday morning. The item, only faintly remembered because she had not composed it herself, had read in effect:

> Miss Marion Fordman and Gerard Drexell spent the week-end in San Antonio visiting friends.

At that moment the telephone rang and as she arose to answer it, Dick appeared in the doorway.

"Expecting a call," he explained, as he walked across the room and lifted the receiver.

"Yes," he said into the mouthpiece. Then, "Yes," and in a few moments another "Yes" closed the conversation.

Joan told him about the item that she had recalled.

He returned to the living-room, resumed his seat, and said to Drexell, "Were you in San Antonio last week-end—on Saturday, to be more specific?"

"Last Saturday?" repeated the man curiously.

"Yes."

"Well, let me see. Yes, Miss Fordman and I drove over."

"And yesterday at noon, Mr. Drexel!—where were you then?"

"Another alibi?" asked the man. He was not annoyed.

"Call it that," agreed the detective.

"Well, I talked with you at the airport at about twelve-thirty, wasn't it?"

"Twelve-fifteen," corrected Fields.

"Then I came in town and had luncheon here at this hotel. After that I drove out to the oil field. Got there about two, I believe."

"Thanks," said Fields. "You seem to resent my questions less today than you did last night," he remarked.

Drexell laughed easily. "I was pretty upset last night," he said in way of apology.

"Yes, I can imagine that you were," agreed the detective. "I asked you a question then that I'd like to ask again," he continued quietly. "I refer to the information that I have concerning your acquaintance with Mrs. Lawrence." He paused, then added: "Don't think that I'm prying into your personal affairs to no purpose, Mr. Drexell. Everything pertaining to Mrs. Lawrence is of interest to us in this investigation. Surely you must understand that?"

Joan peered through the crack to stare at Drexell. His face was expressionless, but the girl felt that he was trying to come to some decision in his mind. Then he shrugged his shoulders and suggested, "Why don't you wait and question Mrs. Lawrence?"

"We may not be able to do that," answered Fields.

The man's jaw tightened, but he made no comment.

Fields opened an envelope and flicked the snapshot that he and Joan had found the evening before across the table. Drexell picked it up and glanced at it. Then he tossed it back to Fields and laughed rather unpleasantly.

"Look here," he began, "I'll tell you about that, but I'd rather tell you alone. I don't want it all over the town." He looked pointedly at Millbank, who began to puff and protest.

Dick said, "I'm sure that the Judge and the sheriff wouldn't think of repeating anything said here—in confidence, you know." But Joan thought: "You don't know 'em. Old Millbank is the worst gossip in town."

Evidently Drexell had the same idea, for he remarked, "Take it or leave it."

Fields said, "How about it, Judge?" And presently Millbank and Read and the stenographer left the room.

Drexell sighed. "I didn't want this to be known in view of the circumstances until Fordman's murder had been cleared up," he stated, "but it'll be better if you know the truth."

"Much better," encouraged the detective.

Without any further preliminaries the man plunged into his story. "Mrs. Lawrence," he declared, "was not going to marry John Fordman. She was going to marry me. She still is going to marry me," he added.

Fields interrupted, "Did Fordman know this?" he asked.

"No," answered the man. "I don't believe that Glieth had told him. She said that she would tell him while she was here on this visit."

"And what caused this change on her part?" inquired the detective.

Drexell rubbed his hands together between his trim brown-clad knees. "Well, you couldn't say it was a sudden change, exactly. You see the Old Man—Fordman, I mean—rather rushed her off her feet last year. Their engagement hadn't been announced. He just took it for granted, I think, and told everybody. You know, Fordman was always apt to get a thing by wanting it hard enough."

"But I don't see just where you come in, Mr. Drexell," remarked Fields curiously.

The man caught his lower lip between his white teeth and considered his next words carefully. "Well, you see I met Mrs. Lawrence a good many years ago. I knew her husband in France and, when I came back to the United States, I looked her up. She was living in New York at the time. We kept up our acquaintanceship over a period of years, even after she moved back to Houston, which had formerly been her home. Then, when Marion went abroad last year and Glieth was in New York at the time of her return, I wrote to them both and had them meet. John went East to meet Marion and she introduced him to Glieth. He fell pretty hard for her, of course." The man stopped talking and leaned back in his chair, glancing at his wrist watch.

Fields said, "And Fordman didn't know that you knew Mrs. Lawrence?"

"No, I don't believe that he did. You see we had very little personal contact and, though I went down to Houston several times to see Glieth, I'm sure that he didn't know, or care, why I went."

"Weren't you surprised when you found that Mrs. Lawrence was considering marriage with Fordman?"

The man laughed shortly. "I certainly was," he admitted readily.

"And did you do anything to cause Mrs. Lawrence to change her mind?"

"Yes. I went down to Houston and we talked it over. She decided that she had made a mistake."

"In not having accepted you?"

"I hadn't asked Glieth to marry me, until then," stated the man quietly.

"Oh." Fields was a little nonplussed, but he rallied quickly. "But you did ask her then?"

"I didn't exactly ask her," said the man, smiling. "We just took it for granted—both of us."

Joan thought, "He's terribly in love with her!"

"So Mrs. Lawrence was going to break the news to Fordman during her visit here?" asked Fields.

"Yes."

"Why were you afraid to admit that you and Mrs. Lawrence knew each other?" asked the detective. "You told Miss Shields that you did not know her at all."

"It was a mistake to believe that we could keep our relationship quiet until things had blown over," admitted the man.

"And did Mrs. Lawrence agree to this secret between you?"

"She thought it wise," declared Drexell.

"After you suggested it?"

"All along."

"Why was Mrs. Lawrence in San Antonio during the past week?"

"She had been visiting friends."

"At the El Patio Hotel?"

"Not that I know of. She was visiting friends on a ranch several miles south of the city." Drexell was growing restive. He had picked up his hat from the floor and was twirling it in his hands.

Fields said: "Thanks, I guess that's all for now, Mr. Drexell. Do you stay here at the Fredrick, by the way?"

"No. I've moved over to the Mesa. The service here's rotten lately and the prices are too high."

"Thanks. You can go now."

Drexell left hurriedly.

Immediately Joan heard Harte say: "Mr. Fields, here's Mr. Fordman's secretary. He wants t' see you."

"O.K." came Dick's voice.

The newcomer walked hesitantly into Joan's line of vision and sat down. He was a small, sandy-colored man, thin and stooped. He looked around at Judge Millbank, who had followed him into the room.

"I didn't know about Mr. Fordman until yesterday, Judge," he said.

The Judge introduced Fields, who began his questioning with "Where have you been?"

"Why, I've been out in New Mexico, near Ruidoso, to be exact, fishing. I go every year."

"When did you go, Mr. Squires?"

"I left a week ago Monday," stated the little man. "I wasn't due back until the coming Monday," he added hurriedly.

"How was it that you failed to hear of your employer's death?"

"I don't get the paper up there. You see I stay in a cabin back up in the hills with some friends. We came into the village yesterday morning for supplies and I saw a paper. I was horrified. I still don't know much about it. The paper that I saw was a Tuesday edition of the El Paso *Times* and it had nothing at all about Mr. Ross's death. I found that out only this morning. Of course I left Ruidoso right away and drove in. I drove all night," he added.

"That was the thing to do, Mr. Squires," commented Dick absently. "We'll probably need your help soon. Right now I want to know about Mr. Fordman's bank accounts. Did you draw his checks and keep the stubs?"

"Oh, no. He drew them himself, from his personal account, and never filed the stubs at all. If he overdrew, he was notified and made further deposits from other accounts." The man looked worried. "It wasn't very business-like," he added, "but I couldn't do anything with him."

"Of course not," agreed the detective. "The records will be at the bank, anyway. Did he keep statements?"

"He didn't, but I did," answered Squires promptly. "I have them all. They cover about seven years."

"How long have you been Mr. Fordman's secretary?"

"Just seven years come this September."

"Like him?"

"Like him? Why, yes, sir!" The man looked frightened.

"Yeah?" remarked Fields. Then, "Squires, what is a photostat?"

"A photostat?" The little secretary was bewildered at the sudden change in questioning. "Why, a photostat is a—you know—you have a photostatic copy made of a check if a payment is in question," he finished hesitantly, peering at Fields through his pince-nez.

"That is right. Have you had any made lately?" asked the detective.

"No, sir," was the positive reply. "Nobody questioned Mr. Fordman's payments. You see I always keep receipts on file. I have ever since I started working for Mr. Fordman."

"Do you know what 'hot oil' is?"

"Yes."

"Did Mr. Fordman ever 'run' any hot oil to your knowledge?"

Squires blushed and looked at the Judge. Clearing his throat he answered loudly, "No."

Dick grinned and nodded. "Of course. Can you think of anything that might help us out, Mr. Squires? Even something that might seem of little importance to you?"

"No, sir. I'll think, though," he promised.

"Where do you live?" asked Fields.

"At the Mesa Hotel now, since Miss Fordman has returned. Usually I live at the Fordman house."

"Well, keep in touch with us. You can probably help Miss Fordman and Mr. Drennan now. You'd better report to her."

Squires left, and Dick came in to talk with Joan.

"Waiting on the Joneses," he said. "What did you think of Drexell's story?"

"You could have knocked me over with a feather," admitted the girl.

"There are holes in it."

"Poor Marion," commented Joan. "No wonder he wasn't interested in her."

"Well, it looks as if Mrs. Lawrence was just playing Fordman to get Drexell to tumble. He's a reticent fellow, isn't he?"

"Very."

"Still, Fordman died mighty convenient. Saved her a nasty scene with him."

"Do you suppose that Drexell's story is true?"

"We can't check on it until Mrs. Lawrence comes out of the coma she's in," said the man. "He may have exaggerated when he said that they had come to an agreement. It looks like it when you remember that she started to recognize him out there at the airport and he shut her off. She hadn't been tipped to keep quiet then."

"I like her," stated Joan irrelevantly. "That was a slick suit she had on yesterday."

Fields laughed and walked to the window.

"What on earth is that?" he called suddenly.

She came and stood beside him, looking beyond the fringes of the town and out across the high prairie land that lay in the north. A low, reddish-gray cloud hung along the horizon, stretching as far to the east and west as one could see.

"Oh, hell!" said Joan warmly. "It's a sand-storm." She watched the huge curtain of yellow dust advancing slowly toward the town. "Why does there have to be a sand-storm? It's so hot now that I can hardly breathe and that will be the last straw—unless it brings rain. Then you'll witness the edifyin' spectacle of a rain of mud."

"How long will it be before it hits here?" inquired Dick.

"Oh, it's a long way off. Probably four or five hours yet. This is an odd time of the year for one. They usually come in the spring so that they can ruin the young crops, but I guess that the drought is responsible."

Fields turned from the window. "You know," he remarked, "I can't make up my mind whether that fellow Drexell is a bounder or not. You can't grasp him, somehow."

"That's so," agreed the girl.

He shrugged and changed the subject. "I got reports from Dallas. The bullets were fired from the guns I sent, all right. Expected that. Oh, yes. The prints on the cartridge clip of the large automatic belonged to Ross, just as I had expected. The others were Drexell's, as he stated."

ADA E. LINGO

"Nothing helpful," Joan said.

"No. Most of the trails end like that—in blind alleys."

The sheriff rapped on the door and opened it at the same time. "Howdy, Miss Joan," he said vaguely, and to Fields: "The Joneses come. You gotta handle 'em. I can't think of all th' things to ask like you do," he complimented.

He and Fields re-entered the living-room and Joan adjusted the door so that she could look directly at Clarence Jones as he sat in the chair in front of Dick's desk.

"Looky here—" began the groceryman.

But Dick broke in with: "Now, Mr. Jones, we'd appreciate your help. Just answer a few questions. You made a statement as to your whereabouts at the time of the shooting of the Fordman well. You were sitting in your car. Correct?"

"Yes," answered Jones. "I was with my wife, Mildred, my daughter, and Ed Frank, the editor of the paper."

"Very good. How long had you been there before the explosion occurred?"

"Why, I was there all the time. I never got out of the car. Neither did my wife."

"Was there someone with you all of the time?"

"No. We just sat there by ourselves."

"How did it happen that you and your family attended the shooting of the well, Mr. Jones?"

"Why shouldn't we of gone?" countered the man.

"No reason," replied Fields. "It's a routine question, you know."

"Well, I'm a stockholder in the Fordman Oil Company an' I gotta right to see th' wells shot," explained the man. "Besides, John asked me to come," he added.

"You said that your daughter was in the car with you when the explosion occurred, but she was not there all of the time. When did she leave you?"

"Mildred?" the man repeated stupidly.

"Yes. Did Miss Jones leave the car?"

"I believe she did," said the man slowly. "She and Frank came up just before the explosion."

"Together?"

"Yes."

"But neither you nor Mrs. Jones left the car?"

"No." The man was patently nervous. His small, sharp Adam's apple slid quickly up and down as he swallowed and he bit his lower lip with his squirrel-like upper teeth.

"What were your relations with Mr. Fordman, Mr. Jones?"

"I don't know what you mean."

"I mean, were you friendly?"

"Yes, friendly."

"You had nothing against Mr. Fordman?"

"No, of course not. Why should I?"

"*I* don't know, Mr. Jones. That's what I'm trying to ascertain. Where were you between twelve and one on Tuesday?"

"I was home."

"Who else was at home?"

"My wife."

"A servant?"

"No. My wife gave her the day off. You see she was going to a party, but after Mr. Fordman's death she didn't think she should. They were old friends, you know." The last statement was made quickly. Jones was pale, but not quite so agitated.

"Then you were alone with your wife?"

"Yes."

"She got lunch—I mean dinner—for you?"

"No. I got something myself from the icebox. She felt ill and went to bed."

"Did you see her between twelve and one?"

"No. I don't think so. I talked to her, though, through the door."

"What did you talk to her about?"

"I asked her if she wanted some tea or coffee, or anything to eat."

"Did she?"

"No."

"Why not?"

"I think she was asleep," Jones admitted slowly.

"Then she didn't answer you?"

"No."

"Did you look in to see if she was asleep?"

"No."

"Why not?"

"Why should I? Besides, the door was locked."

"Then you did not see your wife between twelve and one, and she didn't see you?"

"Well, if you want to put it that way."

"Your daughter wasn't at home?"

"No. I don't know where she was."

"Where were you last night before I saw you at the club upstairs?"

"At home."

"You stay at home a great deal, don't you, Mr. Jones?"

"Nothing wrong in that," answered the groceryman indignantly.

"No," agreed Dick, "but why did you leave home and go to the club at such a late hour? When, exactly, did you leave your home, by the way?"

"About ten, I guess," answered Jones sullenly.

"Then it wasn't your car that was seen turning into the road up to the Fordman estate at nine o'clock?" asked Dick in conversational tones.

The man stared at him and jumped to his feet. "No," he shouted, "it wasn't! You can't prove it! You're just trying to get me to say something that will ruin me."

"Why *ruin* you, Mr. Jones?" interrupted Dick.

"*I* know that somebody tried to murder Mrs. Lawrence. Everybody in town knows it. By God, you'd better catch whoever's doing this. It's awful! I'm nearly crazy, anyway. You'd better watch that man Drexell. He's no good. He gets ten thousand dollars and he'll get the girl, too. But, by God, he'd better stay away from my wife! I'll kill him! I'll kill him!" Jones screamed the last in sheer rage, pounding on the desk in front of Dick. Joan had arisen and was peering through the door.

Something made her glance toward the hall, and there she saw Agnes Jones, staring at her husband with loathing and contempt.

"Clarence!" she said sharply. The man halted his tirade, fist high in the air. He looked around at the woman and smiled foolishly and uncertainly.

Dick waited for something to develop, but no other word was spoken. Jones dropped back into his chair and Mrs. Jones returned to the room across the hall.

Harte's face popped in. Looking flustered and angry he said: "Hell's far, boss. *I* couldn't do nothin' with 'er. She wuz quicker'n a wild cayuse."

"It's all right, Harte." Dick gestured Jones out and asked him to send his wife in. The grocer hesitated at the door, but finally did as he was told.

Agnes Jones came in immediately and sat down. She was well dressed in a smart black-and-white linen suit. Her heavy dark-red hair had been waved that morning and lay close to her head under a crisp white linen hat. There were smudged purple shadows under her gray eyes, but her poise was complete and certain.

"I shall be direct with you, Mrs. Jones," began Fields. "I'll tell you what we know about you and I hope that you'll give us some help."

"You are investigating the death of John Fordman and Samuel Ross?" questioned the woman quietly.

"And the attack on Mrs. Glieth Lawrence," stated the detective.

"Yes?"

"You didn't know that Mrs. Lawrence was attacked, Mrs. Jones?"

"I have heard talk," said the woman frankly, "but I don't believe all that I hear."

"Your husband believed it."

"Yes?"

Joan felt that Dick wasn't getting much 'forrarder' on this line and he evidently decided the same thing because his next question, rapped out suddenly, was most unexpected.

"Where were you on Tuesday between twelve and one, Mrs. Jones?"

"I was at home," came the calm reply.

"Alone?"

"No, my husband was there also."

"Your husband states that he did not see you between twelve and one. Where were you?"

"In my bed."

"Asleep?"

"No."

"Did you hear Mr. Jones come to your door and speak to you?"

"Yes."

"Did you answer him?"

"No."

"Why not?"

"My husband is a fool. I preferred not to talk to him."

There was a short silence. Joan smiled to herself. Chick Jones was a fool. He probably drove his wife crazy with his endless questions and his hangdog air.

"What time did your husband leave home last night, Mrs. Jones?" began Fields again.

"I could not say. I was in bed, asleep," answered the woman flatly.

"You were John Fordman's mistress for several years, weren't you?" asked Fields casually.

"Yes," was the non-committal reply.

"What were your feelings when you found that he was planning marriage with Mrs. Lawrence?"

"My feelings are my own business and have no place here," stated Mrs. Jones.

"Did John Fordman provide for you when he broke off the affair?" was Fields's brutal question.

The woman went white and her eyes narrowed, but her reply was clear and low. "You are insulting, Mr. Fields."

Dick rustled some papers on his desk. His next words were deferential. "I'm sorry. There are things I must know. Is this your signature?"

Agnes Jones leaned forward and sat back in her chair holding a slip of white paper.

"Yes," she said. "Where did you get this?" Her composure was somewhat shaken.

"That check came in too late to be mailed to you with your regular monthly statement, Mrs. Jones. It was still in the bank. It tells us that you withdrew yesterday three thousand dollars from your account in the Fordman National. Are you planning to leave town soon?"

"No," said the woman. "I am making an investment."

"Payable in cash?" inquired Fields.

Mrs. Jones looked at him for a moment, and then said calmly: "I don't know why I *should* tell you. It is my own business. But I will tell you. I withdrew my money, yes. I withdrew it to get out of this Goddamned nasty little town. I've had enough. I'm sick of it. I'm sick of the lying, the pretense, the peering, self-righteous women. I'm sick of my husband. I was sick of John Fordman long before he tired of me. All I wanted was money—enough money to get me out and away from here. Well, I've enough now and I'm going. My daughter can stay here with her father. She hates me, anyway." The woman's voice rose exultantly. "I got enough out of John Fordman and I'd have had more—" she stopped suddenly.

"What do you mean, 'more'?" asked Fields.

"Nothing," was the cautious, sullen reply.

"Oh, come, now, Mrs. Jones," said Fields sharply. "You must have had something else in mind. Unless you tell us, we have only one thing to think, and it's not so nice."

"What do you mean?"

"Blackmail," was the detective's incisive reply.

"Blackmail? Oh, no. I'd never have done that to John." The woman's voice rose, "Not that," she repeated.

"What else can we think, Mrs. Jones? Fordman was about to marry. He stopped your allowance. You admit that the money meant much to you. You could easily get more, probably a large sum, from your former lover, by threatening to go to his fiancée with the story of his liaison with you . . ."

"Oh, no," she protested, "there was nothing wrong about it. I didn't mean that I could get more money *from* John. I meant that my knowledge of his life and of his character would have yielded me a great deal. You see," she explained, "someone here wanted to buy my knowledge of John's past life . . ."

"Someone?" interrupted the detective. "Who?"

"I don't know," stated the woman promptly.

Fields stared at her, disbelief in his eyes and she protested: "But I don't. I never did!" She clicked the fastener on her white handbag rapidly, open and shut, open and shut. The silence irritated her and she went on sullenly:

"You can believe it or not. A lot I care! Anyway, it was over a year ago when I heard from him last."

"How?" asked Fields.

"How?"

"Yes. How did you hear from him?"

"Oh! By letter."

"Do you have any of these letters?"

"No. I was directed to return each letter in my answer."

"Return them? How did you do this? By mail?" The man leaned forward over his desk.

Mrs. Jones giggled nervously. "I sent them to Louie's Tire Company, Box 2162, I think the number was," she answered, pushing at her hair under the edge of her hat and watching the man for his reaction.

Fields grunted and wrote on his pad.

"What was the offer made to you?" he asked. "Tell us the whole story."

"Well, this bird—man, I mean," she corrected hastily—"I guess he was a man. Anyway, he wrote me about three years ago, first. The letter was typewritten on a piece of gray wrapping paper. I remember it like it was yesterday. It said something like this: 'When you are through with John Fordman, keep me in mind. This is a simple proposition. I only want words from you. For instance: who are his friends on the state oil commission board? What does he think of proration and is he trying to beat it?'" She stopped.

"That's about all in the first one," she said.

"Did it give the return address then?"

"Yes. I sent back the letter and a note with it."

"What did you say in the note?"

The woman looked tired, and opening her handbag took out a vanity case. Her voice was low as she answered:

"I said, 'Go to hell. I love John Fordman and I won't sell out on him.'"

"Did you mention this to Mr. Fordman?"

"No, I didn't. He was out of town at the time and when he got back I decided not to."

"Why not?"

"I don't know. I just decided. He was a little cold toward me."

"And the next letter?" prompted Fields.

"It came about six months later," she admitted.

"And found you more interested?"

"I'll say it did," the woman answered firmly.

"You agreed to help this blackmailer?"

"Blackmailer?" Mrs. Jones shook her head. "I tell you it wasn't blackmail. He was writing a book, he said, and needed my help in filling parts of it out. You know these books they write about rich men now—they tell everything, especially the bad things. And it seems to me the meaner the men were the better the book sells."

Fields nodded and smiled a little. "How much did he offer you for your help?" he asked.

"Ten thousand dollars," admitted the woman reluctantly.

Fields whistled faintly, and Joan could hear both Read and Millbank make quick, incredulous ejaculations.

"And has he paid?" pursued the detective.

"Only two thousand dollars," Agnes Jones said flatly.

"The rest?"

"Was to be paid when the book was published."

Fields laughed and said: "Surely you knew that such a book could never have been published, Mrs. Jones? The publisher and the author would have been sued for libel . . ."

"Why libel?" asked the woman reasonably. "There was to be nothing untrue in it. The publishers wanted a personal story of Fordman's life and John had told me everything important. I knew how he did business, who he bribed and how he still sold his oil, even after the field here was prorated. I knew where his bootleg pipe-lines were because he showed me, and I knew why the officials never found them. I knew about his marriage. He never loved his first wife. His whole ambition was to make money and to pull wires that made the politicians jump. Oh, I knew John Fordman." She stopped and smiled maliciously in the direction of the county attorney. "I know a few things about you, Judge," she said.

The man cleared his throat several times and muttered weakly: "My dear lady. Look here, Fields. You don't believe all this, do you? John Fordman was our most respected citizen. He couldn't have . . ." His voice trailed off.

Fields grinned at the Judge and motioned to Mrs. Jones. "Go on," he said.

"Well, I wrote back and said I'd help with the book," she continued. "The second note was a lot like the first, but it was written on a different typewriter." She looked shrewdly at the detective.

"How'd you know?" he prompted obligingly.

"Well, the first one was big type like an office machine and the second was small type like on a Corona portable. It looked just like the type on my own machine."

"Good," commented Fields.

"Anyway," continued the woman, "the second note said, 'I think you've changed your mind, haven't you? Well, get your stuff together and answer these questions.' There was a long list of them and some about trips that John and I had taken together. I answered them and the next letter had five hundred dollars in it in hundred-dollar bills—old ones."

"Did you try to find out who was promoting this business?" asked Fields.

"Well, I wondered," admitted the woman, "but how could I find out? There wasn't any Louie's Tire Company or garage in the 'phone book. After I wrote my letter acknowledging the receipt of the money, I went to the post-office and located the box by its number. My letter was there. At least, I guess it was my letter, but I couldn't watch it all the time. I stayed several hours, off and on, that day. Next day it was gone and I had a queer note in reply, or rather, in warning."

"How do you mean, queer?"

"It was made up of words and letters cut out of magazines and newspapers and pasted on cardboard. It said, 'Don't watch the box. Something might happen!' There was a great big eye pasted under the words."

"Eye?"

"Yeah, just an eye, cut out of a magazine too. It gave me the creeps."

"What color eye?" asked the man, grinning.

"Green. I think it was a cat's eye," answered the woman solemnly. "It had a pupil that was a slit—you know—up and down."

Dick quit smiling and remarked, "Gave you a scare, eh?"

"It did." Mrs. Jones was quite serious.

"And then—?"

"Well, some more letters came with questions. I answered all I could and he sent five hundred dollars three times. About the first of this year I quit hearing from him. I wrote once or twice, but my letters were returned marked 'not box 2162.' I asked about it and they told me that the box was vacant for three months, then rented to somebody named Hicks. I found out that he was with Shell Oil Company and had just come from Pennsylvania, so . . ." She paused and shrugged her shoulders.

"Good work," was the detective's comment. "So he owes you eight thousand dollars and you can't collect?"

"Yeah," agreed the woman listlessly.

"And you returned every letter?"

She nodded.

"Too bad." Fields turned to Millbank. "Have one of your men get onto this right away, sir. Get them to check the post-office files and find out how payment, application, and so forth were made. If there are any handwriting samples, they'll be invaluable."

The county attorney made a notation of the request and hurried out, glancing back at Agnes Jones as if she were a new and horrible species of rattlesnake.

The woman lighted a cigarette and grinned suggestively at Fields.

After Millbank had left there was a short silence in the room. Joan could see Mrs. Jones nervously smoking her cigarette, tossing it away only half finished. The detective was sorting papers, making notations. He seemed to have forgotten the woman. She shifted restlessly and remarked: "If that's all, I guess I'll be going."

But Fields shook his head. "Wait a moment," he commanded. "Have you ever seen this?" Joan leaned forward and saw him hand her the bridge clipping.

The woman glanced at it, turned it over and looked at the other side. Then she said, "What has this to do with the case?"

Fields, evidently anxious to impress her with the seriousness of the business, said grimly, "It was found, after John Fordman was shot—not far from his body!"

The woman looked again at the fragment of newspaper and pulled herself together with an effort. When she answered she spoke firmly. "I'm afraid I can't help you, Mr. Fields. I've never seen this before."

Dick took the clipping and dismissed her. When he came in to see Joan a few moments later, he rebuked himself warmly.

"Hell," he said, "I told her too much. She lied about that clipping. They all lie about something. If that fellow Drexell had caused Mrs. Lawrence and Marion Fordman to meet in New York, why should he pretend here that he doesn't know the woman? It's senseless."

Joan suggested, "Let's eat and talk about it later."

They ordered sandwiches and coffee and, after the sheriff had departed for his own lunch, they had a drink. When the sandwiches came they sat on the divan together and ate them. They talked in a desultory fashion and had just finished their lunch when Jimmie returned. He took a package from his pocket and handed it to Dick, saying: "Belinda says that you could have saved yourself a lot of trouble by asking Miss Fordman about the handkerchief. It's one of a dozen that she gave her father for his birthday. They all had different colored threads and Mrs. Smith cautioned her not to boil them. That's how she knew."

Fields laughed and put the square of linen aside. "That's the way with clues," he remarked. "Take that telegram you found in Mrs. Lawrence's room, for instance," he said to Joan. "We had it traced and found that it was from her sister Louise, a Mrs. C. E. Cunningham in Houston. The telegraph people made a mistake in the signature and left off the last letter of her name."

"But what was she doing in San Antonio, Dick?" asked Joan.

"I haven't found that out yet," answered the man. "I've got a call in now for her sister and I expect that she'll know." He turned to Jimmie. "Go see if you can find Read, will you?"

The boy left and they waited for the sheriff. Dick remarked: "The Federal examiners made a quick check-up at the bank yesterday. They told Millbank that we could put aside any idea that there might be something wrong there. The institution is in fine condition."

"What are you going to do this afternoon?"

"Have a few more interviews to finish—" He broke off as the sheriff thrust his head in and called:

"Say, Stephens and that feller Goetz has come, Mr. Fields."

Joan returned to her post and Stephens was ushered in first. He was a tall, rawboned farmer with a lined, unhappy face. Hooking a thumb under his overall bib he stood and stared at Fields.

"Have you seen Mr. Drexell lately?" asked the detective.

"Yep," was the reply.

"When?"

"He come out to see me yest'day."

"What for?"

"T' git a watermelon an' some fryin' chickens."

Fields looked puzzled. "You live north of town, don't you?"

"Yep."

"Does Mr. Drexell come to see you often?"

"Nope."

"Did he ever buy any chickens from you before?"

"Yes. Him an' Miss Fordman come onct an' bought some."

"Recently?"

"Not so recent."

"What time was he there?"

"Long after dinner."

"D'you mean about seven o'clock?"

"Hell, naw. We eat dinner about eleven-thirty."

"Did Mr. Drexell speak of the happenings here in town?"

"Ef'n you mean these here murders, he shore did. We talked about 'em fer nigh onto half an hour. He said he'd jist come f'm th' inquest. I was int'rested becuz I was out to th' field th' day Mr. Fordman was shot."

"Did Mr. Drexell remind you of the fact that he talked with you that day?"

"I didn't need no reminder."

"Then he did speak of it?"

"Yeah. He told me when it was. I'd forgot th' time."

"When did he say it was, Stephens?"

"Jest after th' well was shot, he said. I rec'lected it when he mentioned th' fact."

"Was he standing with you when the nitroglycerine exploded in th' well?"

"Yep."

"How long had you been talking?"

"I dunno."

"Come, now—surely you can say five or ten minutes, or longer?"

"Say 'bout ten minutes, then."

"No longer?"

"Well, it might of been."

"But you wouldn't swear to it?"

"Swear to what?"

"Swear to the fact that Drexell had been with you at least twenty or thirty minutes before the well was shot?"

"I'd swear that he was talkin' to me, but I wouldn't want to go to co't an' swear to th' time."

"Did Mr. Drexell tell you why he wanted you to remember that he was talking with you at the field?"

"Yep. He said bein's he was with Mr. Fordman he had to give a alibi as to his whereabouts when th' shootin' come off. Ain't that so?"

"Yes," Fields replied. "That's so." He took the man back over his testimony swiftly and then let him go.

Goetz, the caretaker at the Hathaway place, came in next. He, too, was a weather-beaten man, but small and stooped. He spoke with a faint accent, carefully, and was quite intelligent. Telling his story again, he said that the man had come down the walk not exactly running, but rather in long hurried strides. At Fields's insistence, Goetz finally remembered that the man had worn a dark felt hat.

"Felt," repeated the detective in surprise. "On the Fourth of July?"

Millbank put in: "People around here wear felts all year 'round, Mr. Fields. Sort of hang-over from the days when everyone wore ten-gallon Stetsons. Most of the boys think straws are sissy. The sheriff, for instance, wears his Stetson all of the time, though it's not quite as big as some the old-timers still affect."

Fields let Goetz go on, and asked the sheriff to get Joseph Levy for him. He came in to Joan and said, "It'll be half an hour before Levy comes, if you want to do anything else."

Joan took her car key from Dick and drove down to the office. The heat had moderated with the approach of the sand-storm, but the air was heavy and dead. Small funnel-shaped whorls of dust twisted crazily about the streets, and these miniature cyclones, swirling papers, weeds, and dead leaves, dipped from lawn to roadway, caught at flowers, and twisted the tops of trees. Joan looked across the north at the reddish wall of approaching dust. It had grown in height and would probably envelop Fordman within an hour or two. She looked at the clock on the dashboard. It was four-forty-five.

At the newspaper office, Mitch, in shirt-sleeves, brown hat tilted to the back of his head, was regarding the news on the A.P. printers.

"Hi, honey," he called to her gaily, "where've you been?"

"Busy," she replied. "Did Ann get all of the society in?"

"Guess so," he said. "She was around until about twenty minutes ago. Gone home."

"Mitch," she inquired, "how'd you know that Gere Drexell and Marion were in San Antonio last week-end?"

"Saw 'em,' he replied briefly, tearing strips of paper from the printers into 'takes' for heading up.

"Were you there?"

"Yeah. Ed and I drove down Saturday night. He hadda see a fella at th' paper there for Fordman. I went up to th' El Patio roof to watch th' dance and saw Drexell and Marion there. I couldn't dance because I wasn't dressed," he added ruefully. "Say," he demanded, "you don't think she's fallen for that bird, do you?"

"How would I know?" answered the girl.

"She'd tell you," he stated positively. Then, "Helluva sand-storm comin' up."

"Yes," said Joan absently. She read proof on a few scattered society notes that had been set up late and left within the hour.

Returning to the hotel she let herself into the bedroom. Jimmie was lying across one of the beds, peering through a crack in the door. He gestured to her for silence and Joan peered through the crack. Joey Levy was in the witness chair and his round face wore a most unhappy expression.

". . . you got me wrong, Mr. Fields," he was protesting. "I always say, 'Let bygones be bygones.' John was just smarter'n the rest of us."

"But it is true that the land on which this last well is located once belonged to you?"

"Yes, but that was a long time ago. John, he bought it fair an' square. I don't say but what he didn't fox all of us at th' time, puttin' in that test well an' lettin' it be known it was a dry hole—then we all sold out cheap. But you got to admit it was a smart trick." There was admiration in the man's voice.

"You mean," Fields said incredulously, "that Fordman sunk a well on his own property, struck oil, closed up the well, and denied that he had hit anything?"

"Yes. He let th' old derrick stand there for months an' then even took it down and carted it off. He didn't have much property, you know; only forty acres. Then he began to buy up land all around him—through an agent, of course. I didn't know who'd bought my property for a year or more. I guess he did everybody that way. Then, when he had bought or leased half of the basin, he begun work on number one well again and it wasn't a month before it come in, a good producer. Of course people didn't get wise for a long time, but it leaked out. One of the crew got sore at Fordman an' talked. But the business wasn't never really confirmed, you might say." Levy scratched himself under the left arm-pit and continued, "But, as I say, I don't hold no hard feelin's. Bygones is bygones an' . . ."

"You own a store here, don't you?" interrupted Fields.

"Yes, the Quality," answered the man.

"How's business?"

"Oh, fair, fair."

"You've a big loan on the business, haven't you?"

Levy squirmed a little. "Not so big," he protested. "Everybody nowadays has had to borrow some."

"Was your loan from a bank?"

"Well, not exactly. You see I had a loan from the bank at the time, so John just let me have a small amount personal, to tide me over."

"What collateral did you put up?"

"None. I just signed an I.O.U. Fordman did a lot of business like that."

Fields grunted. "Did anybody else know about this deal?"

"Sam Ross did."

"So the matter stands now that you owe the Fordman estate—uh?" Fields paused suggestively. "How much, did you say?"

Levy stared at Fields. "I didn't say," he answered. "I don't see what all this has to do with the murders," was his protest.

Fields ignored the comment. "You won't say how much your indebtedness is?" he demanded.

"I won't," stated the man stubbornly. "It don't have no place here. Their lawyers can talk to me about it," he added.

"O.K.," said the detective. "If that's the way you feel about it."

Levy left, and Fields came into the other room. "That's a slick bird, Levy," he remarked. "I was trying to get a statement as to what he owed Fordman down on paper with witnesses and all."

"Why?" asked Joan.

"Because the I.O.U. he was talking about is missing. I've an idea that it was with that stuff taken from the filing case," Fields answered. "I couldn't tell from what he said whether he suspects that it's gone or not, but you can bet your bottom dollar that if he finds it out, the Fordman estate will never see a penny of that loan."

"Did he give you an alibi for the fourth, when Mr. Ross was killed?"

"Yes. He said that he stayed at the store until about twelve-forty-five and then went home for luncheon," replied the man. "He also says that he was over in San Antonio on the week-end with his family. That makes four of them, to say nothing of Mrs. Lawrence—Drexell, Miss Jones, Miss Fordman, and Levy."

"And you can add two more names to that list, Dick," informed Joan. "Mitch and Ed were there Saturday night and Sunday."

"Good Lord."

They laughed and Fields sat down at the table. "I'm going to make a chart out of those alibis right now," he said. "Read is out on some work for me and Millbank is busy too. We'll have something more definite to work with when we can see them more clearly. I'll take the seven main people in the case and we'll work them over first. If it was someone else I can just admit that I'm stumped. These are the only people that Fordman had a great deal

SUSPECT	JULY 3 12.45–1.15	SUPPORTED BY	JULY 4 12.45–1.15	SUPPORTED BY	JULY 5 9–9.30 P.M.	SUPPORTED BY
Clarence Jones	In his own car	Wife Daughter Frank	At home (not seen, but heard)	Wife	At home	Wife
Agnes Jones	In her own car	Husband Daughter Frank	At home (neither seen nor heard)	Husband	"	Husband
Mitchell White	In mesquite thicket	Rea Levy	In two hotels ('phone call at 12.50)	Mrs. Lawrence	Alone at boarding-house	
Joseph Levy	In car with wife (?)		At store until 12.45 At home by 1.15		Lodge	
Gere Drexell	With farmer (?)	No support	At luncheon (?)		Working in office (?)	
Ed Frank	With Mildred Jones		In sheriff's office	Sheriff	In rooms at Mesa	Clerk
Val Day	In truck	Several witnesses	Barber shop	'Jack'	At lease	Helper

to do with, that is, intimately. The list includes business associates, personal friends, and employees. We decided that it could scarcely be an outsider, a stranger in Fordman. Every act indicated prescience on the murderer's part, especially in the murder of Ross, and to some extent in the attack on Mrs. Lawrence. If our murderer isn't in this list—well, I guess the Governor's men will have to try."

"I can't believe that any of those people would kill anyone," said Joan. "I've known most of them so long."

Fields was silent for a few minutes as he worked and then handed her a roughly drawn chart, with columns for each of the three attacks and names of all of the suspects listed down the left-hand side of the page.

Joan studied it for a minute and then said, "Well, there's not a person who doesn't have at least one pretty good alibi for each of the three times, is there?"

"Notice the Joneses, how they alibi each other," remarked the man.

"Yes. There are a lot of things to be checked. We can let the Jones family go for the time being, I suppose, and Mitch. He's been checked and double-checked for the third and fourth, anyway."

"Levy," said Fields, pointing, "needs checking in two instances. He has no absolute alibi for the time of Fordman's death, but I'll leave that and concentrate on the last two he gave. Drexell's much-prompted story told by that fella Stephens sounded awfully thin and we're checking up on the lunch he was supposed to have had there. He left the airport ahead of us, I remember; before twelve-twenty, wasn't it?"

"Yes," agreed the girl.

"Well, he'd still have had plenty of time."

"But he had a good alibi for last night," reminded Joan.

"So-so," contradicted Fields. "He was on hand when Mrs. Lawrence got the letter and left soon after. He says that he was in his office working with his secretary from seven until nine, but she says that he was in his private office and that she didn't see him all of the time. She won't swear as to when he left, either, because she

ADA E. LINGO

stayed on and worked until eleven o'clock and had to find out from
Western Union what time it was then. I don't consider him to have
any ironclad alibis, to tell the truth."

"No, I guess not," admitted Joan.

"Then take that fella Frank," continued the man. "I don't like
him and I'd like to break his alibis all to pieces, but it can't be
done. He hasn't a very good one for the Fordman murder—yes, he
has, too. Mrs. Jones, Jones, and the daughter all swear that he was
in their car with them when things began to happen. That would
tend to clear the whole bunch, if they aren't in cahoots! Then, when
Ross was killed, Frank says that he was with the sheriff. At least,
we can't accuse the good officer of being in cahoots with the bird,
can we?"

"Well," said Joan a trifle coolly, "I don't see why it would be
any more ridiculous to suspect the sheriff than to suspect Ed."

Fields laughed loudly, and Jimmie, who had been lying on the
bed listening eagerly, remarked, "I always thought she carried a
torch for that guy."

"That's a revolting expression," reproved Joan. But they only
laughed at her again, so she said, "Well, where was he when Mrs.
Lawrence was attacked?"

"He said that he was in bed," answered Fields. "The night clerk
at the Mesa saw him go up and routed him out about an hour or
two later when White called to tell him about Mrs. Lawrence. What
I want to know is, why did he go to bed so early?"

"He'd been up all night, for two nights running, you nit-wit,"
said Joan crossly. "I know just how he felt."

Fields tactfully left the subject. "Day's alibis have not been broken so far," he continued. "The sheriff is working on them now."
He stopped and put down the paper.

Jimmie said, "There's somebody knocking at the other door."

It was the sheriff. His heavy face was gloomy and he sat down
on the divan as if he were both tired and disgusted. He brightened
somewhat as Dick began to explain his alibi chart, and caught its
significance at once.

"Wall, that's real smart," he said. "Hit's a darn sight easier to see 'em all wrote down than it is t' keep 'em in yore head."

"Did you check up on Levy?" asked Fields.

"Yep. He was to lodge meetin', all right. Leastways they've got him marked present on th' roll."

"How about Day?"

"Looks like we got to let him out, anyhow. There's three men ready t' swear that he was in Jack's shop on Tuesday. An' he was out to th' lease last night. I phoned out there an' got holt of that boy that helps him. They had a lot of trouble with th' well an' had t' work almost all night."

"And Ed Frank?"

"Oh, him? He was with me all right on Tuesday, playin' poker with th' boys. Went out to th' Ross's place in my car. I'd swear t' that."

"O.K.," said Fields. "It looks like White's in the clear."

"Yeah."

"Then that leaves us Drexell without a good alibi in any case. And the Jones pair, both could be lying. They haven't any proof to bolster up their stories at all. The routine investigations are well under way now, aren't they?" he asked briskly, opening his notebook.

"Yeah. Millbank has his men checking bank accounts, withdrawals, an' any rumors they kin scare up. An' like you said we've sent out inquiries to all th' photostat places anywhere near."

"How about the inspectors of the state oil commission? Have any luck yet finding out if any have resigned or been fired within the past few years?"

Read shook his head. "I wired the Governor last night to get that information," he answered. "We ain't heard yet."

The telephone rang suddenly and Fields lifted the receiver of an instrument that had been installed in the living-room that morning. He motioned Joan to the extension in the bedroom. She grabbed her pad and pencil and was in time to hear the operator say:

"Ready, New Orleans."

A heavy voice inquired, "Fields?"

Dick said, "Yes," and the man in New Orleans began to talk.

"This is Malloy of the Southern Agency. Got your wire last night. You wanted to know if we'd had anybody tailing a bird named Fordman?"

"Yes," came Dick's voice.

"Well, we went back several years like you suggested and found this in the files. I guess it's what you want. I'm gonna read. Ready?"

"O.K.," said Fields.

"It's a letter dated June 21, four years ago last month, an' says:

> Southern Agency
> 2132 Canal
> New Orleans, La.
>
> Dear Sirs,
> Enclosed find $200 as a retainer.
>
> Within a day or so a man named John Fordman, of Fordman, Texas, will arrive in New Orleans. He will undoubtedly stay at the best hotel. He is about thirty-seven or thirty-eight years old, big, good-looking, blond. Shortly after his arrival I have reason to believe that a woman will join him. She is handsome, red-headed.
>
> Please put a man on these two and find out what you can as to their relations. I will pay another $200 for a snapshot of the two together or for any photostatic record that can be used in a court of law.
>
> The woman is my wife and I need proof of misconduct to obtain a divorce.
> Yours truly
> Louis Bell
> Box 2162
> Fordman, Texas

Malloy paused and Fields spoke: "That's it. That's just what we want. Did you people take the case?"

"Yeah," said Mr. Malloy. "It all turned out as this bird said it would and our operative got a swell snapshot of them two on the beach with his head on her lap. And besides that, we got a photostat of th' hotel register. They come in together an' registered John Fordman and wife! It was easy."

"And you sent the data to this fellow Bell?" asked Fields.

"Sure. We wrote first and sent a bill for three hundred dollars more to cover expenses and evidently the fella paid it because we sent out th' stuff. Funny thing, though—I see here in th' records that he paid in cash and his letters come registered."

"How about the handwriting?"

"Letters written on a typewriter. Signature round backhand like a child's writing."

"Send the stuff over airmail, will you, Malloy?" asked Fields.

"Sure. What's it all about?"

"Extortion and probably murder."

"Humph. Then this guy Bell wasn't the husband at all?"

"We don't know yet. Anyway, the name wasn't Bell. Her name is Jones."

"Yeah? Well, good luck, guy. I'll send this dope off right away."

Malloy hung up and so did Dick and Joan. The girl re-entered the living-room and at the detective's request read her shorthand transcript of the conversation.

When she had finished he said, "Everything leads to box 2162, but that won't get us anywhere, I'm afraid."

The telephone shrilled again and Fields answered it. His face brightened and he said, "Thanks."

Turning to the others he cried: "Mrs. Lawrence is conscious and the doctor says that I can talk with her for a few minutes. She's been asking for me."

Sheriff Read sighed gustily. "Well, that's somethin' t' be thankful for, ain't it?" he asked the room in general.

Fields arranged with the officer to stay and answer any calls that might come for him, and he and Joan, with Jimmie at their heels, set out for the Fordmans'.

The sunshine had a peculiar flat quality and the cool air smelled of rain and dust. Joan looked across to the north and noted that the approaching sandstorm was much nearer.

"It won't be long now," she said as they climbed into the roadster. They didn't talk during the drive. Fields was slumped down into his corner, hands in pockets, his face moody, his red hair blown into a tangled mass.

Joan noticed that people were putting cars away, taking potted plants into the houses, and the few pedestrians who trotted homeward were clinging tightly to their hats and bundles as the first quick gusts of wind darted around corners and across the streets. As they topped the hill on which the Fordman house stood, the sun, like a gigantic orange, began to slip quickly down behind the black horizon. Before they had got out of the car, a quarter of it was gone and the little floating fleecy clouds above it began to look as if each had been dipped in blood.

Inside they found Marion and Doctor Ross waiting for them, and shortly Joan and Dick stood beside Mrs. Lawrence. She lay very still and looked utterly spent and weary. Her head was bandaged and there were great blue concussion circles under her closed eyes.

When Dick spoke to her, she looked up at him and smiled. Her voice, still cool and even more remote than ever, came faintly.

"Was the letter gone?" she asked.

"No," answered the detective, "I found it under the seat."

Her eyes widened a little in surprise. "Did it help you?" she asked.

"A little," admitted the man. "Do you know to whom Fordman referred?"

She closed her eyes and moved her head slightly in negation. "He didn't know who the blackmailer was himself," she said, "when he talked with me."

"And you have no idea who struck you?" asked the detective hopefully.

She moved her head again. "I was opening the gate when I heard a movement and then felt the blow." Her voice was weaker now, and Fields reluctantly signed to Joan that he was through. Doctor Ross came in and before they had left the room Mrs. Lawrence was sleeping.

They went into the living-room where Marion was waiting and the doctor soon followed. He was tired and haggard, but cheerful.

"She'll be all right now," he assured them. "I didn't like to submit her to the strain of questioning, but she was worried more about not seeing you," he told Fields.

"She didn't know a thing," declared the latter ruefully. "Just socko from behind—then black-out."

The physician shook his head. "I can't understand it," he said.

Fields turned to Marion and asked, "Where is that secretary, Miss Fordman? I'd like to see him."

"He's been here all day," answered the girl, "but he went to dinner at six. We are going through all of Dad's papers and trying to get things straightened out." Marion looked rested and cool in a white linen dress, but Joan could see that she was more nervous than she had been the night before. There was an unhappy shadow in her blue eyes and Joan was not surprised when she beckoned her away from the men and took her out into the empty hallway.

"Listen, Joan," she said. "I sat with Glieth this afternoon while the nurse was getting some sleep and she talked—talked about Gere."

Joan said nothing, but her heart contracted. The girl continued:

"She knows him, Joan. She's known him for a long time, I believe."

"Why do you think that?" asked Joan.

"She called him. She said: 'I know. I know how you feel. I've loved you for years, Gere.'" The girl repeated the woman's words quietly and looked at her friend.

Joan swallowed with difficulty and changed the subject slightly. "How did you meet her, Marion?" she asked.

"That was rather odd, now that I think of it," answered the girl. "I had just got back from France and was staying at the St. Moritz, buying clothes and just seeing things. It was late in August, you know, and I'd decided to get an apartment in New York and go to

Columbia for the winter. Dad didn't like the idea and came up to try and persuade me to come down here and spend the winter. One day I was waiting for him in the lobby when Glieth came up to me. She said, 'You're Marion Fordman, aren't you?' and I said yes, of course. She looked perfection itself and I remembered having seen her in the hotel before. Then she said, 'I'm Glieth Lawrence of Houston. Some friends of mine at home wrote and told me that you were here at the St. Moritz and since we are fellow Texans I just couldn't resist introducing myself.'"

Marion smiled at Joan and continued: "I liked her at once and was glad to have someone to dash about with. Dad was busy most of the day and Glieth and I had a marvelous time. Dad just went goofy over her, and I thought that it was sort of funny at first, but after a while I thought that it was swell. She didn't encourage him, but she was so sweet and kind that he was completely in love with her before he left. I stayed, after all, you know, and Glieth didn't go home for a month or so. After she did go, Dad wrote that he'd been to Houston several times to see her and hinted that they were going to be married. I didn't write to Glieth about it, because she hadn't mentioned it in her letters."

"Then you didn't know for sure when you came home this summer whether they would be married or not?" asked Joan.

"No, I didn't," answered the girl. "But I believe now that Glieth wasn't going to marry him and just hated to tell him. It would have hurt him badly."

"Do you think that she is in love with Gere?" insisted Joan.

Marion smiled a little. "I've made an idiot of myself over him this summer," she admitted. "I know darn well that he's just been sweet and polite with me, and if he loves Glieth I think he's got good taste."

Joan was relieved. "It'll all come out in the wash," she said flippantly, and at that moment the telephone rang.

Marion said, "Please answer it, Joan. It's probably a reporter."

But it was the sheriff, his voice harsh with excitement.

"Miss Joan," he cried, as he recognized her voice, "something else has happened. You listen and then tell Fields to meet me right away." He calmed his voice. "A minute ago one of the telephone girls called and said that a light on her board begun to flash on an' off as if someone was a-jigglin' th' hook. She was busy an' didn't answer right away. When she plugged in, she said all she heard was a loud yell an' a thump, like somebody'd dropped the 'phone. She didn't know if it was a man or a woman, but it scared her so she reported it right away."

The officer paused to get his breath, and Joan asked:

"But where *was* it, Sheriff?"

"It was out to Chick Jones's house. You tell Fields t' git there right off and I'll come fast as I kin git my car." He hung up, and Joan ran across the hall to find Dick.

The doctor and Marion had returned to Mrs. Lawrence's room and Fields was smoking a cigarette and staring out a west window at the brilliant afterglow.

He listened to the short message and grabbed her roughly by the arm. "The damned fool!" he said. "It was that bridge clipping. She knew where it came from. I thought she lied." He started for the door, still talking: "You see! She's tried to shake this bird down for that eight thousand he promised her and got caught in her own trap."

They ran down the hall, out onto the porch, and were suddenly caught up in a swirl of wind and dust. Jimmie, sitting on the steps, yelled, "Where ya goin'?" and when they did not answer him, he followed them to the car and vaulted into the rumble seat. Joan raced the roadster down the long hill, out into the highway.

Dick screamed over the roar: "Let me out at the house, kid, and then drive away. I don't want you in on this."

Joan nodded and stepped on the accelerator. Jimmie clung to the sides of the dickey and they spun around corners. Luckily the streets of the town were deserted, for as they reached the outskirts both darkness and the sand-storm descended upon them. The air was thick with swirling dust and the three in the open car crouched low to avoid the stinging particles. Joan could scarcely see the road, but she knew the turns by heart and swung the car through the gates of the addition in which the Jones's house stood.

Fields motioned her to slow the car. "Stop across from the place," he said.

The house was a small brick bungalow on the corner nearest them. It was dark. Next door a party was evidently in progress. Every light was on and a dozen cars were parked in front of the house, some of them blocking the Jones's driveway and standing along the Jones's curb. Above the steady rush of the wind, Joan could hear a radio blaring. The sand was driving thicker and harder, filling their eyes, making it difficult to see or breathe.

Fields, standing on the running-board, said sharply, "Wait for me. I'm goin' in."

He dropped off and ran toward the house. Joan could not see him after he gained the yard.

Jimmie leaned over and yelled: "Say, I'm goin' too!" He prepared to clamber out of the rumble seat, but Joan caught his arm and declared firmly, "You are not!"

He muttered, but subsided, and they waited for several long, uncomfortable minutes, stung by the sand, peering uselessly into the darkness.

Then, as Joan began to worry, the light in the living-room was turned on. She felt certain then that Fields had found no one in the house. So she got out of the roadster, told Jimmie to stay and watch for the sheriff, walked across the street and up the sidewalk. The wind was roaring steadily now and the sand beat against her face and arms, stinging like a thousand needles. She reached the shelter of the small terrace and groped along the rough brick wall for the front door.

A lighted window was on her right and she stooped to peer inside, but the shade had been drawn and she could see only a small area of polished floor.

Her left hand found the screen door and she drew it open. She reached to find the knob of the inner door, but her hand waved forward into empty space. The door was already ajar.

Thankful to be sheltered from the storm, she stepped inside and pushed the door shut behind her. The hallway was a black infinity, and the girl stood still, her pulses pounding, her ears ringing. After the chaos of the sand-storm the quiet stability of the house was overwhelming. The only sound that she could hear was the closed-out roar of the wind.

Down the hall on the right a thread of light shone under the living-room door. Farther down, on the left, another thread shone under what Joan knew to be a bedroom door. She walked quietly, opened the first door. The living-room, lighted dimly by a shaded bridge lamp, was empty.

Leaving this door open so that the light would shine into the hall she moved toward the bedroom. She was frightened now. The silence and the emptiness had stirred her to a certainty that something was wrong.

Panic tempted her to call out, to seek the reassurance of Dick's voice, but caution stayed her. She reached the door, opened it slowly, stepped inside. It was the largest of the three bedrooms in the house and Agnes Jones had furnished it in pseudo-modernistic style. The twin beds, of some black wood, were dressed as usual in their slick white oilcloth 'spreads,' with a jagged streak of vermilion lightning jerking diagonally across the top. The ridiculous room affected Joan again as it had when she had first seen it—with active nausea—and she was about to hunt farther for Fields when a slight noise beyond the far bed made her glance that way.

What she saw terrified her beyond coherent thought. A scream tried desperately to force its way between her clenched teeth, but the muscles that would have released it were rigid. She could not move her eyes that were fixed with such awful certainty upon a pair of groping, clutching hands, bound cruelly together at the wrists, that rose above and caught hopelessly at the slippery white cover of the bed. Up and down they moved, the fingers writhing, and they filled the room with the soft, smooth, sliding noise of their endeavor.

But another noise, sharp and even more terrifying, caused the girl to turn, leap backward, and pound desperately at the door that had been closed so suddenly behind her.

She was trapped, locked in that room with a pair of large futilely waving hands! Reason began to return as she leaned against

the door. The hands were bound—they surely could not hurt her.
A low, strangled sound spurred her to movement. Cautiously she
walked around the first bed, then the second, and stared down at a
figure on the floor.

It was Dick Fields, tied firmly hand and foot, and most securely
gagged. His eyes blazed up at her and he made wild animal noises
deep in his throat as the girl did no more than gaze stupidly down
at him.

Then she began to laugh, dropped by his side, and untied the
cord that held a silk stocking as a gag.

He spat it out, cursed thickly, held up his hands.

The knots were too tight for her fingers and he said, between
swallowing and cursing, "Knife. In my pocket!"

She finally got the rope cut and the man struggled to his feet,
pushed her aside, and ran for the door, Joan called, "It's locked,"
and turned to the French doors that opened on a side terrace. They
gave easily and she stepped out, Fields behind her, his automatic
drawn. The sand-storm still roared, stronger than before, and Joan
was blinded, thrown against the man.

He yelled, "Look out! Go back! Go back!" and ran across the
terrace toward the rear of the house, disappearing in the darkness.

The girl followed the wall toward the front, ran down the steps,
and out toward the roadster. It was a black shape, standing by the
far curb. As she started across the street, the strong white lights
went on, the exhaust roared.

Puzzled and confused, she called, "Wait! Wait!" and ran toward
the low racer. Reaching the side she foolishly jumped on the running-board, but the driver of the car swept out a dark arm and
pushed her away. She clawed desperately at the folded top, lost
her hold, felt the fender strike her hip, and fell heavily into the
paved street. The sand-storm engulfed her and she dimly heard a
shout and the roar of a gun before a sickening blackness blanked
out the world.

XVII: THURSDAY, JULY 6: 7.40 P.M.

Joan was conscious first of a great deal of unpleasant noise; men's voices, hoarse and loud, pressed down upon her. Suddenly something very wet and cold was dropped across her face. She tried to move, to cry out, and the noise about her increased. Then it receded, was hushed, and she came to her senses with a start. She was bruised and aching in every bone.

Dick's face, strained and anxious, swam out of the haze above her and she realized that she was lying on a divan in the living-room of the Jones house.

The whole affair swept back and engulfed her mind. Dick's face blurred and swung sickeningly and his voice came from a long distance. She could faintly hear him saying, "Joan, Joan . . ." and the rest was a mumble.

Someone bathed her forehead with a cold damp cloth again and she reopened her eyes. Things were clearer now and did not swoop and swing so alarmingly. Doctor Ross knelt at her side holding her wrist.

"Atta girl," he said. "Drink this."

She was held up and swallowed a sickening dose from a glass. Almost immediately the room ceased its swinging. Fields was looking down at her and a group of men stood ringed about her.

She grinned up at Dick because his face was so white under his tumbled red hair.

"I'm all right," she said. "Don't look so scared."

He sat down abruptly and wiped his face with a dirty handkerchief.

The sheriff stepped forward.

"You sure had us worried, Miss Joan," he declared. "Listen," his voice was eager, "didja see him? In th' car, I mean?"

The girl remembered suddenly what had happened and tried to sit up.

Doctor Ross pressed her back and shook his head. "Take it easy," he advised.

"No!" cried the girl. "I didn't see who it was!" Consciousness as to what her eyes had glimpsed before she had fallen returned to her. "There were two . . . two of them in the car!" she said suddenly.

Fields exclaimed: "Two? Are you sure?"

She thought for a moment, then repeated firmly: "Two. I know I saw two people. The one at the wheel shoved me off."

The sheriff said abruptly: "Well, boys, we'll git goin'. Miss Joan can't help us none."

The men moved out the door, talking among themselves.

"Where are they going?" asked the girl.

"It's a posse," explained Read, shifting his big Stetson in his hands. "They're goin' after that devil." He turned to the detective. "You'll stay, won't you? Somebody has got to take charge of things here."

"Yeah," agreed Fields. "I'll stay here. There's plenty to be done. I don't believe you'll catch him, anyway."

"We'll try," answered Read grimly and left the room.

Cars roared in the street, voices sounded, then things grew quiet.

Fields came to Joan's side and took her hand. "You sure scared me, kid," he said.

"Was I out long?" asked the girl.

"Not much over ten minutes," was the reply. "Read and his bunch drove up just as I got you in the house."

Joan said, "It seems like an age."

The doctor stood up. "You pretty near got him this time, Fields," he commented.

"Got him!" repeated the man bitterly. "He got me. I walked right into a trap, Joan," he explained. "The front door was open and I came in. He slugged me, and the next thing I knew there I was trussed up like a turkey, behind a bed. Helluva detective," he added.

Joan sat up suddenly and exclaimed: "Jimmie! Where is Jimmie? He was in the rumble seat!"

Dick stared at her, horror in his eyes. "My God!" he cried. "I forgot about the boy."

The doctor exclaimed involuntarily. "Surely," he said, "the boy couldn't have been in the car or they'd have seen him and not tried to take it. Maybe he got out after you did, Joan."

"No," stated the girl positively. "I told him to stay and direct the sheriff. The last I saw of him he was crouching down in the rumble seat to avoid the sand. With his head down and in the darkness and the storm, I don't believe anyone would have seen him." Her voice broke as she realized that the boy's predicament was of her own making.

The doctor regarded her kindly and attempted to reassure. "Don't worry, Joan," he advised. "The posse is out now and they'll catch him soon. Read got a report that the car had been seen on the South Highway."

"Leaving town?" asked the girl.

"Heading toward Mexico, I expect," affirmed the detective. He stood up and stated: "I must get on the 'phone and warn all of the towns below here."

He went out, leaving Joan alone with the doctor. They could hear his voice in the hall.

The doctor questioned her. "And you've no idea who this madman is, Joan?"

"Not a glimmer, Doctor. Where are the Joneses?" she added.

Doctor Ross shrugged his shoulders. "Mildred and her mother are seldom home, anyway, but Chick ought to be here."

Fields called from the hall, "How much gas was in the car, Joan?"

"A little over nineteen gallons," replied the girl. "I bought twenty gallons today. They ought to get about one hundred and fifty miles on it, anyway."

"How far's Del Rio?" asked the detective.

"More than one hundred and fifty miles," answered Doctor Ross.

"Then he'll likely stop somewhere for gas," declared Fields, and returned to his telephoning.

"This state ought to have radio patrol cars," remarked the doctor. "They are the only effective method of combating outlaws."

Dick returned. "South of here the wires are down," he stated disgustedly. "I got through to Austin by way of Abilene and they will relay the messages." He looked down at Joan. "If you feel better now, I'll take you home," he said.

The girl struggled to her feet. "No, I'm going with you," she said. "I couldn't go home and face Mom until I know about Jimmie. I couldn't stay there, anyway, not knowing what was going on. Where are you going?"

"To the newspaper office, first," said Fields thoughtfully.

"Well, I'm going too," she repeated, walking cautiously about the room and locating her injuries.

Fields and the doctor protested, but she had her way and the three of them went out and got into the doctor's car. The sandstorm had blown over and it was raining large warm drops that hit the ground heavily. Doctor Ross let them out at the newspaper office and with difficulty they got through the large crowd of townspeople and reporters jammed about the glass front of the building.

White opened the wicket to the office section and they helped Joan to a chair.

"Any news?" she asked Mitch.

"Not yet," was his reply. He and Dick retired to the A.P. printers and stood watching them. The noise was almost deafening as members of the crowd outside shouted to one another and to Fields and White.

Joan realized that several deputy policemen were keeping the reporters back and she recognized the Dallas *News* man as he struggled to gain her attention. She smiled at him and waved a limp hand.

Dick climbed upon a chair and motioned for silence.

"Please," he began, "be a little quiet. Miss Shields has had a very harrowing experience and cannot answer questions at present. You know as much as she does, for she has been unconscious since she fell from the running-board of her car.

"The only thing that I can add for publication is that Miss Shields's brother, who was in the rumble seat of the roadster as it stood before the house, has disappeared and we are afraid that he has been kidnapped by the fugitive."

The noise burst forth afresh at this information and Fields was forced to amplify his statement and give the story in detail.

He finally came over with Mitch and sat down beside Joan who inquired, "Where's Ed?"

The reporter laughed shortly. "Hell," he complained, "he's in on th' fun. He's with th' posse and here I am tryin' t' get out a paper single-handed."

Fields asked sharply, "How do you know Frank is with the posse, White?"

"He called in a few minutes ago and said he was goin'."

"Where'd he call from?"

"He was at Sam's place, a speakeasy out south of the town. He said a car was waiting for him."

Fields took up the telephone on the desk asking, "What's Sam's number?"

Mitch referred to a card thumb-tacked to the wall over his desk and soon gave the detective the number.

Fields got the operator and Joan moved to her ow n desk to listen over the extension. The speakeasy proprietor at the other end of the wire soon confirmed White's statement.

"Yes, sir," he said positively, "Mr. Frank was in here 'bout twenty minutes or so ago. He told me he was with a posse.

"What'd 'e do? He 'phoned his paper. Yeah, I heard 'im. He come back to my office instead of usin' th' public 'phone. Yeah, there was a lot of customers here. Leave? Yeah, I heard 'im leave. He went off south."

Dick grunted and hung up. "That checks, anyway," he said.

Joan laughed. "You will suspect Ed, won't you?"

"I suspect everybody, even myself," retorted the man.

"What do you suspect yourself of?"

"Idiocy."

There was a shout from the group in the corner by the A.P. printers. Mitch ran over to them with a slip of paper and Joan read the printed words;

A621   FORDMAN

EDITOR'S NOTE: WORD HAS BEEN RECEIVED FROM CORRESPONDENT IN ROCKTOWN THAT A LARGE PACKARD ROADSTER, BELIEVED TO BE DRIVEN BY THE FUGITIVE WANTED FOR MURDER IN FORDMAN, RACED THROUGH THERE AT 8.06 P.M. HEADED TOWARD DEL RIO.

ROCKTOWN OFFICIALS HAD NOT AT THAT TIME RECEIVED WARNING ACCOUNT DAMAGED WIRES NORTH OF TOWN, THEREFORE NO ATTEMPT WAS MADE TO STOP THE CAR.

Farther down on the slip was another message:

FORDMAN PLEASE COMMUNICATE ANY FURTHER DEVELOPMENTS. PAPERS HERE WAITING.
    SIGNED   KEANE

This was from the home office of the A.P. in Dallas and meant that they were waiting for word from Mitch or from their special correspondent. The latter, somebody volunteered, had struck out south after the sheriff when it was learned that a posse had left.

Mitch said, "Hell, I can't spend all my time wirin' th' A.P. We gotta paper here too." He ran his hand through his hair and dashed for a typewriter.

Dick got up and read the message to the reporters, who received it with disgust.

The Dallas *News* man remarked, "We might as well be home. They know more'n we do." He began to harangue Dick, who shook his head and returned to Joan's side.

To her he said: "I can't give this stuff out yet. Millbank's officially in charge. Let him issue statements."

Two men came through the back-shop door. One was Joan's father and the other was Doctor Ross.

The girl remembered her mother when she saw Mr. Shields's anxious face.

"Does Mom know?" she asked.

"About you?"

"About Jimmie."

"She doesn't know anything yet, sister," assured her father. "Are you all right? Ross came up and told me."

"I'm all right," she answered impatiently, "but I'm worried sick about Jimmie. And it was my fault."

"I should think he'd have popped up yelling," remarked the doctor. "How would he know that the fellow in the car was friend or enemy?"

There were no answers for that and they all sat in silence several minutes. Fields had retired to the glassed booth at the back of the room and Joan could see his mouth move as he talked. Soon he emerged and beckoned.

"Millbank's heard from Read," he told her. "They reached the county line without any luck and are coming back."

The man looked thoughtful. "I'm worried about that fool Jones woman," he admitted. "Something happened out there. I couldn't find any evidence of violence, but I think that she got it in the neck. I've a feeling."

"I hope not," said the girl. "Too much has happened now."

"Well, where is she?" Fields inquired. "Her car's there in th' garage. That's why he took yours. He couldn't have got the Jones car out, with those others parked there in the drive."

"Maybe she ran away," suggested Joan.

Fields shook his head. "Her clothes are undisturbed as far as I could tell and there were two handbags in her closet that she'd been sure to take if she'd gone for good. No, I'm sure that she knew who dropped that clipping. She evidently threatened him with exposure and the fellow, cornered, attacked her. Naturally she tried to get away, reached the 'phone and knocked it down. After that, of course, there wasn't any chance for him to remain anonymous. He had to get away and get away quick. I expect that he came to her house prepared to go. . . ."

He was interrupted by the printer bell.

Everyone rushed for the corner where the black machines stood. Mitch tore a strip of paper from the carriage and Joan read over Dick's shoulder. It said:

A621   FORDMAN
BULLETIN
ROCKTOWN, JULY 6 (A.P.). THE BLACK ROADSTER WHICH PASSED THROUGH HERE THIRTY MINUTES AGO WAS HALTED SEVERAL MILES SOUTH OF TOWN BY OFFICERS. IN THE CAR, REPORTED TO HAVE BEEN DRIVEN BY THE FUGITIVE WANTED FOR MURDER IN FORDMAN, WERE TWO YOUNG WOMEN MOTORING TO AUSTIN.

THEY WERE RELEASED AFTER QUESTIONING.

NO TRACE HAS BEEN FOUND TO INDICATE THAT THE WANTED MAN HAS PASSED THIS WAY.

Mitch snorted disgustedly. "They've let him slip through their fingers," he said.

Fields nodded and rubbed his chin. "He's outsmarted them somehow." He walked across the room to the map of Texas hanging on the wall and studied it for a few minutes. Joan followed him and he said, "I don't believe that he's making for the border at all. There's San Antonio and Austin, both large enough to hide a man, and close. He may have had a hide-out already fixed up."

Fields flung himself into a chair. "I'll stay until another report comes in," he said, "or at any rate for thirty minutes longer. I want to run over the whole thing as I can see it now with all of the pieces fitted in.

"First, there was the situation that Fordman's letter explained: that of the blackmailer who had successfully extorted various sums of money from Fordman over a period of a year and whose grand coup, that of selling his collected evidence to his victim for a quarter of a million dollars, had just been accomplished. Of this we are sure.

"Next, we have Fordman planning secretly to double-cross the blackmailer and bring about both his downfall and the return of Fordman's money. But it is obvious that if Fordman would tell Mrs. Lawrence of his plans he might tell someone else, and the blackmailer, constantly on the alert, undoubtedly learned that something was in the air.

"Then, assuming this, we have Fordman's murder, for he is the only person who knows that the money is marked, and how—and the only person who could threaten the safety of the blackmailer." Fields stopped and lighted a cigarette.

"That brings us to Mr. Ross," prompted Joan.

"Yes, Ross," agreed the man. "Fordman's letter clears our motive for that too. I thought the man was killed because he knew something, but I believe now that he was killed so that the blackmailer could retrieve his papers and forestall any discovery that might expose him. If that document had got into the hands of any detective, even the dullest one could have traced it to its source."

"How?" asked Joan.

"Paper, typing, contents, style of writing, and finger-prints," stated the man rapidly. "Any paper worked over as much as that must have been would carry a million prints. He's bound to have handled the snapshots and the photostats and they hold prints nicely. Osmic acid vapor or iodine vapor will develop prints on paper even after they are months old. Swan ink will develop prints three years old. This is common knowledge now."

"But how would he know that Ross had the stuff, and where?" asked Joan.

"That I can't say," admitted the man. "Likely Fordman told him. But however he knew, the fact remains that he did and that Ross had to go. He waited for the banker, killed him, took his keys and, entering the bank, probably that same night, cleaned out the Fordman file. We found Ross's keys on his desk and I thought of it at the time, but it fits in nicely now. It was safer to leave the keys than to keep them and risk having them found."

"It sounds very reasonable," commented Joan. "And, too, the attack on Mrs. Lawrence fits in nicely. When he knew that she had a letter written by Fordman, probably after his suspicions were tangible, he had to have it—to know what it contained. Fordman might have told the woman how the money was marked or revealed his plans for exposing the blackmailer."

The man nodded and continued, "Then we can assume, I think, that the blackmailer is not mentioned in the Fordman will . . ."

"I don't agree with you," argued the girl. "We haven't any proof that Fordman knew *positively* with whom he was dealing. And if he made any changes it might become known and excite the man's suspicions."

"That's so," agreed Fields.

"Then," suggested Joan, "suppose the blackmailer didn't murder Fordman and one of the legatees did . . ."

But Fields interrupted. "No, no, no," he said impatiently, "you forget that Ross was killed solely for the stuff in the filing case. It was the blackmailer covering up."

"I grant that," said Joan, "but you must remember that the blackmailer would have had to cover up even if Fordman had died a natural death at that time. Fordman's death, no matter how brought about, would have left him open to prosecution, or at least to exposure and to certain suspicion."

The man thought this over and admitted: "Well, it's an angle, all right, and a plausible one. But it isn't probable. It would have been too much of a coincidence for Fordman to have been murdered by another enemy while he was trying to cope with the first one," he stated. "Your mind is certainly ticking better than mine is, though," he added. "It's all worked out too fast. There are so many trails that it's become a maze. It would take weeks to run down every clue and most of them would end in blind alleys. The only chance I had was to get him into the open and make him run, but it seems to have been a dangerous procedure at that." He looked at his watch. "I've some other things to attend to now," he said. "I'm going out the back way. I'll call you soon or come back." Waving his hand he went through the back-shop door and was gone.

Joan turned her attention to the office. The crowd of reporters had thinned to two or three sitting on benches, half asleep. Most of the curious townspeople had gone, convinced that nothing exciting was happening there. Mitch was reading galley proof and Joan got her red pencil and began to help. An extra was ready to run save for the first page and that would be made up as soon as any definite word was received.

After the odds and ends had been cleared away, they sat about and smoked cigarettes. Mitch went to the Greek's and brought back a big pitcher of hot coffee and they drank it in paper cups. At ten-thirty the county attorney called to say that he was going to bed. He asked for Fields and merely grunted in tired disgust when he learned that the detective was not on hand.

He had hardly hung up when the printer bell began a frantic ringing. Joan and Mitch read the message as it was tapped off, with Mr. Shields peering over their shoulders. It said:

A621 FORDMAN
BULLETIN
DEL RIO, JULY 6 (A.P.). THE FLEEING FUGITIVE
SOUGHT BY POLICE FOR THE MURDERS OF TWO
PERSONS IN FORDMAN SLIPPED THROUGH THE
TRAP SET FOR HIM 85 MILES NORTH OF THIS
CITY AT 10:30 P.M. AND CONTINUED HIS FLIGHT
TOWARD THE BORDER. A SMALL DETACHMENT
OF RANGERS FAILED TO HALT THE BLACK
PACKARD ROADSTER ON A LITTLE USED DIRT

ROAD THAT IS A SHORT CUT BETWEEN ROCK-
TOWN AND DEL RIO. THE MAIN BODY OF MEN
HAD BEEN STATIONED ON THE STATE HIGH-
WAY AS IT WAS THOUGHT THAT HE WOULD BE
SURE TO USE THE BETTER ROAD, BUT HE LEFT
THE HIGHWAY THREE MILES SOUTH OF
ROCKTOWN AND CONTINUED ACROSS THE
COUNTRY ON A DIRT STRETCH THAT CUT FIF-
TEEN MILES FROM THE REGULAR ROUTE.

THE FUGITIVE MUST HAVE HIDDEN FOR SEV-
ERAL HOURS BETWEEN FORDMAN AND
ROCKTOWN AND OFFICIALS HAD ALMOST
ABANDONED THE THEORY THAT HE WAS
HEADED SOUTH. WHEN THE CAR FLASHED
THROUGH THE RANGERS WERE GATHERING TO
RETURN TO HEADQUARTERS AND HAD RE-
MOVED THE WOODEN BARRICADE THAT HAD
BEEN ERECTED ACROSS THE ROADWAY. THE
FUGITIVE WAS RUNNING WITHOUT LIGHTS
AND DROVE SQUARELY INTO THE GROUP
OF MEN ON THE ROAD. ONE TROOPER WAS
KNOCKED DOWN AND SEVERELY INJURED.
SHOTS WERE FIRED AT THE CAR, BUT NONE
TOOK EFFECT. STATE PATROLMEN FOLLOWED
THE CAR, BUT WERE UNABLE TO OVERTAKE IT.

IT IS THOUGHT THAT THE WANTED MAN WILL
ABANDON THE CAR NEAR DEL RIO AND MAKE
HIS WAY ACROSS THE BORDER BY SWIMMING
THE RIO GRANDE BELOW OR ABOVE THE IN-
TERNATIONAL BRIDGE. BORDER PATROLMEN
AND RANGERS ARE GUARDING THE BANKS OF
THE RIVER FOR SEVERAL MILES NORTH AND
SOUTH OF HERE.

When the message had come through entirely, Mitch ripped it out of the machine and cried: "I'll get a paper on the streets with this to feature and we can re-plate and run another batch when some more dope comes in. It'll create a demand for a later edition." He grabbed paper and began scribbling headlines.

Joan looked at her father. "He got through after all," she said despondently.

"They'll catch him in Del Rio," stated Mr. Shields positively. "It's only a matter of time."

Joan sighed. "No mention of Jimmie, of course," she said.

"Why does this come by way of Dallas?" asked Mr. Shields.

"It's the way the loop's hooked up," explained Mitch, pushing his dirty hat back off of his forehead. "The A.P. man in Del Rio is on the job and he's shooting the stuff straight to Dallas."

They hung over the printers anxiously, but no more news came through. The presses roared and the extra went out. People telephoned to ask for news and another crowd gathered. The reporters came back and filled the room with noise and the smell of whiskey. Marion telephoned and complained that she had not been told about anything, that Dick had been there, talked with Mrs. Lawrence and gone.

Mitch complained that the back-shop men were just sitting around playing cards and drawing time-and-a-half pay. "An' here we are," he said, "drawin' nothin'. When Ed gets here he can take the blamed paper over himself for a change. I'm goin' home to bed."

"Did Ed say to stay?" asked Joan.

"Yeah. He said to squeeze th' thing dry an' not mind replating, that nobody'd kick about th' cost. That's true!"

They were both weary and hollow-eyed. Mr. Shields, more anxious about his son than he would admit to Joan, worked crossword puzzles in old papers and phrased and rephrased a story for his wife.

Things were very quiet for another half-hour except for the telephones that never ceased ringing. Then hell began to pop. The printer bell rang madly and they rushed to the machines. The first message was a short one.

A621 FORDMAN
BULLETIN
AUSTIN, JULY 6 (A.P.). THE FUGITIVE WANTED
FOR MURDER IN FORDMAN IS THOUGHT TO BE
IN THE HANDS OF THE POLICE HERE. CONFIR-
MATION LACKING.

EDITORS: STAND BY

The machine was silent for a few minutes and then began again.

ADD A621   FORDMAN

AUSTIN, JULY 6 (A.P.). CHIEF OF POLICE AARON
WATTS OF THIS CITY IS POSITIVE THAT HE IS
HOLDING THE MAN WANTED FOR MURDER OF
TWO IN FORDMAN. THE FUGITIVE ENDED HIS
HEADLONG FLIGHT TONIGHT AS THE PHAN-
TOM BLACK ROADSTER IN WHICH HE MADE HIS
GETAWAY CRASHED IN A RESIDENTIAL DIS-
TRICT OF THIS CITY THIRTY MINUTES AGO.

WATTS DECLARED THAT THE LICENSE NUMBER
CORRESPONDED WITH THAT SENT OUT BY
FORDMAN OFFICIALS, BUT HE WOULD NOT
COMMENT ON THE RUMOR THAT THREE PER-
SONS HAD BEEN FOUND IN THE WRECKED CAR,
ONE OF THEM A WOMAN.

Immediately following this flash came another one.

ADD A62 I FORDMAN

AUSTIN, JULY 6 (A.P.). SCOTT RUE, A SPECTATOR
WHO SAW AND REPORTED THE ACCIDENT THAT
WRECKED THE ROADSTER BELIEVED TO HAVE

BEEN DRIVEN BY THE FORDMAN FUGITIVE, STATED POSITIVELY TO REPORTERS HERE THAT THREE PERSONS HAD BEEN TAKEN BY POLICE FROM THE CAR AND RUSHED TO A HOSPITAL. HE SAID THAT ONE WAS A WOMAN.

'I WAS WALKING DOWN FEDERAL STREET,' STATED RUE, 'WHEN I HEARD A CAR COMING BEHIND ME. IT WAS COMING PRETTY FAST, ABOUT THIRTY OR FORTY MILES AN HOUR. IT PASSED ME AND BEGAN TO SLOW DOWN A LITTLE ABOUT A BLOCK AHEAD. I COULD SEE THE HEADLIGHTS. THEN IT TURNED SUDDENLY AND RAN UP ON THE SIDEWALK AND HIT A TREE. THERE WAS AN AWFUL CRASH AND I RAN.

'WHEN I GOT THERE I FOUND A YOUNG KID ON THE GROUND NEAR THE CAR. HE WAS CUT BUT BREATHING. IN THE CAR, WHICH HAD TURNED OVER ON ITS RIGHT SIDE, I FOUND A MAN AND A WOMAN, BOTH UNCONSCIOUS. I TRIED TO FIND A 'PHONE, BUT COULD NOT AND WAS RUNNING FOR A DRUGSTORE DOWN THE STREET WHEN I MET A POLICEMAN WHO CALLED THE AMBULANCE.'

The machine was silent.

"Why in hell don't they quit flashing rumors," said Mitch. "That police chief won't give out a statement and the reporters are wild."

But a fuller story was coming through at that moment.

A621 FORDMAN

AUSTIN, JULY 6 (A.P.). POLICE HAVE TENTATIVELY IDENTIFIED ONE MEMBER OF THE GROUP OF THREE WHICH THEY SAY WERE

RIDING IN THE 'GETAWAY CAR' OF THE
FORDMAN FUGITIVE WHICH CRASHED IN A
RESIDENTIAL DISTRICT HERE THIS EVENING.
HE IS SAID TO BE JAMES ESTES SHIELDS, OF
FORDMAN, HIGH-SCHOOL FOOTBALL STAR OF
THAT CITY. HIS IDENTITY WAS REVEALED AS
DOCTORS AND DETECTIVES OF THE CITY HOS-
PITAL EXAMINED HIS CLOTHING AND FOUND
NAME TAPES IN HIS SNEAKERS.

ALL THREE VICTIMS OF THE CRASH, ONE A
WOMAN, ARE STILL UNCONSCIOUS, BUT NOT
SERIOUSLY INJURED, ACCORDING TO DOCTORS
AT THE CITY HOSPITAL.

The machine hesitated, returned to starting position, then
tapped out:

NOTICE TO EDITORS: FULL DETAILS FORDMAN
STORY SOON.

After this promise it was still, and the three in the office sat in
anxious silence. Joan called Millbank and found that he had been
in touch with the Austin officers. They declared that none of the
victims of the accident were badly hurt. Millbank told her that he'd
caught Sheriff Read at Midway and that he and a few of the posse
had started immediately for Austin.

The printers had started another story before she finished talking with Millbank, and Mitch brought it to her when she hung up.
It read:

A621   FORDMAN

AUSTIN, JULY 6 (A.P.). HIS IDENTITY STILL A
MYSTERY TO LOCAL OFFICERS, ONE MEMBER
OF THE ILL-FATED GETAWAY CAR USED BY THE

FUGITIVE WANTED IN FORDMAN WAS TAKEN
TO THE PRISON HOSPITAL HERE TONIGHT.

UNTIL HE CAN BE IDENTIFIED BY PROPER AU-
THORITIES HE WILL BE HELD FOR RECKLESS
DRIVING IN CONNECTION WITH THE ACCIDENT
IN WHICH TWO PASSENGERS WERE INJURED.
HE IS STILL UNCONSCIOUS, ACCORDING TO THE
POLICE.

Following this was the message:

FORDMAN PLEASE NOTE: FILE IMMEDIATE
STORY ON JAMES ESTES SHIELDS, MEMBER OF
THE ESCAPE PARTY WRECKED IN AUSTIN. IS HE
JIMMIE SHIELDS, FLASH HALF-BACK CAPTAIN
OF THE CHAMPION PANTHER TEAM? IMPERA-
TIVE THAT WE HAVE DETAILS AT ONCE. PAPERS
WAITING. WHERE IS HURLEY?
KEANE

Mitch yelped: "Where is Hurley? Yeah, where is Hurley! Where
is Ed? Where are all those guys? On the way to Austin. That's where
they are."

"*Who* is Hurley?" asked Joan.

"Their special correspondent," explained the reporter, sitting
down in front of his machine.

Mr. Shields said: "I know the mayor of Austin. I'm going to
'phone him to see that Jimmie is properly taken care of." He hurried to the booth. Fifteen minutes later he came out grinning.

"The brat's O.K.," he called. "He's come to, the mayor says.
They're certainly excited down there."

"Do they know who it is yet?" Joan asked impatiently. "I'll go
crazy with the suspense!"

"No," replied her father. "The mayor didn't know yet. Things
are in a big mix-up from the way he talked. They are waiting for

the officers from here. He said he'd have me notified as soon as everything was straightened out." He picked up his hat and buttoned his coat. "Let's go home, sis," he suggested. "They'll 'phone me there and you need some rest."

The girl sighed. "I expect I do," she admitted. "Can you hold it down, Mitch?"

"Yeah," he assured her. "You go on. We'll replate as soon as the next flash comes in."

Wearily she followed her father to his car. They drove home in silence and found Mrs. Shields anxious and excited. Some kind neighbor had called to impart half-truths and she had not known what to think. Joan left her father to explain and threw herself down on a bed. She tried to stay awake, but could not. She had no will to grapple with the puzzle, and her last conscious thought was that she did not care. The bed felt too good.

XVIII: FRIDAY, JULY 7: 7.15 A.M.

It was after seven the next morning when Joan awoke. The events of the night before were blurred and unreal. She remembered that her mother had made her undress, had told her that there was no news. She realized with a start that she had slept through the entire night and that she had not been awakened. As she started to get up a paper rattled and she found the late extra edition of the Fordman *Daily News* across her chest. A screaming seventy-two-point headline smote her eye:

SCHOOLBOY FOILS FUGITIVE

Unknown to Fleeing Murderer Kidnapped
Kid Rides 200 Miles Locked in Rumble;
Escapes, Slugs Abductor with Tire Tool

HERO JIMMIE SHIELDS, FOOTBALL STAR

Police of 5 Counties Failed to Halt Escaping
Man Wanted in Famous Fordman Case as
He Made for Austin Hide-out

Joan read the story, spread down two right-hand columns in ten-point type. Aghast and unbelieving, she read it again, threw the paper to the floor, and got out of bed. As she was groping for her slippers, the door was flung open and the family 'hero' stuck in his head.

267

"Get up, you lazy wench!" he yelled. "You ain't gonna get outa seein' 'em crown me with th' laurel wreath!" A grin split his brown face and a bandage wound picturesquely around his head almost covered one blue eye.

"I'll crown you with a monkey wrench," promised his sister mechanically. Then, "Jimmie, is this true?" indicating the paper.

"Sure," he said, "I did everything they got in there. Looka my head. Three stitches. You oughta see th' other papers!"

"Darling," commented Joan caustically, "how we'll ever live with you from now on is a mystery to me."

But he would not be insulted. "Th' boy slooth, that's me!" he whooped, and galloped down the hall.

Joan put on her robe and slippers and hurried to the living-room. Her father and Dick Fields were reading papers and threw them down as she came in.

"It's all over but the shouting," said the detective.

The girl nodded. "Tell me all about it," she commanded.

"Jimmie wants to do that," said Fields, "while we have breakfast."

They went into the dining-room and found that the boy had finished eating. "Sit down," he invited, "and I'll give you the lowdown."

Joan looked at her father and mother. "Haven't you heard it yet?" she asked.

"No," answered Mr. Shields. "He just got here about ten minutes ago."

"I've heard it," commented the detective, "but I want to hear it again. Maybe I can pick up a few pointers."

"It sure was lucky," the boy began, "that you made me stay in the car. I never woulda got 'im if I hadn't, and nobody else would have either," he added seriously.

"Go on," urged his sister.

"Well, after you got out I laid down on th' seat to get out of th' wind. It was pitch-dark and noisy as the devil, what with the wind and sand. I figured you two would be right back an' I couldn't see anything that was goin' on, anyway. So I was layin' there listening for th' sheriff's car when right at my ear I heard a guy say, 'Get in quick!' I'd read about it, but it was th' first time I really heard a fella, you know, snarl.

"I was pretty near paralyzed an' I couldn't of hollered, anyhow, things happened too fast after that. I felt the car move and somebody got in and sat down. Then this guy got in and started the motor, real easy. But just as he threw her into first, you came bustin' out like a crazy person, yellin'. I tell you I never was so scared in my life. I expected him t' shoot you then and there, but th' car started fast an' I heard a shot from back of you. It hit th' fender and scared me worse than ever."

Fields shook his head. "I shouldn't have tried that shot," he said, "but I thought I'd get the tire. Joan was lying in the street and I could see her white dress, so she wasn't in danger."

"Well, you didn't miss the tire much, nor me either," conceded the boy. "We turned the corner on two wheels and then, instead of hittin' it outa town like I expected, he just drove up that alley behind the Jones place and parked!"

Jimmie paused for effect and got the desired results. His listeners exclaimed incredulously, and he continued:

"That's what he did, all right, and smart, too. Nobody'd ever think of lookin' out in th' alley. It was so darn noisy an' dark that he was safe. Well, by that time I was down on th' floor, all curled up in a knot, because I was afraid he'd look in th' back. I couldn't figure what he was goin' to do next, but he just sat there . . ."

"Listen," interrupted Joan. "Did you know who it was?"

"Sure," answered the boy. "I knew Ed Frank's voice and I suspected him all along, anyhow."

"Yes?" remarked his sister skeptically.

"An', boy, was I scared! I knew he'd killed two people already and I figured he wouldn't stop at me. But he just sat there quiet an' I was tryin' to decide who the other person was when he said, 'Well, Aggie, I've got a good plan for you,' and laughed. She didn't answer and it dawned on me that he had Mrs. Jones and she was all tied up and gagged. She made some funny noises and I'll say this for her she didn't sound scared, just awful sore.

"He laughed again and asked her, 'You didn't really think you could shake me down for eight thousand dollars, did you? And with the game up like this?' Then he said, 'You sure have got guts, anyhow.' Pretty soon then he got out of the car, walked around back and plunk, down came the rumble-seat cover. There I was, locked in a space about four by three feet square an' not more than two feet high, but the worst of it was I couldn't hear anything else."

"You were a little warm, weren't you?" asked Fields.

"Slightly," agreed Jimmie, "an' there were a lotta tools and other junk in there with me too. It was hot as Hades an' I couldn't turn over until he started again for fear of makin' a noise. Pretty soon, though, he started and drove real slow for about fifteen minutes. It was durin' this time I found that door in the side where you put golf clubs in was unfastened. It was shut, but the lock hadn't caught good. I pushed it open and got some air, but I knew I couldn't get out of it, it was too little for my massive frame." He stopped and grinned at them.

"Go on," urged Joan.

"Don't rush me," he teased. "I'm nervous."

"Hooey," said the girl.

"It was lucky for me," he continued, "that my head was up that way, but I was scared to open it too much. We drove a little while an' stopped again. He got out an' left th' car. I couldn't tell where we were because it was so dark, but th' wind had almost died out an' it was beginning to rain.

"I could hear him walk away an' I waited a few minutes an' took a chance. I stuck my head out and said, 'Mis' Jones, can you hear me? Kick on the floor if you can.' She almost kicked the floorboards through! I told her who I was and asked her if she could move at all—to kick once for no and twice for yes. She kicked once. Then I said, 'Can't you even move your hands?' and she kicked twice at that. I said, 'Could you screw around and unfasten this rumble seat?' I could hear her wigglin', but I guess she couldn't make it because pretty soon she thumped once. So I said, 'Look out and if you get a chance unlock me, and I'll bean him with a wrench that's

back here.' She thumped several times after that and pretty soon
Ed came back.

"I heard him say to her, 'I'd untie you, Aggie, but I don't trust
you.' Then he started the car and we shot off about eighty miles an
hour. I guess we drove for about an hour before he stopped again
and turned down some sort of lane or off across the prairie. When
he stopped, he said to Mrs. Jones, 'We'll just wait here until that
posse comes back. They won't go outa the county.' And sure enough
in about fifteen minutes they passed by. I could hear the cars and
see th' headlights about a quarter of a mile away.

"Then he asked Mrs. Jones did she want a cigarette. I guess he
took off the gag since he wasn't worried about her yelling any more,
but she didn't say much, just how'd he ever expect to get away with
such a thing.

"He said he expected t' get away with it all right—that he had
everything fixed in Austin t' beat it. He didn't say where to. Then
she asked him why he killed John Fordman in the first place, an'
he laughed, not like he thought it was funny, but like it was a joke
on him. He said it was sort of self-defense, though nobody'd ever
believe it or look at it that way. I remember his words. 'That self-
righteous old devil,' he said, 'there he sat with everything a man
could ever want, power, money, people scuttling when he said, an'
had the nerve to tell me that by the next night I'd be in jail. He had
it all worked out. I should have got out of the car and hustled out
of town, but it made me so mad that I picked up a little pistol that
was lying on the seat beside me and shot him right in the belly.'"
Jimmie looked around the circle of faces, caught his mother's expression, and hurried on with his story.

"Mrs. Jones didn't say anything, but he kept on talking. I guess
he couldn't stop. He told her how he got out of the car an' put the
gun in the spare tire because he didn't want to throw it away—
there were too many people about. He said, 'I couldn't help thinkin'
how surprised that nigger would be when he found it.' Then he
went on, rather proud, and told her how he worked everything else.
He said that he just walked into the bank at midnight, unlocked

that filing case back of Mr. Ross's desk, and took out everything he wanted . . ."

"How did he know where the things were?" asked Joan.

"Fordman told him that he'd put the stuff in a safe place—that he'd given it to Ross on Sunday and told him to put it in the vault. He knew that the time lock was on Sunday, that Ross was out at the field Monday morning and at the investigation Monday afternoon and all Tuesday morning he was in a directors' meeting, so he couldn't have got the stuff in the vault. I guess he'd had enough to do with Fordman's business to know that Ross kept a file in that cabinet. He should have known."

Jimmie stopped to catch his breath. "I'll make it shorter," he said.

"He started the car after a while and drove back to the highway. Then he sure stepped on it. About an hour later I heard somebody shout an' some guns go off. Somebody got hit by the car too. They told me later it was a patrolman. I began to get scared again because I could see he wasn't taking any chances. But I was gettin' mad, too, bein' cooped up in that place so long.

"Then we had a flat on a front tire. I was pretty near crazy for fear he'd look in the back for tools. He stopped the car and cursed and told Mrs. Jones to get out. She said she couldn't since he'd tied up her feet, so he must of untied her, for in a few minutes she got out. 'Don't try anything funny,' he told her. She said she wouldn't and asked if she could sit up on the back fender. He let her, and then I heard him move the seat and find the tools.

"Then, while he was workin' on th' tire she got the rumble seat open. I was more frightened than ever for fear he'd notice it, but he didn't. He just threw the tools back in the car, made Mrs. Jones get in, and we started again. He left the wheel with the flat tire right there in the road.

"Well, we drove for hours, it seemed, switching back and forth on country roads. From what he'd said to Mrs. Jones I knew we were headed for Austin. I expected him to ditch the car somewhere soon after he got there and beat it. I knew he'd fix Mrs. Jones up so she couldn't get to the police, so I figured that if I was goin' to do something, I'd better do it quick.

"I didn't think that I could hit him with the car stopped, he'd see me or hear me. So I decided to hit him with the car moving. I got that big flat piece of spring we use for a tire tool and tried to decide whether to use the edge or the flat side.

"When we hit Austin, though, we were goin' so fast that I didn't have a chance. He shot through town and out toward the University. On Federal he went slower like he was hunting for a place to turn, and when he dropped it to about twenty I got up on the seat and kept my head down. I figured to catch the wheel after I hit him and keep the car straight.

"So I popped up quick and was just goin' to hit him when he saw me in the mirror. He ducked, but I beaned him, anyhow. I had to hit him twice because he let go of the wheel and tried to turn. It was too late to grab the wheel and we hit something smacko. All I remember after that is flyin' through the air as pretty as you please!"

Jimmie waved his hands and grinned. His mother sighed and said, "I only hope that I don't dream about it."

There was a rattle of comment and question from the others and Joan could scarcely make Jimmie listen to her. "Was he hurt very badly?" she asked.

"Naw," answered Jimmie. "He broke a leg an' a shoulder, but that's all. Mrs. Jones was knocked haywire for a while, but she's O.K. now."

Mr. and Mrs. Shields arose from the table and the cook called from the door, "'Phone fo' yo', Mist' Jimmie." He rushed out importantly, leaving Joan alone with Dick.

"Hit you pretty hard, kid?" he asked.

"It's a shock in a way, of course," she admitted.

"You weren't in love with the guy?" persisted Fields.

Joan smiled at him and shook her head. "No," she declared firmly.

He looked relieved. "Well," he said, "I guess I take a licking on this one. Three false alibis and I didn't bust one of them."

"You didn't have time," protested the girl.

"I should have taken time," he declared, "but when the *sheriff* swore that the guy was with him when John Ross was shot, there wasn't much use in worrying about the other two alibis. You see he killed Fordman before the explosion, as we figured, with the gun Miss Fordman had left lying on the seat . . ."

"Lying on the seat?" interrupted Joan.

"Yes. When she got out of the car she took it out of the pocket to get a tin of cigarettes and didn't replace it. She just tossed it onto the back seat near her handbag and hurried off to watch the shooting of the well. He found it there and used it."

"And the newspaper clipping, Dick? How did Agnes Jones know that he had it?"

"He cut it out of the San Antonio paper when he was there. At the field he showed it to Mrs. Jones, who had already seen it in the local paper. She asked him to show it to White and he said that he would. When he returned to their car just before the shooting, she asked him what White had said. He looked through his pockets and admitted that he'd lost it. He couldn't go back to look for it, because the sheriff's men were all over the place and you found it the next morning."

Joan was thoughtful. "All but a few things slip into place perfectly," she said. "But I still can't see how he knew that Mrs. Lawrence had the letter; how the sheriff thought he was in his office; how he worked the other two alibis and why Mr. Ross was killed with his own gun."

Fields grinned. "Well, the last first—Ross was killed with his own gun to make the death look like a suicide. And it did, or would have, if he'd taken the time to press the dead man's fingers on the gun, thus leaving finger-prints. But he thought that the water idea was safe enough."

"Were you sure that the water hadn't obliterated the prints, Dick?"

Fields looked guilty. "No," he admitted. "Sometimes it does, but the water wasn't very hot, and then I noticed that Ross had fresh green paint on two fingers and the thumb of his right hand. He had touched the newly painted screen door downstairs when he came in and had gone directly to the bathroom to wash it off. If he'd handled the gun, the paint would have stuck."

"Of course," said the girl. "I remember that the door had just been painted."

"You see, he planned carefully. You had already told him that Mrs. Ross would be at a luncheon the next day . . ."

"I?"

"Yes. In a casual conversation, and he remembered it. So he waited for Ross in his home on Tuesday, killed him, and took his keys. He went there with a gun of his own, but on looking around found that one of Ross's and it suited his purpose exactly.

"Then, as to how he knew that Mrs. Lawrence had the letter— you may remember that she called the sheriff's office, the newspaper, and the hotel when she was hunting for me? Unfortunately, she got him at the newspaper office and asked for you or for me. He was immediately alert, realizing that something had happened. He offered to take the message, but she refused, saying that she'd go to the hotel, as she wanted to see me personally. Then, as we know, Frank went there ahead of her, watched her write the note, watched the desk clerk take it. How he got it we already know."

"And the alibis?" prompted Joan.

"He met Mildred Jones and was with her before and during the shooting of the well. The night Mrs. Lawrence was attacked, he was seen to go to his room by the desk clerk who awakened him when the rumor came in. He merely went down a fire escape at the back of the building."

"But the sheriff," insisted Joan. "I don't see how he fooled him."

Dick laughed sourly. "He's easy to fool. That's what put me off so badly. I let him check Frank's alibi and took his word for it. I was so busy that I didn't get around to checking it myself. And instead of talking it over with his men who were there in the anteroom playing poker, he just relied on his own memory that Frank was there. The truth is that he had been there and left unobtrusively, saying that he was going to 'phone. Nobody missed him, they were so used to having him come in and go out. He just slipped in again, about a half-hour later, and was there when the call came from the Nelsons' that Mr. Ross had shot himself! Imagine the nerve of having the sheriff swear to your alibi during the time of a murder."

Joan nodded; then she said: "I'm ashamed of myself for suspecting Glieth Lawrence of anything wrong, but I would like to know where she was when Mr. Fordman was shot and why Gere acted like such an idiot when he met her."

"She was visiting some friends on a ranch south of San Antonio," explained the man. "I went out there last night and had a long talk with her. She had a room at the hotel and they sent the message out to her when it came. She and Drexell are going to get married next month, she says. He's been nearly crazy since Fordman was killed for fear he'd be accused. He'd no alibis worth talking about, benefited by ten thousand dollars, and was broke. He knew that when we found that snapshot of him in Mrs. Lawrence's bag we'd suspect him more than ever. I believe he was afraid that she'd think he did it. Then, too, he didn't want to hurt Marion with the knowledge that he was in love with Mrs. Lawrence." The man finished this long explanation rapidly and smothered a yawn. "I'm going to sleep for a while," he said suddenly. "I'm worn out. They've called a special session of the grand jury for this afternoon and there's sure to be an indictment. I have to get everything in order for Millbank. Can you help me?"

Joan nodded and Jimmie burst in upon them.

"I been havin' my pictures taken for the news reels!" he yelled. "They want you too, sis."

The girl shook her head. "No, sir," she said. "*I* object to being gawped at by a million people and, besides, I have to get to the office. Poor Mitch must be almost crazy down there trying to get a paper out by himself. I expect that Marion will let him take Ed's place and I'll bet that it will make a man of him."

"Say, listen," Jimmie broke in suddenly. "A woman came by this mornin' just as I was drivin' up an' left you a note." He drew a folded paper from his pocket and flicked it across the table at Joan.

She read:

Dear Miss Shields,
I have looked all over the paper for the write-up
about my party I gave for the Laff-a-Lot Bridge Club

Saturday and I can't find it anywhere. I know the ladies will blame me for not having the write-up in, but you remember I told you all about it on the telephone Monday afternoon, so it wasn't my fault. Then I called you again Tuesday and you promised me it would be in that day.

I don't see how you can expect anybody to read the paper if you don't put some news in it and I'm sure my bridge party is just as important as anybody's.

Yours truly
Mrs. W. H. Shaw

COACHWHIP PUBLICATIONS

COACHWHIPBOOKS.COM

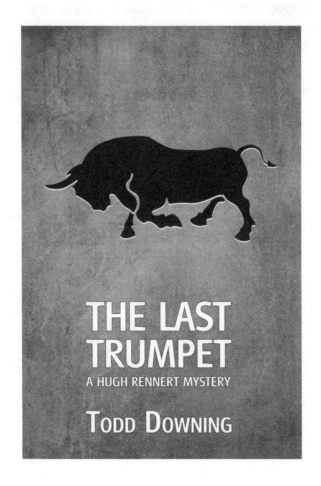

THE LAST
TRUMPET

A HUGH RENNERT MYSTERY

TODD DOWNING

ISBN 978-1-61646-152-2

COACHWHIP PUBLICATIONS

COACHWHIPBOOKS.COM

BLOOD ON HER SHOE

MEDORA FIELD

ISBN 978-1-61646-275-8

COACHWHIP PUBLICATIONS

COACHWHIPBOOKS.COM

THE
DARTMOUTH
MURDERS

THE
WAILING ROCK
MURDERS

CLIFFORD
ORR

ISBN 978-1-61646-323-6

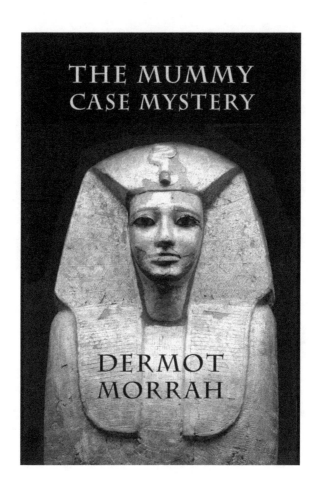

THE MUMMY
CASE MYSTERY

DERMOT
MORRAH

ISBN 978-1-61646-250-5

COACHWHIP PUBLICATIONS

COACHWHIPBOOKS.COM

LOUIS F. BOOTH

THE BANK VAULT MYSTERY
BROKERS' END

ISBN 978-1-61646-326-7

MYSTERY AT
LYNDEN SANDS

J. J. CONNINGTON

ISBN 978-1-61646-320-5

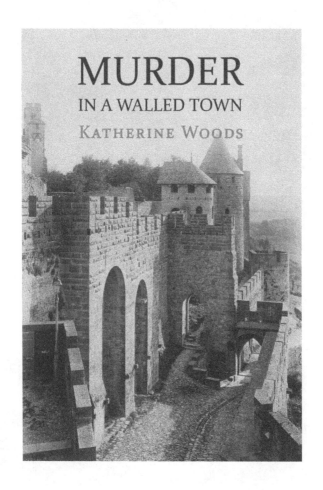

MURDER
IN A WALLED TOWN
KATHERINE WOODS

ISBN 978-1-61646-326-7

COACHWHIP PUBLICATIONS

COACHWHIPBOOKS.COM

ANITA BOUTELL

DEATH BRINGS
A STORKE

CRADLED
IN FEAR

ISBN 978-1-61646-334-2